CW01622332

Dreamforest

DREAMFOREST

Dalene Matthee

PENGUIN BOOKS

PENGUIN BOOKS

Published By the Penguin Group
80 Strand, London WC2R 0RL, England
Penguin Putnam Inc, 375 Hudson Street, New York, New York 10014, USA
Penguin Books Australia Ltd, 250 Camberwell Road, Camberwell,
Victoria 3124, Australia
Penguin Books Canada Ltd, 10 Alcorn Avenue, Toronto, Ontario,
Canada M4V 3B2
Penguin Books (NZ) Ltd, Cnr Rosedale and Airborne Roads, Albany,
Auckland, New Zealand
Penguin Books India (Pvt) Ltd, 11 Community Centre, Panscheel Park,
New Delhi – 110 017, India
Penguin Books (South Africa) (Pty) Ltd, 24 Sturdee Avenue, Rosebank,
Johannesburg 2196, South Africa

Penguin Books (South Africa) (Pty) Ltd, Registered Offices:
24 Sturdee Avenue, Rosebank, Johannesburg 2196, South Africa

First published in Afrikaans as *Toorbos* by Tafelberg Publishers, 2003
First published in English by Penguin Books (South Africa) (Pty) Ltd 2004
This edition published 2006
Reprinted 2009, 2010, 2011

Copyright © Dalene Matthee 2004

All rights reserved
The moral right of the author has been asserted

ISBN 9780143025153

Typeset by DCW Design in 10.5/12.5pt Galliard
Cover design: Mouse Design
Printed and bound by Interpak Books, Pietermaritzburg

Except in the United States of America, this book is sold subject to the condition that it shall not, by way of trade or otherwise, be lent resold, hired out or otherwise circulated without the publisher's prior consent in any form of binding or cover other than that in which it is published and without a similar condition including this condition being imposed on the subsequent purchaser.

For my daughter
Hilary

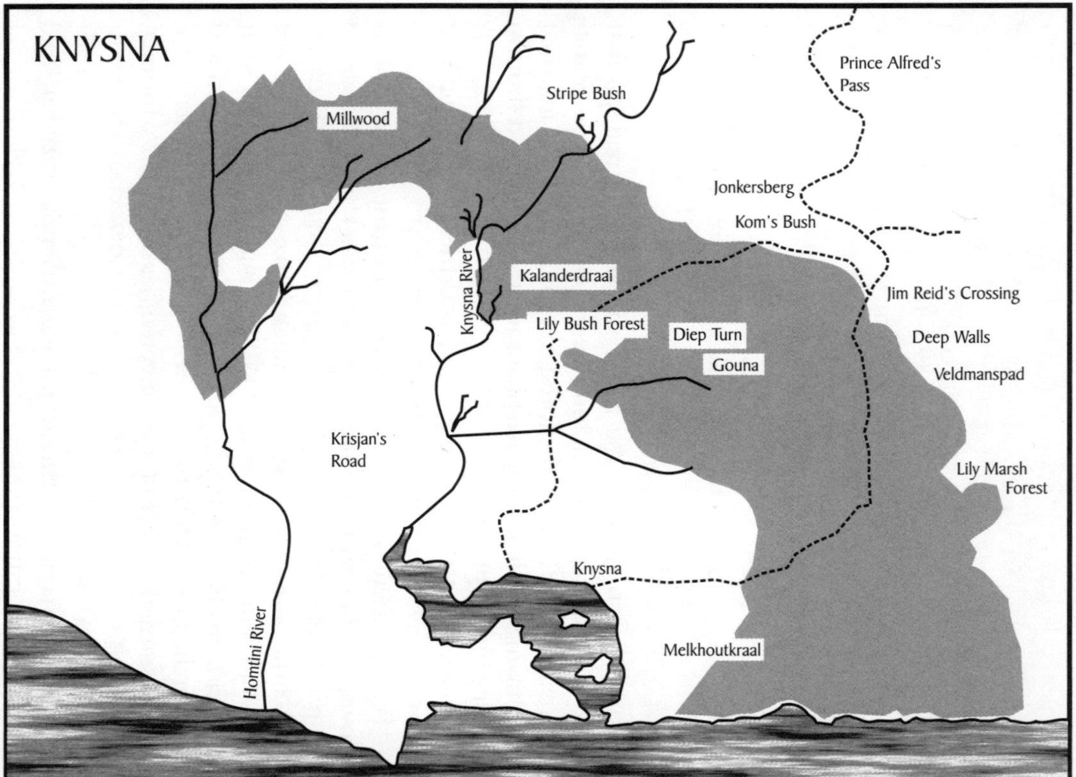
KNYSNA
Prince Alfred's Pass
Stripe Bush
Millwood
Jonkersberg
Kom's Bush
Kalanderdraai
Jim Reid's Crossing
Knysna River
Lily Bush Forest
Diep Turn
Deep Walls
Gouna
Veldmanspad
Krisjan's Road
Lily Marsh Forest
Knysna
Melkhoutkraal
Homtini River

1

AS SHE WALKED through the forest she suddenly realised that there was an elephant watching her from the thicket. Somewhere above her head in the forest canopy a lourie was gurgling and hissing to warn the elephant that there was a human walking along the sledpath.

Lourie: the bird was the elephant's friend, a telltale that always alerted him when a human was close by.

Perhaps there was more than one elephant in the undergrowth. It didn't matter, the wind was on her side, she would get past safely.

A little further on she came upon three woodcutters: the two Van Huysteen brothers, Willem and Koos, and their mother's brother, Jan Zeelie, all of them wearing their tattered and patched work clothes.

She startled them, and they greeted her hurriedly. 'Morning, Karoliena!'

'Good morning.'

'The elephants are surely going to trample you yet!' old Zeelie gravely cautioned her.

'Indeed.' She had heard that warning many times.

There was a bridge between the world of the forest and the outside world which was sometimes difficult to cross. It was like knowing you had to wake up but were reluctant to open your eyes. She wanted to walk quietly past the woodcutters before she entered the outside world, but Koos stood in her way.

'Did the man find you?' he asked.

'What man?'

'The one who was looking for you. An important man in a pinstriped suit, said he was urgently looking for Karoliena Kapp, he has to speak to her. He drives a motor car.'

Old Zeelie laughed, showing toothless gums. 'Don't worry, we threw him off your track nicely. Told him it would be best if he tried your mother, Meliena Kapp, in Long Marsh Forest. Perhaps *she* had seen you, we seldom do.'

'What man?' she repeated.

'What was it he said?' Koos asked Willem, breaking off a piece of dry bread from the chunk that lay on the ground between them. There was a bottle of cold black coffee too. Their knapsacks hung from the branch above them. Three axes and two saws leant against the trunk of a Cape beech.

'Naudé, I think he said his name was. Some or other official from the government.'

Naudé. It must have been the same man who had come enquiring about her from Oldman Botha a few days before. She had watched him closely through a narrow crack in the front wall of the little plank house. He was thickset, out of breath and sweating after the short climb from the hard road up to the house. She had prayed that Oldman Botha would not take it into his head to invite the stranger in; he had a habit of shamelessly asking for a ride in any motor car that stopped near the house. Riding in a motor car gave him enormous pleasure – even if it sometimes took him hours to walk back home again.

'The man said he's in the forest on a very important

mission, Karoliena.'

'If you meet him again, tell him I'm not available.' She had to get away, she had to catch the timber train to the village.

'He asked us about you.' Old Jan Zeelie continued to detain her. 'He asked us if we knew you,' he added somewhat spitefully.

'I suppose you had a good gossip about me.'

'He gave us each a nice yellow apple,' Willem added apologetically. 'But we didn't tell him you ran away from your husband.' A smile crossed his face. 'We only told him that your father had been struck by lightning in Gouna Forest and that a spark must have hit you too.'

'There's an elephant in the thicket behind you, he's watching you.' One grabbed the bread, another the coffee and the knapsacks.

'You lie, you little imp!' old Jan shouted as he limped towards the nearest white elder in case they had to get up a tree.

She turned away and walked on, the little wooden box containing the moths firmly pressed against her body. She dared not miss the train, she had to get the moths to the village. Anna van Rooyen had to have a blanket, the old woman was shivering to death and it wasn't even winter yet. The church nurse had promised to make a plan, but nothing had come of it yet. There was no money.

What important mission brought Naudé to the forest? According to Mister Fourcade enquiries were being made about the circumstances of the poor whites in the forest. A Commission of Investigators, appointed in America, was to come and investigate the wretched poverty of the woodcutters. Maria Rothman, an important woman from Swellendam, had been appointed to come and talk to the forest women. Talk about what? Women-matters, she supposed.

Poor white. She hated the term. She had been in primary

school when she first heard the words. They were like a blow that knocked you into the gutter and turned you into an inferior being.

About a month after that she saw the tree-spirit. It was a mystery – and it had changed her for ever.

She knew she had not imagined it.

*

Shortly after her father was killed by lightning, her mother sent her to the church nurse in the village to ask for some medicine for shock. Her mother just could not get back on her feet after the funeral. It had been a big funeral. Karel Kapp was a good man and a lot of people followed his hearse. He'd been a woodcutter like his father and grandfather before him. Her mother had told her: Take the timber train to the village, ask Nurse for a place to sleep, then take the train back again tomorrow morning. Don't come back on foot, it's March and it's damp in the forest, and the elephants are restless; I won't survive another death.

Karoliena was the only child.

Long before the railway for the big train was built from George to Knysna, there was a narrow rail built into the forest from Knysna to Deep Walls to carry a little timber train. It was built so that the wood from the forest could be transported faster to the sawmills in the village. Ox-wagons had become too slow. Tom Botha, who was the guard on the little train, never made the woodcutters or their wives or children pay to ride on the train as long as they sat on the floor of the open trucks or on the wood. On Mondays, Wednesdays and Fridays they hooked on a little passenger coach with a roof and window openings and wooden benches and you had to pay two shillings to ride in it. Well-dressed strangers visiting Knysna took the train specially to visit the forest, picnic baskets in their hands. They were people from the ships that anchored in the village to load the wood and people who came to the village on the big train. The wood brought in to the village by the little train was reloaded on to the big train or on to the ships. The big train could not go into the forest because of the narrow gauge rail. And there were people who came to the forest in motor cars. Important people. Then her mother used to say: sit tight, hide yourself, don't let them stare at us. Later she learned to make them gape at her, deliberately …

She got the medicine, as well as a place to sleep with the church nurse, Miss Crouse. Early the next morning she went to the small station to catch the little train back to the forest. There was a fine drizzle in the air. The passenger coach was hooked on right behind the engine, with four empty trucks behind it and two empty trucks *in front* of it – these were the push-trucks. When the train came back from the forest, the empty trucks would have been left behind and heavily loaded ones hooked on in their place. The engine seldom got the cumbersome load to the top of the slope called Tough Rise on the other side of Veldmanspad in the forest. So the driver unhooked the trucks at the back, pushed the two front ones to the top, unhooked them, drove back to the bottom, hooked the back ones on again, pulled them to the top, hooked the two front ones on again – and away they went. It was said that there was not a man in the forest who could drive a span of oxen as skilfully as Tom Kennet drove the timber train.

She got on to one of the empty trucks behind the passenger coach and sat down close to the wooden side, looking for shelter from the rain. But the guard Tom Botha walked down the rail and saw her.

'Go sit in the coach, Karoliena, or you'll be soaking wet by the time we get to Deep Walls.'

'I'm all right, Uncle.'

'Don't argue! You can see we're going out with Number 4, we're going to have a hard time getting there.'

'I don't have two shillings to pay, Uncle.' She didn't want to ride in the coach, she'd rather get wet.

'I won't charge you. Just go and get into the coach!'

Tom Botha was a good man, but a gruff one. Especially on a wet day when they had to fetch wood in the forest with the Number 4 engine. There were three engines that pulled the timber train. Number 1 – he was the Coffeepot and a little old already; he could only pull trucks around the station yard, or take things over to the other side of the village to load on to the big train with its bigger wheels and wider rail. Strangers sometimes came to take photos of the timber train's engines, especially the Coffeepot, which they proclaimed was beautiful. Then Tom Kennet took off his cap and posed proudly alongside the engine.

Number 2 engine could no longer go out to Deep Walls either, it was also too old. It could still pull heavier loads than Number 1, though, mostly transporting wood to Parkes' sawmill in the centre of the village, or across the causeway to Thesen's sawmill on the island in the lagoon. Number 3 was very strong. The problem engine was Number 4, the strongest of them all, the one the forest people called Old Elephant because he always caused trouble in wet weather. If the rail was wet, its wheels slipped on the steep slopes and round the bends like a beast that could not find its footing; then the sander on the first push-truck had his hands full keeping sand on the rails in front of the engine's wheels so that Old Elephant could keep its footing. In wet weather they always took an extra drum of sand along. Coming down, when the trucks were heavily loaded with the bodies and limbs of dead trees, there were fortunately only two rises where he usually slipped.

She didn't want to sit in the coach.

'Karoliena.' It was Tom Kennet, the driver, who walked past. 'Didn't you hear Mister Botha tell you to go and sit in the coach?'

'Yes, Mister Kennet. Sorry, Mister Kennet.'

She gathered her skirts, and lifted her leg over the side of the truck, reaching for one of the iron wheels with her foot. Mister Kennet put his hands around her waist and lifted her down. 'I heard that your father passed away; I'm sorry for you and your mother.'

'Yes, Mister Kennet.'

'His wagon wood was amongst the best we ever loaded.'

'Yes, Mister Kennet.' She didn't want to ride in the coach. She didn't want to talk about her father either. She was angry because he had died and left her behind with an emptiness inside her. Like the place where a big tree had been down cut and a hole in the forest roof remained behind.

Her father had been like a big tree. When she had finished crying for him, she had the terrible feeling that she would never again know what it was like to be sheltered, because she no longer had a father. Then she cried in the night. When her mother asked why she was crying she said she had stomach ache. The pain deep inside her could not be put into words.

When the pain did not go away, she decided she should find herself another father. Perhaps Uncle Gieljam at Gouna? No, his feet were always dirty. Her father had always scrubbed his feet at night. Uncle Wiljam Stander from Veldmanspad became her father for a while. She wanted to watch him milking one of his cows one morning, but he chased her away, saying the milk was not flowing because she was disturbing the cow. Her father would never have chased her away. Her father had been strict, but never unkind.

Six well-to-do people were already sitting on the benches. Three women, two men and one of the distinguished village women. They had a picnic basket. The strangers' faces were alight with excitement, but the woman from the village looked disapproving.

When Karoliena sat down on the bench furthest away from them, the strangers stared at her curiously and one of the women whispered something to the village woman behind her hand.

'One of the forest children,' the village woman said loudly, nose in the air. Then she added: 'Poor whites. An enormous problem.'

'How sad,' the strangers muttered sympathetically.

Poor whites.

In those days she was at school at Veldmanspad and she asked Mr Heunis the following morning what the words meant. White people who are very poor, he replied. Like most of the woodcutters. It was not that she could not understand the English words, she just wanted to make sure. The only thing she could not understand was why the words had made her feel so bad, so crushed. Perhaps it was because the strangers stared at her all the way to the forest. As if she was some sort of curiosity. When Number 4 started slipping on the first hill outside the village one of the men jumped up and pushed his head through the window to see what was going on. When he pulled his head back, he had a worried look on his face. He told his companions that it seemed to him that the train would not get up the hill. His voice filled with anxiety, he asked the village woman if she thought they were in any danger. No, said the woman, she didn't think so. The timber train had never had a serious accident – not as far as she knew.

Then all five strangers had their heads out the window, the men holding on to their hats, the women on to the headscarves that were tied under their chins around their fancy hats. Then they were all back inside again. Wet. They evidently thought she could not understand a word they said. One man kept asking why the engine had been linked up in the *middle* of the train and not in front like other trains. It was ridiculous. He said he would have a word with the driver, and then he turned to *her*. 'Young girl,' he asked, 'are you not afraid?' She pretended she didn't understand him, and stared at the floor of the coach. The village woman said: 'They don't understand English; they're very backward.'

*

She had to deliver the moths to the village.

When she came to the clearing in the forest at Ironwood Ridge, she was relieved to see the train was still standing at Deep Walls station. They were having trouble getting an enormous yellowwood block on to the open truck at the back. It was a truck without sides, and it was a massive block. It must have been a giant tree when it was alive; not even a hundred of the strongest woodcutters in the forest would have been able to roll the block on to the truck. So they were trying to pull it up a ramp of poles with the help of twelve oxen. The oxen were spanned into leather thongs lying across the truck and fastened to the block on the other side of the truck.

It was Freek Stander's span and he drove them himself. 'Slowly, my beauties, slowly!' The bodies of the oxen strained with the effort. Freek deftly reached the rear oxen with his whip. 'Pull it up! Hold it!' The block started to move. 'Stay on your feet!'

Freek Stander was no longer a poor white. He was making a good living with his wagon and oxen and vegetable gardens at Old Place close to the village. He had a good house and two of his children had trained as teachers.

'Hold it, my beauties! It's climbing!'

She no longer wanted to watch. She walked round the block and got on to one of the trucks where she found a place to sit on the load of tree trunks. Yellowwood, ironwood, candlewood, stinkwood. She turned her face towards the forest. It was Tuesday, they didn't hook the passenger coach up on Tuesdays. It was only a wood train.

There was an old red alder in full bloom on the edge of the forest with its long strings of tiny white flowers. To the left, above the platform, a forest woman leaned on the corrugated iron wall of the station shop; she was holding a child by the hand, a baby on her arm. She looked tired. It was woodcutter Jan Koen's wife. She was probably waiting for the train to leave before she went into the shop to ask for something more on credit. The shop was also the butchery and post office – all under one roof. It was the wood-buyers' shop. And the wood-buyers' train …

'Good afternoon, Karoliena.'

'Good afternoon, Mister Fransen.' He was the Deep Walls

stationmaster, postmaster, shopkeeper and butcher – as well as the wood-buyers' right hand and spy. Not a splinter of wood left that part of the forest without his knowledge. He had a book and a pair of spectacles in his hand.

'There was a man at the shop the day before yesterday, looking for you.'

'What man?'

'A man by the name of Naudé. I've never seen him before. He said he was on a very important mission in the forest and will be addressing the woodcutters at Small Clearing tomorrow afternoon. He'd heard about you from the church nurse and he would very much like you to be there.'

'Tell him to go to hell.'

The outside world was a confusing place. She no longer belonged there.

*

Six months after her father's death, her mother married Freek van Rooyen. For a while she thought she had a new father. But then she discovered that he was stupid, he could not even read. Her father had been a clever man, he could read. Her mother had been married to Uncle Freek for about a year, when an elephant trampled him to death in Kom's Bush. Six months later her mother married another Kapp. Cornelius Kapp. The forest people used to say: 'Had your mother been a rich woman, Karoliena, she would have been a beautiful woman. Pretty face, just like you, when she was young.'

They moved to Long Marsh Forest to her mother's new husband's three-roomed house with a proper stove in the kitchen. But her mother did not have any more children. She always said that God saw the misery that lay ahead for her with the one she already had.

And Uncle Cornelius did not become her father either. He was a good man, but not a father in the way her own father had been. So she decided that she would live without a father, even though it hurt …

⁂

She put the box containing the precious moths on the stinkwood stump next to her. She never looked inside the box after she had caught them, just hoped they would quickly be smothered. Sometimes they were still alive when Mister Ferndale took them out. Then he quickly pinched their heads between his thumb and forefinger, killing them instantly. In her heart she apologised to the moths. Everything in the forest, like everything on earth, had a price. A pound for a moth. Three moths, three pounds. Sometimes she caught more. It depended on circumstances. Almost every time she took moths to Mister Ferndale, he asked her the same question: Are you sure you did not tell anyone about the moths? No. Promise you never will. I promise.

The moths were a secret. He sold them overseas and some he sent to museums. Or so he said. Sometimes he badgered her to bring more, but she refused. She had a contract with the trees where she caught them: not too many at a time. He would laugh at her and ask her to show him where she caught them. No. Was she *sure* they emerged from the bark only between February and April? Yes.

Ghost moth. Swift moth. *Leto venus*. She knew all the names of the moth. Mister Fourcade had taught her. He was the cleverest man in the forest, although he no longer lived there but somewhere on the coast, east beyond Plettenberg Bay. A few times a year he came to collect plants in Deep Wall Forest or back in Gouna Forest; put them in his wooden plant boxes, wrote their names in his book. When you mentioned his name, the woodcutters spat in disgust and said: Fourcade? Bloody fool, he's the one who was sent years ago by the government to measure out the forest so it could be sectioned. A pity the elephants didn't kill him!

2

THE OUTSIDE WORLD.

Where she and the moths always found a place to stay overnight at Miss Claassens's house in the village. She was the new church nurse, or mission nurse, as she preferred to call herself. The old church nurse, Miss Crouse, decided one day that she just could not carry on working among the woodcutter families.

'It takes me six months and more to get to the worst cases. My feet can't take it any more. What am I doing this for?' She packed up and got on the big train. And she was gone.

At least Amelia Claassens still had courage.

'It's good to see you, Karoliena. You have no idea how often my only consolation is the fact that you are at least keeping an eye on the people up in your part of the forest.'

'Don't be too sure of that. There's many a night I decide never to set foot in a forest clearing again. There are now two hundred and forty-six woodcutters left. Old Jan Tait died last week. He simply sat down under a candlewood and breathed his last. They say he still had his axe in his hands. He and two of his sons were cutting wood for sleepers at Kalanderdraai.'

'How are things with Marta Barnard at Black Earth Clearing?'

'Awful. She chased me out of her house because I threatened to catch all those skinny cats, put them in a bag and drown them in the river.'

'Mrs Stopforth, the head teacher at the Sourflats school, says more and more children come to school without food nowadays. She feeds them when she can, but it's not always that she's able to do so.'

'Yes, and I suppose the shop does not want to give any more credit, either. It's had to advance money for wood licences to many of them.'

'There are children in Mrs Stopforth's school who come from as far as Millwood. It's a six-mile walk there and back and it's almost winter again. They don't have enough clothes and arrive at school cold and wet.'

'Isn't there anyone who can knit jerseys for them?'

'Where will they get the wool? What happened to the Zeelie girl at Veldmanspad?'

'She's doing domestic work here in the village. The extra money helps. Toon Barnard's two oldest boys, who were wood-draggers in Gouna Forest, have gone to Port Elizabeth where they've found work in a tyre factory.'

'At least some of the unregistered ones are finding work. Two girls from Sourflats have also gone to Port Elizabeth to work in a clothing factory. Reverend Odendaal went to a lot of trouble finding work for them.' Amelia dropped her head in her hands. 'I don't know what's going to happen. Poor Relief simply does not have the funds to help everywhere. There just seems to be no answer to the problem.'

'Perhaps an answer is on the way. I've heard there are people making enquiries about the poor whites in the forest.'

'Yes. Reverend is expecting a whole team of delegates. He will have to accompany them to the clearings in the forest. He reckons it's not going to be easy, their time in the forest will be rather limited.'

'Philanthropists have come rushing to the forest for years, Amelia. They come with good intentions, but run away fast when they see what's going on – and then they tell the outside world the elephants chased them.'

'Shame on you, Karoliena, you shouldn't mock. But at least it's good to see someone laughing for a change.'

'I've been laughing for a long time.' She ignored the shock on the good woman's face. 'Ampie Stroebel and his cousin Jakobus left by train the week before last for government land somewhere upcountry. Magaliesberg. They will apparently be given a room to live in and a plot of land on which to grow ground nuts.'

'The government is doing its best.'

'On the one hand the government is causing all the trouble, then on the other it has to appease where it has no choice.'

'How can you say a thing like that, Karoliena?' Amelia asked, shocked.

'Mister Fourcade says so. The country needs wood, lots of wood. Wood grows in the forest, it has to be cut and dragged out. It's hard work. Who must do it? The woodcutters. Not the wood-buyers, they're far too rich and important to do it themselves. How do they keep the woodcutters cutting? By keeping them poor. The government does not really care, it only wants the wood. Now and again they appease the woodcutter by giving him an extra tree to cut, but actually the government is tired of the woodcutters' complaints. The problem is, they can't think of a better way to get the wood from the forest. Or they can't be bothered to make another plan. They no longer grant cutting licences to new woodcutters, but they can't get rid of the old ones because they're dying out too slowly. They're too tough.'

'Karoliena, that's dangerous talk! Reverend Odendaal says the danger that's slowly creeping up on us is Communism.'

'Reverend doesn't know what he's talking about.'

'Karoliena! No wonder I hear complaints that you are causing trouble in the forest.'

'That's not true. The problem is that since my eyes were opened I tend to open my mouth too much.'

'I saw Johannes at the shop yesterday.'

She knew Amelia had been waiting to get to Johannes. To bait her. 'How is he doing?' she asked.

'How do you think a man whose wife keeps running away is doing? He's a good man, Karoliena. I don't think your eyes were opened, I think you were struck blind!'

'It's time you paid a visit to old Elmina Vlok at Barnard's Clearing to see how simple miracles sometimes are. She's even keeping the house tidier now.'

'Don't change the subject.'

'There is no subject. Let's go to sleep. I must be up early.'

'How are you managing to survive in the forest, Karoliena? People are talking.'

When the timber train pulled out of the station the next morning, there were seven strangers in the coach with her. And Anna van Rooyen's blanket, some wool and knitting needles, a packet of tobacco and one pound, eight shillings and sixpence in her pocket.

The strangers in the coach fidgeted like children who had been set loose: one moment they hung out of the windows facing the lagoon, the next they hung out of the windows on the forest side. They asked the questions strangers always asked.

When are we getting to the grave of the king's child, George Rex? They say it's just outside the village.

Another mile or so.

How much further to the forest?

Another twelve miles or so. The train first has to unload at Bracken Hill.

Is it true that the train sometimes kills elephants?

No.

Are we going to see any elephants?

No.

Why not?
Elephants hide when they hear the train coming.
Are we going to see any of the forest people?
Perhaps.
Is it true that they are wild?
No.

Sometimes she talked to the strangers, sometimes she merely gave the answers.

*

She'd had great fun when she was still at school and used to go to Deep Walls during the holidays to wait for the train. She made sure that she had her oldest dress on and was barefoot, with hair dishevelled so that she looked wild. But she put on her sweetest face, helped with the picnic baskets, and gave the assurance that the train would be stopping for at least two hours to hook on the wood-trucks. She spoke in a mixture of English and Afrikaans. Yes, there were places in the forest where one could have a picnic. Was it dangerous? Very dangerous. At that point it sometimes happened that the strangers simply got back into the coach and sat there for the whole two hours. The times she liked best were when they asked if she would show them a safe place to have a picnic.

Then she led them along a footpath into the forest, her body slightly tensed as she took long slow steps. She looked around constantly, as if she expected danger at any moment, watching to see if the faces behind her were showing fear. She enjoyed every minute of the game. The best days were those when a lourie started its loud kok-kok-kok nearby and put proper fear into them.

'What's making that noise?'

'Don't worry, it's only a bird. A lourie. He won't harm you.' If luck was with them they spotted the lourie as it glided from tree to tree with its large green body and red wings. They stopped, amazed, to watch it clamber along the branches.

Then she took them deeper into the forest until they reached the big old stinkwood tree where there were two tree stumps on which they could sit and unpack the picnic baskets. There were the nicest slices of bread with butter and jam. Boiled eggs. Meatballs, slices of tomato. Sometimes thick slices of meat or a roast chicken. Little cakes. Most of them gave her something to eat, a rare feast for her. They asked her about the forest, the elephants, the forest people. About herself. How old are you, dear girl? Twelve, Auntie. They listened in awe to her lies, that she was one of twelve children – one of whom was crippled. Not that it was really a lie, she had just borrowed it from some of the other forest people who lived in the clearings.

'What do you poor people live on?'

'Mostly on bread and sweet potatoes.' Then they gave her all the left-overs. Perhaps even a shilling or two.

She never mentioned that woodcutters had lucky days that kept them going: days when they caught a bushbuck in a snare. Or a little blue buck, or a wild pig. Nor did she mention their vegetable gardens.

But there were days when she was more afraid than the strangers. Like the day the two Englishwomen and their husbands sat down to have their picnic. They had even brought a servant to lay a 'table' for them with a white starched tablecloth. They didn't invite her to sit down with them and just pecked at their food with silver forks and curled little fingers, as if it was nothing special. They were ecstatic about the forest; stared at the orange fungi growing from dead wood; a half-moon red fungus growing from a tree trunk, the brown and cream striped fungi as big as dinner plates on the shady sides of the trees; little mushrooms on thin stalks standing up from the leafy forest floor, the ferns. They said it was magic, a fairy land ...

Shafts of sunlight fell through the leaves across their bodies, across the food, across the women's incredibly beautiful hair bundled on top of their heads. She wondered how anyone could be so elegant. The fine blouses with lace collars, the pearls around their necks …

Then she saw the big black shadow behind them in the thicket and her heart began to race. Elephant. Motionless. No, two elephants, there was an even darker patch to the south. Only the week before old Mrs Perkes at the station shop had warned her not to take the strangers too far into the forest. 'If the elephants don't trample them to death, they'll get lost!' She had pulled a face behind the old woman's back and told her she was jealous because she was too scared to take them into the forest herself and never got any of the picnic left-overs.

The old woman said: 'I've told your mother you're a nasty brat with no manners!'

At that time her mother had already married Cornelius Kapp and they were living in the clearing in Long Marsh Forest, east of Deep Walls. Her mother was always glad when she got home with the food the strangers had given her, and she shared it with the other woodcutters and their families. She was glad to have the shillings too.

Karoliena told the English people to make haste and finish their meal because the train would not wait for them. One of the men took out a watch on a long gold chain and checked the time. According to his watch, he said, there was at least another hour before the train would leave. Then a lourie started hissing and gurgling in the tree above them. She called to the bird, asking it to go and ask the elephants not to make trouble. The strangers burst out laughing. Was she talking to the trees? Yes, she said, and the trees said they must get out of the forest because there was fog on the way.

The lourie hissed and gurgled.

The English people wanted to know what was making the strange hissing noise. She told them it was the bird in the tree above them, and *he* also said they had to leave. Could she speak bird-language? Yes. Could all the wild people of the forest speak bird-language? Yes. Especially *that* bird's language.

The servant in his white starched uniform started to clear the 'table', packing everything back into the wicker basket. He did not give her so much as a crumb to take home. Just before they got back on the train, one of the men gave her a sixpence.

When she got home, her mother and the sister of her mother's second husband, Freek van Rooyen, were sitting in the front room crying fresh tears for Freek who had been so tragically killed by a cantankerous elephant in the forest the year before.

⁂

She got off the train at the second last station, Veldmanspad, not going as far as Deep Walls. Tom Botha got off too.

'How are you, Karoliena?'

'Well, Mister Botha.'

'Who's the blanket for?'

'Anna van Rooyen.'

'I've heard she is no longer able to get out of bed.'

'That's right. Her legs have given in completely.'

'I was saying to Mister Kennet that I don't know what's going to happen in the forest, it seems to me that everything is going backwards. How long have you been back in the forest now, Karoliena?'

'Almost three years.'

'Are you going on to Deep Walls? We still have to hook on three trucks here.'

'No, I have to see to a few things here first. I must give Anna her blanket.'

'If only there were more charitable people like you, Karoliena.'

'I'm no one's charity, Mister Botha. Only my own.'

Words, words. So that she need not tell him that she was actually going to take a short cut to Small Clearing to hear what the man called Naudé had to say. But first she had to see Anna van Rooyen.

The little house of corrugated iron and wood stood on the edge of the forest, like so many of the forest dwellings. The houses seemed tired of standing there, tired of living; they had an air of loneliness that clung to them like lifeless moss. Three chickens, a pig; three snot-nosed children, their mother sitting listlessly and crookedly on an old chair in the front room. She was Anna's daughter-in-law Fransina. Not yet thirty. Her husband Martiens, Anna's son, was somewhere in the forest cutting wood.

'Don't you knock?' the daughter-in-law asked angrily when she walked in after kicking the pig out of the way.

'No. I've brought the blanket.'

The earth floor made the house damp. A roughly made bed stood in a corner; there were bundles of bedding lying around, and smaller bundles pushed into the window openings kept the light and the air outside. A table, two chairs, an assortment of rubbish, a guitar on a rope hanging against the wall. Poverty and bad smells hung like dust in the air. She looked, but refused to *see*.

'Ma's sleeping.'

'When last was this place tidied up? When last was that bed made?'

'Listen here, Karoliena Kapp, don't you come and open your mouth in my house!' Fransina jumped up out of the chair. 'If you have something to say, go say it to yourself in the mirror and go find the husband you've thrown away. Or is that dim-witted Oldman Botha better than the decent Johannes Stander?'

'Is that you, Lina?' the old woman called out from the second room.

'Yes, Auntie, I'm coming.' The second room was no better than the first, only darker. Two beds, Anna van Rooyen on one, bundles on the other. 'I've brought the blanket.'

'The Lord bless you, child. Thank you. With my whole heart. Where's Fransina?'

'Inside. I must go.'

'No. Tell Fransina to give you a sweet potato first.'

'I'm in a hurry.' She had to get away. This place was too close to the outside world.

Fransina was waiting for her in the front room, her attitude one of challenge. 'Don't think you can just come in here … '

'Can you knit, Fransina?'

'Knit what?'

'I asked if you can knit.'

'Where will I get the wool?'

'I'll give you wool. Can you knit neatly?'

'Where will I get needles?'

'I'll give you needles. Two shillings for a child's jersey.'

She saw the disbelief in the woman's eyes. And the sudden hope.

Outside on the road she took deep breaths of the clean forest air.

A short distance before she turned off on to the footpath that would take her to Small Clearing, there was another forest dwelling at the side of the road. It was woodcutter Salie van Huysteen and his wife Martjie's three-roomed house made of a pole network, covered with branches and then plastered over with trodden clay. A veranda of corrugated iron was patched on to the house. It was a friendly little house with a lush vegetable garden on one side and a flower garden in front. And Aunt Martjie at the wooden gate was glad to see her.

'Karoliena! We never see you! How are you?'

'Well, Aunt Martjie. Where's Uncle Salie?'

'Gone to Small Clearing. The forest men have been summoned for a meeting there; God knows what for this time. Did you hear about the milk?'

'No. What about the milk?'

'There's news that the milk the government gives the children in school doesn't mean a thing. Knysna milk apparently has no strength.'

'That can't be.' At least the little mug of milk each day was something extra in the stomachs of many of the children.

'I'm not joking. They say the children should rather be given cheese.'

Better than nothing.

'You'll have to excuse me, Aunt Martjie, I must be going.'

'Watch out for the thick-legs, they're very cantankerous at the moment. Pushed over all the mileposts along the railway line, a telegraph pole as well. On Deep Walls side. Of course, they've done it before.'

'I'll keep a lookout. Your garden looks good.'

'I'll say so myself.'

There are two kinds of poor people: the good poor and the bad poor. Fortunately there were more good poor than bad in the forest, and if plans for some kind of assistance should be announced at Small Clearing that day …

When she left the footpath for the sledpath shortly before the clearing, she noticed the wheel tracks of a motor car deeply scored in the leaf-strewn path. More and more sledpaths were becoming roads for motor cars. More and more strangers were coming to the forest. Especially on Sundays.

The stranger in the clearing was standing on an ironwood stump, dressed in a black suit like a preacher. It was the same man she had watched through the crack in Oldman Botha's plank house. His shirt collar curled up at the ends and he was wearing a grey-black tie. Around him sat about twenty shabby woodcutters, faces grim with anticipation; a few sat on folding stools, others on tree stumps, most of them on the ground. Jan Koen, Martiens van Rooyen, Salie van Huysteen. Koos and Willem van Huysteen. Salman Fransen from the station shop was among them – he always had to be in on everything. Jan Zeelie. And many others.

'Good afternoon, dear friends.' The stranger opened the meeting. There was a lordly air about him. 'On behalf of the Carnegie Commission of Investigation, I welcome you all.'

'Who?' Jan Zeelie asked brusquely.

'The Carnegie Commission. In short, your concerned friends in America.'

'Don't know them.' The others nodded their heads in agreement.

'That is exactly why I'm here, Mister. To give you advance information. I am Mister Naudé, assistant to one of the main investigators and delegates of the Church, the Reverend Albertyn of Kimberley, who was specially appointed to look into your interests.'

'Then you're a miracle, Mister!' Jan Zeelie again, this time with open scorn in his voice.

'I can assure you that the Church is looking at your problems with great concern.'

'The Church doesn't bother about us,' snorted Jan Koen. 'Now and again it sends a holy one through the forest to come and see if there might be a soul to be saved. The children run away and hide. So do we.'

'The time for hiding is over, Mister. As a result of pressure by the Church's Poor Relief Committee, I bring you the good news that the government is seriously looking into establishing a Department of Social Welfare.'

'Does that mean we'll be paid more for our wood?' It came hopefully from a few of the men.

'That I am not qualified to answer.'

'We're worn out, Mister.' It was Toon Barnard. 'The hope in our hearts is as thin as the clothes on our backs – and our children's backs.'

'There will be no solution to the poor white problem unless a thorough investigation is made into the *cause* of the problem,' the man said.

Martiens van Rooyen jumped to his feet. 'That's it! Now you're talking straight, Mister! About causes you can tell us nothing; *we* can tell them to you by the dozen. We're poor because for years the wood-buyers have seen to it that we are paid as little as possible for our wood. They give us seven pennies a spoke and then sell it to the wagon-builders for almost three shillings. They pay us a penny for an axe-handle …'

'Just a moment … '

'Martiens is telling the truth, Mister.' It was old Jan Zeelie again. 'This forest was Common Woods for years and years. As it was in our fathers' and grandfathers' time. No one needed to buy a licence in order to cut in it. A man was a woodcutter if he could swing an axe, pull a saw and slave all day long to cut and saw and drag the wood out to the village to keep the wood-buyers' sawmills running. We were paid poorly, but at least we could make a living in the old days. Not like now.'

'If you would give me a chance … ' Naudé waved his arms for silence. Karoliena could not help feeling sorry for the man – the woodcutters would not make it easy for him, they were only too pleased to have the opportunity to give vent to their feelings for a change.

'One day we were simply informed that it was now the government's forest,' Martiens van Rooyen said, reproachfully. 'Forest that the government bought from whom? From God? All wood now suddenly belongs to the government!'

'A government with two tongues,' Jan Koen added. 'With the first one they say we can no longer cut as we wish, the forest must be preserved. With the other they shout: you will have to cut *far* more wood; the country needs it for railway sleepers and ox-wagons that must get to the Free State where the diamonds were discovered. Then gold was discovered somewhere up there too. More railways. Believe me, Mister, in this forest hundreds of thousands of sleepers have been cut and dragged out; every railway in this country lies on this forest's yellowwood and stinkwood and beech wood and Cape ash, and the woodcutters' sweat and blood! They pay us sixpence a sleeper and argue for ever that we've brought out second-hand quality while everyone knows that's a bloody lie. Meantime government appointed keepers and conservators to spy on us, to see that we don't cut as we used to, they hung one restriction after another round our necks. They suddenly announced that we had to *register* as woodcutters, or else we would not be allowed to cut at all. In order to register, we first had to prove that we were bonefeet cutters.'

'I beg your pardon?'

She stepped out from the edge of the forest. '*Bona fide* woodcutters,' she said and enjoyed the shock on Naudé's face when he saw her.

Jan Koen continued. 'Our names were entered in a very thin book and we were told plainly and clearly that no new names would be added until enough of us had died. There were too many of us. We had no say, we merely had to go along with it. And then? The moment they had our names in that book, they said we now had to buy a licence to cut. And Mister says this Committee wants to come and look for *causes*?'

'The object of the Committee is to come and listen to your problems, find out why you've become so poor.'

Suspicion grew on their faces. One of them asked: 'What did the government tell Mister to come and tell us?'

'I was sent by the Commission, not the government. We will be responsible only for submitting our reports to the government so that solutions can be found.'

'So that it can become a government matter?' asked one. Woodcutters were not stupid.

'Yes. For in the end it will be the government that has to make the necessary decisions.'

'A forest snail, Mister, is a slow thing. But compared to government decisions it has great speed – and if Mister doesn't keep still, he's going to fall off that stump.'

'I can assure you it won't happen. All I ask of you is a reasonable chance to inform you about the work of the Commission.'

'I thought Mister said they were coming to find out why we are so poor,' Willem van Huysteen reminded him. 'We told Mister ourselves, but perhaps Mister is a bit hard of hearing.'

That brought Jan Zeelie stiffly to his feet. 'Perhaps Mister wants more causes. Like the day the government decided to have this whole damn forest measured off and cut into sections; every section divided into four and numbered, and they painted a red stripe on the trunk of every tree which *they* thought could be cut. As a result, we now have to go to the nearest forestry station on a particular day of the year to draw lots for a tiny piece of the forest and take whatever red stripes luck throws at us. We must be thankful for it a whole year long. We may not put an axe to any tree with seeds or fruit on it! We say to the keepers, it's not an orchard, it's a forest! But it makes no difference. It's the government's law, is what they throw back at us. But government keeps demanding wood, wood, wood. We're not even allowed to take a splinter from some of the sections because the forest has suddenly become a reserve that the government wants to conserve for people coming from outside to see what a forest looks like.'

Naudé's patience was running out, one could see it from the way he twitched his shoulders. 'If only I could get through to you people!' he shouted. If only I could convince you about how important the work of the Carnegie Commission is for you!'

'I thought Mister said they were coming to listen to our problems,' Salie van Huysteen reminded him, turning to the others around him. 'Do you remember that year when the whole country was crying out for wagon wood and we had to cut assegai for spokes as a matter of urgency? But the government's bloody conservator would not give us permission to cut because the assegai trees were in blossom.'

At that point Naudé insisted on making himself heard. 'It has now been almost two years since the Commission started travelling through the country in the most difficult circumstances in order to interview all the poor whites. They have had discussions with the trek farmers, the peasant farmers, the diamond diggers, the gold diggers, the hunters in the bushveld ...'

'Mister ... '

'This is a fact-finding mission of enormous proportions

that's costing thousands of pounds and that's being paid for by concerned people in America! In short – and at last – the Commission is coming here to interview the impoverished people in this forest. We *have* to have your cooperation!'

'Mister! Someone gave you the wrong address. The gold diggers that came to this forest years ago are long gone or dead. The only remains the gold diggers left behind is the damage to the real forest back in Millwood.'

Some of the men stood up and started gathering up their knapsacks. Naudé tried to stop them with dignified annoyance. 'The Carnegie Commission brings you a chance of survival that you dare not let pass!'

'It sounds more like a doctor who comes to see what's wrong with you, but doesn't have the medicine you need.' It was Old Salie.

'Don't keep interrupting me!'

Then he fell off the stump.

And she turned around and walked back into the forest.

She did not know how Naudé was going to get through to them. Woodcutters were woodcutters. They were a different kind of human being. Unholy two-legged oxen with a different kind of intelligence in their heads. And only when it suited them. They were as mysterious as the deepest forest gorge where few dared to venture, they could converse with one another in a secret code so that one of them could quickly drag away the bushbuck – under the keepers' noses – that lay strangled in an illegal snare. They admitted their deepest fears with the frankness of children, shared their last piece of bread or sweet potato with each other; took the axe from a weak one's hands and hacked his wood for him. They climbed the highest cliffs in the foothills of the mountains to reach a beehive for a little sweetness – or to brew some honey beer for a little gaiety.

Two of them had once threatened to drag her before the magistrate because of a beehive.

'To accuse me of what?' she asked.

'Attempted mutilation!'

On that particular day she was hiding near a stream in Gouna Forest watching the butterflies that always came to eat the sandy mud in the afternoons. Suddenly she heard axes. Two axes, two men. It was late in the day for woodcutters to start felling a tree. At first she did not pay much attention, her eyes fixed on the strip of wet sand on the side of the stream where at least a hundred, or perhaps two hundred, large butterflies were dipping in to eat the mud. Wing to wing. All alike. If one flew up, another took its place. Beautiful butterflies with soft brown wings with yellow dots and squares painted all along the edges. Only long afterwards, when she picked up a dead butterfly one day, did she see the blue and orange dots, like eyes, also painted on the wings. But on that particular day she was only watching them in amazement, dozens of them gliding in the air above the stream as if at play; dozens landing on the branches of a tree-fuchsia overhanging the water and dappling them with spectacular colour.

The noise of the axes continued. After a while she heard not only the chopping, but distant voices as well. She got up, told the butterflies she would be back the next day, and asked that they should be there too.

She had not gone far when she found them on the footpath that led from Diep Turn: two men cutting down a white alder in order to get to the beehive in the forked branches at the top. She became angry and shouted at them, asking if they had gone mad. They dropped their axes, and one – she thought he was a Tait – shouted back at her: No, there's only one mad one in the forest and that's Karoliena Kapp who prowls around where no girl should! She told them that she hoped the bees would swarm and sting them to death for cutting down the poor tree; why didn't they go looking for honey on the mountain? The second one threw down his axe in a fury: Go to hell, Karoliena! No wonder the strangers think we are wild people – just look at you! Your poor father must be turning in his grave! She bent down and grabbed his axe, and in one movement swung it at his legs. He leapt into the air, howling. The other one wrenched the axe from her hands, shouting: Are you bloody mad, you could have mutilated him!

No, the Commission of Strangers would not understand the woodcutters.

They were indeed a different kind of human being. They were able to cut down the largest of trees and make it fall precisely where *they* wanted it to fall for sawing up and dragging out. They could 'see' inside a tree simply by looking at a tiny knob on the bark and know they would find trouble inside if they were to cut it: worms, red veins, gum – that the wood-buyer would not allow them to unload the wood in his yard; would send them back empty-handed to the forest.

Woodcutters were tree-sharp. Wood-sharp. They could work a piece of wood with a left-axe so smoothly that you would swear it had been done with a plane. In their lifetimes they cut thousands of spokes with an adze for hundreds of wagon wheels; hundreds of all kinds of wagon parts. They cut and dragged mountains of yellowwood and stinkwood railway sleepers – though few of them had any idea what a real train looked like. They knew only the little forest train. They had no knowledge of a telephone, yet they cut hundreds of telegraph poles. Thousands of pickaxe handles. Floor planks. Beams.

Woodcutters sometimes made the most beautiful pieces of furniture for their simple homes without realising they were works of art.

Woodcutters: trapped for life in the snare of poverty because they did not know how to free themselves. Neither the good poor, nor the bad poor. They feared the world outside the forest and they feared the elephants that sometimes kept them up trees for hours, or blocked a sledpath so that their oxen could not move an inch further; elephants knew that oxen feared them too. Devilish creatures, said the woodcutters. Creatures that would trample you to pieces if they could, in the same way that the whole world was crushing you. But the world still wanted the wood that you cut!

'And what about the day when you've cut down the whole forest, Uncle?' Karoliena once asked one of the old woodcutters.

'I'll be long gone.'

'Then you'd better not take too long to go. According to Mister Fourcade, the little that's left of the forest is going to be taken care of now.'

'Tell him I say he can go to hell. You too. Now get going!'

'They say the forest used to be twenty times the size it is now.'

'Just think of all the wood one could have cut!'

'What's the strangest thing you have ever seen in the forest?'

'You. Why are you always sneaking around? What's wrong with you? How could you walk out on a good, decent man?'

'It's been more than two years, Uncle, but you people simply won't let it go, will you?'

'Because we can't believe anyone could throw away the best opportunity that's ever likely to come her way! Especially a chance to get out of the forest.'

'You don't understand.'

She herself did not always understand. There were things she could not unravel, no matter how hard she thought about them.

No. Naudé would not understand the woodcutters.

She followed the sledpath back in the direction of Deep Walls. Back to the forest …

There was a bridge between the outside world and the world of the forest that was easy to cross when the peace surrounded you once more, lifting you to the highest treetop while a redchested cuckoo called to its mate. The forest world was where the frogs on the forest floor talked endlessly to one another. They even talked to you. Asked where you'd been, told you that leopard had been there the night before. They were looking for something to eat and walked silently on soft-padded feet. They caught one of the wild pig's children. Look in front of you, see its spoor. And its droppings.

In the forest world you could look up and see a crowned eagle circling slowly against the sky – searching, searching for an opening through which he could fall noiselessly to grab a monkey or a little buck. One's heart pleaded: please, not a blue buck today, they're still nursing their lambs.

Then, slowly, you started coming down from your own flight, landing softly in the twilight of the forest where you found the footpath that led to the Tree. *Her* tree. She had given it many names, but none was really suitable. Kalander, Yellowwood, King, Oldest, Most Beautiful, Greatest.

She had almost reached Deep Walls when she turned away from the hard road and into the forest and started to push open a path through the undergrowth and monkey ropes with her body. In the deep and shady places the rain of the previous night still lay in every hollow and the wet branches whipped against her hair.

Good day, Tree, she said when she reached it, bowing her head in reverence.

*

There was something Karoliena knew but could tell no one because no one would believe her. Perhaps she would tell Mister Fourcade one day. The only person she had trusted with a bit of it had been old Abel Slinger.

On that day, many years ago, she had taken a short cut through Deep Walls forest from Barnard's Clearing. It had taken her about two hours. At the time she and her mother were living below the forestry station at Deep Walls. Her mother had sent her early that morning to borrow the red dress she had given her sister Maria, who lived in Barnard's Clearing. Her mother needed the dress because she had started to dress up for the evening visits of Uncle Cornelius Kapp from Long

Marsh Forest. They sat in the front room while Karoliena went to bed in the back room. Her mother would call out to ask if she was asleep and she always pretended that she was. Then they blew out the candle in the front room and she heard all manner of strange noises. When the bed began to creak faster and faster she wanted to run into the forest and never come back. But she was afraid to go out into the dark forest.

The day that she walked back from Barnard's Clearing was a very hot day – swelteringly hot – the second bergwind day in a row. She was streaming with perspiration; the forest was dry, the smallest twig snapped beneath her feet, even the trees creaked strangely. They sounded as if they had teeth. The air was different, the light was different, everything seemed clearer, as if one could see deeper than usual into the forest. It was very quiet. Eerily quiet.

When the first bolt of lightning struck, she got such a fright that she started to run as fast as she could. When the second bolt struck she cried out loud in terror, fearing that it had come to kill her as it had killed her father. She was almost at the giant old yellowwood just before the hard road at Deep Walls when she remembered that one should never run in thundery weather. She was so tired and frightened that she threw the dress down in the sledpath and stumbled towards a fallen tree. She leaned back against it, trying to catch her breath. Then the third bolt struck. She looked up and saw a movement. As she watched, a strange ghost-like apparition slowly rose out of the top of the yellowwood like something that wanted to stretch itself and look out over the forest. A long green-grey robe, not of cloth but of something finer, legs and arms under the folds. The shape of a body. A head with long strings of green-grey hair. It was crystal clear, not at all like a dream. And somewhere in her mind the words formed: That, Karoliena, is the soul of the tree.

Afterwards she remembered that the tree-spirit emerged as far as its feet and that she could not tell if it was male or female.

That night, when her mother called out to ask if she was asleep, she was already outside in the dark and the rain. Earlier, when the stupid old man had come to visit, she had opened the wooden shutter in the back room and quietly climbed out to go and hide in the forest.

She was never again afraid of the forest in the dark.

⁂

Long, long afterwards she asked Oldman Botha what was the strangest thing he had ever seen in the forest. He said Dr Phillips' face the day he showed him the three little stinkwood trees.

Nobody knew the forest like Oldman Botha. She sometimes felt that he had not been born like other human beings, that he had just started to grow out of the forest floor from the seed of a tree.

A red alder seed with its soft brown shell. His wild grey hair was the colour of a red alder in blossom, and he had a long unruly beard. Strangers sometimes asked him to pose against the edge of the forest so that they could take a photograph of him.

⁂

Markus Josias Botha, of Jim Reid's Crossing above Deep Walls. Oldman Botha, they called him. He was a bachelor. He lived in a neat little plank house less than a stone's throw from one of the main elephant paths through the forest. He was not afraid of the thick-legs. He had a contract with them: they did not trouble him, he did not trouble them. Sometimes they came and rubbed their bodies against a corner of the house and his few pieces of crockery rattled and shook, but they caused no damage. They knew a very important man had given him permission to live there.

He loved to talk about the important man who had arrived at his home on horseback one morning. He introduced himself as Dr Phillips. Oldman Botha said, pleased to meet you, it so happens that I have a nasty pain behind the shoulder. No, said the man, not *that* kind of doctor; I am a plant doctor. Newly appointed at Deep Walls by the government to conduct important research in the forest. He was a Research Officer. He said that Oldman Botha could no longer stay where he was; in any case, everyone was going to be removed from the forest.

'I did not panic. But I warned him that I had seen an elephant run faster than a horse in that very same forest, the horse got away just in time. Now Mister-doctor could not say that he had not been warned. The elephant is very clever, I told him. We did not even call him by his name in the old days, we were afraid he'd hear and come put us in our place. Unfortunately Mister-doctor will not be able to put me out of the forest, for I am the one who will have to teach Mister-doctor about the forest.

'A few months later he sat on that tree stump in front of my house. He had come to discuss a plan with me. The government wanted to replant all the open spaces in the forest, where the trees had been cut out. I told him: The forest was not planted by human hands. God planted it long ago. Clever God. He waited till it was waist-high before he chased in the bushbuck, otherwise it would have been eaten away. Where the forest has been cut out, the undergrowth takes over. It was the same with the elephants they kept shooting. They won't come back. Dead is dead. Mister-doctor said he could not accept it. He needed proof. I, Oldman Botha, had to provide proof here at Jim Reid's Crossing, for a shilling a day, in the little clearing that was once used as a depot for wood dragged from Kom's Bush and where I had cleared a space for my vegetable garden. I always have something to throw in a pot with a piece of meat. I agreed to his plan. Then he said: This is how things will be from now on: one row of vegetables, one row of saplings. Especially stinkwood. I said: Mister-doctor, I'm not so sure about stinkwood, for stinkwood does not like to be planted. But I'll try.'

*

Good, gentle Oldman Botha. He didn't ask questions. But he gave her a roof over her head when she had nowhere else to go. And he was always so grateful for the pouch of tobacco she brought him.

When she ran away from Johannes the first time, his little plank house was the only shelter she could find.

3

FOREST PEOPLE MARRY forest people. Only once in while did it happen otherwise. As with her and Johannes.

If she thought back carefully, she could remember the day she had first seen him.

*

She and her mother had embarked on the ten-mile walk from Long Marsh Forest to the village to buy Karoliena some shoes and material for a few dresses. Halfway there a horse-cart caught up with them and the driver stopped to ask if he could give them a lift. Her mother said, yes thank you, Mister Stander, we're on our way to the village on important business. They got on to the cart. She sat at the back, her mother sat in front next to him. He was a tall man, his head almost touched the canopy. The horses trotted along nicely, it was downhill. Her mother suddenly assumed an air of importance as she told the man that they were going to the village to buy clothes for her child who would be going to the high school at Wittedrift the following year.

Is that so? said the man. He turned around and looked at her with surprise. He was clearly not used to hearing of forest children being sent away to high school. There were a few forest boys in the industrial school at Knysna, but they had to have standard six before they could be accepted there, and very few had that, because long before they reached standard six they were already working in the cutting teams. Two girls from Veldmanspad attended the housecraft school in Knysna; a school mainly for poor white children.

'How old is your daughter, Missus?' the tall man asked.

'Fourteen, she started school a bit late. But she's very bright. Reverend Odendaal pleaded so nicely … '

Her mother didn't tell him the whole truth about the day the Reverend turned up at the house in Long Marsh Forest. It was a Saturday. He told her mother he was there because of a serious request from Mister Heunis, headmaster of the school at Veldmanspad. Oh, said her mother. Fortunately the house was clean and tidy. The Reverend Odendaal was a difficult man; it was said that if things weren't to his liking in the forest people's houses, he simply started throwing stuff out. Reverend, her mother said, if you were sent to find out why the child misses so much school, you can hear for yourself how her chest is wheezing because of the damp and cold we have to endure. No one has mercy on us forest people. If it wasn't for the plank floor poor Cornelius himself put in, Karoliena would have had TB long ago; only my prayers keep her alive and she is all I have. Lightning struck her father years ago and left me to cope on my own. I send her to school every day, but then she gasps so from shortness of breath that she has to sit down along the way.

It was a lie. School was a stupid place. She did not always go back inside after break because she found schoolwork boring and she knew it by heart in any case. She preferred to go and play on the railway line, waving to the people in the coach, and to Mister Kennet and the fireman in the engine and to Mister Botha on one of the trucks. Or she went looking for places where the elephants had crossed the line during the night. Clever-footed, they never trod *on* the line. They knew they would be shot if they dared to break the line. It was the wood-buyers' line; Mister Thesen and Mister Parkes of the mighty rich allowed nothing and no one to trample on *their* belongings.

One day she played a bit further down the line than usual, to the south of the school. She came upon the fresh heap of dung right alongside the line, vapour still rose like smoke from it. She jumped between the lines, knowing no elephant would trample her *there*. She stood very still, listening. She was frightened, for it was said elephants could slap you to death with their trunks. She waited, she listened. The forest on both sides of the line was quiet. Only now and then came the call of a bird and the wind in the treetops sounding like the sea. It was dense forest, the part where strangers usually hung out of the passenger coach staring in amazement, hoping to see an elephant in the thicket or one of the wild forest people. The next moment she heard wood snapping. It was a slow, long snap, as if a tree had fallen over. But a tree did not just fall over by itself and the wind that day was not strong enough to blow one over. Still she waited, still she listened. She heard nothing. She could not see very far down the line, because there was a sharp bend right ahead of her. She started to walk towards the bend. Slowly, keeping between the lines and stepping from sleeper to sleeper. She made a mental note of a white alder tree that she would be able to climb if an elephant decided to chase her . . .

When she came to the bend, she saw it: a tree lying across the line, completely obstructing it. Mister Kennet would never see it in time when he came down with the train from Deep Walls. Not with the two trucks he'd be pushing ahead of the engine. She had heard the train whistle moments before up at Veldmanspad; there was not much time before it would round the bend and hit the tree. She turned round and started running back. The moment she saw the train coming, she stopped and jumped off the line, waving her arms and shouting. She waved, she jumped up and down, she screamed, but the fireman was on her side of the line and the stupid man only waved back. There was no coach hooked on, it was a timber train day. Mister Botha was standing between the logs on one of the trucks at the back. She waved, she screamed, she jumped up and down. All he shouted back was a warning that the school was looking for her …

So she started running along behind the train.

The collision with the tree knocked the first push-truck off the rails, leaving it hanging rather foolishly to the side, but fortunately it did not fall over. Mister Kennet and Mister Botha and the fireman had to saw and drag away the branches to get the rail open for the train again. They took two heavy jacks from both sides of the engine and started to jack up the truck with a long iron pole, winding and winding until the wheels were back on the rails. It was hard work and it was almost dark when they finished. Mister Botha was angry. He said it was an old trick the bloody elephants played, they always pushed trees over the rails at the very spot where the driver would not see it in time to apply the brakes. And it was always an elder tree. Could you not have tried to warn us, Karoliena?

Her mother was not shy about lying to the Reverend that day. He said: I'm not here because of your daughter's absence from school, Mrs Kapp. Mister Heunis asked me to come and speak to you because she is a very bright pupil who ought to be sent to high school next year.

'Then I suppose the school had better send her, I don't have money for it.' Her mother was immediately irritated.

'Mister Heunis assures me that she is very strong academically.'

'What does he know?' Afterwards her mother asked her what the word meant.

It means I'm clever, Ma.

Oh.

'I'm here with the suggestion that she should go to the high school at . . . '

'I'm not sending the poor child to the high school in Knysna with all those English children. She gets mocked enough by them in the street when we're in the village.'

'Don't be overhasty, Mrs Kapp.'

'No, Reverend, and nor will I allow her to go to the housecraft school in the village where all they do is teach poor white girls to be servants for the rich.'

'We want her to go to the high school at Wittedrift, on the other side of Plettenberg Bay.'

First her mother's mouth fell open. Then the shock hit her. 'Wittedrift school? Where will I get the money? She'd have to live in the hostel, have new clothes and all sorts of things that no woodcutter can afford even half of!'

'She will be given a bursary which will enable her to stay in the Church hostel adjoining the school. The Church is even prepared to help her with clothing.'

Her mother enjoyed boasting to Johannes Stander that day about her daughter going to high school.

Karoliena did not pay much attention. Living was much like sleeping then. Except that one could dream as one wished. One could dream that one was pretty and smart like most of the village girls, or like the strangers that took the timber train to explore the forest. You could dream, as you walked along a footpath through the forest, that you had high-heeled shoes on; all you had to do was keep your head and your shoulders high like a real person. Not like a poor white.

Johannes Stander dropped them off in front of Smith's shop in the Main Street and raised his hat when he said goodbye to them. As he drove away her mother said: 'There's no point in him trying to be so important. His father grew up in the forest, just like me.'

Wittedrift was like a restless slumber. She knew she must not wake up, for if she did she'd surely run away. She slept in the Church hostel on a strange little iron bed among other poor white children and ran the twenty miles home night after night to tell her mother that she did not want to be in the high school. The forest was better than the gap between the mountains where the red-roofed school stood half-hidden like something ashamed of itself; grass everywhere on which the school's cattle grazed and dropped large green heaps of dung from under their curved tails. There were no high trees. No thickets. No elephants. No forest train that came past so you could wave to the people in the coach, or to Mister Kennet or Mister Botha. Or linger at Deep Walls station in case any strangers wanted to go into the forest.

The only good thing about the school was the lonely, half-dark room where they kept the rows of books which you were allowed to read. Books with difficult words, not like school work. Mister Johnstone, the English teacher, always let her borrow a book to take back to the hostel on Fridays. She wrapped the book in a cloth and hugged it to herself, as if it were a secret.

However, she first had to get out of school.

Books helped to pass the time, the never-ending school terms.

When school holidays came, the teachers looked for a lift home for her – even if it was only as far as Knysna. From there she could walk to her mother in Long Marsh Forest. The other two forest girls at the school never bothered about finding a lift, they simply walked home on their own. It took them a whole day. They walked all along the kloof behind the mountain until they reached the Uniondale road that went over the Prince Alfred Pass from the Long Kloof, then across the mountain and into the forest from the back. Her mother never wanted her to walk home with the other girls; she said they were low-class. The teachers didn't want her to walk home either. When the holidays were almost over, Uncle Cornelius started looking for a lift back to Wittedrift for her.

One day the headmaster, Mister Cronje, sent for her in the middle of the day. He told her to gather her things quickly because there was man willing to give her a lift to the forest. She was delighted. She ran to the hostel, threw her clothes into the suitcase the Church had given her, washed her face, put on her shoes, combed her hair.

She rushed back to the headmaster's office. He said the man would be back shortly, he had just gone to have a word with one of the teachers about a certain wild flower that apparently grew in the hills above the school.

'The man is an authority on plants,' said Mister Cronje. 'What do we call such a man, Karoliena?' As if she was in class.

'A botanist, sir.'

'Correct. Although school only breaks up the day after tomorrow I have decided to give you permission to leave today because Mister Fourcade has kindly offered to give you a lift as far as Deep Walls.'

'Thank you, sir.'

Mister Cronje – he was not so bad. It was *she* who didn't want to be in his stupid school. But the Church had said she must be educated, for the biggest problem that faced the poor whites in the forest was illiteracy. Uncle Cornelius said it was a bloody lie. Deacon Van Zyl said the woodcutters' biggest problem was their ungodliness; they would walk to the village for sugar and coffee, but not to attend church. One of the woodcutters dared him to take off his frock coat and repeat what he had said; after all, woodcutters went to church at the Veldmanspad's school every Sunday and to prayer meetings on Wednesday afternoons, usually led by one of the foresters, depending on how far from home we're cutting. So keep your mouth shut.

Suddenly Mister Cronje asked her a rather strange question: 'Karoliena, are you happy here at school in Wittedrift?'

No, she said to herself. 'Yes, sir,' she answered with her mouth.

'Then promise me you will not leave school.'

I will. 'No, sir.' Where was the man who was going to give her a lift?

The man arrived. From the sudden change in Mister Cronje's manner, she knew that he must be an important man. They spoke only in English and Mister Cronje walked outside with him, thanked him for taking pity on the poor girl; she did not have an easy life, her father was a woodcutter.

She said to herself: that's not true, my father's dead.

The most wonderful thing of all was that the man had a *motor car.* A car with a folding hood, much like a horse-cart, but with wheels instead of horses and the car's registration number was CCO 10. She had been in a car few times before; it was nice and fast. Uncle Wiljam Stander, who lived above Veldmanspad, had four milk cows and a motor car that had cost him forty pounds, but people had to pay to ride in it. Uncle Wiljam used to smile and say he sometimes made more money in a month from transporting people than from selling milk.

Mister Cronje walked around the car and opened one of the back doors for her, telling her to get in. The Englishman said: No, let her sit in front.

So she sat in front.

Then they set off. It was wonderful! They followed the road behind the mountain and after a while she began to wish that the road would never end and that the kind old man would never ask her to get out. He spoke English, she spoke Afrikaans, they understood each other perfectly. The frames of his spectacles seemed to be made of the same stuff as her comb. The suit of clothes he was wearing was of the same blue-grey material as a blue buck's coat. To tell the truth, from the side he looked rather like an old blue buck with glasses. And he talked to her as if she was an ordinary human being, not a poor white to whom he had given a lift.

How many children have you got, Uncle? Unfortunately he had no children. Where is your wife, Uncle? He did not have a wife either. She said: No wonder you don't have children. He laughed and asked her how long she had been attending school at Wittedrift. Almost two years, she said, she was in standard eight by then. He asked if she enjoyed school. No. From which part of the forest did she come? Long Marsh Forest. Did she love the forest? She replied: How can one love a forest? It's only a forest. Where do *you* come from? From Witelsbos, it's quite a way to the north of Wittedrift. Did she know the Deep Walls Forest? Most of the footpaths, yes. Had she ever seen an elephant? Many tracks, she said, lots of dung, but not many elephants; they were dangerous, it was always best to keep in sight a white alder or a stinkwood tree to climb in case they chased you – the other trees in the forest were too difficult to climb. Have *you* ever seen an elephant, Uncle? Yes. He used to work in the forest. Were you a woodcutter? No, he was the surveyor who had surveyed the forest into sections many years before. Do you know what a section is? Yes, uncle, it's a *wêrrie*. The woodcutters have to draw lots to obtain a *wêrrie* in which they are allowed to cut because they are no longer able to cut anywhere as they used to. He said that he knew that. The people of the forest were getting poorer and poorer, Uncle. He said that he knew that too.

Is old Mister Botha still living up at Jim Reid's Crossing? he asked. I don't know, Uncle, there are many Bothas living in the forest; a strange wild old man lives in a little plank house up at Jim Reid's Crossing. That's him, he said, and smiled, his face wrinkling.

'When next you see him, tell him Mister Fourcade sends regards. He knows me.'

When they got to the fern bend at Buffelsnek he stopped and got out of the car to look closely at a tree next to the road.

'It's a Cape redwood, Uncle,' she said when he got back into the car. He looked up in surprise, as if noticing her for the first time. 'We call it paper tree because its bark peels off like pieces of paper, but Abel Slinger – who is a very old man who lives in the forest – calls it cold wood because even on the hottest bergwind day it is icy cold to the touch or behind your back if you lean against it to rest.' She wanted to add that Abel's wife always carried a splinter of its wood on a thong around her neck because it kept away evil. Or that one could make snuff of its bark to treat a headache.

'Do you know all the trees in the forest, Karoliena?'

'Most of them, I suppose, but not all.'

'And the plants in the undergrowth?'

'Not all of them. But most of them, I think.'

'Where does Abel Slinger live these days?'

'Close to Dirk's Clearing – if you know where that is … '

'I do. I surveyed the area. Abel was my cook boy.'

'Oh. What's the strangest thing you have ever seen in the forest?' Perhaps …

'A very rare orchid.'

'I don't know about them, but I once saw the strangest little wax flowers growing from the bark of a yellowwood.'

'Those are orchids.'

4

THE SECOND TIME she saw Johannes Stander he was getting out of his car at Deep Walls station.

It was school holidays and Mister Fransen had sent for her one Wednesday morning to accompany a man into the forest – a man who had come to write an article about the little forest train for a newspaper or a magazine. His name was Mister Speight. He jumped eagerly off the train at Deep Walls shortly after twelve – nimble-footed, bag over his shoulder, book in his hand, a camera round his neck. Young, with thick hair so heavily oiled that the teeth of his comb had left lines like footpaths through it. When Mister Fransen introduced him to her, he almost crashed her fingers with his grip. He was from the South African Railways and Harbours magazine, he said, and could they please set out immediately? His time was somewhat limited, the car fetching him to take him back to village would be there at about one o'clock. He said rather rudely to Mister Fransen that it was a pity that there was not a *gentleman* to accompany him as he had come a long way to get the information he needed.

Mister Fransen stood around nervously doing his best to

assure the man that Karoliena Kapp was a child of the forest and had escorted many strangers there before, and that he should have no doubts about her knowledge of the forest.

She silently hoped that the three elephant cows that had been grazing on the edge of the forest that morning were not in a hurry …

Unfortunately the cows were gone. The only signs that they had been there were the browsed-off tops of the tree ferns on the other side of the first forest stream; there was not even a heap of dung with which to impress the man. The only thing that amazed him was how dense the forest was and that anyone could have dared to build a railway line through such wilderness.

'Have you any idea how they did it, girlie?'

She didn't think it was really a question, but answered him nevertheless. 'They brought in a Swedish engineer to show them how.'

He looked at her, surprised. 'Do you perhaps know what his name was?'

'No.' It was something like Westfeldt, but she was not sure. Moreover, the newspaperman did not bother to remember *her* name, she was simply *girlie* – something far beneath him.

'The building of the railway must have been an enormous task.'

'Yes.' The man irritated her.

'And a most dangerous one as well for the construction workers, I imagine. What about the elephants?'

'Most of the elephants went into hiding in Gouna Forest; they only came out afterwards to do an inspection.'

'I'm not here to write a story, girlie. I'm looking for facts.'

He should be glad the cows had gone the other way … 'The construction teams often had to work in the rain. Fill up, excavate, put the sleepers in place, nail the heavy iron railway bars in place with dogspikes and special hammers.' Many of the old woodcutters had worked as youngsters on the building of the railway and loved to tell how they got the 'train-path' up to Deep Walls. 'It was not only a heavy task ... '

'Leave the construction, girlie, I can read up on how a railway line is laid if I want to. I'm far more interested in the results of the railway line. Damage over the years from forest fires, for instance. Locomotives throwing out live coals that caused fires.'

'Not these engines. Each one is fitted with a wide-mouthed spark catcher round the smokestack that catches the coals. It's government law, to prevent fires. The forest belongs to the government. The whole country needs wood. That's why the law also stipulated that a strip ten feet wide be cleared of trees and undergrowth on both sides of the rail. A strip, twenty-two miles long, from the village to Deep Walls. It took one team two years to get it done. The wind blew over the rest of the trees.'

'What do you mean by that?'

'Let me cut half of your feet off and see how difficult it is to stay on your feet.'

'I don't have time for jokes, girlie. I've arranged to be fetched at Deep Walls.'

The next moment they walked into an open patch where about twenty forest workers and woodcutters were crawling about like huge tattered moles, trowels in hands. 'And *this*?' Speight asked, surprised.

'Planters.'

'Planting what?'

'The government is having all the open patches in the forest replanted.'

'Replanted with what?'

'Pumpkins.' She couldn't help herself.

'Who are these people? Why do they look so dreadful?'

'That's the way they look.'

'Good day, Karoliena!' One after the other they saw her and greeted her. Small stinkwood trees protruded from one sack. White pear seedlings from another, little yellowwoods from a third.

'Will these poor things ever grow, Uncle?' she asked the old man standing closest to her. She knew his face, he was a woodcutter from Gouna. 'Aren't they too small?'

'Doesn't bother me, they're paying me a shilling a day to plant.'

'Why aren't you using spades and pickaxes to get through the roots? Why struggle with trowels?'

'The foreman says it's the cheapest way.'

Speight was suddenly in a hurry. 'Let's go, I'm not here to write about replanting and poor whites!'

'Of course not.'

Stupid man.

The timber train was pulling out of Deep Walls station when they came to the edge of the forest. Slowly, tiredly – a dark monster entering a dark green world with tons of dead trees on its back. The newspaperman took a photograph.

'I believe the timber industry is the entire basis of the village's prosperity,' he remarked. 'And that the sawmills are the largest providers of employment in this area.'

'Yes. But you can be sorry that you're not taking the train back to the village. Number 3 is never going to get that load out in one haul today.'

'I think my lift has arrived. I'll get the rest of the material for my article at the village.'

A car stopped at the side of the road that ran past the station and Johannes Stander got out.

'Aren't you … ' he said questioningly and put out his hand to greet her.

'Yes, I am.'

' … Meliena Kapp's daughter?'

'Yes.'

'I once picked you and your mother up on the way to the village.'

'Yes.'

'You've grown up. Did you go to high school then?'

'Yes. You remember well. Mister Speight is in a hurry to get back to the village, and I must go home.'

'Long Marsh Forest?'

'Yes.'

'Ride with us. I'll drop you off on the way.' He looked at her with undisguised admiration in his eyes and she got the feeling that he didn't want to let her go yet …

'Thank you. The road up to the house is very bad, but I'd be glad of a lift as far as Petrus Brand Road.'

When they reached Petrus Brand Road, which was actually a sledpath, he simply turned off and drove up to the house, while Mister Speight groaned loudly in the back of the car because of the bone-shaking and unexpected delay.

When they drove away, her mother waved after them with a silly sort of gleam in her eyes.

'When I saw the car coming, I knew there was something on the way … but I never thought it would be *this*.'

'Don't imagine things, Ma.'

'I'm not. When I saw the car approaching, I hurried to make myself presentable – and when you stopped, I was ready. Johannes will not be able to say he dropped you off at a low-class door. Imagine, driving a motor car now! He must be doing well out of that little shop of his. It's just as well you washed properly this morning, and that you put on your blue dress. He could not keep his eyes off you. Not the one at the back, though. Did you see how he sat with his nose in the air?'

'Don't overreact, Ma. Johannes only gave me a lift out of pity.'

'Pity does not look like *that*, Karoliena. Believe me. Take that piece of material out of the sideboard in the front room and take it to Aunt Martjie Salie at Veldmanspad; ask her to make you something nice. Tell her I'll give her some sweet potatoes and a nice piece of bushbuck meat. Mark my words, Johannes Stander will be stopping at my door again before Sunday.'

He came on the Sunday afternoon.

But the Thursday and the Friday before that were bergwind days that made her restless. When the thunderclouds started rolling in over the forest on the Saturday, nothing could stop her. She took the road to Deep Walls in case it should be a day on which the spirit would again emerge from the yellowwood …

Three times before she had gone looking on days when the weather had been like that first time. She was anxious for it to happen again, yet afraid it would not. Afraid that it had been only her imagination – yet she knew that was not true.

The last time when the weather was right had been during the short school holidays in April and it was almost time for her to go back to Wittedrift. She squatted down under the Tree while lightning struck the forest around her, changing it as if by magic into a brilliant world of shining green. When the weather started blowing itself out, she cried angrily: Wake up! I know you're in there! Wake up!

Nothing happened, apart from the feeling that the Tree was making a fool of her, while the heavy drops of rain started thudding down. Two woodcutters coming up the sledpath from Gouna stopped dead in their tracks when they saw her and stared, wide-eyed.

'Is anything wrong, Karoliena?' one asked.

'No.'

It was Gieljam Botha and Daantjie Zeelie wearing their best clothes as if they were going to church, not in the usual tatters they wore for cutting wood. They were not carrying axes either.

'Why are you in your Sunday clothes instead of your work clothes?'

'Don't ask, Karoliena. All we know is that we're in trouble and we don't even know why.'

'What did you do?'

'That's what we're on our way to find out,' said Gieljam Botha. 'The chief warden of the forest, Mister Keet, has sent for us to see him urgently at Deep Walls forest station. I have a knot in my stomach that won't go away. It's been more than a month since I trapped the little blue buck. Why send for me now?'

'Exactly,' added Daantjie Zeelie. 'If it was one of the wood-buyers reporting me because of the wagonload of wood I smuggled out from Gouna to the village to save on train fare...'

'Perhaps it's nothing serious, Uncle.'

'Mister Keet only sends for you if it's serious, Karoliena. But perhaps fate sent you to us today; we believe you're an educated person now, you even write letters to the magistrate for the woodcutters.'

'Unfortunately I can't write to Mister Keet on your behalf.'

'But you could come with us to the station to help us understand what's going on.'

They were unashamedly terrified. 'Mister Keet will want to know what I'm doing there. He didn't send for me.'

'I'll say I'm related to your mother.'

In the end she went with them out of sheer curiosity.

Keet received the two frightened old men outside the door of the building. He did not invite them in and paid no attention to her.

'I believe you are two men who *know* wood,' Keet said, looking down at them from the top step. He could just as well have asked if they knew how to breathe. 'I believe you're amongst the oldest woodcutters in the forest.'

'As you say, Mister.'

'Then I need not tell you how important the wood from this forest is to the state ...'

'No, Mister.' They were uneasy, shuffling around like children awaiting punishment. To her it sounded as if Mister Keet was postponing the real issue – that he was still on his introduction.

'And which kind of wood, as we all know, is the king-wood in this forest?'

'Stinkwood, Mister.'

'Exactly. Stinkwood not only adorns our most graceful national buildings, but also quite a few important buildings overseas. Why? Because it is one of the most exclusive kinds of wood on earth and grows only in South Africa. What's more, it is one of the most expensive woods in the world.'

'Why then are we, who cut and drag it out, paid so little for it?' Gieljam sounded as though his spirits were recovering a little.

'You always receive a good price for first-class stinkwood.'

'Where does one find first-class stinkwood? According to the wood-buyers we cut only second-rate wood – that's if we're lucky enough to draw a section with stinkwood in it.'

'You people will always find something to complain about. What I am about to tell you today could spell disaster for our timber industry. It has come to light that so-called *stinkwood* is being imported from Brazil by the ton for furniture that is being made and sold to compete directly with our wood.'

'I thought Mister said it grew only in South Africa … '

Mister Keet turned and shouted to someone inside: 'Sampie, the wood!'

His clerk Sampie appeared with a large piece of wood under his arm and placed it on the bottom step. It was a pretty, light dark wood. The two old woodcutters stepped closer, looked at the wood cautiously as if to make sure that it was not a snake.

'So?' asked Mister Keet. 'What kind of wood would you say that is?'

'I'm afraid you've got us, Mister. If it had a bit of bark on it so one could identify it by the skin … '

'Would you say it is stinkwood?'

'No, not stinkwood, for that we'll give Mister a paper with a stamp on it.'

'Exactly. But *that* is the so-called stinkwood that is now being imported from Brazil.'

'No!' old Daantjie Zeelie snorted with disgust. 'It has not even been stained properly. We could have done a better job with skunk bush brew. If the wood-buyer told us the stinkwood we'd brought out was too light, he would not give us much for it. So we'd take it back and put it in a concoction of skunk bush. The week after that he'd buy the same wood as dark stinkwood. And at a better price.'

Then Keet turned to *her*. 'Miss, I don't know what you're laughing at, but I find it most irritating!'

'Sorry, Mister Keet.'

On her way home, she saw Mister Fourcade's car approaching in the distance from the village. She waved and waved so that he would see her because it was always her greatest joy to see Mister Fourcade.

He threw back his head and laughed when she told him the story of the stinkwood and the skunk bush brew. She could see down his throat, and his beautiful small teeth; he wiped the tears from his eyes with a large white handkerchief, his eyes glittering like a blue buck's.

'Woodcutters? They're brilliant people!'

He asked if she was in a hurry to get home. No. To herself she said: don't go away, stay a while in the forest with me. He asked if her mother would worry. No. Her mother knew she always returned home.

'You're a very special child,' he said.

She replied: 'And you're a very special old man, but I'm no longer a child; I'll be seventeen on my next birthday. I started school a bit late.'

When he came to the forest to gather twigs and leaves and flowers to preserve in his plant-boxes she walked with him all day. He always wrote their names down in his book, sometimes making a sketch, and he told her they were *working*. He was teaching her. She was intelligent. Sometimes he would scold her, saying she was not paying attention. She would tell him that she did not really care about the things growing in the forest, she cared only for him. Then he would give her hand a little squeeze.

He drove back to Deep Walls that day, past the Yellowwood, the car shuddering down the sledpath that went towards Gouna and along which the two old woodcutters had come that morning.

She asked him what was to become of the woodcutters. He said he did not know, but that he often worried about them. Why, she wondered, could they not simply be paid more money for their wood.

'Karoliena,' he said, 'life is the same the world over because people are the same. Believe me. If I have something that you want, you will try to get it from me for as little money as possible, so that you can ask the next man who wants it for much more. So it goes on.'

'What you're actually saying is that the woodcutters are not going to be paid more.'

'No. Some other plan will have to be made to accommodate them.'

'What would *you* do? You're clever, *think* of something!'

'Don't worry your head with adult problems, Karoliena. Just look after yourself. The government has most of the say, the ordinary man has very little. It's best to find your own place on earth and listen to what your heart tells you.'

'Where is the place where *your* heart has its say?'

'Witelsbos.'

'The woodcutters have no place.'

'I know.'

'Jesus, Uncle!'

'It's not necessary to swear, Karoliena. It diminishes you.'

'My mother's husband, Uncle Cornelius, has joined the planters for a shilling a day. If I could take the hostel money that the Church is giving me and give it to my mother, they will be better off and I won't have to go back to Wittedrift either.'

'You must stay in school.'

'One of the woodcutters from Gouna cut a stinkwood illegally in the government reserve at Lily Bush Forest and a forest keeper dragged him and the wood to the magistrate. He was fined ten pounds, but because he could not pay it, he is now spending a month breaking stones for the roads. Other people are feeding his wife and children. What are you laughing at?'

'The skunk bush brew again. Had the government not closed all doors to the woodcutters years ago, things would be different today. They should rather have sold the forest to the woodcutters in small lots and taught them how to become businessmen, to look after the forest instead of destroying it, to market the wood properly. Things would have been different for them and for the forest today. But the government is not really interested in the conservation of the forest, they're only interested in how much money they can make from it. They will see to it that this so-called imported stinkwood is destroyed as quickly as possible so that real stinkwood remains the king-wood.'

'And the woodcutters?'

'I don't think the government is totally without a plan, Karoliena. I believe, for instance, that plans are being made to establish an old-age pension.'

'Most of the woodcutters are so old, they don't even know when they were born. The government will want proof of their correct ages. Uncle Cornelius reckons the government keeps on hoping they'll just drop dead from fatigue.'

'Enough, Karoliena!' As if he was putting a hand over her mouth.

Then he stopped the car and became the other Mister Fourcade: a shrewd old bushbuck with a human head.

'And what are we looking for today?' she asked when they got out of the car. It was as though she was slipping through a secret gate and no woodcutter or government or Wittedrift or poor white could follow.

'Today we hope to find a yellowwood or a candlewood with an orchid growing from its bark. It is time for orchids to come into flower. Tree-orchids. They take nothing from the trees on which they grow, they just need something to hold on to.'

'Then I am your orchid because I don't take anything from you either. You're something for me to hold on to. Sometimes.'

'We all need something to hold on to, Karoliena.' Was it her imagination, or did the old man sound sad? Probably her imagination, for he was back to the orchids again. 'Everywhere in this forest little gardens live in the air – tiny ferns, small and perfect orchids, sometimes as many as twenty on a spray. We call them epiphytes.'

I don't want to learn big words today!'

'Don't be lazy, Karoliena.'

Suddenly she knew she had not got through the gate; the woodcutters were standing in her way. 'I'm confused, Mister Fourcade.'

'Why?'

She was reluctant to explain. She hadn't realised until then that she had found herself another father. Mister Fourcade was her father. The truth hit her so suddenly and so strongly that she had to say something to get away from it.

'The woodcutters are cutting the forest to death, and the forest is killing the woodcutters. Now they've started replanting the forest so that they can cut it to death again one day!'

'Dear child, don't think yourself into a corner. Keep your eyes open for your own opportunities in life. There will be some relief for the woodcutters too. And for the forest.'

'How? What?'

'Always, when it is almost too late, people start to wake up. From what I hear, the first delegates of the Carnegie Commission are already in the forest.'

Silly answer.

'What's the strangest thing you have ever seen in the forest?'

'You've asked me that before, Karoliena.'

'I know. Something stranger than an orchid.'

'No, nothing stranger. Only something as beautiful and as perfect as a *Mystacidium capensa*.'

'I'm not in the mood for complicated words!'

'You're stubborn today, Karoliena. What's bothering you?'

'I don't want to go back to school. And I don't want to be a poor white.' She had to say it. She had to get the words out of her head.

'If you do not want to be a poor white, you will have to go back to school.'

'Everyone keeps chaining me to the school gate!'

He was not really paying attention. He was slowly reaching out a hand to the quar tree in front of him, gently touching the plant-thing that grew from the bark. *Mystacidium capensa*, he said softly – almost as though he was christening the stupid thing with his fingertips.

And there was not even a single flower on it.

5

ON THE SUNDAY AFTERNOON Johannes Stander's motor car again drew up in front of Uncle Cornelius's house in Long Marsh Forest.

When the sun went down that evening Karoliena had the feeling that life had suddenly started to climb upwards. Suddenly she knew how it must feel to be cleansed of mud; how it was when a glimmer of light started to break through the dark ...

If only her mother had not been so presumptuous! Bow in her hair and two spots of rouge on her cheeks. And dressed up in Uncle Cornelius's only white shirt tucked into her ugly purple skirt, and the pair of green shoes that had come in the church nurse's charity parcel shortly before Christmas. They were three sizes too big. She did not stop talking and boasted shamelessly. She told Johannes that the Church had started nagging about Karoliena again; they now wanted the child to go to Oudtshoorn to study to become a teacher. Where would the money for this come from? Woodcutter Andries Koen from the forest at Salt River said it had cost him thirty-two pounds to send his daughter to Oudtshoorn for the first year; sixty-four pounds for the second year. Not everyone was like Andries Koen who could rent extra land and keep cattle. She'd heard that he'd recently rented more land from the English Church. While he cut wood, his poor wife had to herd the cattle like a servant. His other daughter had married well to a man in Johannesburg.

'Ma ...'

'Pour Johannes some more coffee, Karoliena, and straighten your dress, the hem is dipping.'

The only way out was to ask Johannes if he would like to go for a walk.

The louries had already begun to settle in the trees for the night, but it was still light enough to find the footpath into the forest. They had not gone far, when Johannes suddenly took her hand, looked into her eyes and cried out passionately: 'Karoliena, you've *got* to get out of the forest!' Almost as if he wanted to take her by the hand and *drag* her out.

'I don't know how,' was all she could say. He had the most beautiful blue eyes ...

'You're no ordinary girl, you don't belong here!' They were like words out of a dream. Cleansing words. She didn't want him to stop. He had the most handsome face ...

'I have to go back to Wittedrift, they don't want me to leave school.'

'Go until the end of next year. Standard ten is enough. Parkes is appointing more and more girls in his office, I have good contacts. You must get out of the forest.'

'I have no place to stay in the village.'

'There are nice young people at Miss Ann Macmaster's boarding house. You'll learn to speak English.'

'I *can* speak English. Mister Fourcade speaks only English to me.'

'I want you to stay away from that old Communist. What does he want with you? I'm sure I saw you with him in his car one day.'

'He sometimes gives me a lift to Wittedrift. Or home.'

'I don't like it at all. Next week I'll take you back to school myself.'

Life started climbing upwards.

She kept on walking in her sleep, letting the most beautiful dreams play through her mind.

But then the devil disturbed the peace of Long Marsh Forest when it was least expected. At four o'clock one morning when Uncle Cornelius opened the front door to set out at dawn to assemble with the other planters, he found Hestertjie Vermaak from north of Deep Walls sitting outside in the light of the lantern. She was weeping bitterly.

Uncle Cornelius said he did not have time for nonsense; the foreman would not allow him to start work if he was late. Meliena came out of the house with a blanket wrapped around her and helped Hestertjie inside; the girl could hardly stay on her feet. Karoliena appeared in the doorway to see what was going on.

'Aunt Meliena,' Hestertjie cried, 'I'm in the family way.'

'Jesus!' Meliena shrieked, and pushed Hestertjie on to the bed in the front room. 'Could you not have kept your legs together? Isn't there enough trouble in the forest? Karoliena, get her a sweet potato!'

She could not move. Terrible black waves rolled through her head, pushing away the dreams, leaving just the wretched Hestertjie in a heap on the bed.

'Karoliena!'

'Yes, Ma.'

She and Hestertjie had been in the same class at school in Veldmanspad, although Hestertjie was two years younger because she had started school at the right age. Hestertjie's father was a woodcutter too, and there were eleven children in the family. Mister Heunis had often said he wished he could divide them in half: half of Hestertjie's sweetness for half of Karoliena's intelligence. She sometimes walked home with Hestertjie after school, curious to have yet another look at

Hestertjie's mother. She was fat and wore an old black hat on her head. The children said her hair was terribly matted, she didn't have a comb. When they reached Hestertjie's home, and always within earshot of the old woman, she asked what smelled so bad. Then Hestertjie's mother became furious and shouted: Bloody pest, don't come sniffing around my house! Ever since your bloody mother married a man with plank floors and a stove, she thinks she's the bloody queen! But she forgot to teach her bloody child decent manners! I'm an educated woman.

Hestertjie's mother had a book. A red book. It was a bit shabby but it was always lying on the shelf in the front room, and when the church nurse or the Reverend came calling the old woman always opened the book on her lap and started reading attentively. One day Hestertjie told her that her mother could not read. Then Karoliena saw that it was an old school history book. At least *her* mother really *could* read.

Late that afternoon, when her mother came back from Deep Walls where she had taken Hestertjie to tell her mother of her plight, she sat down on the couch with a strange worried look in her eyes. After a while she said: 'You must get out of school, Karoliena. You must take Johannes Stander.'

'Yes, Ma.'

If she could have, she would have run to the village to Johannes.

She had to get out of the forest.

But Johannes said she must finish her last year at school.

It was a long year, a bitter year. On the one side her mother was tugging to get her out of school; on the other Johannes was insisting she stay.

'Education, Karoliena, is becoming a social requirement for girls today. You will thank me for it yet.'

Her mother even went to see the Reverend Odendaal to give him a piece of her mind because the Church would not allow her to daughter to leave school. If she lost Johannes

Stander as a son-in-law as a consequence, she would take the Church, pulpit and all, to court. See if she wouldn't! When Karoliena accompanied Mister Fourcade on his trips into the forest during the school holidays, her mother carried on like a brood-hen who saw a hawk in anything that moved.

On the last day of the last year of her school life, Johannes came to fetch her and her suitcase at the hostel at Wittedrift. Behind the mountain, when they had almost reached the crossing to Uniondale, he stopped the car and took her face in his hands. His eyes plainly said he was taking her for himself.

'From here on we walk together, Karoliena. I'm going to take care of you, I'm going to take you out of the forest and place you in my care. Do you understand what I'm saying?'

'Yes.' Although she did not quite understand. But she knew if the angels had come to fetch her to heaven at that moment, she would have told them to pass her by, for she was in heaven already.

'I've talked to your mother and she has given her consent for me to take care of you from now on. As from Monday you will be boarding with Miss Ann; she will look after you. She is a cultured lady and has a heart of gold where the poor are concerned. Mrs Cuthbert – her house is also in the Main Street – will start making you suitable outfits. I'm in the process of renovating the house adjoining my shop. The floors will be laid tomorrow.'

'Are you telling me that I'm not going home to Long Marsh Forest?'

'You're going home to your mother and Uncle Cornelius for the weekend.'

'I thought you were going to find me work at the sawmill?'

'I've decided against it because it is not necessary that my wife should work – unless, perhaps, I should need you in the shop.'

'How old are you, Johannes?' He seemed to have a few grey strands in his beautiful black hair …

'I'll be thirty-four on my next birthday. Your mother says

you'll turn nineteen on the eighteenth of January.'

'Yes.'

'I want you to become my bride on that day.'

Life started skipping upwards. One moment she had been nailed in a box on which POOR WHITE was painted in large letters; the next Johannes Stander had begun to free her with his bare hands.

When she got home it seemed that a ray of light was casting a glow over the whole forest.

Her mother was different. Uncle Cornelius was different.

'The wheel's turning, Karoliena. The wheel's turning.'

'That's true, Ma.'

'Behave yourself properly and stay in the house. I've promised Johannes that I'll look after you.'

There was a strange holiness about her mother, a sort of beatitude. About Uncle Cornelius too – though perhaps a little less holy, rather more contented. Her mother sat stringing a dish of green beans; Uncle Cornelius was sharpening a hacking-knife with a flat file just outside the front door.

'We've had good news in the forest,' he said.

'What?'

'Forestry is going to give us work at a fixed rate of pay.'

'How did that come about?'

'Plantations are going to be planted as far as the eye can see. On government instructions. Mister Keet says it's to create work for the poor. They will be state plantations. Of pineapple trees.'

'*Pine* trees,' her mother supplied the correct word.

'What happened to all the replanting you were doing? The open spaces in the forest?'

'Bushbuck devoured the lot. Jan Westraad tells me there's not a leaf left where we replanted in Deep Walls Forest. It was a waste of time.'

'Hestertjie has a baby boy,' her mother said.

'Has she said who the father is?'

'No. You must behave yourself properly, I don't want Johannes to find any blemish on your character. Why are you so fidgety?'

'I'm going to become a village person, Ma.'

'He told me, yes. He also said I may come and choose a piece of material from his shop for a new dress. He thinks you'll be useful in the shop. I told him he's getting a hard-working woman, that you've always helped me in the garden and in the house. But, I'm telling you now, I want some of those orange sweets in the glass jars in his shop. And a few of those tins of sardines. Uncle Cornelius must have a new pair of trousers too.'

'Ma! I can't simply take things from the shop!'

'Why not? What's his is yours. It's the law. The Reverend was here again. Wittedrift sent him to ask that you should study to become a teacher. I said: Reverend, you can plead till you're purple in the face. Karoliena is about to marry a very rich man. Uncle Cornelius and I took the train into the village last week to go and have a look at the house he's fixing up for you. He's building on an extra room. I said to myself that I would need more than one piece of material. I can't allow you to be ashamed of the fact that your people come from the forest. One of the women who works behind the counter in his shop turned up her nose at me when she asked if she could be of assistance. I said: No thank you. I'm just looking. Mister Stander is about to become family.'

Uncle Cornelius spoke again. 'It's not everyone who will be able to move over to the plantations.' There was a touch of malice in his voice. Or maybe it was pride. 'Hans Stroebel tells me that the men at Veldmanspad who cut in Parkes's forest are trapped. Most of the houses at Veldmanspad were put up for them by Parkes. It's as good as a life-long contract.'

'Really? I think it's rather Parkes who is getting worried that the woodcutters will all run to the plantations. The law says only registered woodcutters may cut wood – even in Parkes's forest. And the government no longer registers new woodcutters.'

'Tom Botha asked about you,' her mother told her. 'Tom Kennet too. They say they miss you on the train, and there's no one at the moment who can take strangers into the forest and scare them. I told Tom Botha you're grown-up now and educated, that you're about to get married to Johannes Stander. He said he's not surprised, you've always been a very pretty girl. Like I used to be.'

Uncle Cornelius's mind was evidently already in the plantation. 'Many new roads are going to be made through the forest, and the sledpaths will be gravelled; Hans Stroebel says about twenty of the unregistered woodcutters and wood-draggers will start road-making next week. They'll earn fixed wages. Strangers are complaining about the state of the roads in the forest. Their cars break down. One had a wheel fall off in Kom's Bush. He could have been killed. One of the keepers at Deep Walls told me that two men covered the distance from George to Knysna in three and a half hours last month. I said to him, gone are the times when it took us seven days by ox-wagon from George to Knysna … '

'My father always said it was fourteen hours by horse, if you had a good horse,' her mother added. 'Pa had a good horse, we weren't always so poor. By the way, Karoliena, that foreigner came to the house with his car last week. He wanted to know how you were. I did not invite him in.' She was clearly offended.

'Mister Fourcade?'

'Yes. I told you to stay away from that old goat and stop following him into the forest!'

Mister Fourcade.

'What did he say? When's he coming again?'

'Coming what for?'

'Don't be nasty, Ma! I miss him.'

'Jesus!'

Karoliena got up and walked outside because she suddenly felt as if she would suffocate in the house. She was anxious. A strange fear threatened to overcome her and it suddenly occurred to her that one had two hearts: one for the night and one for the day. At night her heart ran to Johannes, in the day her heart turned to Mister Fourcade.

'Karoliena, where are you going?' her mother called after her in alarm.

'Leave me alone!'

6

MONDAY ARRIVED.

One of the few things she remembered about her father was that he had always scolded her when, as a child, she had wanted to climb up a tree. He would say: Get down from there, Karoliena, you're going to fall and hurt yourself!

Miss Ann's boarding house was a tree she *had* to climb. *Wanted* to climb. Because Johannes wanted her there. That was why she did not have a moment's hesitation when he dropped her there that day. No – when he *handed her over* that day. Like leaving a kitten in a good home.

Miss Ann was a dear old lady who wore her hair in a bun on the top of her head; she had small feet, small hands and wide eyes that missed nothing. Miss Ann received her with kindness and showed her the stoep-room that had been prepared for her. There was a single wooden bed with a crisp white coverlet spread over it and a little bubble-cloth mat on the floor in front of the bed. A glass jar of nasturtiums stood on a beautifully embroidered doily on top of a chest of drawers. A washstand with a marble top; a porcelain washbasin, jug and chamber pot; dark red curtains. A beautiful old stinkwood chair, a stinkwood-and-yellowwood wardrobe. A porcelain soap-dish. What else? A yellowwood table in the corner with a stinkwood drawer; another stinkwood chair, a candle in a candlestick. There was a large standing mirror in a frame. She could see her entire reflection in it!

The first few days were spent getting used to a new routine – a hundred times better than what she had to get used to at the hostel. First she had to get used to the sounds, learn to distinguish each one; the creaking of every floorboard, the human noises, the village noises: the sounds of revelry when the street lights came on at night and the coloured children came to play under the lamp posts. There were lots of moths. Horses were in their stables and most people were inside their houses with the shutters closed. Cars no longer drove past, kicking up the dust. Only occasionally the doctor's car came past.

In the late afternoons Johannes came and sat with her on the stoep. He told her what ships had entered the lagoon through the Heads that day; what goods for his shop had been offloaded at the mooring place. The same mooring place at the wooden quay where the ships came to load the mountains of wood from the forest. Woodcutters' wood that had been carried from the forest by the little train. Pieces of dead trees.

'Are you happy in the village, Karoliena?'

'Very happy.' Life had become like a box of gifts; every day she opened a new one.

'Miss Ann says you are having your hair cut tomorrow.'

'Yes, I'm looking forward to that.'

'Are you missing the forest?'

'No.'

'I believe Mrs Cuthbert is going to start making your outfits next Monday.'

Somewhere in her being she wanted *clothes*, not outfits. 'Miss Ann says she'll go with me to choose the material.'

'That's good.'

He brought her the most beautiful box of handkerchiefs, a

little silver brooch, a new comb and brush, a toothbrush to replace the one the Church had given her when she had gone to the hostel.

'Why did you bring me to Miss Ann, Johannes? Were you ashamed of me?'

'Not in the least. You simply didn't have the opportunities the village girls have had; they are sent by ship to Cape Town to fancy schools, or to finishing-schools – often overseas. Miss Ann's place is like a finishing-school and I'm giving it to you as a gift so that you will adapt to your new environment with ease – and also adapt to life as my wife. We're getting married in seven weeks' time. Do you realise that?'

'Yes.' Fortunately it still seemed a long way off. After all, one did not *jump* up a tree … one climbed slowly and carefully.

'Miss Ann says that you need very little "finishing". She says some of the other boarders are surprised to learn that you're from the forest.'

'She told me so.' Hope they go to hell … .

'There are, however, a few small things I want established in my house right from the start.'

'Such as?'

'Absolute neatness. The use of starched table napkins at every meal.'

'Then you'd better see to it that there are table napkins and starch in the house.' Did he think she did not know about table napkins?

'I will.'

She might not have learned about table napkins in the forest, but there was not a picnic basket opened at Deep Walls that had not contained the starched articles. Nor had the food-baskets Mister Fourcade sometimes brought with him.

'Another thing, Karoliena.'

'What?'

'I expect my wife to dress smartly at all times.'

'In the kitchen as well?' It came from her mouth a bit sharply.

'Yes, in the kitchen as well. In case of unexpected guests.'

How many hundreds of dresses did one need to be smart every day? She did not ask, but it crossed her mind. And what would 'outfits' look like in a kitchen? Did one have special aprons too?

The only difference she had with Miss Ann was about her habit of wandering off into the village. Miss Ann said it was not proper for a young lady to walk in the streets on her own. She told Miss Ann she was used to walking on her own. Miss Ann replied: This is the village, not the forest! Mister Stander had asked her to keep an eye on her. But she couldn't just sit on a chair the whole day long, doing nothing. Besides, if one lived in the forest, one had to make sure one knew the forest; if one lived in the village, one had to make sure that one got to know the village.

And so she simply walked off.

Past the old stone church in the Main Street. Past the magistrate's office. Quickly past the large sawmill in the middle of the village where the saws screamed in your ears and gobbled up enormous logs and spat them out as planks and heaps of wood chippings. The chippings were dragged away to be thrown into the furnace which had brought the water to the boil to make the steam that enabled the saws to gobble up the next dead tree. It was like braiding a rope on which to hang yourself. She kept on walking until she heard the sound of the next sawmill. Then she went down one of the side streets. And up the next. Such beautiful gardens. Pretty little whitewashed houses with thatched roofs. Double-storeyed houses. There were cattle along the side streets, devouring people's gardens. A smartly dressed woman came out of one of the houses and angrily tried to drive away two oxen at her hedge. The beasts took no notice. They just kept on eating. Karoliena picked up stones and threw them at the cattle, which frightened them and sent them galloping down the street. The woman looked at her in amazement, said a quick thank you, then hurried inside. Surely she could not have thought that she might have thrown the next stone at *her*?

It was a rich people's village; they wore nice clothes and drove motor cars. But the trees on either side of the Main Street looked dreadful. They were poor crippled things, trying to be brave. Gaps where one was missing, others just stumps. Like most of the forest people's teeth.

'Why do the trees along the Main Street look so awful?' she asked Johannes that evening. 'What kind of trees are they?'

'Oak trees. A town has to be made beautiful, it attracts people.'

'They're anything but beautiful.'

'You're very observant. The Council has recently decided that other trees will have to be planted. There were people from England in the shop today, they want to buy property here. They say the place is like heaven. The problem is that development has become a nightmare. There is no way the Council can extend the village boundaries because the owners of the land on the outskirts of the village do not want to sell off their land, nor even part of it; they don't pay rates at the moment, and they are standing in the way of progress. Places to build are becoming very scarce.'

It didn't bother her, her mind was still on the trees. 'I doubt if such stupid trees as those along the Main Street will be tolerated in heaven.'

'You still have a lot to learn, Karoliena. It's the price of progress. When those trees were planted, the Main Street was a road for ox-wagons bringing wood from the forest into the village – not a street for motor cars and street lamps.'

'Miss Ann says the dust is getting her down.'

'It won't be for much longer. The street is going to be rebuilt and tarred next year. The problem is to decide whether or not the main road should run through the village. There is increasing traffic on the roads. By the way, Miss Ann says you're a bit cheeky.'

'I have to have a *say*.'

'I understand.'

The next day Mrs Cuthbert came to take her measurements and show her sketches of dresses from which she had to choose. Padded shoulders, flower patterns cut out on the bodices. She told Miss Ann that they looked a bit like old people's clothes. Miss Ann said they were the latest fashion.

The following day they bought material at Johannes' shop. The two ladies behind the counter had a good look at her while they weighed rows of little paper bags with the usual tickey's worth of salt and sixpence worth of sugar – ready for when the forest and sawmill workers came to spend their week's wages on Saturday afternoons. She recognised the little brown paper bags. There were rows of them on the shelves of the shop at Deep Walls.

A few days later Johannes showed her and Miss Ann the house he was getting ready alongside the shop. It was spacious and beautiful, but still empty and full of hollow sounds. There were two bedrooms. An enormous four-poster stinkwood bed. A stove in the kitchen where cupboards were being installed along one entire wall. Taps for water, ready to be turned on. A bathroom with an iron tub resting on feet shaped like a cock's claws. Two water tanks outside.

'Johannes,' she said that evening when they were sitting on the stoep, 'I'm worried about all the money you're spending.'

'Nothing is too much for you, Karoliena. I can't keep my eyes off you. You are looking so lovely, your hair, the colour in your cheeks, that pretty outfit you're wearing.'

'I'm afraid to look in the mirror. It feels as though I don't have hair any more, my neck is too bare. Do you remember the oak tree they took out with pickaxes next to the bank last week? They've planted a petrol pump in its place today. A red one.'

'I know. Miss Ann says Mrs Cuthbert has started work on your wedding dress … '

'Yes. It will be very pretty.' The colour of an elephant's tooth. A dream that was coming true. The only problem was the shoes that Miss Ann made her wear. She told Miss Ann her feet did not such have such sharp points. Miss Ann said they'd get used to it.

She sat on her bed that night, bent down and picked up the bubble-cloth mat. Again the strange fear came over her. Something was not quite right. She was going to wake up …

When she was still at school in Veldmanspad she used to see old Anna van Rooyen sitting in front of her house cutting out round pieces of cloth. Dozens of them. Day after day. Week after week. Year after year. She was always begging for cloth or old garments to cut up. Then she worked the pieces together with needle and thread to form little cloth bubbles which were again sewn together … year after year. One day she stopped and asked the old woman how many thousands of those pieces of cloth bubbles she was still going to sew together. She said she did not know. But it was better than doing nothing.

Perhaps it was from all the sitting and cutting out of pieces of cloth that, in the end, her legs gave in.

All through the forest one found articles made of the bubble-cloth. Mats, pillow cases, bed covers, floor covers, table cloths.

Bubble-cloth things were poor white things. Johannes must never put any of them in their house.

The next day she walked as far as the small station where Mister Wilson, the manager of the little timber train, was surprised and glad to see her.

'Karoliena!'

Mister Wilson kept the train's books, wrote everything down, negotiated prices with the woodcutters when new sleepers had to be cut to replace the older ones on the line. The woodcutters said Wilson was becoming as corrupt as the wood-buyers and in some ways just as stupid too. He decided one day that he was no longer going to boil the sleepers in tar to protect them against pests, it was too expensive. Instead, the woodcutters had to cut insect-resistant wood. They asked him, what's that? He said white pear and hard pear. They asked, are you sure about that, Mister Wilson? He said: Yes. He wanted a thousand of each. They said nothing. White pear and hard pear were the favourite food of worms and bugs. They just went into Kom's Bush to cut the best white pear and hard pear they could find, sawed every tree into seven-foot lengths from which they cut the sleepers and dragged them out to Deep Walls for the train to take to the village. When it came to paying for the sleepers, however, Mister Wilson was suddenly very embarrassed. The sleepers, he said, were unfortunately all of second-hand quality. He could not offer much for them. Hans Stroebel said: Mister, if this is second-hand quality, you haven't seen rotten yet – wait until the worms and the bugs get their teeth into them!

'I've heard that you're now living in the village, Karoliena. How are you doing?'

'Very well. And how are you, Mister Wilson?'

'How shall I put it? Between being mayor of the town and manager of South Western Railways, there is little time for anything else.'

They sat on the bench in front of the station office. 'What's that they're putting up across the line down there?' she asked. It looked like a shed on iron legs planted on both sides of the line.

'That, Karoliena, is a weighbridge. So that we can at last teach the woodcutters that it will not pay them to try to cheat us. From now on, every truck of wood that comes from the forest will have to come in over that weighbridge to be weighed. The woodcutters are charged railage per ton-mile for the wood, but their estimates are always short. Which means that we lose and they win.'

'The woodcutters say the railage is the last worm that eats them.'

'Woodcutters, Karoliena, always have something to complain about. You should know.'

'They're having a hard time.'

'Everyone's having a hard time. The government is taxing the timber train off its very rails! We've already had to pay off workers. If we dare look the other way, the woodcutters will span in their oxen and start bringing out the wood by ox-wagon again! They have no sense of progress. The main problem for us, however, is the lorries that sneak into the forest to bring out wood. How are we to compete? And I haven't even mentioned the losses we've suffered since the introduction of the big train between George and the village. The survival of our harbour is at stake. Most of the wood is no longer shipped out, but hauled out by the big train. The ships now mainly transport sugar and drums of petrol – for as long as the government will allow it, of course. We are making representations to the government.'

'The last I heard was that the woodcutters in Gouna Forest were unhappy because two of the sawmills in the village refused to buy any wood that did not come into the village on the timber train.'

'We have no choice. Ask Johannes Stander. He has an amazing head for business – and for choosing the right wife.'

So he knew about her and Johannes.

On her way back to Miss Ann's that afternoon, she met Hestertjie Vermaak and two of her younger sisters on the street in front of the Royal Hotel. One of the sisters was carrying the baby. She wanted to turn back and cross the street again, but Hestertjie's eyes had already widened when she recognised her.

'I'll tell your mother that we've seen you. The baby is fretting, we took him to the church nurse.'

What had Mister Fourcade said one day? When you meet someone without a leg, don't cut yours off in sympathy – for then not one of you will have two legs. She wanted to take off her clothes and give them to Hestertjie. Give the brooch to one of the little sisters. Anything. To make her feel better.

'Pa and the team are cutting in Kom's Bush,' said one of the sisters. 'The elephants chased them yesterday.'

'Is it nice to live in the village?' asked the other sister.

'Yes.'

'Your mother says you and Johannes Stander are going to

get married,' Hestertjie said, not looking up. 'She says she and Uncle Cornelius are coming to live with you so that Uncle Cornelius will no longer need to work in the plantations.'

She lay on her bed that night, but she could not sleep. She wanted to cry, but she could not cry because she did not know if the tears behind her eyes were tears of pity for Hestertjie, or because she was glad to have escaped from the forest. In her mind she started combing Hestertjie's hair, dressing her in new clothes, putting shoes on her feet. But Hestertjie would not look up.

The following day she asked Johannes how much he paid Miss Ann for her board.

'Three pounds a month.'

'I'll come and work for you in the shop.'

'After we're married there may be times when it will be necessary, Karoliena. But not now. Why do you sound so depressed?'

'I met some people from the forest in the street yesterday.'

'You're done with the forest, Karoliena. Next time simply walk past them.'

'What's going to happen to my mother?'

'We can drive out to Long Marsh Forest once a month. Perhaps take her some meat.'

'I'm afraid that she will want to come back with us.'

'I'll make sure that it does not happen.'

But things nagged at her. Hestertjie. The clothes Miss Ann had had made for her that were too tight. The people who stared at her when she and Johannes took their places in church on Sundays. The bad feeling that would not go away because she had disappointed Miss Ann one day at a grand woman's tea party in a grand house above the village, because she did not know she was not supposed to take her empty cup to the kitchen and wash it. On top of that she had slipped out the back door to have a word with Moos in the garden. She knew

Moos, he used to be a woodcutter at Veldmanspad. Miss Ann's face was red with anger afterwards. She said guests were *not* supposed to talk to the hostess's servants! And a guest *never* told the hostess that the tea was too weak!

'It was weak as piss.'

'A lady does not use words like that!'

Inwardly, she ached. Like the day she fell out of the stinkwood tree and had to pretend for days that she was not hurt so that her father would not notice.

Johannes sat with her on the stoep on a Monday evening. She told him she was sorry, she knew she was failing him. He said she was imagining things; everywhere he went people congratulated him on his beautiful fiancée. It didn't make her feel any better. She asked if she could go and visit her mother at Long Marsh Forest. He offered to take her there the next Sunday afternoon. But she said she had to go alone. Why? There was something she had to ask her mother. Urgently. She wanted to go by train. Alone. He said it would be all right on condition that she waited until the Wednesday when they hooked on the passenger coach that came back the same afternoon. Would he please explain to Miss Ann? Yes.

When he left, he gave her five shillings.

She kept two shillings for her train fare; with one shilling she bought thirty bananas for Uncle Cornelius; with another shilling she bought her mother a bag of the orange sweets that looked like apricots. The last shilling she put away. Just in case.

There were five strangers in the coach. They were from England, getting away from the winter across the sea. It must be wonderful to live in Knysna, they said. Had she lived there all her life? Did she think they would get to see any of the wild people of the forest? Would she point out George Rex's grave when they went past it? They didn't think he was really the king's son, there was no proof. Were any of his descendants still around? Yes. One of his grandsons used to be stationmaster at Deep Walls in the forest, and there were other Rexes too. Some white, some brown. Did she think they would see an elephant?

All the usual questions.

She encountered the first 'wild people of the forest' on the other side of Veldmanspad shortly after she had taken the footpath to Long Marsh Forest. Dirk Bouwer from Dirk's Clearing and Neels Barnard from Black Earth Clearing, husband of Martha Barnard, formerly of Gouna. Each man had a knapsack swung over his shoulder, they appeared to be in a hurry and had worried faces. Karoliena was glad that the English people on the train had not seen them, because they would then for ever after have said that they *had* seen some of the wild people.

'Good day, Karoliena. Your mother is at home, we went past her house a short while ago.'

'Where are you going?'

'To Deep Walls, to find out whether a rumour is being spread through the forest to frighten the last bit of courage out of us.'

'What rumour?'

'Hans Stroebel says the government has counted the trees in the forest and worked out how long we will still be allowed to cut. Those doing the sums say not for long. What are we to do? We have wives, we have children … '

'How is Aunt Martha, Uncle Neels?'

'Miserable. Your mother reckons *her* salvation is on its way, because you're getting married to Johannes Stander. I knew his late mother well when they were still poor people – before his father started slaughtering pigs and getting ahead.'

'How are things at Uncle Dirk's house?'

'If it wasn't for the things we get from the garden and occasional luck with a bush pig for a little meat … '

'I'd better be on my way, I have to catch the train back to the village. You didn't really tell me what it is you want to find out at Deep Walls.'

'They say that from now on the woodcutters are going to be allowed to cut only 300 cubic feet of wood a year. No longer 700 cubic feet. That's as good as a death sentence, Karoliena.'

'That's true, Uncle Dirk.'

It surely could not be true. They could never survive on that. The government would not allow it. When were the Carnegie people coming? Or was that also just a rumour …

Her mother got a fright when she saw her at the door.

'Karoliena? Jesus, my heart!'

'Don't upset yourself, Ma. I'm only visiting.' The house was in disarray. It had clearly not been swept for some time. 'How are you, Ma?'

'Not well. Uncle Cornelius is working in the plantation up at Buffelsnek. He leaves before dawn each morning and doesn't get home until it's almost dark.'

'I see there's not much in the garden.'

'Where do you think he finds time to pick up a spade? Sundays? That's the only day he has to rest.'

'Ma can dig.' She and her mother had always worked in the garden.

Her mother became angry. 'What are you saying? You sit all high and mighty with your arse in the village and come and tell *me* to pick up the spade?'

'I brought Ma some sweets. And bananas for Uncle Cornelius.'

'There's not a bit of meat in the house. Johannes promised me material for a dress … but that's how it goes. The moment they've got you, they hang you out to dry like a piece of meat! But I can see that you're wearing something new and decent.'

'I can't stay long, I have to catch the train back to the village.'

'Oh. When will you come again?'

'I don't know.'

'Bring us some meat next time. Mutton. A nice piece of rib.'

'Has Mister Fourcade been again, Ma?' She had to know he had not forgetten about her …

'Why are you still bothering about that old man?'

'Has he been?'

'No.'

'Don't lie to me, Ma.'

'See that you get your train, and don't give Johannes any trouble.'

'Was Mister Fourcade here?'

'Once you start badgering you never stop!'

'*Was* he, Ma?'

'Yes! He came here with a string of stupid small waxy flowers that he asked me to give you. I threw it away as soon as he turned his back.'

When she got to the railway line at Veldmanspad, she heard the train whistle up at Deep Walls station. And Uncle Salie's wife Martjie was pulling up carrots in her garden.

'Karoliena, child! You're a proper village lady now, smartly dressed and all! Your mother is so proud of you, she says you're marrying a very rich man. I say: good for you!'

'We're getting married on the eighteenth of next month. Your garden is looking good. Tell Uncle Salie I say hello.'

'I will. He's cutting wood for Parkes, they don't want to let him go. Lord knows what's going to happen – rumour has it that they are now going to get less than half the usual wood to cut.'

The five strangers in the coach were exhausted and dirty and happy. They all talked at once, telling her she had no idea what she had missed, *it was so beautiful*! But also very scary. One couldn't really get *into* the forest, it was too dense. But, best of all, they had seen a few of the wild people and their children at the station shop. They looked terrible. Really wild.

7

THEN THERE WERE only two weeks till the wedding.

Miss Ann came to her room one day to ask the question everyone was too scared to raise. Even Johannes. Should her mother and Uncle Cornelius be invited to the wedding? No, she said. Her mother would prefer a side of salted mutton. The only person she would have liked to invite was Mister Fourcade, but she didn't know his address and Johannes did not actually know him.

Miss Ann and three of her friends had taken it upon themselves to cater for the reception. Mrs Cuthbert had made all the curtains for the house and had hung them. Karoliena helped her. Then the furniture started to arrive, some of it by ship. The house looked more and more lovely. Johannes grew more and more handsome. Her wedding dress, which was hanging against the wardrobe in Miss Ann's room, became more beautiful by the day.

Long afterwards, when she was able to think more clearly, she realised that she had been asleep all the time – asleep and dreaming. She had moved higher and higher up the tree, and was holding on more and more tightly.

There were few days on which she was not invited to tea by someone, even the English-speaking women of the village paid attention to her. It had apparently become fashionable to invite Johannes Stander's fiancée to tea. What they did not know was that when she arrived the fiancée could intuitively sense whether she had been invited out of curiosity to see what a poor white looked like in village garb, or out of genuine kindness.

What she was doing without realising it, was throwing her laundry in the dam … like Kristiena Botha had done after she married the widower Jakob Niemand with his four orphans, and then found the laundry too much to handle. She made a plan. If she threw it in the dam, it was gone and she need not wash it. It was also out of her mind. And the sun still came up each morning and others would scrape together something for the children to wear …

The day she came back from Long Marsh Forest after visiting her mother, Johannes asked her why she looked so despondent.

'Not despondent. Only ashamed – of my people.' When she told Mister Fourcade that she was ashamed of the woodcutters, he had laughed and said she was ashamed of the most beautiful people he knew. 'I'm afraid that you will also be ashamed of me,' she told Johannes.

'About that, Karoliena, you need never fear. You have become my whole life and you need never be ashamed of yourself, either. You're done with the forest and its people. You've risen above them.'

Like the tree-spirit … which she had so badly wanted to see rise out of the tree one more time. And to work in the forest with Mister Fourcade just one more time …

'What is going to happen to the woodcutters, Johannes?'

'Alexander Wilson has invited us to lunch on Sunday. Mister Werdt, our representative in parliament, will also be there. I'll ask him about the government's plans for the woodcutters.

Incidentally, I don't think the little stinkwood table should stand under the window in the lounge. It would look better in the passage just inside the front door.'

'I'll have it moved tomorrow.' She thought it looked rather good under window.

The man from parliament was very distinguished looking. A rather handsome, middle-aged man with a loud voice, oozing confidence. His watch chain stretched across his potbelly. Everybody congregated around him to ask questions, hanging on to his answers. What made *her* move closer was when she thought she heard him mention the poor whites. But when she found herself standing opposite him, he was issuing a serious warning to everyone, his arms waving dramatically.

'The Second Great Trek has begun, my friends – the trek to the cities! The poor are moving to the cities in their hordes to try and make a living because of drought, pests and plagues, lack of money.' She knew that the woodcutters would not run to the cities; they hardly wanted to come to the village. 'Our nation must be rescued from the creation of slums!' he declared. And from the forest, she added silently. 'The biggest danger awaiting the poor in the cities is the trade unions of the Communists which will absorb them, teach them new values: encourage hatred of our white leaders; hatred of the church; ridicule of our moral values and family traditions. Have you any idea how many of our young boys are fleeing to the mines in their destitution, how many of our young girls flee to the clothing factories ... ' It felt as if a cold wind had blown over her; two of the forest girls, Maria and Anna Tait, had gone to work in a clothing factory ... 'The trade unions are becoming enormous organisations and more than half are under Communist control – as government analysts can prove. The aim of the Communists, dear friends, is nothing less than world domination. It is our duty not to be blind to this.'

Johannes was standing next to Mister Werdt. She looked him straight in the eyes and told him to *ask*.

He must have heard her. 'Mister Werdt,' he said, 'you mentioned the poor in the slums of our cities; what about the woodcutters in the forest around this village? This is a group of people that is becoming more and more of a problem.'

'The Church, Mr Stander, is in the process of appointing a Commission of Investigation in collaboration with the Carnegie Corporation in America to look into the poor white problem in this country. The forest workers are included in this survey.'

They were married on Saturday, 18 January 1931.

She woke before dawn on Sunday the nineteenth feeling that she had to keep as still as possible; if she moved, Johannes would wake up and discover that he had been deceived, because it was only Karoliena Kapp from the forest who was lying with him in the huge bed. She had fallen out of the tree. The other Karoliena was still standing in the church in a beautiful satin wedding dress while her heels and toes were on fire from the blisters forming on them ...

Somewhere, something terrible was wrong. She did not know what it was, she only felt it deep inside her. Like when you're walking through dense forest and decide to take a new short cut and you walk and walk without knowing where you're going to come out. But you keep on walking. The words of the old people mocked her: the quickest way to get lost is to think you can't get lost.

No, it wasn't the old people's words that were mocking her. It was the words of the man from parliament – that the poor were stumbling to the cities in search of relief. She had stumbled after Johannes to get out of the forest, to get out of her poor white skin; she had followed him for seven weeks – long past the point where she should have turned around.

By then it was too late.

Fear overcame her only when she stood dressed for her wedding in front of the large mirror in the stoep-room and she suddenly realised that it was not her in the mirror. It was someone who had been created by Miss Ann and Mrs Cuthbert; the two old women danced around her like proud hens, pulling here, tucking there.

'Absolutely wonderful!' they cried and embraced each other.

She was a doll they had made and dressed.

She had no say. Except that she had said yes, when she should have said no.

⁕

She had always dreamed of one day getting married in a flower-dress. A wild olive dress.

When she was a child she had imagined the most beautiful weddings in October, when the wild olive was in full bloom. Every year a more handsome man. A better man. A richer man. Never a woodcutter. Every year a prettier dress. The flowers of the wild olive were balls of creamy white lace; she picked armfuls to pin to an old sheet which she hung around her body. She stuck them in her hair, smelled the sweet honey scent. When she got home, she told her mother she was a bride. Her mother said: You're making a mess in the house with all the flowers falling off you, go and play outside and see that every pin gets put back in the tin!

One year she decided to have a winter wedding and she almost froze to death because she wanted to wear a different dress. An elder-tree. Elder-trees only flowered in winter – clusters of lacy, creamy-white flowers. They were even prettier than the wild olive flowers and they were sticky so she could simply press them on to her body. No pins. All she had to do was to walk very slowly and carefully and keep her bloomers on so that her fanny would not show. When she got home shivering, her mother cried: Do you want to catch your death? Go put on your clothes, the time for being indecent will come the day you really get married!

*

Many people attended the church service and many photographs were taken. Johannes was a handsome bridegroom: straight back, head held high. A proud man. Everyone said she was the prettiest bride they had ever seen. She smiled and smiled so that no one would notice that she was clinging to a branch that had started to creak and tear loose. Dream and reality had started to merge, faster and faster, till she could no longer separate them.

At Wittedrift there was an old woman who helped to scrub the floors and benches at the school; it was said that years before she had turned back in front of the pulpit on her wedding day.

Only a very brave person could do such a thing.

The reception was held in the church hall. There was a lavish feast, and lots of flowers. Johannes had seen to it that a whole sheep was sent to Veldmanspad on the forest train for her mother and Uncle Cornelius; he had arranged that Uncle Salie van Huysteen would take it to them.

Day was breaking. She knew she had to get up and make the fire; Johannes wanted tea in the mornings. Fortunately she was not naked. She had waited until he was asleep the night before, then got up and put her nightgown back on. Hestertjie Vermaak was pregnant when she got up . . .

It was painful when he struggled to get into her; he had blocked her nose with his neck until she thought she would suffocate, then he made the strangest noises and suddenly rolled off her. Was that what it was like to be married? Don't think about it, she told herself.

There was something terribly wrong with her. Something was telling her to get out of bed, walk to the door and keep on walking till she was back in the forest where she could hide and no one would ever see her again. She felt like part of a dream that had played itself out. Everything was a lie. She was the lie

– *she* had made the lie!

She wished she could close her eyes and quietly die.

But she lay there. She knew from his breathing that Johannes was still asleep. Her head told her she had to get away before he woke up. A strange fearlessness rose in her. Her old shoes were in the storeroom behind the kitchen, one of her old dresses from the hostel days was also there. She tried to quell the impossible thoughts that raged through her mind. It was said one could *think* oneself out of one's mind and she didn't want to go mad. She cried out with her whole heart: Lord, help me!

Uncle Salie van Huysteen swore to this day that the Lord heard him cry out the day the elephant cow chased him in Lily Bush Forest.

When the huge raindrops started exploding on the iron roof above her, it was like help falling from heaven. She could not go back to the forest in such heavy rain. She had to get up and start living her new life. Johannes had said that he wanted them to go to church that morning, and that he wanted her to put on the pretty little hat with the net that fell over her eyes.

Johannes did not take kindly to being opposed. A few days earlier he had had an argument with one of the women who worked in his shop about the price of a tin of jam – part of a consignment that had just arrived. His face had grown red with anger when he told her that *he* decided the prices, and no one else!

Miss Ann said that Mister Stander was a man who stood by his principles – and she always made it sound like a warning.

She had to get up. He said he wanted his tea as early as possible.

If only she wasn't so frightened. Suddenly so afraid …

After church people came to the house to congratulate them and have a cup of tea. Gifts were left on the stinkwood table in the passage. There were quite a few envelopes which she guessed contained money.

Why she did it, she did not know, but she surreptitiously pushed three of the envelopes into the little drawer in the table. Perhaps there was a dishonest streak in her; it was always said that forest people were cunning.

Her thoughts became more and more confused, but she concentrated on being pleasant to her guests so that no one should notice there was something wrong with her …

Afterwards Miss Ann said she could see Karoliena wasn't looking well when she stood in front of the pulpit. Still later she said she always knew it was not going to be easy to get the forest out of the girl that Johannes Stander had landed her with. The dear man didn't realise that the gap between the forest and civilisation was well nigh unbridgeable.

8

THE THOUGHTS GOING through her mind became rebellious. And the feeling of fear was so intense that by the Tuesday she thought she would collapse under the strain. Then, suddenly, she could endure it no longer. God might have heard Uncle Salie's cry and made the elephant turn away, but God most definitely wasn't hearing *her*!

As day broke on the Wednesday, she took the short cut through Dam Forest outside the village. It was like being released from a trap that was strangling her; escaping from it enabled her to breathe easily again …

The first bird to wake up was the brown canary with its shrill call that sounded like 'Why-why-why'.

No concern of yours!

Far behind her the village dogs began to wake up. Although she had the urge to run she had to walk slowly, making sure she stayed on the footpath. It was still dark in the forest. Once she got through Dam Forest, through the gorge and on to the hard road, she would be able to walk faster. When she had taken the short cut through Kruisfontein Forest she would feel safe and would go and hide …

'Why-why-why?'

⁂

When she was a child she sometimes mimicked the noisy bird all day. It was a little brown-green bird that made sure you never saw it, you only *heard* it. Until the day she decided she *would* see it, she'd hide in the undergrowth and she'd catch it out. The problem was, it never seemed to be the first to stop calling. The moment she thought she'd won and took a bite of her bread it started again, making her spit out the bread so she could start mimicking it again. Before it thought it had won.

⁂

It was not, however, the brown canary's teasing that troubled her. It was the words in her head that asked, over and over: what-are-you-doing, what-are-you-doing …

She didn't know what she was doing. She only knew that she had to do it. Perhaps there was a spirit inside her, like the tree spirit she had seen that lightning-filled day, and it was telling her to go back to the forest.

The next moment fear intervened, telling her: *You must go back!*

No. She would make that decision when she got to the hard road.

It was starting to get light.

She walked stiffly so that she did not to slip. The earth was still soggy from the rain of the previous day. They had been taught in school that half the days of the year were rainy days in the forest.

At least the rain had stopped. Only a squall of tree-rain now and then when the wind blew through the trees.

She would decide what to do when she got to the hard road. By the time she got to Kruisfontein Forest, it would be too late.

'Why-why-why!'

⁂

She always won against the bush-lourie. She simply hooted eight times through her lips and hid herself in the undergrowth. The bush-lourie is inquisitive and will always come closer to see where you are. Somewhat dim-witted, it always hooted again to find out if you would answer. But when it saw you were a human, it didn't want to play any more.

⁂

Please, she mustn't be pregnant ...

She did not take any of the new dresses Johannes had had made for her. Nor did she take one of the nice pillow cases to put her few things in: she took one from the spare room, without lace. 'The spare room is for the times when your mother might want to sleep over for the night,' Johannes explained the brownish bed linen to her. Miss Ann said he had it made specially by one of the women in the shop.

She was not going to feel guilty about the three envelopes she had taken. Three guineas, and three guineas, and five pounds. She had counted it in the bathroom before dawn. It was not stealing; it had also been meant for her. After all, what was she to live on while she decided how she was going to live? One could only live on wild grapes and wild olives for few days, then one became weak. She was not a bird.

She hadn't touched the other five envelopes; in any case she didn't know where Johannes had put them, because they were gone the night before when she had wanted to hide another in the drawer.

Johannes would be furious. She knew that.

But she didn't want to turn back. Nor did she want to go to Long Marsh Forest. Her mother didn't have to know. Not yet.

When she got to the hard road, she had to rest; give her

shaking legs time to recover, give the turmoil in her head time to subside. A voice was telling her: turn back! Another voice said: run! The conflict had been going on in her mind for days.

Perhaps she had some kind of mental illness. Like Aunt Betta had when she lived at Old Place just outside the village. They said she was out of her mind for five years because of a 'conflict' inside her. Her mother had remarked: it was not enough of a conflict to keep her from having thirteen children!

Please, she mustn't be pregnant!

One day at Wittedrift she had read a beautiful sentence in a book. She wrote it down in her Bible so that she would always remember it. *All wild things must be wary in order to survive*. She translated the English words into Afrikaans. She thought that whoever had written it was referring to the forest people.

She no longer had the Bible, there had been no room for it in the pillow case. In any case, it had been the Church's Bible.

She would live warily.

Johannes had been a dream that could not possibly come true. It was not his fault; it was she who hadn't known how to dream properly. She had left him a note on the stinkwood table in the passage. She had written: *I've gone back to the forest. Karoliena*.

She was almost out the back door when she went back and added: *Thank you for everything*, and put her wedding ring on it.

'Why-why-why?'

Shut up!

Above White Fountain and just before Earth Dam she twice had to hurry away from the road when cars drove past. Strangers, forest visitors, slowly creeping up the winding road through the forested hills. Fortunately she heard them coming and had time to hide in the undergrowth. She didn't want to be offered a lift. She wanted to walk, she wanted to think, and she was becoming more and more frightened about the terrible thing she had done. What had possessed her? She had really wanted to be a good wife to Johannes, she had really wanted to become a good village lady, not to mind when the high and mighty looked down on her with disapproval in their eyes. Not to mind when people laughed at her.

She was in trouble. All kinds of trouble. The road was wet and muddy and her shoes were coated with mud. It didn't help to try and wipe them clean against the bushes, because a few steps later they were caked with mud again. She felt her feet would slide out from under her at any moment.

Then reality caught up with her once more. It was mindless to be running away from Johannes because she was running away from her only salvation. One didn't need a 'conflict' to realise *that*! She had to turn back and beg him to forgive her.

⁕

She had once run away from school at Wittedrift late on a Sunday afternoon. Run back to her mother. She had already gone a few miles when the sun started to go down. She went faster and faster. When fear came walking behind her, she went even faster. But when fear started walking on both sides of her, she turned around and ran back.

⁕

And now fear was once more walking on both sides of her. If she turned back, it would be downhill all the way to the village. Johannes would not be too angry yet. She would plead with him as she had pleaded that Sunday with Mister Cronje. Please, sir, I will never do it again, my mother will kill me, the Church will kill me, they said I must be good and study hard, I'm costing the Church a lot of money. I just wanted to go to my mother for a while. I will never run away again, I'll be good and study hard. Please, Johannes, I'll obey you, I'll keep the house clean and tidy, starch the table napkins, prepare good food, never boil the sweet potatoes in water again, not resist you every time you want to take off my bloomers; not refuse to put on that silly hat with the net over the eyes, even though it makes me feel like a chicken in a coop. I will obey you and always wear a hat when I go into the village because you said a smart woman must cover her head with dignity. I promise not to be so friendly towards the people who work in your shop.

Please, please …

She could not shake off the feeling that something was terribly wrong. Somewhere in her heart she loved Johannes. But her love had become weaker and weaker after she had gone to live in the village. There was something hollow about him, like the ragdoll her mother had once made for her but did not have quite enough stuffing …

Shortly before High Peak, where the forest opened a little, she saw the two cars that had passed her earlier. They were parked alongside the road. The occupants were standing in the road behind the cars; something must have disturbed them. When one of the men looked around and saw her approaching, he hurried towards her, an expression of relief on his face. Two of the women followed him; the other man and woman started following *them*. And they all started talking at once, arms waving, but she already knew what had happened. It could only be elephants.

The first man said he had almost driven into the animal. The elephant was lying in the road, blocking the way. Fortunately he had been able to reverse. Then the second car had arrived and fortunately that driver had been able to brake in time. It was an enormous elephant, and it was impossible to tell if it was wounded or sick. The road was narrow; it was not possible for the cars to turn around.

She suddenly felt that she was really back in the forest. It was as if she had come home. Human fear left her. She even found pleasure in seeing that the strangers' shoes were as caked with mud as her own, seeing their eyes wild with fear. One woman's hat had sagged on to her forehead, the golden hatpin about to fall out.

'Are you one of the forest people?' the first man asked.

'Yes.'

'What are we to do? Can you call someone to come and help us?'

The hatpin woman started to cry.

'They won't come. You will just have to be patient, the elephant might lie there for a long time.'

'I beg your pardon?'

'It has rained, the forest is wet, the elephants come and lie in the road to get a little sun. Your hatpin is going to fall out, Madam.'

It took three hours.

A third car turned up, another four people to be terrified. The fear that had abandoned her had seemingly transformed itself into elephant-terror in *them*. Eleven people. From Cape Town, from Port Elizabeth, and people from the Long Kloof who often drove over the mountain on their way home and had come across the signs of elephant many times before, had seen broken-off branches next to the road, but had never *seen* an elephant. Was she sure they should not throw stones at it so that it would get up and go back into the forest? Sir, she said, you may try that, but if the elephant gets angry, you're in trouble.

Back in Brook Bush an elephant had once tossed old Hans Stroebel up into a tree with one slap of its trunk. Hans said he came upon the elephant without warning; it was happily feeding on fruit from a stinkwood. He surprised the elephant, and the elephant surprised him. They both got a fright. The elephant swung round, slapped him with its trunk and – as true as God – he landed halfway up a candlewood tree. The elephant disappeared before he could blink, it did not even wait to see if he fell to his death.

The elephant in the road was in no hurry.

She showed the men how to gather bedding-bush along the side of the road and how to pack it in a heap against the damp.

They fetched the travelling rugs from the cars and threw them over the bush so that they had somewhere to sit. Two of the cars had picnic baskets, and the Long Kloof people had also brought food for the journey. In the end she got the best of the food because all their concentration was focused on the elephant, as if they expected him to come round the bend at any moment. Every creaking branch, every twig that snapped, every kok-kok-kok of a lourie – any sound at all – made them jumpy. She didn't tell them that they were actually quite safe, that the wind was coming from the direction of the elephant, and he would not get their scent.

But she kept a white elder in sight for herself, should anything unexpected happen.

Every now and then two of the men tiptoed to the bend to see what was happening and hurried back to report that the elephant had not moved.

The women started talking to one another, mostly about their husbands. One of the men was a school teacher. The other had something to do with ships; they had been visiting Knysna in connection with a government investigation that concerned the harbour. The Long Kloof man was a fruit farmer.

Then they started asking her questions. Where did she live? Long Marsh Forest. Had she been born in the forest? Yes. They would never have thought so. Had she gone to school in the forest? Yes. Her hair was very pretty, who had cut it? A woman in the village. What was her name? Hestertjie Vermaak.

The expressions on their faces told her that to them she did not quite fit in with the forest. The Long Kloof woman openly admitted that she had been under the impression that there were only poor whites left in the forest.

Every time one of them had to have a pee, she had to go with them and stand guard. She did not tell them that, had she been alone, she would have been past the elephant long ago; where the first car had stopped a footpath turned away westward and took one back to the hard road just below

Veldmanspad. It was an old short cut the woodcutters used when they went to the village. She waited patiently with the strangers; secretly glad of the delay because it had brought time to a standstill. It gave her time to try to comprehend what she was doing.

As far as she was concerned the elephant could lie in the road for ever and life could stop right there. Then she need not think about where she was going.

At last she decided to go and have a look at the elephant herself. What if it was dead? No, the old forest people said the elephants had a secret place in the forest where they went to die.

When she set off into the forest, the strangers were immediately alarmed.

'Where are you going?'

'I'll be back shortly.'

The forest was dense. She had to push open a path through the undergrowth with her arms and her body and mark her route so that she would be able to find her way back again. She did not want to turn towards the hard road too late and come upon the elephant on the wrong side of the wind …

*

She and her mother once had to make a detour round two elephants in Kom's Bush in order to get home. Two bulls. They were lying on their sides in the sun on a sledpath, tusks in the air. It was winter, the forest was cold and wet. It was not long after the elephant had trampled Uncle Freek to death – her mother was still in shock. She said she had a feeling that she would die that day. Don't talk like that, Ma, she said, come on! She led the way, her mother right behind her. After a while her mother asked: Where are you taking us, Karoliena? She said: Don't worry, just follow me. Through forest streams, through a forest gorge, across a dale covered with ferns, a river. Her mother became more and more agitated and kept asking where she was taking them. Don't worry, Ma, just follow me. She didn't say that she herself no longer knew where they were, that she was hoping that they would somehow arrive at some familiar place, because they were following an old footpath.

They came out on the hard road at Buffelsnek. Her mother was angry. Jesus, Karoliena, you almost had us in the Long Kloof!

*

When the forest started to open before her after she had changed direction towards the hard road, she saw the huge grey mountain in the road. There was not *one* elephant in the road, there were *three*.

Panic took hold of the women when she got back and announced what she had seen. They burst into tears, bit their lips, stamped their feet, held their heads in their hands, and asked over and again if there really was *no one* who could come and help them.

'Do what? Drag the elephants out of the way?' she asked the woman who had said she thought there were only poor whites left in the forest. What she enjoyed most, however, was observing how smart women could also fall out of trees. Hats askew, powder washed from their cheeks, hair untidy, shamelessly pulling down their bloomers to pee beside the road.

The man from Cape Town said he had been under the impression that the government had had the elephants shot out a long time ago. Didn't they appoint a man, years ago, to come and shoot them? Pretorius, his name was, if he remembered correctly. No, said the Long Kloof man, his name was Potgieter. Although it was now clear that he had missed a few.

'It *was* a man called Pretorius,' she corrected them.

Her mother always said that if you heard ten words about a forest matter, erase nine of them as lies. 'He had the government's permission to shoot one for a museum. But he enjoyed himself so much that he kept on shooting until he had killed five.'

'How many of the creatures are left in the forest?' the Cape Town man wanted to know, clearly shocked.

'No one knows for certain. Adam Barnard's father counted thirty-one bathing at the seep-hole below Deep Walls. It was a very hot bergwind day.'

'Really?'

'Yes. Of course they may no longer be shot, they've been declared crown property.'

'What's that?' one of the women wanted to know.

'That only the king or a member of his family may shoot them.'

Anxiety had begun to creep up on her again. She had to find a place to sleep and get past all the prying eyes at Veldmanspad. As if he could read her thoughts, the man from Port Elizabeth asked: 'Have you far to walk to get home, young lady?'

'No, not too far.' She could not decide whether to call him Sir or Uncle. Miss Ann had forbidden her to call people Uncle or Aunt, saying it was a forest custom that she had to unlearn if she wanted to live in the village.

She no longer wanted to live in the village. The next moment a plan formed in her head.

'You can give me a lift as far as Deep Walls, if you don't mind, sir,' she said to the Long Kloof man. 'To the forestry station.'

'Is your father connected to Forestry?' his wife asked.

'No. An elephant killed him.'

She could not stop the lie. It simply fell from her mouth all by itself.

Shortly after midday, they dropped her off at Deep Walls.

When she got to the Tree, a bittersweet feeling of gladness swept over her. Mister Fourcade once said that mountains talked to each other. If mountains talked to mountains, surely trees talked to trees?

'Tree,' she said, leaning against him and holding back her tears, 'please tell the other trees that I'm back in the forest; tell them I've done the most ridiculous thing, and I don't know why.'

She could have sworn that something put its arm around her. Even if it was her imagination, it lifted the heaviness in her heart just a little. And gave her the courage to take the footpath north to Kom's Bush without having to take to the hard road where others might offer her a lift. It was Wednesday, inquisitive people in motor cars usually came on Sundays ...

If she could get to Kom's Bush, she decided, she could walk to Faan Mankvoet's clearing and ask to sleep overnight with him and Susanna. They owed her a favour. She sometimes helped their eldest child Willempie with his arithmetic during the school holidays. Faan wanted a better education for the boy than standard six at Veldmanspad. So that he would never have to cut wood, Karoliena, he told her, because it breaks a man's body and his courage.

She had been following the footpath for some time when she suddenly realised that there was someone else in the thicket. She took another footpath, one that turned to the right – and came to a wire fence. But there were no fences in the forest! The next moment she stopped in her tracks in sheer astonishment: she had reached a little camp fenced in with chicken wire. Almost on the edge of the forest, it was about the size of six forest dwelling gardens and in the middle of the camp someone was kneeling as if he was praying. No, he was mumbling. Talking with his eyes open to something in front of him.

It was Oldman Botha, the strange old man who lived above Jim Reid's Crossing in the little plank house. Wild hair, wild beard, tattered clothes. He was talking gravely to something in front of him. A wounded buck, perhaps? Surely not a mouse? He was strange, but not mad. He seldom talked to anyone; when one occasionally met him at the shop at Deep Walls station he hardly greeted one.

'Uncle?' she called out softly, afraid she might startle him. She did. He got up on his haunches and glared at her as if his eyes were deceiving him.

'Yes?' he asked, abruptly.

'I'm on my way to Faan Mankvoet's place, I just stopped to say good-day.'

'Oh.'

There were rows of cabbages. Carrots. Pumpkins. Sweet potatoes . . .

'I see you have a nice garden here in the middle of the forest.'

'Yes. And I see you're Meliena Kapp's daughter.'

'Yes.' It had not been a question.

'Faan's not home. He's cutting in Lourie Forest.' As if telling her she might just as well turn back.

'Then I'll go and visit Susanna.'

'She's gone to visit your mother.'

'How do you know?'

'I know everything.'

'What are you doing?'

'It has nothing to do with you. Mister Fourcade was here looking for you.'

Mister Fourcade had been looking for her! The news was balm to her weary mind. 'When?'

'Can't remember. I told him you went off to get married. Are you having a baby?'

'No.' Please, no . . .

'Why did you get married then?'

'You don't perhaps have a place for me to sleep tonight?' She had not planned to ask, just suddenly knew she had to. So she could hold on to him and not be alone when she fell out of the tree. Somewhere between the beard and the hair and the bushy eyebrows two dark hawk's eyes looked at her sharply. She would go down on her knees and beg him for a place to spend the night. 'Please, Uncle.'

'I still have carrots to pull up.'

Was it a yes?

'I'll help you.'

'Walk down the fence, there's a gate on the other side.' She found the little ramshackle gate.

It was a yes!

And it wasn't a buck or a mouse he was talking to, it was a little stinkwood tree.

'It wants to die, this tree. I've told it not to, my livelihood depends on it. See down there, at the bottom of the garden, see my little Cape beeches, my little red alders, my little ironwoods. I'm trying to prove something to a very important man at the Deep Walls forestry station. But he keeps pestering me for stinkwood. Says the forest must be replanted with stinkwood where it has been cut out. That's what the government wants.'

'Uncle … '

'I planted about twenty stinkwoods. I went to a lot of trouble, but I could only pull six through. Forestry gave me the wire for the fence when they saw that the bushbucks were eating up all my evidence. Now there are only three of the little trees left, and this one looks as if it wants to give up as well.'

'Did Mister Fourcade say he would come back?'

'He always comes back. I want to go to Lily Bush Forest to collect a new batch of small stinkwoods, because I've got a brilliant plan. I also want to pick up a few stinkwood seeds and plant them in boxes. Some time in the future this forest will again be full of stinkwood trees like in the days when every tenth tree was a stinkwood – as Mister-doctor says. It's a pity Mister-doctor is not a clever man. I told him stinkwood needs plenty of room for its feet; it doesn't like growing on the toes of others. But he wouldn't listen. He sent a couple of men to Gouna Forest to clear a huge patch of tree-ferns; said he had never seen tree-ferns grow as luxuriantly as there, so it must be very rich soil. I told him Gouna had always had the tallest tree-ferns in the forest. He wouldn't listen. He had more than a hundred stinkwoods saplings planted there, and they all died.

He came crying to me. I said, see where skunk-bush grows, *that* is where stinkwood will take – after I've brought them on for a year or two in my camp.'

'What did Mister Fourcade say when he heard I had gone off to be married?'

'Just shook his head. While I pull up the carrots, you can come and talk to the little stinkwood, tell it to breathe properly!'

'Yes, Uncle.'

She would have gone on her knees and kissed the little tree if he'd told her to.

9

OLDMAN BOTHA'S LITTLE plank house took her by the hand and invited her inside. It offered her safety, shelter; and a door that closed behind her while a stormed raged outside. It was one large room, with a home-made bed with a straw mattress in the corner for her to sleep on. 'If a man lives along the hard road, he has to have room for a lost soul who comes knocking on his door,' the old man said.

'I'm not lost, Uncle. Only confused.'

'The whole forest is confused. You'd better see to it that you sort yourself out.'

'Can I stay with you tomorrow as well? Please.'

'You can stay as long as you want to. As long as you talk to the little stinkwood again; we've got to pull it through.'

She had to get used to the sounds. The owls. The frogs. The creaking of the trees. The old man's snoring. Feet that walked past in the night and made her sit up in bed, terrified.

'I had a terrible fright during the night, Uncle! People walked past in the road below the house.'

'Plantation workers on their way to Buffelsnek.'

'Just before dawn a lorry went past.'

'Forestry's lorry. Transporting gravel for the roads, and sometimes the whetstone and other implements. But it's not permitted to pick up the plantation workers even if it is empty. Government's lorry. Government's orders. You have to go and tell your mother where you are.'

'I will.'

The following day, shortly before midday, a horse-cart pulled up at the house. An old man was at the reins, the church nurse next to him. Karoliena and Oldman Botha had just returned to the camp. She had been to talk to the little tree, he had been doing some hoeing.

Oldman Botha and the nurse were pleased to see each other. Obviously they knew each other well.

'How are you, Nurse? Getting on any better with the forest people?'

'Here and there, but it's still challenging work – and who, if I may ask, is this stranger with you today?'

'It's Karoliena Kapp. Karoliena, this is our new church nurse, Miss Claassens.'

'Call me Amelia. Karoliena *who*?'

'Karoliena Kapp,' she said – and could just as well have knocked the woman over.

'Meliena Kapp's daughter?' she asked, clearly both shocked and surprised.

'Yes.' The woman knew something. Her big brown eyes asked the questions that her mouth did not dare to.

'But I thought … ' She did not complete what she had thought, just left the unfinished question hanging in the air.

Then Oldman Botha asked: 'Where are you on your way to today, Nurse?'

'Barnard's Clearing, Uncle. I did not get there last month.'

'Is Elmina still in bed?'

'Yes, Uncle.'

'I don't understand that kind of stuff, Nurse. But then I don't understand woman's stuff, in the first place.'

Amelia turned to her. 'You don't perhaps feel like coming

with me, Karoliena?'

'I don't know the people of Barnard's Clearing, although my mother's sister lived there before she died.'

'Come with me.' It sounded like an order.

'Yes, feel free to go,' Oldman Botha pressed. 'If Nurse had a car, I would not have minded going myself.'

She didn't know whether to say yes or no.

'Come with me,' the nurse repeated. 'It's quite an interesting case.'

Nothing looked interesting to her when they stood in front of a miserable little clay house on the edge of the clearing. She didn't want to go inside, she didn't want to see what was inside, she only wanted to run back along the footpath to where old Lewies was waiting for them with the horse-cart on the hard road. She didn't want to see the woman Amelia Claassens had to visit. She didn't want to see the inquisitive eyes watching from the other houses. There were about seven houses altogether, some built of plank, others of clay. Some were better than others, with vegetable gardens, flower gardens. There were children dressed in rags and chickens scratching around.

'Come,' said the nurse and pushed open the door.

The next moment she stood beside a wooden bed on which a woman was lying – a beautiful woman with the most serene smile on her face – under a snow-white bedspread. Around her was the dirtiest and most unkempt room imaginable.

Elmina Vlok. At least sixty years old, the nurse had said, but the dim light in the little house concealed her years.

'How are you, Elmina?' the nurse asked, sternly.

'I'm well, Nurse. I'm hoping it will be a little girl. I think my time is getting close now.'

According to Amelia Claassens the woman had taken to her bed more than a year ago, and seldom stood up for fear that the baby she was 'expecting' would fall out her bottom. Married for almost forty years to the woodcutter Samuel Vlok, she had been childless – until she had declared herself pregnant. The coloured woman who lived next door, and whose husband was also a woodcutter, did necessary chores for Elmina out of the kindness of her heart. The rest her husband did when he got home at night. At least he was making a better living since he'd been given plantation work – two pounds, five shillings a month – although he regularly lost a day's wages when Elmina sent him to the village to buy things for the baby. Everything was stowed in a drawer. Nappies, napkin pins, dummy, blankets, bootees.

'Do you remember our last conversation, Elmina?' The nurse sat down on the bed alongside the woman.

'Nurse said I would have to take good care so that she doesn't get nappy rash. I sent Samuel to get some Vaseline. It's in the drawer.'

'I told you to get out of bed every day, Elmina! You can't just lie here, you'll get weaker and weaker!'

'I get up to use the pot. Samuel empties the pot every night, and he brings me water so that I can wash.'

The nurse got up. 'Let's go, Karoliena,' she said. 'This case is past redemption. While there's still a bit of sense left, one can try, but once that is gone, one's wasting time and patience. Come!'

'Is she going to lie like that till she dies?' she asked when they got outside.

'Possibly.'

Barnard's Clearing was surrounded by beautiful forest. A huge old yellowwood stood on the edge of the clearing, its head way above the forest roof as if it didn't want to look down.

Old Lewies was holding the horses by the reins so that they could get on to the cart.

'You say she's been in bed for a *year*?'

'It could be even longer. There's no use talking to her. Reverend Odendaal came and talked to her, everyone tries to get her out of bed, but she doesn't want to. She's waiting for the baby.'

'There are many mysteries one can't solve.'

'That's true.'

They were almost at the end of Kom's Road when the nurse turned to her and looked her straight in the eye. 'At least you can solve one mystery for me before we drop you off.'

She knew what the woman was about to ask. 'What?'

'According to your mother, you are living in the village and you recently married Johannes Stander. She boasts about it to anyone who'll listen.'

'Don't ask me about that.'

'I have to. I have to know which story to believe.'

'Believe whatever you want to.' Only pray that *I'm* not expecting a baby!

She could not sleep that night. The storm would not stay outside, nor would the fear that was tugging at her. Oldman Botha scolded her from his corner, asked her to stop tossing around. It was Elmina Vlok who was tossing around in her head. Elmina must have been young and pretty once, she must have loved a man and married him in happiness. Then she died. Why? What was love *really*? She did not know the answer. She only knew she wanted to run away again, but she did not know where. Perhaps she was running away like Elmina, only in a different way. A stone that had started to roll and roll – and then stopped. Dead. She wanted to get up and run to Barnard's Clearing and pull Elmina from the bed and shake her till she woke up.

So that she could wake up herself?

Was Johannes looking for her? How angry was he? What if she was pregnant?

No. Please, no!

When would it be daybreak? The plantation workers had gone by long ago. The lorry had still to come …

When she woke up, Oldman Botha was making the fire.

She got up and started to tidy the house, swept the floor,

went outside to fill up the water bucket at the tank.

She knew she had to go to Long Marsh Forest. And to the village. The two journeys were like two mountains she had to cross before she could start living, one day at a time; until she knew whether or not she was pregnant. If she was, she would have to go and plead with Johannes to take her back. If she wasn't, she would walk into the forest – walk and walk and walk, until she felt peace inside her again.

Her mother was sitting on the sofa in the front room, her arms folded. She had dozed off, her head falling forward on her chest. The old green shoes were on her feet; her hair, in two plaits, had stray strands standing up on her head that said they had not been combed properly for days. The garden looked neglected, the house was untidy. Should she let her mother sleep and quietly turn around and leave? No. It would not make the mountain go away.

'Morning, Ma.'

Her head jerked up, eyes half open and bewildered, then she woke up as if filled with a sudden gladness, which was quickly replaced with apprehension. 'Karoliena?'

'Morning, Ma.'

'Why so unexpected?'

So Johannes had not come looking for her … 'How are you, Ma?'

'As it always is with the poor, nothing but misery.' Suddenly her eyes glinted with suspicion. 'Why are you dressed in your old clothes? Where's the pretty dress and fancy shoes you had on last time?' There was a sudden wariness about her. 'Where's Johannes?'

'Ma … '

'Jesus, Karoliena, you gave me such a fright!'

'I'm sorry, Ma.'

'Sorry about what?'

About Ma, about Elmina Vlok, about myself.

'I've left Johannes.'

Her mother uttered a single curse. Then she leapt to her feet, took a step forward, cursed a second time, took a step backwards and sank down on the sofa again. 'Are you out of your bloody mind?'

'I could not cope with life in the village.'

Then the curses tumbled from her mother's mouth, one after the other. It seemed as if every part of her was cursing – her eyes, her body, her hands; even her feet, as one of the green shoes flew past Karoliena's head. She was like one possessed, unable to contain her fury.

'Ma, please … ' She did not know that her mother even knew such words.

'Don't please-Ma me! You'll get back to the village and go on your knees before Johannes or I'll get a stick and drive you back to him myself!'

'Please, Ma.'

'God will punish you, Karoliena! Do you hear me? He will punish you!'

'Please, Ma.'

'Wretch! You've brought disgrace on all of us!'

'I didn't mean to upset you, but thought it better that I came and told you myself.'

'Did he hit you?' She was grabbing at straws.

'No, Ma.' She went to the kitchen to make her mother some sugar water. She was beside herself, making the most awful noises, crying and moaning at the same time. 'Drink this, Ma. Will Uncle Cornelius be coming home tonight?' Her mother slapped the cup out of her hand.

'I'll come back another day.'

'Don't you ever set foot in my house again! Do you hear me? Ungrateful bitch!'

She knew it was shock and disappointment that had made her mother hysterical. She could still hear her down on the sledpath, where the footpath turned away to Veldmanspad. But she had crossed the first mountain.

The second one was different.

No one screamed at her. But there were shocked eyes when they recognised her coming down the street. Halfway into the village she felt as if her legs would give way, yet at the same time a strange calm possessed her. She stared ahead of her, stubbornly ignoring any face that looked familiar.

Past the first sawmill. Passed the second sawmill where a wagon from Gouna was turning into the yard. Tired oxen with heads hanging, four woodcutters in threadbare clothes, three half-grown boys wearing tatters. They had brought in a load of finely worked yellowwood beams, weeks and weeks of heavy work.

On the next corner men were digging a hole apparently to plant the pole that lay to one side; a pole with a big flat head on which the word SLOW was painted in red letters. On the next street corner a similar pole had already been planted – with the word STOP painted on it.

Motor cars kicked up clouds of dust in the street.

She looked neither left nor right, just kept walking.

Past Miss Ann's boarding-house. Past Johannes's shop, her heart thumping. Two smartly dressed village women with pointed shoes came down the steps in front of the shop – they hesitated, shocked expressions on their faces when they saw it was her. She didn't look around; she just kept walking.

To Smith's shop.

Where she bought the doll for eight shillings.

She took a short cut through Dam Forest to get out of the village.

'Why-why-why!' mocked the brown canary.

I don't know.

All she knew, once more, was that she didn't want to turn back.

Johannes had not gone looking for her.

'I was worried about you, Karoliena!' Oldman Botha scolded her when she got home shortly after sunset.

'I had to cross two mountains.'

'You look as if you have. What have you got in that brown paper parcel?'

'One of the mountains.'

'It looks as if we're going to pull the little stinkwood through.'

'I'll talk to it again tomorrow morning.'

First she needed sleep. To erase the mountains she had left behind her and to reflect on the one that lay ahead …

When she woke up it was already light and Oldman Botha was busy in the garden. She washed herself and dressed, made her bed, swept the house, washed the plates and mugs from the night before. Then she went into the garden and knelt beside the little stinkwood. The old man was digging in the corner of the camp.

The little tree looked better. It was she who did not feel any better, who could not shake off a feeling of hopelessness.

'Uncle … ' She stopped to talk to him on her way back to the house a while later, 'how long will it take for that little stinkwood to become a proper tree?'

'At eighty it ought to be a fine tree.'

'Then you're going to all this trouble for something you'll never see.'

'If God took the trouble to plant the whole forest, I can surely take the trouble to help replant a bit of it. The year before last I took Mister-doctor into a deep gorge up in Stripe Bush. The forest is so dense there that although the sun was high above us it was dark as night around us.'

'Why did you go there?'

'To find the old stinkwood that I'd visited with my father when I was child. Pa said that no human being would ever get it out, not even with a hundred oxen – but we would have got quite a few pounds for it! It took us the whole day to reach the tree, and we had to sleep over in the forest. Fortunately it was summer and Mister-doctor had brought food for us. The tree was still the same old giant I'd seen as a child, it was impossible to tell whether it had added so much as an inch to itself. Mister-doctor was overawed, he was so deeply moved that he was speechless. He said the tree must be at least a thousand years old. He measured it, wrote the measurements down in a book, kept touching it, kept staring at it. I suppose the tree is still there today, unless it's toppled over. Part of it grew in a little stream, happily scooping up water for itself for a thousand years. We stayed up in Stripe Bush an extra day so that Mister-doctor could measure and gape at the other stinkwood giants in the gorge. We had to leave when we ran out of food.'

'What do you think it's like to be a tree?'

'I suppose like a tree. What a strange question to ask.'

'I'm going to Barnard's Clearing.'

'Why?'

'I don't know. Perhaps to try and keep a stinkwood alive, like you're doing.'

'There are no stinkwoods left around there. Just a lovely old kalander.'

She took the doll out of the brown paper, wrapped it in one of her jerseys and set off. She could only try.

She had hardly entered Kom's Bush when a brown canary started mocking her with its 'Why-why-why!' She didn't answer. She let the old feeling of joy at being in Kom's Bush slowly surround her. It had always been her favourite playground. She didn't want to move to Long Marsh Forest when her mother remarried again.

A Cape robin gurgled in the dense undergrowth on the side of the road. A lourie began its kok-kok-kok nearby and another called in the distance towards Old Fire. A Rameron pigeon cooed asthmatically somewhere in the forest roof above the road. It was like walking through a great green tunnel.

'Good morning, good morning,' she greeted the trees out loud as she walked; ironwood, candlewood, ironwood, yellowwood, ironwood, white elder, yellowwood, ironwood, white elder, elder, knobwood, ironwood, white elder …

When she was a child returning home from a day in the forest, her mother used to ask: What did you do in the forest the whole day long? And she would reply: I made up a game for myself.

It was years since she had last made up a game. 'Good morning, good morning.' *Good morning, good morning*, the trees answered back, rustling like the wind. 'I see that my friend Yellowwood at Deep Walls has sent word that I'm back in the forest.' Ironwood, kamassi, stinkwood, ironwood.

There was plenty of ironwood, but it was heavy to work. When the forest bosses needed sawyers at the forest station, they always got unregistered forest workers to come and do the work. A penny a foot for sawing ironwood. The sawyers said it was the cheapest way to hell.

Johannes had ordered a load of ironwood for the fireplace, declaring that there was no better fire than an ironwood fire.

How long would she be able to stay with Oldman Botha?

She did not want to stay with her mother again. An old forest woman had once told her that the girl-elephant stayed with the cow for life; it was only the boy-elephants that took themselves off when they grew up.

Where was she going to get money when she had used up the wedding money?

What was she going to do if she was pregnant?

Don't think about it!

Good morning, yellowwood; good morning, red alder; good morning pretty Cape beech …

Just before the footpath turned towards Barnard's Clearing, she sat down to rest a while. She knew, though, that she really wanted to cling to the peace around her just a little longer and to postpone seeing Elmina …

Mister Fourcade often complained because she could not sit still in one place for any length of time. He told her that if she would only sit still in one place for long enough, the forest would come to her. She said: Nonsense, the forest can't walk!

When would the Carnegie saviours arrive?

If she ever saw Mister Fourcade again, she would sit quietly with him for hours. He understood everything.

Two blue-beaks with their long red tails swished through the air – as if they knew she was thinking of Mister Fourcade. Whenever they had come across blue-beaks he scolded her for not calling them by their proper name. 'Not blue-beaks, Karoliena! They are paradise flycatchers! You were given one name, and so were they.'

'Then they were given the wrong name. Their beaks are blue.'

Somewhere to the north she heard a bush-lourie hoot. The bird that had earned her four shillings, although she had never told Mister Fourcade that story.

*

One day, when she was still at school in Veldmanspad, a man and a woman got off the train at Deep Walls Station. They were strange-looking people, both wearing the same peaked caps and the same jackets. They carried books tied with a strap, wore binoculars around their necks, and had a huge tin lunch box with a strap handle. They stood around like two lost souls. She straightened her dress, put on her sweetest expression, walked up to them and asked in English if she could be of any assistance to them. Take them into the forest, perhaps?

No, they said, they weren't there to see the forest – they were bird-watchers. They had come specifically to look for and observe one particular bird. She felt she'd been offered a gift from heaven! What kind of bird? A Narina Trogon. The gift shattered. There was no such bird in the forest, she said. Oh yes, they argued, there was! She told them she lived in the forest, she knew the birds of the forest, and there was no such bird. They hurriedly undid the strap round the books, took one out, flipped through the pages, found what they were looking for and turned the book to her as if saying: Told you so! It was a plain and simple drawing – nicely coloured in – of a bush-lourie! She told them the bird was called a bush-lourie. They became very excited and asked if she had ever seen one.

Rich people smell different from poor people. She could smell that they were rich. Yes, she said. I've seen many. They became flustered with excitement. Did she know where they would have the best chance of seeing one? Yes, she did, but she would have to take them into the forest. Would she do that? Yes. Bush-lourie, she thought, you'd better play your part today!

To the bird-watchers she said: Unfortunately, we will first have to come to an agreement. I want to be paid a shilling for every bush-lourie I find for you. They looked stunned. You've made the price too high, she thought, better come down to sixpence. The woman shook her head in disbelief and asked if she knew that it was one of the most difficult birds to spot in the forest. Yes, she knew that. What was the other name Auntie had called it? *Narina Trogon*. A famous man had discovered the bird many years ago and thought it so beautiful that he named it after one of the Hottentot women in the forest. No, she said, there could not have been any such Hottentot woman in the forest, for they were very ugly. The bush-lourie was beautiful. The only Hottentot woman left in the forest was old Abel Slinger's wife, and she was anything but pretty.

Wait! Wait! they cried when she was about to walk away, they were *dying* to see a bush-lourie. They agreed: a shilling a bird – *if* it was the right bird.

She led them deep into the forest. After they had crossed the first forest stream she stopped, cupped her hands round her mouth and hooted eight times through her lips. The bird-watchers' mouths fell open. What are you doing? they asked. I'm calling the bird. They couldn't believe it. She waited. Walked a little further, called again. Nothing. Kok-kok-kok, an ordinary lourie called from somewhere. They knew that bird. After a while a marsh-lourie started to doo-doo-doo somewhere behind them. No, they knew that bird too.

At last she heard a bush-lourie. It was far away. She called again. Waited, listened, hoped. Called again. Eight times exactly, bush-louries could count.

It called back – she called again – it called back. Closer …

She made four shillings that day. But the bird-watchers didn't wave to her from the coach when the train pulled out. They were upset. She had told them that six bush-louries in a pot with a sweet potato made a very decent meal. Did the forest people eat those incredible birds? Yes. They mimicked their call until they came close enough to shoot. Gieljam Botha, a woodcutter from Gouna, could conceal himself so cleverly in the thicket that he could kill one by throwing a stone at it.

⁂

She could no longer put off seeing Elmina Vlok.

She did not knock, simply slipped inside the house. Elmina was asleep, her thin bony body covered with the white bedspread. She took the doll from the jersey. It was a fat doll, as big as a baby, more or less. Its body was rather rigid, but she could only try …

'Elmina?' First one eye opened, then the other. She sat up. She had beautiful thick yellow-grey hair. 'Your baby has come, Elmina.'

'When?' the strange woman cried and reached out for the doll, joy radiating from her face. She gently handed the doll to her. Elmina took it and hurriedly put it under the bedspread. 'She's cold! You didn't keep her warm!' she said reproachfully.

She was at the door when Elmina asked: 'Was it an easy birth, Nurse?'

'No.'

10

ONE SUNDAY MORNING Oldman Botha asked her to go outside when she had finished drinking her coffee and eating her sweet potato. He wanted to wash, because he was going to church at Veldmanspad. She could come too, if she liked.

'I'd rather stay home, Uncle. I'll go and see how the little stinkwood is doing.'

'No, the stinkwood is having a day of rest. It's the Sabbath. And don't touch the hoe, the hoe is also having a rest.'

'Yes, Uncle.' She had helped with the hoeing the day before.

'What are you preparing the new ground for?'

'That's a secret.'

After he had left for church, she washed herself and tidied the house. He returned shortly after midday, said it was a very good sermon, the forester from Deep Walls had read it. It was about the prodigal son. Next Sunday would be Communion, and the Reverend himself would come and serve it; he only came out to preach at Veldmanspad four times a year. Her mother and Cornelius had been in church and her mother wanted to see her urgently. She had good news.

How did her mother know where she was?

Did Johannes also know where she was?

'I'm going to the station shop at Deep Walls tomorrow. I can't keep on using your coffee and sugar, and we need flour as well, I've used the last for the griddle bread. I'll visit my mother on the way.'

'I'll make a plan to get some meat.'

She took herself off for a walk along the old elephant path behind the house and into the forest. She walked until she reached the top of Deep Walls Forest where she had often played as a child when they lived near the forest station. That was when her mother was married to Uncle Freek van Rooyen.

She walked faster and faster, but she could not quell the anxiety that burned like a fire inside her. If she was pregnant, she would have to go back to Johannes. Or to her mother. Oldman Botha did not have room for her *and* a baby. Why did her mother want to see her urgently? What good news could she have? If she was pregnant and Johannes did not want to take her back, she would be alone with the baby. She did not have sisters, like Hestertjie Vermaak, to help her. What would she do?

She left the elephant path, taking the footpath that turned away to the left. She did not want to, she had not planned it, but it was as if she wanted to punish herself ...

She heard the baby crying even before she reached the house. Hestertjie's mother was sitting at the door, the baby was crying in one of the rooms, the other children were squabbling; it sounded chaotic. The cooking area was alongside the house under a corrugated iron roof; a thin puff of grey smoke rose from the ash. Sweet potatoes were baking under the ash; a blackened pot stood to one side. Hestertjie's father was sitting next to the house, his legs outstretched, his back resting against the dried-out plank wall. A woodcutter's Sunday: weary and dispirited, more dead than alive.

She should not have come, she had to turn back before anyone saw her ...

But it was too late. Hestertjie appeared in the doorway.

'Karoliena?' Surprised, and hostile at the same time. Her dress was too big for her, she was barefoot and dirty.

'Good afternoon, Hestertjie.'

Hestertjie's mother had also seen her. 'I'll be damned!' she said with a sneer. 'Look who's come to visit. If it isn't Meliena's daughter, the one who married the important man, I'll eat my hat!'

Karoliena stepped closer, feeling ill. The same old black hat over the matted hair, the same fat, bulging body, the same unpleasant look in her eye. 'Perhaps you should take that hat off for a change and wash your hair!' She could not stop herself. The old man looked up in alarm. Hestertjie's mother twitched angrily.

'What did you say?'

'I said ... '

'No wonder he hit you, you little shit! Who gave you the right to come and open your mouth in *my* yard? Look at you, you're a bloody disgrace! It's all over the forest that he drove you away. Why didn't you keep yourself clean for *him*?'

'Careful, woman.' The old man stood up, his cracked feet spilling from broken shoes. 'We heard that you'd come back, Karoliena. Hestertjie, bring her a chair.'

'No, thank you, Uncle, I don't want to sit down.' She had to get away. The two sisters she had seen in the village with Hestertjie peered around the corner anxiously. 'Are they still going to school?' she asked.

The old woman snorted. 'When I see what school has done for *you*, Karoliena Kapp, I'm thankful for having taken mine out of it!'

'Why is this yard such a mess? I'm going to bring the church nurse to see what it looks like.'

'She was here last week,' one of the sisters chirped.

'We saw her coming and hid,' piped the other one.

Hestertjie said nothing.

'Get out of my yard!' the old woman shouted. 'You're not welcome here!'

'I'll go. But I'll be back, I promise. To burn all the rubbish in the yard – and your hat.'

'Jesus! Anneries, did you hear what she said?'

'Karoliena,' the old man warned her, 'I think you'd better go now. Please.'

When she got back to Oldman Botha's house she saw Johannes's motor car parked down in the road. He was sitting on the tree stump in front of the door. Her heart started to beat so fast that she could not speak. Johannes was wearing the suit in which he had married her. Antipathy blazed from his eyes, from his whole body; his hands, white-knuckled, gripped his knees.

He stood up. 'Karoliena.' It was not a greeting, more of a warning growl.

'Johannes.'

'Where's Oldman Botha?' she asked.

'Gone to Jonkersberg to visit his brother.' His words were brusque. 'And I'm here to ask you one question, Karoliena.' He spoke slowly, emphasising each word, as if he was throwing stones at her.

'What?'

'Why?'

Only that. His voice was cold. 'Answer me. *Why?*'

'I don't know.'

'Karoliena, I've had enough time to think about things, enough time to decide that I will not lose my temper. *Why?*' He looked her straight in the eye. 'I'm waiting for an answer.'

'I'm sorry.'

'About what?'

'About everything you've done for me.'

'But it was obviously not enough!' He was angry, very angry.

It was too much, Johannes. The words formed silently in her head.

'I beg your pardon?'

'I'm sorry, Johannes. You're a good man.'

'But not good enough! No wonder you forest people are in such a wretched state! No wonder all efforts to improve your situation come to nothing!'

'Yes, Johannes.'

'Look what you look like! I had decent clothes made for you, I gave you a chance you almost certainly would never otherwise have had!' Sweat had started to break out on his forehead. It was hot; she wanted to tell him to take off his jacket. He got up and came to stand right in front of her, waved a finger in her face. 'I used just about my last penny to see that you had everything you needed!'

She was not afraid of him. Not at all. But she felt guilty. Did he know about the wedding money? 'I'm sorry, Johannes.'

'You forest people don't know the meaning of the word!' he shouted. 'You want to live irresponsibly, cutting and sawing wood, keeping a few oxen, planting some sweet potatoes and corn, finding honey in the forest, and then you turn to the state for support when the Church can no longer help you!'

'I don't think we are all like that.'

'You want to live like tramps in the forest, out of reach of the law, because when a woodcutter has paid for a licence to cut, he thinks he can do as *he* pleases, live where he wants to. The government should drive the whole lot of you from the forest, the sooner the better! As long as you are allowed to do as *you* please, I see no hope for any of you, and that includes you, Karoliena!'

'Yes, Johannes.'

'Have you any idea of the embarrassment you've caused me?'

'I'm sorry.'

'If you say that once more … !'

'I am really sorry.' She *wanted* to say it again. To bait him, because she thought he had come to ask her to come back to him. In spite of everything. She knew with sudden finality that she would not be able to go back to him if she was pregnant, and realised that she was in terrible trouble. 'Johannes, I found out too late that it was not *me* who was trying to live in the village. It was someone Miss Ann and Mrs Cuthbert put together.'

'You're not only insolent, you're ungrateful as well!'

'You said yourself there is no hope for us.'

'And you are brazen!'

'Yes, Johannes.'

'Now you listen to me, Karoliena.' It was a warning. 'The day will come when you will plead with me!' He was furious; the veins in his temples bulged. 'You will come *crawling* to beg me to take you back, but I will not. I give you my word for that.'

'I know.'

Then he turned around and stumbled back to his motor car. Got in, slammed the door shut and pulled away in a cloud of dust.

When Oldman Botha arrived home he admitted that he had not expected to find her there. He thought she would have gone back to the village with Johannes.

'He didn't come to fetch me.'

'I saw he was a bit annoyed when he got here. He tried to look into my house as if to make sure you weren't here.'

'I'm sorry. It means I will have to stay with you a little longer.' Please.

'It might be a good thing. I told you I want to go to Lily Bush Forest to dig up some small stinkwood trees to plant here in the camp. You can help me with them.'

'I went to see the Vermaaks today, above Deep Walls. Things are bad there.'

'Old Anneries Vermaak is a hard-working woodcutter, it's his wife that's such a disgrace.'

'What's to become of them?'

'Nothing. That's how life sorts us out: bad does not become good and good does not turn bad. You are what you are.'

'I can't believe that.'

'Believe what you wish.'

11

AT DAYBREAK ON the Monday she spent some time with the little stinkwood while the old man dug in the garden.

'Do you know Lily Bush Forest?' he asked her when she had finished talking to the tree.

'I've been there, but not to the marsh. My father always promised to take me when the lilies were in bloom, but he never got around to it.'

'Are you afraid of the forest in the dark?'

'No. Why do you ask?'

'Because we'll have to come back in the dark. Otherwise my plan won't work.'

'What plan?'

'For now, it's a secret. I have to prove to Mister-doctor that I'm the only one who can help him to return the stinkwood to the forest. We'll take the lantern. If we get there before dark, you'll be able to see the lilies. They bloom in February.'

'Today is the first day of February.'

'I know.'

She had worked out that she would know whether or not she was pregnant around the tenth of February. It was like working out in advance the day you would die. 'I'll go and visit my mother now, Uncle.'

'Good. The little tree looks stronger every day. You talk well to it.'

When she got back to the little plank house, she found Faan Mankvoet sitting outside the door with a piece of paper in his hand. Someone would have to make a plan to take Faan to the church nurse in the village so that she could get the doctor to have a look at his foot. He could hardly walk these days. Apparently he had been bitten by a wild pig when he was a child. One of the good poor, he and his wife and two children lived in a little clearing in Kom's Bush where there was too little sunlight for them to make a proper garden. The two lice-infested children attended school at Veldmanspad and were always hungry.

'Uncle Faan?'

'Good morning, Karoliena.'

'Why are you looking so troubled?'

'I've come to ask you to have a look at this letter, please. I dictated it to Willempie. You see, I never went to school. All you have to do is check the spelling.'

'Let me see.'

It was a letter to the magistrate in Knysna written on a page torn neatly from one of Willempie's exercise books. In the letter Faan told the magistrate that the rumour going through the forest – the one about the woodcutters being given only ten trees instead of twenty to cut each year – was of great concern to him because it was impossible to make a living from ten trees. Did the forest keepers have no feeling for the poor?

'I'll get a stamp and an envelope at the station at Deep Walls and post it today. But I first needed you to check if Willempie had done it properly.'

'I will. But I think it would be better if I rewrite the whole letter.' She did not have the heart to tell him that one could not possibly send such a letter to the magistrate. Too many words misspelt. Also, one did not ask to be excused for writing in pencil because one did not have the money to buy ink; and one did not close a letter with the words 'I greet you in *constipation*'. She knew the forest people loved elaborate English words, but they seldom knew what they meant.

'I'd be most grateful to you, Karoliena. Tell me when I should fetch the letter so that I can go and post it.'

'I'm on my way to visit my mother. I know there is writing paper and envelopes left over from my school days there. I'll use them and then post the letter on my way back.'

He stood up and took a penny from his pocket. 'This is for the stamp. Make sure you stick it on properly, it's an important letter.'

She took the penny to put his mind at rest. 'Don't worry, I'll see that it gets on to the train to the village.'

'Thank you.'

Her mother was not home when she got there. A slow anger grew in her when she noticed that the bed had not been made, the house had clearly not been swept for some time and there were dirty dishes in the kitchen. Everything was a mess.

Why?

Her mother used to be a respectable forest woman, especially when men came courting her. During her schooldays too. The best roof her mother had ever had over her head was Uncle Cornelius's house in Long Marsh Forest – which now suddenly seemed like the home of a poor white. Why? Did she just give up when the tribulations of life in the forest became unbearable? Was *she* supposed to keep the house clean? No. She was not going to.

Perhaps Oldman Botha was right – *bad does not become good and good does not turn bad*. She found it hard to accept. Her mother was not bad.

According to Mister Fourcade there was a woman with the Carnegie delegation who was talking exclusively to the forest women. Someone needed to *talk* some caring back into them. When would the Carnegie people arrive?

Faan's letter. She found the writing pad and a few envelopes among her old school things, a drop of ink in an inkpot, a pen with a half-loose nib. She cleared a space on the kitchen table and rewrote the entire letter, neatly and correctly. As she was writing a question formed in her mind: was the greatest chance she had thrown away in her life the chance to become a teacher? How would she ever know?

Her mother wasn't bad. Perhaps one simply stopped caring when there was nothing left to care for …

'And why are you sitting at the table?'

'Good day, Ma. It looks as if you've had a long walk.'

'I've come from Black Earth Clearing. The angels fetched Neels Barnard last night, they saw that his burden had become too heavy. God knows when it will be our turn. No one has the courage to carry on.'

'Don't say that, Ma.'

'Who have you been writing to?'

'I've rewritten a letter from Faan Mankvoet to the magistrate.'

'Write one from me as well. Tell the magistrate he should take off his jacket and join the plantation workers on starvation wages; perhaps he'll understand us better then. The plantation is killing Cornelius.'

'What will Aunt Martha do now that Uncle Neels is gone?'

'She'll keep on breathing, what else?'

'One can't live for nothing, Ma! The least one can do is see that one keeps things clean and tidy.'

Her mother flared up immediately. 'Are *you* trying to spit in my face? You, who can't even tell the difference between shit and sugar? What do you hear from Johannes? Will he take you back?'

'No, Ma.'

'Don't blame him. The man is poisoned. You must go back to him and draw the poison out.'

'What nonsense are you talking?'

'It's not nonsense, Karoliena! It's your salvation. I read it with my own eyes in Martjie Salie's newspaper. His blood is poisoned. It's especially bad in the mornings. All he needs is a good dose of Eno's fruit salts every morning. It says so in the paper, you can go and read it for yourself. They say it's every woman's solution to an obstinate man. It washes every bit of irritability out of his system.'

'Johannes is not irritable.'

'Then you're the one who needs it! What the hell is wrong with you?'

'I thought you had good news.'

'You're bloody stupid as well! I've just given you the news about the Eno's, but you weren't paying attention! You can buy the stuff from any of the shops in the village.'

'Ma, please.'

'Don't *please* me. You're on your way to hell and you don't realise it!'

'I must go and post Faan's letter. Why not tidy up the house for a change?'

'I will not be dictated to by a brainless child!'

When she left, she took the writing pad and the envelopes with her, the ink and the pen too.

There was an unusual amount of activity at Deep Walls station. A lot of strangers were drifting around, their faces anxious: they wandered in and out of the shop – something was wrong. The first thing she noticed was that there was no coach hooked on for passengers, but *three* open push-trucks in front of the Number 4 engine and on the third push-truck, right in front, rows of chairs had been arranged on which a few of the strangers had already taken their places. It seemed to be a picnic outing of some sort.

'Karoliena!' Somewhere in crowd she heard Salman Fransen call her. It wasn't a greeting, it was more like a call for help.

'Good afternoon, Mister Fransen.'

'Karoliena, I am so glad to see you!'

'What's happening?'

'They specially fitted out an open truck for sixteen tourists from England who wanted to visit the forest, and now three of them are missing! They haven't come back from the forest. I said to Tom Botha, just now, remember the days when Karoliena used to take strangers into the forest; she never lost a single one.'

'Has anyone been to look for them?'

'Where does one start looking?'

'Has anyone been calling them?'

'Where does one go to call? The problem is, the driver can't wait much longer. What are we going to do?'

'Leave them.'

'Karoliena!'

'It will teach them a few things about the forest.'

'They're important people. We can't just leave them!'

'Tell Mister Kennet to keep on blowing the whistle so that at least they can hear in which direction they should be walking. That's if they've got enough sense to stay on a footpath; otherwise they'll never find their way out.'

'Kennet has already blown the whistle a few times.'

'Tell him to keep on. I've got to get to the shop to buy a stamp.'

'Don't try to pretend that this is not a serious matter!'

'It isn't.' She had no intention of going to look for the lost visitors.

Uneasy passengers were milling around in the shop. Old Mrs Perkes was standing behind the counter looking worried. She asked Karoliena if she could not make a plan to look for the missing people.

What sort of plan? she retorted.

'At least you're used to getting lost!' Mrs Perkes was rude and reproachful. 'If Mister Parkes and Mister Thesen hear about people getting lost, there'll be big trouble!'

'Has the mail bag been closed?'

'Yes.'

'I need to get a letter to the village.'

'Have you got money for a stamp?'

'Yes. And I need flour and sugar and tobacco as well.'

'Have you started smoking now?'

'It's for Oldman Botha.'

'No wonder Johannes chased you away.'

There was sudden cheering outside the shop; obviously the lost ones had found their way out of the forest.

Two men and a woman, terror written all over their faces. The woman's stockings hung in tatters around her ankles, her hair was streaked with dirt. One of the men had to support her to keep her on her feet. The other man threw his jacket over the side of the truck and sagged down on his haunches, as if overcome by nausea.

Salman Fransen came and stood with her as the train pulled out of the station. At least the Number 4 engine should get them to the village without slipping. It was dry in the forest.

'Karoliena,' he said as the last truck loaded with wood passed by, 'we're getting more and more people wanting to visit the forest. Can't you come and accompany them like you used to? I'll send someone to call you. I believe you've moved in with Oldman Botha … but I always say one should never judge …'

'Don't bother to send for me, I won't come.'

12

WHEN SHE REACHED the Tree in Deep Walls Forest, the thought came to her for the first time that there were actually two worlds: a world of people and a world of trees. The outside world and the forest world. Poles apart. Trouble lurked in the outside world but in the forest world there was peace; elephants and bushbuck and birds – and not one of them cared whether or not she had run away from Johannes.

She sat down on one of the thick buttress roots under the tree.

'Tree,' she said out loud, 'I wish I could go and stay somewhere deep in the forest until I can see the light again. It's so dark around me that I can hardly see a step in front of me. Can you hear what I'm saying?'

Talking to the tree didn't seem strange to her. It felt good to release the words that were dammed up inside her, allowed her to assemble them in neat rows – even if it was around a tree. But then the Tree was not just any tree.

'I don't know if you can see how muddled everything is in the human world outside. I think you probably can. You're big and you're old, your feet are somewhere under the earth, you have a spirit inside you. I know because I've seen it. You know I have. My problem is that I don't understand what human life is all about. Nor do I know about good and evil, my eyes and my ears acknowledge that there's a difference, but I don't understand where they come from. Perhaps they both live together inside us and we are meant to unravel them like a ball of tangled string. I wish I knew what it was like to be a tree.'

Suddenly she heard a sound in the dense undergrowth, a sound like pebbles rolling together. Then, with a whir, a little bird flew out of the bush, passing so close to her face that she felt the wind of its wings against her cheeks. It came back again and almost touched her face! It was a stonechat, the size of a sparrow and quick as lightning. When she was a child she once came across the nest of a stonechat in the fork of a tree. There were three little pink-spotted eggs in it. She took one home and broke it open. Inside there was an ugly little chick with huge bulging eyes but no feathers. Before she threw it away, she sang a hymn for the unborn bird, trying to console herself. But it didn't make her feel any better.

Suddenly the stonechat sped from the thicket again, this time so close to her that she ducked involuntarily.

'What's the matter with you?' she called, waving her arm in its direction.

The next moment it *landed* on her hand. She could not believe it! A wild bird was sitting on her hand – little black head, white spot on its neck, red-brown breast. It had pitch black eyes like tiny beads. The bird seemed fearless, but she was afraid to move, afraid it would notice that it was sitting on a human's hand and be frightened away.

Tree, she said, look, there's a little bird sitting on my hand! She wanted to reach out and touch it with her other hand ... slowly ... cautiously ... *all wild things must be wary in order to survive ...*

Then it hopped boldly on to her other hand.

Oldman Botha was sitting in front of the house when she got

home. He was a tired old man, his tattered clothes damp with perspiration. He told her he had spent most of the day digging. He took the bag of tobacco from her, smiling like a happy child.

She made the fire, filled the bucket at the tank, put potatoes in the pot, and mixed the dough for griddle bread.

'A strange thing happened to me this side of Deep Walls. A little bird came and sat on my hand.'

'It must have been a stonechat.' Was there anything he didn't know about the forest?

'How did you know?'

'They're very tame when they're breeding – but they've finished breeding now, so perhaps he was a little mixed up.'

'It felt so strange to have a wild bird sitting on my hand. When I started walking home, it flew alongside me for a long time.'

'How is your mother?'

'In decline. Please wake me when the plantation workers come past tonight. I want to go with them, see what they're doing.'

'What for?' He sucked contentedly on his pipe.

'Because I want to know. Uncle Cornelius has joined them.'

'A plantation is different from the forest. The one is God-made, the other man-made; one is needles, the other leaves; one stands in rows, the other in freedom.'

'Plantation workers get one shilling and a sixpence a day; what do you get?'

'A shilling a day – but they'll have to raise it for the stinkwoods. You wait and see. You'll have to take food with you tomorrow.'

When Oldman Botha woke her, the men had already gone past and she had to hurry to catch up with them. Almost immediately she regretted not taking the lantern as Oldman Botha had suggested. It was a very dark night. The lighter colour of the hard road was the only glimmer she could follow while her eyes adjusted to the dark. The forest on both sides of the road was like a soaring black wall. An owl hooted on one side, and then on the other side. Frogs called, hundreds and thousands of them. For peace of mind she had to identify every rustle or creak quickly: mice, bushbuck, wild pig. She pushed herself to go faster. Until the next unknown sound disturbed her. A branch tearing deep in the forest. Elephants? Could elephants see in the dark? She came to a little clearing where she almost fell over her feet because she was looking up at the stars.

At last she came to a valley where for a moment she could see the planters' lantern ahead of her. By that time she had no idea where she was, how far from the fern valley – or perhaps they had passed it already? According to Oldman Botha, most of the planters from that part of the forest had at least a four-hour walk to the top plantation.

The road was uphill most of the way. An owl again. Close by. Another owl, far away. Signs of life in the sleeping forest. All those creatures that slept by day woke up and quietly went about their lives. Wild pigs, snouts sniffing for the roots they scratched out of the earth. Strange noises sent shivers down her spine and her imagination played tricks on her. In which tree was the leopard lying in wait? Where was he prowling?

Gradually she began to go downhill into a narrow valley which made walking easier for a while. She went faster. At the bottom of the valley she had no choice but to wade through a stream. There were frogs everywhere. How many frogs lived in the forest? Some appeared in the day, others only emerged at night, each one's call disclosing who he was, where he was hiding. Those nearest the road fell silent when she approached. They were the forest's secrets.

Where were the night-adders? What if she stepped on one?

She had to catch up to the planters!

The road began to climb again, steeper and steeper.

*

One day while she was at school in Wittedrift, she got a lift as far as the small station in Knysna. She sat down on the bench in front of the station to rest for a while and to enjoy the feeling that she was almost home. Someone knocked on the window behind her. It was Mister Wilson in his office. He beckoned her to come inside. Asked how she was, told her she was growing up. A large sheet of stiff paper had been unrolled on his table, the corners held down with an inkpot, a cup, a pot filled with pens and pencils.

Mister Wilson informed her proudly that these were the plans for the railway line across the mountain. What mountain? The mountain between Deep Walls and the Long Kloof. That's not *one* mountain, she said, it's a mountain upon a mountain upon a mountain. True, he admitted, one may look at it that way. But did she realise that a start would shortly be made on the extension of the timber train line across the mountain to Avontuur in the Long Kloof where it would join up with the narrow-gauge railway line from Port Elizabeth? An extension of thirty-eight miles! Could she imagine how much that would benefit the wood trade? Direct connection with a big port city where big ships would dock to take on the wood. She said she doubted if Number 4 with its slippery feet would make it over the mountain. He told her they would be getting stronger engines from Hungary. More trucks as well. It wasn't just wood from the forest that would be transported. Did she want to know a secret? The future was in *pine wood*. In plantations!

*

She caught a glimpse of the lantern light twice in quick succession; she was catching up with the planters. They were planting the pines that the new timber train would carry over the mountain. She had told Oldman Botha about the new train one night; he said that he'd eat the train that managed to cross *that* mountain, fire and all. It was nothing but wood-buyers' dreams.

The swinging lantern was visible in front of her most of the time now; she even imagined that she could hear the planters' voices. At least she no longer felt so terribly alone in the night-forest …

There were fireflies in the undergrowth on both sides of the road. Hundreds of them, each with its own glimmer of green light. Somewhere an owl called mournfully. Frogs, and more frogs. And no sign yet that day was breaking. Where did the birds sleep? Most of them had finished breeding. Oldman Botha said the trees woke up in the morning when the birds started calling them.

Suddenly she could no longer see the lantern. Had the planters taken a short cut? How was she to know? What would she do if she lost them?

The next moment a voice called out in the dark, its tone threatening.

'We know you're there! If you're alive, we're waiting for you; if you're a ghost, we call you to rest in the name of the Cross!'

She had trouble controlling her laughter. They had evidently heard her footsteps behind them in the dark. Forest people had an inborn respect for and fear of *things*. Ask them what *things* and they couldn't give you an answer. Apart from old Anna van Rooyen at Veldmanspad – if you chose the right moment to ask her. The best time was late in the afternoon when she sat sewing cloth bubbles together in the fading light. You asked: Auntie, tell me again about the ghost-child, please. The old woman stared into the distance and then said: She was my most beautiful child, seven years old when diphtheria drifted into the forest and stopped at my house. She got sicker and sicker. When the fever was at its worst, I set out on foot to take her to the doctor in the village – Wiljam Stander didn't have a motor car in those days. I had to carry her. She was heavy. I prayed harder and harder, and I walked faster and faster, my legs aching. I took a short cut around High Peak, and as I went through Quar Bush I swear the child suddenly felt lighter in my arms. The next moment she was skipping in front of me. It was a double fright for me: I was carrying the child in my arms, but at the same time I saw her disappearing into the forest ahead of me. Skirt swinging gaily round her thin little legs. I looked, and saw I was carrying a dead child in my arms.

There were people who said that they never took a short cut around High Peak, for late in the afternoon the ghost-child always skipped through the forest.

'Light the lantern, it's me, Karoliena!' she cried out.

Six planters. Uncle Cornelius among them, six shabby ghosts with yellow faces in the lantern light. They looked both angry and embarrassed.

'We knew it wasn't a ghost!'

'You ought to be glad we weren't waiting for you with a hacking-knife!'

'Why the hell are you following us?'

'My heart almost stopped!'

'What are you laughing at?'

'I didn't mean to give you a fright, I only want to go with you to see how a plantation is made.'

'The foreman will chase you away, it's no place for a woman.'

'I'll look after myself.'

At the fern valley another five planters joined them from a side path; and another nine shortly after the turn-off to Buffelsnek. By that time it was light and the birds had come to life everywhere. Which probably meant that the trees had woken up too ...

And then it was no longer forest. Just bare hills and ravines where straight rows of little trees covered the foothills of the mountain. The lorry with the whetstone on the back passed them and waited for them behind a rocky outcrop where the road came to an end. When the foreman got out, he glared at her, an angry frown creasing his forehead.

'What are *you* doing here?'

She knew him, he used to be a woodcutter in Deep Walls

Forest. 'I came with my mother's husband, Cornelius Kapp. I want to have a look.'

'A look at what?'

'How a plantation is made.'

'There is no room for spectators.'

'I will work if you want me to.'

'Don't give me that clap-trap! This is no place for girls! Just go away.'

'I can't go back on my own, I'm scared of the elephants. I won't get in anyone's way. I'll just watch.'

'If the inspector comes here today … '

'I'll hide.'

'There is no place to hide. Get out of my way.'

A few of the men got on to the back of the lorry and started to offload boxes of little trees. They lifted the heavy whetstone down and placed it on the ground. Lots of implements too: axes, flat-headed pickaxes, hatchets, hacking-knives. Two men started sharpening axes at the whetstone: a huge round stone with a whole in the middle for the handle, a tin tray for the water through which the stone was turned. One turned the handle, another did the sharpening. Sounds of iron on stone. No one actually spoke – apart from the foreman who gave orders and made notes with a pencil in a grubby notebook.

About ten of the men set off down the slope and into the undergrowth with sharpened hatchets, axes, hacking-knives. Each had a knapsack. This team had to clear the ground for the planters. The second team – the largest one – started to climb the hill in front of them. Two carried the whetstone, the others carried boxes of seedlings, knapsacks and flat-headed pickaxes slung across their shoulders. One carried a heavy chain, folded double, across his back. The foreman hurried them on. Uncle Cornelius was in the second team, and she fell in behind him.

Some way up the slope, she realised that they were in an area that had already been cleared of growth. There were just stones, rocky outcrops, the remains of the shrubs that had been cleared, and little mountain flowers bravely trying to survive.

No one spoke. Each one evidently knew exactly what he had to do. The two carrying the whetstone rested every few minutes. When they reached the first row of saplings, they piled their knapsacks in a heap. The foreman measured out where the end of the chain should be placed; two men evened out the chain. It was a long chain and some of its links were painted red. The first planters moved in and dug holes next to the red links, the second team followed with the boxes of seedlings, made the holes deeper and planted the trees. When the row was finished, the chain was moved to the next position and the pattern was repeated. Hole-makers ... holes made deeper, trees planted ... The sun rose higher and higher ... it became hotter and hotter ... the chain was moved ... hole-makers ... planters ... the foreman shouting to the planters not to fall behind ... Far below them lay the forest, dense and green ... still further away were the Heads where the sea began ... a strip of blue sea ... The chain shifted ... holes were dug ... the planters fell behind, and the foreman rebuked them angrily ... Crooked feet in broken shoes trying to keep a foothold on the mountain slope, jackets discarded, shirts discarded, but hats kept on heads. Two at a time at the whetstone when their implements had to be sharpened. The foreman shouting orders, out of breath.

At quarter-day the foreman shouted: Stop!

Time to eat and have a short rest.

A few of the men fetched the knapsacks and laid them in a circle below the chain. There was very little talking. She found a place next to Uncle Cornelius and ate some of her griddle bread. Most of the men had bottles of black coffee, sweet potatoes and dry bread. From the air they would look like a group of bedraggled vultures that had landed to peck at a carcass.

'How is my mother?' she whispered to Uncle Cornelius.

'She has given up on life. I don't know what to do any more. And now you, on top of it all.'

She didn't want to defend herself to the old man. 'What

happens on a day like this if it rains?' she asked.

'We make ourselves hoods from grain bags. You don't get paid if you stop because of rain.'

The foreman shouted: Fall in!

And so the plantation day continued. It was a bleak scene: little trees growing alone against the mountain. They were strange trees – like green needles on sticks. Two mountain-adders got in the way, their heads were quickly shattered with the flat side of a pickaxe. Scorpions, stings held high, tried to escape from the axes. Perspiration streamed down the faces of the planters.

She wanted to go home. She was feeling sick.

They weren't planters, they were old ironwoods without bark who were planting new trees to replace all the thousands upon thousands of trees that been cut in the forest without a second thought.

Were they settling some strange account without realising it?

⁕

She did not understand life. Although maybe she had when she was a child. Before she started school she discovered one day that she could count! Everything was one-two-three. Then four. An ox had four legs. Count, count, count. Everything in neat rows. Fourteen oxen pulled her father's wagon.

Abel Slinger could not count. He counted two, two, two plus one. More than seven was *many*. *Many* followed seven, not eight. One day they were coming through the forest with a load of wood. Abel was leading the oxen. She kept getting in the way. Counting, counting, counting.

'What comes after fourteen?'

'Fifteen,' her father called out.

'What comes after twenty?'

'Karoliena, get away from the oxen!' Abel shouted at her.

'What comes after twenty?'

'Twenty-one,' her father answered.

Counting trees presented a problem. 'Abel, how many trees in the forest?'

'Two two two many. Karel, Karoliena is getting in the way!'

It took her days to count the feet of the oxen. But when she had done it, there was not one with a missing foot. Counting didn't lie. Counting was the only thing that did not lie …

*

She went up to the foreman. 'Foreman, how many pine trees have already been planted here?'

'How should I know?'

It was half-day.

Coffee, bread, sweet potatoes. Most of the planters stretched out on the hard ground when they had finished eating.

Until the foreman called: Fall in!

The ironwoods stood up stiffly.

Move the chain, dig the holes, plant the trees …

At three-quarter-day some of them had nothing left to eat. She noticed one of the planters struggling down the slope towards her.

'You're Karoliena.' He was one of the oldest. Everything about him was old. Finished. Particularly his eyes.

'Yes, I am.'

'I'm Samuel. Elmina's husband.'

The church nurse hadn't told her he was *that* old!

'How is Elmina?'

Did he know it was *she* who had given Elmina the doll?

'She is well. But the baby has measles.'

'I see.'

It was awful to see the concern on his face about the 'baby'.

'The foreman gave me the day off yesterday to go and ask the nurse for medicine. It seems that the rash has broken out on the inside.'

Something blazed inside her when the plantation workers

began loading the equipment back on to the lorry, the empty boxes and the whetstone too. One-two-three was no longer one-two-three. There were too many without feet.

The foreman came up to her and said he could give her a lift as far as the turn-off to Kom's Bush.

'I'll walk. Rather give the men a lift.'

'Look, don't try to be smart. I am trying to do you a favour, it's a government lorry and I have to comply with government regulations, I have no say in the matter. I have only my orders.'

'Then get into your government lorry and go.'

'Don't talk to me as though I'm your servant! I've been watching you the whole day; you didn't come to see how a plantation is made, you came to make trouble! I've a good mind to report you to the station wardens!'

'Karoliena!' Uncle Cornelius called out a warning.

She did not cry until she got home, releasing the tears that had been building up inside her the whole day. Tears of relief, tears because she had been shown mercy. She was not pregnant, there had been blood on her bloomers when she had gone to pee behind the rocky outcrop.

'It's no use crying, Karoliena. I told you not to go,' Oldman Botha scolded.

'I'm glad I went. The forest and the plantation are like a human-child and a doll-child.'

'One says strange things when one is overtired. I've had a bit of luck, there's some nice bushbuck liver and potatoes in the pot.'

'I must go and see Johannes urgently. Tomorrow.'

'Take the train then, you've walked enough today.'

'I will.'

But more than a week went by before she could get to the village and to Johannes.

Before dawn on the morning after she had gone to the plantation, there was a cautious knock on Oldman Botha's door. He got up in a hurry. A knock before dawn, he said while he lit a candle, never brings good news.

She pulled the blanket over her head, she didn't want to get up. Her body was still tired.

But then she heard the old man scolding someone outside: 'What are you doing here at this ungodly hour? The thick-legs could have trampled you!'

'The nearest one is in Gouna Forest, Uncle. I'm sorry, Uncle. I have to speak to Karoliena.'

She got out of bed, wrapping the blanket around her. It was the older of Hestertjie's two sisters with a lantern in her hand, adult anxiety written all over her face. The other sister stood back on the edge of the forest like a frightened animal.

'What's wrong?'

'The baby's dying.'

'Why?'

Behind her Oldman Botha lit the lamp and blew out the candle.

The younger sister stepped forward. 'We don't know what to do. Ma says it's from hunger. Hestertjie has dried up, and the baby won't stop crying. Ma tried flour water.'

'Bring them inside and give them something to eat.' Oldman Botha was concerned.

'No. Go sit on the stump and I'll bring you something to eat.' She didn't want them to come into the house. She had to get money out of the chest of drawers – and she didn't want them to see. It was time she counted the money, it would not last for ever …

Oldman Botha scraped the ash from the hearth and started a new fire. She fetched water from the tank so that she could wash and get dressed in the darkest corner of the house. Why had they chosen *her* to run to?

'Why did you come here?' she asked when she took the two bowls of food outside. Two frightened, dirty children in rags, sitting close together on the stump while the first Cape robin began to call behind the house.

'We didn't know where else to go. Hestertjie is crying, she

doesn't want the baby to die.'

'Have you brought any money?'

'Ma said you'd have money, Johannes is a rich man.'

It would have been senseless to get angry – or go back to bed and cover her head, although that was what she longed to do. She was not the church nurse; she was not a miracle-worker, but they had come knocking at her door laying responsibility for the baby at her feet! How many more dawn knockings before the money ran out?

'Finish your food, we've got to get to Veldmanspad.'

'Ma said we were to come straight home.'

'Do you see any cow here that I can milk? You can take the short cut home from Veldmanspad.'

Veldmanspad was the only solution she could think of.

When they reached Deep Walls, the younger sister complained that they were walking too fast. At the station they asked if Karoliena had money for sweets.

'No. Have you tidied up the yard yet?'

'A little. But we've had to look after the baby.'

'Don't let me get there and find things like they were.'

'You mustn't burn our mother's hat; she's angry with you.'

'I don't care. Where's your father?'

'He's cutting in Kom's Bush for Mister van Reenen. He's going to ask the warden to move him to the plantations. It's better.'

'Hestertjie must go and look for work in the village.'

'Ma says we're not servants.'

'What are you?'

'She didn't say.'

Karoliena felt like turning back and leaving them right there in the road – and she would have, if it hadn't been for the baby. She asked when last they had taken the baby to the church nurse.

'The church nurse is rude to us. Just like you. She told Hestertjie she must not bring the baby again unless he is clean. Ma says, her arse.'

Bad does not become good and good does not turn bad – and miserliness never turned into generosity.

Wiljam Stander at first misunderstood the reason they were there; he thought they wanted a lift to the village. He told them there was no petrol in his car.

'Fortunately it's mostly downhill to the village,' Karoliena said. 'It won't be too much of a problem to push it.'

When he finally understood that they were looking for milk and that she would pay for it, he started complaining about how much it was costing him to keep the cows. He was not sure how long he would be able to supply milk because there was a rumour that the government was planning to give schoolchildren milk once more …

'Please, Uncle. Hestertjie's baby needs milk. I'll give you a pound and these two girls will fetch milk every second day.'

'From what I know of the Vermaaks, they'll drink the milk themselves.'

'It's for the baby.'

'They'd better bring a bottle next time. A clean one. Where's the pound?'

'I want a month and a half's milk for it.'

'I beg your pardon?'

'Yes. Or else I'll have to go and ask the Reverend what I should do.' Rumour had it that Wiljam Stander wanted to be elected a church elder …

'Really!' the old man became angry. 'Just remember to tell the Reverend that you've run away from your husband like a shameless hussy!'

'He knows.' When she held out the pound to him, he grabbed it eagerly and called to his wife to bring a bottle of milk.

13

ONLY WHEN SHE got to Deep Walls on her way back home and was sitting at the Tree's feet did she allow the feeling of relief to wash over her. Thank you, thank you, thank you! She was not pregnant. She felt as though she had been pulled back from the edge of the abyss.

She felt cold little feet and sharp little claws on her arm and opened her eyes to find the stonechat perched there. Sheer gladness filled her.

When she got up and started walking, the bird stayed with her – around her, on her head, on her shoulder – almost all the way back to the station. The timber train was moving backwards along the side-line so that the engine was in front again. It was the Number 3 engine. A crowd of strangers alighted from the passenger coach with picnic baskets and rugs, but she walked past. Pretended that she did not see them or Salman Fransen waving at her …

She wanted to go to Ironwood Ridge Road because there was another place calling her – had been calling her for a long time: Dirk's Clearing. She needed to see Abel Slinger and try to gain some insight from him.

The forest concealed so many old things, so much old wisdom. Mister Fourcade said Abel and his old wife were remnants of another era of humankind. Every white elder and red alder in the forest represented tree-remains of a much older forest that stood there thousands of years ago. She told Mr Fourcade that her ears heard what he said, but her head did not understand a word of it. He said: Don't worry, there are many things we don't understand. Then she asked, deliberately disingenuous: What, if I may ask, happened to the old forest? There could not have been woodcutters all those thousands of years ago because they teach us in school that they have only been cutting in the forest for something like a hundred and fifty years. If they cut like they're cutting at the moment, he said, there won't be even one white elder or one red alder left because the forest would be dead. She said: At least the poor whites will be dead as well. Possibly, he replied, but then the highest mountain of all will have to be confronted: the poor blacks. Black people don't mind being poor, she said, surprised. They're used to it. Mister Fourcade stopped in his tracks and looked at her, a shocked expression on his face. Karoliena, he said, you are a very stupid child! But Mister Fourcade, you told me only yesterday that I'm a very bright child!

Abel Slinger and his wife weren't *black*. They were a dark yellow. With peppercorn hair. And Bella, Abel's wife, had the largest buttocks in the forest.

Their tiny clay hut stood on the edge of the forest in a little clearing just before Dirk's Clearing. It was like the lair of a wild animal.

When she was a child Abel and Bella had lived in Gouna Forest in a similar clay dwelling. One day she asked Abel if they were moles. What had given her such an idea, the old man asked her angrily. If moles had corrugated iron doors in front of their earth houses, she replied, they would have been forest-people. Abel turned to her father and said: Karel, this child of yours is a strange one.

Shortly before she reached the mole-house, she encountered

two rather odd-looking strangers walking along the sledpath from the clearing. They were wearing curious leather trousers and boots. One had a sack slung over his shoulder, the other was carrying a leather bag. She startled them.

'Who are you?' she asked. They had also startled her.

'Who are *you*?' the older one asked, in English. The younger one, the one with the sack, looked at her in amazement. She asked if they were lost. No. They had been to see Mister Slinger; he worked for them. She didn't know that Abel worked for anyone; he had always been an independent handyman in the woodcutter teams. Especially when wood had to be hauled out of the forest. The woodcutters always said Abel could see round bends because no load of wood ever got stuck when *he* drove the oxen through the forest to the nearest sledpath. In any event, he understood oxen better than humans; and no ox could hide from him either, because he smelled them out. Oxen were clever. Sometimes, when they were about to be yoked, they wandered into the forest to hide, much to everyone's annoyance. But they could never hide from Abel.

'Where do you come from?' she asked the strangers.

England. They were archaeologists visiting the incredible town of Knysna and its surroundings. Unfortunately the woodcutters had been reluctant to cooperate with them, but Mister Slinger had been of great help. Where did she come from? The forest. Their eyes grew wide. Could she then tell them about the amazing bird with the green feathers and red wings that hissed like a snake? Yes. It's a lourie, and when he hisses like a snake he's telling the elephants that you're close. Not to worry, said the older one, Mister Slinger had assured them that the elephants kept far to the west of the forest; they'd get back to Deep Walls station safely.

Hardly a minute after they had said goodbye, she came upon a fresh heap of elephant dung in the middle of the sledpath.

The corrugated iron door of the mole-house was firmly closed. She had to knock a second time before Bella came and dragged it open.

'Afternoon, Bella. You might not remember me … '

'Your mother said you ran away from the village man.'

'Is Abel home?'

'He does not want to be. Go away.'

'Please, Bella.'

Abel called out from deep inside the house, asking who was at the door. Karel Kapp's girl, Bella answered.

'Let her in.'

It was gloomy inside and smelled of buchu and soot. In the light that fell through the slit at the door she could see bundles of twigs, dried animal skins and strips of leather hanging from the latticed roof. And two thick, square pieces of black skin, that looked like elephant skin. There was a frayed rush mat on the floor on which the old man sat cross-legged, his back against the wall. He resembled nothing so much as a crooked, wrinkled bundle of rags. An animal safe in the seclusion of its lair.

'Sit.' It was an order. 'I saw you coming.'

'Where?' She sat down in front of him. An old, worn walking stick lay at his feet. 'How did you see me coming?' There were people in the forest who believed that Abel Slinger had a prophetic eye. When he said it would rain in three days' time, it rained in three days' time. If he said the god-sickness was sitting on the mountain looking for a footpath into the forest to carry off a few children, an epidemic of measles or whooping cough broke out.

Miss Ann had once read the tea leaves in her cup and said she saw three children for her and Johannes and a long happy life together …

'I saw you coming yesterday.'

'How?'

'With my inner eye.'

'I'm very confused, Uncle Abel.' She could no longer hold back her tears. Tears of relief and joy, and tears of anxiety and sorrow wet her cheeks. She had the strange sensation that she had crawled into a shelter buried deep in the earth.

'I can see that you are muddled.'

'I don't understand about life any more. I have found a place to stay with Oldman Botha, but I don't know what's to become of me.'

'Light the candle, Bella.'

'I must go, it's getting late.'

'One does not leave when one is muddled. Sit.'

'Have you ever seen a spirit rising out of a tree, Uncle?' The question suddenly overtook all the other questions that seethed in her head. The old man looked at her closely. 'Have you, Uncle?'

'If you ask, you've seen what you have seen.'

'Just give me a straight answer. Please.' Bella had lit the candle and his eyes became like two little flames. Old eyes, distant eyes, slits in his wrinkled face. The knowledge of thousands of years burned in those eyes. 'Have you, Uncle Abel?'

'The tree blows out his breath when he falls, just like a human. The spirit is his breath. Some trees don't have breath, because they are the dry trees we need for firewood.'

'Nothing is right in the forest.'

'That's how it is.'

'What's going to happen to the woodcutters? Things are becoming worse and worse for them.'

'Man will always desire other men's possessions. Poor people work for rich people. That's how it is and how it's always been.'

'I'm becoming more and more rebellious because of the way things are, but I feel as if my hands have been cut off; I can only kick a little here and there with my feet. I buy milk for Hestertjie's baby, but I'm angry with Hestertjie and I don't know why.'

'The young ox has shaken off its yoke, it does not want to pull the wagon.'

'I'm not an ox!'

'Daughter of Karel, a human being is just like an ox. Once you've been yoked, you have to pull as you are bidden – or else they get you with the whip.'

The old church nurse, Miss Crouse, once took the Reverend to talk to Abel; she was worried that the old man might die without anyone having gone to the trouble to save his soul. The Reverend read from the Bible and said a prayer. Then he asked Abel if he believed in God. Abel said: Reverend look up and look down and look all around you, then come back and give your opinion.

Miss Crouse said there was nothing they could do for Abel.

'Mister Fourcade says that you and Bella are all that is left of the oldest people of the forest.'

'That's how it is.'

'What people were they?'

The old man slowly lowered his head until his chin was almost on his chest. For a moment she thought he had fallen asleep, but then he suddenly straightened his head and said: 'They were the people I have sold for four shillings to the strangers. My grandfather. My grandmother.'

'What do you mean?'

His head drooped once more, and he did not answer her. Bella was the one who answered, with bitterness and reproach. 'Karoliena, daughter of Karel Kapp, haven't you noticed that Abel is crying? You can't see that he is a broken man? You just come and pester him with your questions!'

'Why is he a broken man?' She suddenly realised that the old man was not crumpled with age, but with grief. There was something wrong. She could see it in the hatred in Bella's eyes. 'What is wrong?'

'He is broken because he has sold his grandfather and grandmother to the strangers from England. He dug them out of the cave next to the sea. A string of beads still round his grandmother's neck.'

The sun was going down when she got back to the sledpath.

And it was dark when she got home.

'I was worried about you!' Oldman Botha scolded.

'I can't talk. I just want to sleep.'

'You should eat something.'

'I'm not hungry.'

'Have you been to Johannes?'

'No.'

She had heard that there were well-educated people from overseas who were keen to buy Bushman and Hottentot skulls and skeletons to display in their libraries. Ancient stone and bone implements too. And beads. Many such artefacts were buried in the caves on the Heads, the huge cliffs where the sea rushed through a narrow channel into the lagoon. But they were difficult to retrieve, because it was not easy to find a way down the cliffs. There was a whole skeleton in the sack one of the Englishmen had been carrying, and a skull and other objects in the smaller case. Abel had dug them out of the caves and sold them for four shillings.

Bella blamed *her* for it. 'You think that because you're white, you can disregard the old laws!'

'That's not true.'

'You know nothing! The old laws say that stealing and deserting your husband are evil deeds for which you should be stoned to death! I told your mother so.'

'Bella … '

'Quiet! You asked. And now I've told you. Abel is grieving because he has broken the ancient law that says one must honour the dead.'

Oldman Botha came to her bed and asked whether she wanted some coffee. No thank you, Uncle. He said he had waited for her to come and talk to the little stinkwood, but when she didn't turn up, he had done it himself.

I'm sorry, Uncle.

She had deserted her husband *and* stolen the money …

The most terrible thing of all had been the sound of old Abel's weeping. Like the leopard cub at Jonkersberg that had lost its mother. Soft, hoarse mews. Except that Abel's mouth had been closed, not open like the cub's. She had tried to take the old man's hand, hoping to comfort him, but he pulled it away. He did not want her to comfort him.

She tried to distract his mind.

'Your people were the Outeniquas, weren't they?'

'No. *You* people came and named my people the way *you* wanted to! They were the Inqua Hottentots. People come and take pictures of us, say we are the last of the old ones. Write about us in their books. Call us Outeniquas. I tell them we are Hout-Inquas – Inquas of the forest, but they don't listen. Most of the Inquas lived behind the mountains in the Long Kloof. The rest lived in the forest. Hout-Inquas. Wood-Inquas. Then rich people came through the forest riding oxen on the elephant paths. Where an elephant can go, an ox can go.'

'Were they woodcutters?'

'No. They kept cattle in the clearings and on the edge of the forest, cows for their milk. They collected dead wood for their fires, branches to make their huts. Then the woodcutters arrived and started cutting and cutting, took whatever their axes and saws fancied. They loaded the wood on to wagons and offloaded it thirty days later in a place called Cape Town. Six, seven wagons at a time. I know, because when I was young, I was first a leader of the oxen, then I became a driver. I was poor, they were rich. Now they are poor and the wood-buyers are rich. That's how it is.'

'How many elephants were there in the forest when you were young?'

'Many. The elephants were rich too. They lived in the forest with the Hout-Inquas, pushed over the trees that had to be pushed over, made the roads. They knew the Hout-Inqua would never kill them, unless it was the right time. They always caught the old ones.'

'Caught?' He had stopped crying.

'Yes. In a snare-pit which they dug quietly and slyly in his path. Once he had fallen in, he could not get out again. They trapped him for his meat and liver and his skin to make better shelters during the winter. Then the hunters came and used the elephant paths to follow them and shoot them for their teeth. Which they sold. The woodcutters sold the wood they cut. Everything was for selling. Hout-Inquas sold themselves for the rich man's brandy. Everything, Karoliena, daughter of Karel Kapp, has its time to live and its time to die. Inqua, elephant, Hout-Inqua, woodcutter. They make their own choices.'

'What choices?'

'To be rich or poor. To live or die.'

'How can you believe that? Woodcutters have no choice, they're simply being paid less and less for their wood.'

Abel laughed hollowly. 'You won't understand. It's the inner eye that sees the snare-pit. You don't have the inner eye; you're too young.'

'Then how did I see the tree-spirit?'

'That I do not know.'

14

WHEN HE GOT up the next morning Oldman Botha was clearly excited.

It was the day of the stinkwood, he announced, with an air of expectancy. When the new stinkwoods are standing all over the forest, he added, they will be the new kings and Misterdoctor would build him, Oldman Botha, a palace at Jim Reid's Crossing! Just wait, Karoliena, you'll see. A palace made of stone. We must set out for Lily Bush Forest at midday.

Obviously, the old man had a plan, but it was a secret he was not ready to reveal.

'New stinkwoods, Karoliena, will stand in this forest and be proud giants a thousand years from now and they will be known as *Oldman Botha's stinkwoods*.'

'Who will know, in a thousand years' time that *you* planted them?'

'They'll know. It will be passed down through the years. Two strangers came by yesterday – one was carrying a sack over his shoulder. I had difficulty understanding them, but one could speak a little Dutch. He said that the giant yellowwood behind the station at Ironwood Ridge must be preserved and never cut down because that tree must have been there when the Lord Jesus walked on earth. I told him I'm not so sure, that was rather long ago. I asked what was in the sack. He told me it was the skeleton of an old woman from about the same time, and that they were going to reassemble her again overseas.'

She was little annoyed with them for having chosen the tree behind the station. *Her tree* – the one on Deep Walls side, was taller. The skeleton in the sack must have been one of Abel's ancestors. And they did not realise it.

They took the footpath to Kom's Bush. She carried the food, half the sacks and the axe, he took the rest of the sacks, a spade and the lantern. Shortly before they reached Barnard's Clearing they came across Faan Mankvoet sitting on a boulder next to the road. He had had a reply from the magistrate, he said; the man wrote that the government was under no obligation to supply the woodcutters with trees. Mrs Perkes at the station had read the letter to him.

She fell in behind Oldman Botha again, but she was troubled about Faan. He had to get to the church nurse to have his foot attended to. Oldman Botha took them along short cuts she didn't know existed, and she began to wonder if they would ever find a footpath or sledpath again. At times they had to push through the densest undergrowth, sometimes crawling on hands and knees.

'You're going to get us lost!'

'You can't get lost in your own bed.'

The old man stopped when they eventually arrived at an old sledpath. He said: 'Karoliena, here's a good example of life inside and outside the forest. Have a look.'

'Where?' Then she saw it. A beautiful yellowwood with the girth of a young ox was being strangled by a monkey rope as thick as a child's arm. It was not the first time she had seen a monkey rope winding itself around a tree, but never around a tree as big as that yellowwood. Round and round the trunk, almost to the top of the tree, every coil cutting deeper and deeper.

'The tree is not going to make it,' Oldman Botha said. 'It's like the woodcutters being choked to death in the forest. Monkey rope may not seem like much, but it's got a strong grip on that tree.'

'Why couldn't the tree shake it off when it was still small?'

'Trees can't run away from danger. Come, let's go!'

'No. Take the axe and cut the monkey rope!'

'It's too late. The tree is already suffocating.'

'Someone will have to look after Faan, before he is suffocated by his struggle.'

'The warden at Deep Walls says there are good things on the way for the forest. I said: You're right; the stinkwoods are going to be replanted by the dozen. The warden laughed. I told him: You can laugh now, but you will see.'

A secret gleam came into the old man's eyes and he started to chuckle to himself.

'Why are you so eager to get to Lily Bush Forest?'

'I want to fetch the baby stinkwoods and plant and nurture them in my camp before I replant them in the clearings. You'll see. I have a very clever plan. When are you going back to Johannes?'

'I want to stay and help you with the stinkwoods.'

'That will be good, for you have to help with the planting as well. Tomorrow, before daybreak, we must have finished the planting.'

'That's fine. It seems to me that Mister Fourcade is not coming back.'

'He'll come.'

They walked past trees and more trees, through undergrowth and forest streams, dense forest and open forest, startling the birds …

'Have you any idea where we are, Uncle?'

'In the forest!'

'There's something I don't quite understand. Some of the

woodcutters say they were far better off in the old days than they are now.'

'Things always seem better in the past; it's ahead of you that the road seems to disappear. I suppose they remember the days when we used to go to Riversdale and Swellendam and Worcester with up to eighteen wagons loaded with wood from the forest. In those days we got five pounds for a twelve-foot stinkwood plank. Today they get between half a crown and five shillings, because the wood-buyer no longer knows the difference between first-class and second-class quality. One wagon brought in fifty pounds in those days, eighteen wagons meant nine hundred pounds.'

'What did they do with the money?'

'That I do not know.'

'Did they buy land?'

'No. Forest land was not for sale. A few of the wood-buyers managed to buy some – but then the government stopped it.'

'Did they build houses?'

'No.'

'Did they give money to the Church?'

'Karoliena, I sense that you are asking some very deliberate questions. But I don't have the answers.'

'Did they buy clothes?'

'One does not need many clothes in the forest. If you get wet when it rains your clothes dry on you.'

'Did they send their children off to be educated?'

'You sound like the church nurse when she's out of sorts.'

'I feel more like that yellowwood with the monkey rope round its body.'

At the bottom of a shallow gorge they stopped at a stream to rest for a while.

An hour later they had to turn back and look for another way: four huge elephants were blocking their path.

'It's an old habit of theirs when the lilies are in bloom,' Oldman Botha said. 'They warn you off in the hope that you'll turn back. The old people believed the little marsh was the elephants' private garden.'

One thing was becoming clear: they were without doubt in the land of the stinkwood. Everywhere about them stinkwood saplings rose from the forest floor, baby ones, half-grown ones about ten years old; the old stinkwoods must have fruited profusely in that part of the forest. On many of the older trees a patch of bark had been removed and the wound was painted red. To indicate that the tree could be cut down.

Oldman Botha shook his head. 'I told Mister-doctor I don't understand how they think. On the one hand they want to preserve the stinkwoods, but on the other they cut out the best ones. What is the use of all my efforts trying to prove they can be replanted? He says it can't be any other way, the government wants stinkwood. I say that the government does not understand about stinkwood. It's a different kind of tree.'

'How is it different?'

'It's a magic tree. Leave a decent bit of stump when you cut him and he won't die. He'll stand there as if dead – quiet and unnoticed – and then suddenly one day he'll rise from the dead and start pushing out three or even five shoots from the stump to become new trees on the old tree's feet. It's miraculous, as if the dead has come alive again. After a hundred years those stump-shoots are beautiful trees which are ready to be cut again. Stinkwoods planted from seeds take at least four hundred years to grow to adulthood. I tell you, it's a magic tree.'

The next moment they were standing on the edge of a little swamp. And the whole swamp was covered with the most beautiful red lilies; she gazed and gazed, but it was altogether too much to take in. So beautiful that it was unreal. Every lily was a cup of red petals surrounded by the deep green of the dense forest. If this really was the elephants' garden, they had chosen the most amazing place to hide it. She wanted to turn around and steal quietly away so that no elephant would ever know she had been there. But it was too late. Across the marsh, on the other side of the lilies and on the edge of the forest, stood the largest yellow-tusked elephant cow she had ever seen.

She was motionless, only her ears moving ever so slightly. She watched them warily.

'I'm going back!' she called out across the lilies, hoping to reassure the elephant.

'What did you say?' Oldman Botha asked behind her.

'We must turn back.'

'Yes. You've seen.'

They walked deeper into the forest, going in a westerly direction. Far below them in a deep forest gorge were the shining black pools of the Knysna River, the river that eventually flowed into the lagoon at the village and became a different sort of water when it met the sea between the Heads.

It was getting dark.

'When are you going to start taking out the trees?'

'They're still awake.'

His ingenious plan – the secret he had been nursing for so long – was to dig out the little trees by the light of the lantern while they slept. And then to have them planted in the camp at Jim Reid's Crossing before they woke up the next morning. Because they had been removed while they were asleep, they would be none the wiser and would simply keep on growing when they woke up. You'll see, Karoliena, Mister-doctor will see, everyone will see my success.

At first she thought they were going to put the little trees in the sacks. No. Oldman Botha explained to her after he had cut two thin poles and started stripping off their bark. 'We are going to make a stretcher with the poles and the sacks; we are going to *carry* them home. You and me. If we put them in the sacks they will get bruised.'

There were many of the little trees, and he dug them out with the greatest care, while she wondered how on earth they were going to get them back to the camp. They would have to stay on the road. No short cuts. In the dark. She would walk in front, he at the back. She hoped with all her heart that the old man's trees really would one day be the new kings of the forest.

He had gone to so much trouble, and he had taken such care.

By daybreak the trees had been planted in long neat rows in the camp.

'Talk to them, Karoliena.'

The storm began around midday. It shook the plank walls of the house and woke her up. Oldman Botha was sleeping like the dead. After they had finished planting the trees, they had been too tired even to eat. She wondered whether she should wake him. But what could he do?

It was a forest storm.

When she was a child and a storm came raging through the forest, she always crawled under the table and put her hands over her ears. Then her father would come and kneel beside her to comfort her and reassure her that the house would not be blown away, and nor would the trees fall on the house. Yes, some of the trees would be blown over, but only in the forest.

He always helped to calm her.

When the storm was over, the forest was in utter chaos and seemed exhausted from the turmoil. Many trees were uprooted, branches torn off. Birds' nests dislodged. Thousands of leaves shaken loose and scattered all through the forest. After a storm a sudden stillness settled over the forest for a few hours and her father told her the forest was resting. It had been a sickle-storm that had come to reap and blow away everything that the forest no longer needed.

Please wind, she begged silently when she looked through the window in the back wall of Oldman Botha's house and saw the wildly waving branches, please have mercy on the little stinkwoods. The old man had worked so hard to get them planted before dawn. She was hungry. The old man would be hungry too when he woke up, but she dared not make the fire, the wind was too strong. If the house was blown over, the fire would blow into the forest and it was very dry. The water tank was almost empty.

Please, wind! She struggled to control her fear. The creaking of the trees, their trunks crashing together, was a terrifying noise – and just as terrifying was the sound of branches being ripped off by the buffeting wind.

Wind, please!

The old man slept through it.

The door shook. The window shook. The corrugated iron roof threatened to break loose from the nails holding it down …

If the two old ironwoods behind the house were blown over, the house would be demolished.

The wind was coming from the direction of the mountain, not from the village. Then, with sudden and tremendous force, the door was jerked open, and someone stumbled into the house. She was crouching under the table but she recognised Ampie Stroebel from Gouna. He pushed the door shut behind him and leaned back against it for a moment till his breathing slowed down.

'It's blowing,' he said if he needed to be sure that she was aware of it.

She crawled out from under the table. 'Ampie?'

His lips moved, but she could not hear him above the noise of the wind. He went down on his knees and crawled across the floor towards her. Oldman Botha slept on. 'I've come from the village,' Ampie shouted. 'I had to climb over trees and branches that have blown over in the road. Nothing will make it over the pass today. Is the old man dead?'

'No. Why didn't you take shelter in the village?'

'The Reverend says I have to have a testimonial from someone I worked for in the forest. You're educated, and I worked for your father a long time ago … Jesus, I don't think this house is going to be able to stand this!'

It *has* to! And the little stinkwoods too. The old man had turned on to his back and they could hear him snoring, despite the noise. She was thirsty. She crawled across the floor to the water bucket and stretched out a hand for a cup. The water in the bucket rocked back and forth and there was sand in it, but she scooped up a cupful and drank. If this was a sickle-storm it was doing a thorough job of reaping. Only God knew if the little trees in the camp would survive.

Please, wind.

The old man had worked so hard.

Deep into the night the wind began to abate.

At daybreak Ampie took the envelope with the testimonial and started out for the village. He was anxious to get back. She had written him something during the night, lying flat on her stomach on the floor while he held the candle for her to see by.

'The forest is killing me, Karoliena,' he confessed. 'I've got to get away. The government is giving some of us poor people a chance to go and plant ground nuts, and Reverend says he will help me get a train ticket.' The storm seemed to have blown new life into him. 'I've got to get away!'

Shortly after Ampie left, Oldman Botha sat up slowly on the edge of his bed. He rubbed his rough, dirty feet together, over and over again. His body was limp, almost lifeless. He said he had to get to the camp across the road, but he was finding it difficult to get to his feet. She knew he was too scared to go.

Only then did it emerge that the planting of the little stinkwoods in the camp was the last work he would do for Mister-doctor, because Mister-doctor was going away. Going away? 'Yes. Another Englishman will take his place, and I don't have a contract with him.'

'I'll go and speak for you, Uncle.'

'No, the little stinkwoods have to speak for me.'

There were no little stinkwoods left. Only a few scattered sticks. Like dead stonechat chicks. The wind had brought only one sickle and it had reaped Markus Josias Botha's experiment and with it the rest of his camp.

A child cries like a child, a grown-up cries like a grown-up. But a broken old man cries with such heart-rending sadness that you have to turn away. Karoliena fled from the destruction and took to the road to see if her Tree had survived. She walked past workers sawing up branches and trees and dragging them out of the way. She greeted no one and no one greeted her. She just kept on walking. She felt as if the wind had shredded her soul.

The Tree was standing, seemingly without a care. The stonechat came and perched on her shoulder. On her head. But she did not want to play.

The roof of the station shop had been lifted at one corner, men on ladders were fixing it. Old Mrs Perkes was blowing her nose on a dirty green cloth which she put in her apron pocket.

Karoliena kept on walking.

Past the wreckage of the storm. An old boekenhout was lying in the road at Veldmanspad, a torn-off stinkwood branch as well. Forest workers dragged branches from the railway line. There was an ironwood lying in the road. Stinkwood … elder-tree … candlewood …

The immaculate Johannes opened the door.

'Karoliena!' Shock and happiness mingled together in his eyes. 'Come inside!' But the next moment the anger in his heart flared, and he glared at her. 'What do you want?'

'Nothing.' The house smelled of polish and affluence. 'I only want the address of the man from parliament.'

'I beg your pardon?'

'The man who had lunch with Mister Wilson on that Sunday.' He did not ask her to sit down. They stood in the passage just inside the door – next to the little stinkwood table with the drawer in which she had hidden the wedding money.

'I'm referring to Mister Werdt who said that a Commission of Inquiry had been appointed to come and look into the conditions of the poor in the forest.'

'That's right. Why do you want his address?'

'I want to go and ask him where the Commission is, how much longer it will be till they get here.' She was too tired to embark on a lengthy explanation. 'I want to tell him that it is most urgent that the Commission comes at once.'

'Mister Werdt is a very important man and a very busy man too. One does not simply go knocking on his door.'

'I will do so.'

'Karoliena, wait!' It seemed as though a grain of concern had started to surface. 'You cannot go to him looking like that. Why do you look so terrible?'

'That's the second reason I'm here. To ask you to lend me one of the dresses you had made for me. So that I can go and see him.' Her legs felt weak, the walk to the village had been a long and hard one.

'You can't just go to him! You have to have an appointment.'

It was the important Johannes speaking. She turned around and reached for the heavy brass door-knob. 'I'll go and ask Mister Wilson.'

'Karoliena, wait!' he stopped her. 'I want to know why you look so dreadful!'

'We've had a dreadful storm.'

'I said that I would not be home the day you came crawling to me.'

His tone was that of one reminding a child of a punishment he had been warned about.

'I have not come crawling. I came only to ask how I can get hold of the Werdt man.'

'His office is in George.' As if he wanted to put her off.

'*Where* in George? I will take the big train.'

'Where will you get the money?'

'I'll steal it!'

'Don't be flippant. Listen to me!'

'Lend me a dress, please,' she implored.

This released a torrent of questions.

How did you get here?

Walked.

Why do you look so utterly awful?

The storm – Oldman Botha has been completely devastated.

Are you hungry?

No.

Come and sit down, I'll get a servant to make something for you.

Thank you.

You can't walk back, it's almost dark.

It does not matter; I have to get home.

This could have been your home!

I know, but it can't be helped; I belong in the forest.

Stop concerning yourself with the damn poor whites!

I don't know how to.

Why are you crying?

Because I'm exhausted.

Here, use my handkerchief. You will sleep here tonight, you must rest.

It was as if the world had suddenly taken her by the hand.

The problem was that she could not reach its hand, because she had been blown too far into the forest.

She slept in the spare room on the brownish bed-linen and realised, some time during the night, that he was standing next to her bed.

The road had been cleared of trees and branches. Shortly before the sun rose and before she reached Veldmanspad, she tore off some branches from a blown-over stinkwood which she took with her. She did not know why she did this; she just wanted the branches. She carried the dress, petticoat and shoes in a pillow-case, and erased the memory of Johannes's face as she walked. His disappointment when she told him that she *had* to go back to the forest.

Uncle Salie's wife Martjie was working in her garden when she passed their house, tying bunches of yellow asters to stakes with strips of cloth – asters that had been blown over in the storm. 'The wind got to everything. How come you're up so early, Karoliena?'

'I had to be.'

A deeply troubled Oldman Botha was sitting at the table.

'Life is not easy, Karoliena. The moment you think you have found an answer, the wind comes and shatters everything.'

'Yes, Uncle.'

She hung the pretty dress and petticoat on the nail behind the door, put the shoes under her bed. She wanted to take herself away from the outside world and walk deep into the forest until life became one-two-three again...

'Where are you going, Karoliena?'

'I don't know, Uncle.'

She wound the first rope around her head, the second one around her body under her arms. Then one around her waist. She started tearing off twigs from the stinkwood branches, pushing them under the ropes until she had a body made of leaves and felt as if she was standing inside a tree. A magic tree. A stinkwood tree, with eyes that could see from deep inside. A tree that started walking slowly along the footpath into Kom's Bush. A human being concealed in a leafy refuge; nothing could touch her. She was alone, free. She was a tree with a new spirit. A human-tree. As she walked further into the world of the forest, a peace grew slowly inside her. The frogs did not stop their calling when she approached. The other trees looked in awe at the tree with feet. A little blue buck ram did not dart away in fright; only tiptoed towards its next morsel of food. A lourie's nest, cleverly disguised in old man's beard stolen from a tree, had been shaken out of a red alder. It was empty. A tiny doublecollared sunbird hovered with fluttering wings in front of a wild pomegranate flower, sipping up the sweetness inside the hollow little flower – it was the smallest bird in the forest. Somewhere above her a bush-lourie called inquisitively from the forest roof.

Mister Werdt. They said one could take the big train to

George for five shillings.

But first she wanted to rest a while in the forest, feel what it was like to be a tree. Step by step. Her body of dark shiny leaves rustled softly while she inhaled the scent of earth and forest. She felt as if she was wearing the most beautiful dress …

The next moment she was looking at an old rough-barked yellowwood tree through a leaf-veil over her face. And from its bark, at the height of the magic tree's eye, hung a long spray of small pure white orchids. It was the tree's most beautiful adornment; sharp-pointed waxy flowers attached to long green stems. At least twenty flowers, if she had counted them. Mister Fourcade's little orchid with the fancy name, deep in the forest, waiting for the magic tree to find it.

She didn't want to leave it. But she had to.

The footpath turned in the direction of an old sledpath which wound towards the forest's edge. Step by step, she went. The human-tree was part of the forest. The human-tree was *inside* the forest.

The next thing she knew, the sledpath had become a hard road – and in the road stood a motor car. Beside the car stood a slight woman in a black dress and flat lace-up shoes covered with dust. Not a forest woman. The woman started and then stared at the human-tree with a slight frown on her face. The man standing on the other side of the car was also a stranger. Both had intelligent, enquiring faces, although the man seemed rather bemused.

The woman came closer, unperturbed. 'And who, if I may ask, lives under the leaves?' She had bright clever eyes.

Tree could not run away. And Tree didn't want to answer. Tree wanted to stand as still as possible, wishing they would disappear …

'Excuse us …' the man tried to say something. The woman stopped him with a small motion of her hand.

'Are you from the forest or from the world?' she asked calmly. She was wearing round-rimmed spectacles, the kind that Mister Fourcade wore. 'I would dearly like to know.'

'From both.'

'And what, if I may ask, is your name?'

'Magic tree.' They were playing a game.

'And your earthly name?' She seemed to understood about playing games.

'Karoliena.'

'Karoliena Kapp?' the man called out in surprise. 'The very girl we're looking for!'

She was trapped. Caught in a snare from which she could not extricate herself. 'I don't want to be found. Not today.'

'What about tomorrow?' the woman asked with a smile. She was as sharp as an axe.

'Perhaps.'

'Where?'

'Jim Reid's Crossing, the little plank house.'

'That's where we've been looking for you. The old man does not look well. He told us to come here to look for you. My name is Maria Rothman. I'm from Swellendam and I'm part of the Carnegie delegation. I'm very pleased to meet you.'

'I'm pleased to meet you too.'

'This is Dr Murray from the Department of Health.'

They were the people from the Carnegie Investigation! The woman was the very one who was coming to talk to the forest women! Her hopes were materialising!

'The forest has been awaiting your arrival for a long time.'

'So have I. To see with my own eyes how beautiful the forest really is. In the mean time, perhaps you can tell me what it's like to be tree?'

'It's different from being a human being.' She had to get out of this fix before they came to the conclusion that she was not right in the head. Although perhaps they had already decided that she wasn't. Especially the man. But a tree could not simply fall over; so she slowly started to pull out the twigs from the rope round her head so that her face was visible.

Maria Rothman looked at her sharply. 'The church nurse

has told me about you.'

'The church nurse does not really understand the forest people.'

'Is that true? Do *you* have the right kind of understanding?'

'Sometimes.' She started to pull out the twigs from the rope under her arms.

'I hope to speak to as many of the forest women as possible in the short time I'm here. Yesterday I had the privilege of talking to quite a few women at Salt River – on the other side of the village. I've already written my report.'

She pulled out the twigs from around her waist. The man had trouble deciding whether or not he should look away – perhaps he was hoping that the tree would not be wearing a dress!

'The women at Salt River aren't forest women,' she informed them. 'They are water-carriers.'

'I beg your pardon?' The man didn't understand.

'I beg your pardon?' Nor did the woman.

'Salt River belongs to the English Church. It is mostly hills. One hill costs five shillings per morgen per year. Every bucket of water for the houses has to be carried from the streams down in the kloofs. It's hard work, all day, every day.'

'You're very well-informed, Karoliena,' the woman said, astonished. 'I found a few progressive families at Salt River, but there is also a great problem with ignorance – among white as well as brown.'

'You will find that right through the forest, Auntie – I'm sorry, I mean Madam.'

'The church nurse says you have a high school education.'

'Yes. And I believe she will have said more than that.' Both the strangers' faces confirmed her suspicions. She had to get away. 'Unfortunately I can't stay any longer.'

'I would very much like to have a proper conversation with you, Karoliena.' The woman was eager to keep her talking.

'I am staying with Oldman Botha at Jim Reid's Crossing.'

'Can I come and see you there?'

'When?'

'I have a very busy schedule, but I'll make a plan.'

'I was hoping you were in the forest to talk to the women. Things are bad for most of them, their lives are very hard.'

'The church nurse is arranging for me to address them as soon as possible.'

'That means she will pick out the best ones so that you do not get to see the worst cases.' She was no longer a tree; she was a forest person who was beginning to get agitated. 'I really must go now.'

'We'll drop your off,' the man offered enthusiastically.

'That won't be necessary. I'll be taking a short cut.' Her joy that the Carnegie people had finally arrived suddenly evaporated. The outside world did not understand the world of the forest. She turned away and took the sledpath back into the forest. But she didn't take the footpath that led to Jim Reid's Crossing; she kept on walking until she found the footpath that led to the Tree. She was feeling flustered because of *how* the Carnegie people had found her. They'd caught her out. Amelia Claassens would not be able to rectify matters because Amelia Claassens would not understand either.

The only thing she wanted to do was get to her Tree and tell him that she was feeling strangely uneasy – uneasy about herself, about Oldman Botha and her mother, Hestertjie Vermaak, Maria Rothman.

Some distance before she reached the Tree, the stonechat fluttered around her head, playfully, merrily; one moment in the air, the next on her head, on her shoulder.

'What is it you're trying to tell me, stonechat? I can't understand you.'

Shortly before she reached the Tree the footpath led her through a patch of dense underbush and she had to turn back twice. The third time she tripped over a protruding tree root and fell down flat in the underbush. For a moment she simply lay there, then she started to laugh. At least the Carnegie people had not been there to witness her loss of dignity. The stonechat on her head, the stonechat pecking at her hair. They would definitely not understand.

She sat up in the underbush. Laughed out loud when she remembered the Carnegie man's face when he saw her emerging from the tree. She laughed at the stonechat that kept coming back even when she shooed it away. She laughed like one who was simply hungry for laughter. And she laughed for the sheer joy of finding herself so *deeply* in the forest that she felt as though she was sitting in its stomach. If she opened her mouth, she could surely bite off one of the large hairy leaves in the underbush!

She laughed at the memory of Mister Fourcade who sometimes played games in the forest to amuse her. She remembered the day when they had to make their way through a dense stretch of underbush and she complained that she was tired. Suddenly he asked her if she knew that witches lived where the underbush grew most densely under the trees. She said there were no witches in the forest; they would never get through it on their broomsticks – it was far too dense. They'd smash themselves to pieces against the tree trunks. Did she knew the proper name for underbush? he asked. Yes. Underbush. The proper name for underbush, he said, was witch-hazel. She couldn't believe it. Why? Because witches made their broomsticks from witch-hazel wood. I don't believe it, she said. He said: If you sit quietly for long enough, you'll see a witch fly through the forest.

The following day he would be puffed up with seriousness again and would give her a lecture about the importance of witch-hazel to the forest. It sheltered all the baby trees until they were strong enough to get along without protection. Then he would pull away the witch-hazel to show her where all the little trees were concealed.

She had to get home to see how Oldman Botha was ...

But she didn't want to. Not yet. She wanted to stay in the forest world a little longer. The stonechat sat on her arm, preening his feathers with his beak. In front of her was a white pear decked out in its beautiful dark, shiny green foliage, sturdy on its greyish, upright trunk, its branches laden with red and green and pitch-black fruit.

'Tell me,' she asked the stonechat, 'why don't you ever eat the fruit of the white pear?' Birds hardly ever touched its fruit and no one knew why; it was not poisonous – it was just one of the forest's mysteries.

On the other side of the white pear was another white pear, its branches entwined with those of an ironwood. As though they were holding on to each other. To her right, deep in the shade, was a kamassi. 'They'll come and cut you down!' she called out to him. Some of the old woodcutters claimed they made more from a kamassi than from a stinkwood. But the wardens only allowed them to touch it in August – that's if one was lucky enough to find one in the section one drew. The wood-buyers didn't mind buying it, paid for it by weight and asked for more; overseas factories where cloth was woven were desperate to get hold of this rare wood that wore so evenly. They used it to make bobbins. And shipbuilders wanted kamassi for their pulleys ...

The idea formed slowly in her mind. It made her get up slowly, shake out her dress, comb her hair with her fingers, and take a short cut to the hard road. It made her walk faster and faster to the forestry station at Deep Walls, all the way holding tightly to her brilliant idea.

The Carnegie delegation would never come to grips with the destitution of the people in the forest. Never.

The chief warden of the forest, Mister Keet, was sitting behind his desk when she walked into his office. Behind her the stupid clerk who had tried to stop her was almost having a fit.

'I told her she can't just walk in, sir!'

'I understand, Vosloo. You may go.'

'Good afternoon, Mister Keet.' She smiled sweetly.

'Good afternoon, Karoliena. I hear from one of my foremen that you caused trouble in the plantation up at Buffelsnek.'

'How old must one be to qualify for the old-age pension?'

'You will definitely not qualify for a long time yet.'

'How old?'

'Karoliena, I don't know what your problem is. I only know that there are many rumours circulating about you.'

'Most of them are lies, sir. Oldman Botha up at Jim Reid's Crossing must be given an old-age pension. He really is too old carry on working.'

'He was appointed by Dr Phillips and will shortly continue his work in the indigenous forest under the supervision of Mister Laughton.'

'How old does one have to be to qualify for the pension?'

'Sixty-five. Proof has to be provided, of course.'

'What if he has no proof?'

'Then someone will be appointed to estimate his age. There are ways.'

'Thank you.' She turned towards the door.

'Wait a minute!' he stopped her. 'What is *really* your problem? Why – in the first place – aren't you living with your parents in Long Marsh Forest?'

'I've got a place to stay.'

'Why do you continue to meddle in matters that are no concern of yours?'

'I look around corners where no else is looking.' It was another case of words simply falling from her mouth.

'A delegation of the Carnegie Commission has just arrived in the forest. I ask you please to stay out of their way and not to interfere with their work. Their Investigation is of extreme importance to the state *and* the forest!'

'They're going to have trouble understanding both.'

'Keep your nose out of their business, Karoliena! They are experts.'

'Yes, sir.'

'Fine. That means we understand each other.' Firm and threatening.

'Yes, sir.' You are very stupid, sir.

'Another matter has been brought to my attention. I believe you assaulted one of the assistant wardens at Askoek Hill in Kom's Bush. Is this true?'

'Yes. With a stick. If he had not run away, I would have killed him.' They evidently gossiped about everything she did. 'The man was painting a stripe on a beautiful young yellowwood so that it could be cut. The paint-brush men who mark the trees in the sections are being bribed by the wood-buyers.'

'Careful! You're making an accusation that could land you in court.'

'The three stinkwoods that have been cut down in Deep Walls Forest should never have been marked.'

'Are you now a self-appointed warden as well?'

'The problem, sir, is that what my eyes see does not correspond with what my ears hear. I don't think the Carnegie people will uncover all the evil in the forest.'

'That's enough!'

'Yes, sir.'

Oldman Botha was down in the camp when she got home, taking in the full measure of the storm's destruction.

'When God strikes, Karoliena, he strikes hard. A man and a woman were here looking for you. In a motor car.'

'How old are you, uncle?'

'I've forgotten.'

'I'm going to the magistrate tomorrow to apply for an old-age pension for you.'

He stood up with difficulty. It seemed as if the only life left in him was but a little warmth under the ash of yesterday's fire. His hair and beard were wild, his clothes old and dirty and shabby.

'I did not ask you to do that!' Stubborn. Perhaps there were more coals under the ash than she had suspected.

'I know.'

'I had one wish. That the day the angels came to fetch me, I would be able to look back and see the forest full of new stinkwoods. Stinkwoods planted by *my* two hands. But God is a jealous God. When He saw that most of the stinkwoods He planted had been cut, He sent the storm to destroy mine! Mister-doctor will surely throw me out of this house now.'

'Come, I'll make you something to eat. And you must rest.'

She helped him across the road and into the house. Made a fire, started preparing the food, and then heard a branch being torn off somewhere behind the house. When she peeped through the crack in the planks, she saw the four elephants come past slowly and disappear down the slope below the house where it was less steep and cross the hard road into Kom's Bush.

'Was that the thick-legs going past?' the old man asked from his bed.

'Yes. Four of them.'

'They won't damage my house, we have a contract.'

'What is the oldest thing to do with people in the forest that you can remember?'

'Like what?'

She had to find something to submit to the magistrate. 'Can you remember when they came looking for gold in the forest?'

'They found it too. In the streams. But the woodcutters were forbidden to throw down their axes and join the gold rush.'

'What else can you remember?'

'Nothing.'

'*Think!*'

'I don't want to think any more.'

'Please, try.' She could not stand seeing him so dejected. 'How old were you when the War broke out?' Old people remembered wars.

'Old. War will come again. They didn't finish fighting the last time. What you don't finish fighting for today, you have to fight for tomorrow.'

'Why do you say that?'

'The woodcutters didn't fight. Years ago, when there were

still bars in the forest, there were some fights. But then Reverend Maclachlan came and did not rest until he had every bar in the forest shut down and the barkeepers expelled. A formidable man, that one. Used his own fists, if he had to. Fought till he had every bar out and schools brought in. Now *there* was a man of God with brains!'

'Come back to the War. I was taught at school that the War began in 1914.'

'War had broken out in the forest the year before that.'

'What war was that?'

'The government made us register if we wished to remain woodcutters. All the woodcutters' names were entered on a list, and the lists were nailed up showing who had the right to cut – nailed up at the forest station, the shop at Deep Walls, at the magistrate's office in the village. The only man who had a good look at the lists was Saul Barnard – he's a rich man today from his furniture factory.'

'I know him. He and his wife live not far from Miss Ann's boarding house in the village. It's a beautiful place with a beautiful garden.'

'His wife's name is Kate. So Saul was the one who brought us the news: the first names on the list were not those of woodcutters, but of shopkeepers and wood-buyers and all sorts of strangers – not one of them had even so much as held an axe in his hand! But, somehow, their names were on the list. Saul was angry, really angry. He rounded up about fifty of us and drove us to the magistrate like a herd of cattle. He said if we didn't speak out, the unregistered thieves were going to steal the bread out of our mouths. When the magistrate came outside, Saul could see we didn't know what to say. So he went and stood right in front of the magistrate, pulled back his shoulders and made a speech that made grown men cry that day. The magistrate was stunned and said the names had to come off immediately.'

'What year was that?'

'The year before the War.'

'It must have been 1913 then. How old were you then, Uncle?'

'They worked out on paper that I was too old to join the war. We cut yellowwood for railway sleepers that year. Felled the giants right here where my garden camp is today. We sawed it up, dragged it out to the village.'

'How old did the papers say you were?'

'Sixty.'

'Then you must be more than eighty today.'

'Then I really should be dead.'

She lay on her bed that night, not sleeping. She listened to the sounds of the forest and the old man's snoring. In her mind she put on her stinkwood dress again and walked back into the forest. She felt cheated because the Carnegie people had interrupted her that morning.

She walked in her tree body until she reached Lourie Bush, through the forest streams in the direction of Marais' Bush. Through the Red Alder River …

When she waded through the river, it was as if Abel Slinger had joined her and was wading through with her.

*

One day her father had sent Abel to Island Bush to fetch two of his oxen that a wood-dragger had borrowed from him. She begged to be allowed to go with him. Eventually her father gave in. They came to a river – she thought it was the Homtini – which was running quite strongly. Abel took her by the hand, bent down, scooped up some water and sprinkled it on her head. 'You're wetting my hair!' He appeared not to hear her. He bent down and gathered some mud from the side of the river and with his fingers drew mud-stripes across her forehead.

'You're making me dirty!'

'Quiet.'

He sprinkled some river water over his own head and drew mud-stripes on his own forehead. Then he said: 'River says we may cross.'

'Can a river speak?'

'Yes. You must always ask his permission; you can't just go through.'

⁂

She solemnly asked the Red Alder's permission before she waded through …

Some time during the night she must have fallen asleep, because she woke up when she heard a car passing and turning in to Kom's Bush. She got up and looked through the back window; saw the lights of the car. It was strange, motor cars never went into Kom's Bush at night. People were too scared of the elephants. Motor cars sometimes passed along the hard road to cross the mountain to the Long Kloof, and in the early mornings the plantation lorry went by.

She dozed off, then woke again – the car was coming back from Kom's Bush.

In the morning she mentioned to Oldman Botha that a car had gone into Kom's Bush during the night and had come back again. He said she must have been dreaming.

At midday one of the wardens came by and asked whether they had heard the news? What news? Faan Mankvoet had slit his throat last night. Faan's wife had run to Veldmanspad and sent Wiljam Stander to call the doctor. The doctor rushed from the village, put Faan in his car and raced with him to George, but he died on the way.

In the afternoon Wiljam Stander came to collect contributions for the coffin. Oldman Botha gave him the yellowwood plank that was lying behind the house, and a handful of nails. The rest of the planks were already tied to the roof of the car.

The next morning, Sunday, a few of the woodcutters made the coffin and at four o'clock in the afternoon one of the forest wardens held a service for Faan at Veldmanspad. Karoliena did not cry for Faan Mankvoet, but for Susanna who followed the coffin with dragging feet, overcome with grief – a child on either side of her clinging to her skirt.

The warden said the doctor told him that the only food he found in Faan's house was a little bowl of wild grapes and a few sweet potatoes.

When she woke up on the Monday morning she knew what she had to do.

'Where are you going this early, Karoliena?' Oldman Botha asked.

'To Faan's wife, Susanna.'

'Take her some carrots, there are still some left in the camp.'

'Later. If the woman from the Carnegie Commission should come looking for me, tell her I'm trying to pull Susanna back from the brink of hell.'

'Karoliena?'

'Later, Uncle. I must go.'

The forest was sparkling with dew. Every drop touched by the sun glittered like fine glass. The smell of every forest herb hung in the air; a wailing cisticola was perched on top of a bush, scolding the forest with his plaintive cry; a flock of bulbuls scratched around in the leaves on the forest floor, looking for food. Susanna could not scratch for food on the forest floor …

But she could say no.

Please, don't let her say no …

She didn't.

'I'm tired of struggling to survive, Karoliena.' Her eyes were swollen from crying, lifeless eyes expressing only grief.

A short distance from the house, she made Susanna and the children wait under a yellowwood tree with their bundles.

'Will you come back for us?' Willempie asked anxiously.

'Yes.'

Her mother was in the kitchen, making the fire.

'Good morning, Ma.'

'If you appear at this time of day with a face like that, Karoliena, it can only mean fresh trouble!'

'I'm afraid it might, Ma.'

'Are you back with Johannes?'

'No. I've come to ask if you'll take in Faan's Susanna.'

'*What?*' She looked at her with shocked disbelief.

'The two children as well. They have nowhere to go.' She asked calmly, lingering before putting down the bait.

'Have you got brain fever?'

'Please, Ma.'

'I'm not boarding house! How can you come and ask me such a thing? We have barely enough to live on ourselves!'

'I'll pay Ma a pound a month.' She offered the bait and saw the surprised look in her mother's eyes. 'Susanna can help you in the house and the garden. Willempie is old enough to help in the garden as well. But the children must stay in school, of course.'

'A pound a month?'

'Yes.'

'And where will you get that from?' As if her mother was scared to believe it too quickly. 'The church nurse is sending old Lewies round with a note saying that a very important woman from the government will be addressing the forest women at the school in Veldmanspad on Saturday. Did Nurse send you?'

'No.'

'Martjie Salie says there are strangers in the forest who have been sent to see why we have become so poor. I can't take Susanna and the children in for nothing. They have to eat.'

'I know, Ma.' She took the pound from her pocket and held it out to her mother.

And next month?' asked her mother, eager hands grabbing the money.

'Then I will bring you another pound.'

'She will have to help me with the washing as well.'
'She will. Thank you, Ma.'

When she walked out of Long Marsh Forest and back on to the hard road, it was too late to walk to the village as well. Her concern about Susanna was alleviated, but a new worry had begun to plague her: money. She had promised her mother a pound a month without knowing how long she'd be able to keep up the payment – how much there was left of the wedding money. She would have to count it as soon as she got home. She guessed that there ought to be enough for about six months. And then? And what about the milk for Hestertjie's child?

The next moment a deep anger welled up in her. She was not the Church or the state or the Carnegie Commission!

What was she going to do when the wedding money was finished?

And who was it that would be addressing the women at Veldmanspad? The Rothman woman? Address them about what? Was there perhaps a glimmer of hope at last?

15

OLDMAN BOTHA WAS sitting on the tree stump in front of the door when she got home.

'The Reverend was here; he says he has to see you urgently. The Rothman woman was with him.'

'See me about what?'

'They didn't say.'

'I've taken Susanna and the children to my mother.'

'That's good. I told the Reverend that there are times when you look after the forest people in this area better than the church nurse does. He reckons, however, that it's time you got out of the forest.'

'If they come again, tell them I'm not here.'

'I worry about you, Karoliena. Mister-doctor came and said I need no longer carry on with my experiment when the new man takes over from him. The new plantings have not been successful. I asked him, what about my house? He told me that all the woodcutters are going to be moved out of the forest. When? I asked. And he said as soon as the investigation has been completed. I wanted to know what investigation. He says important people have arrived in the forest to investigate.'

'Perhaps it is the solution everyone has been hoping for, Uncle.'

'What is going to happen to *you*, Karoliena?'

'I don't know, Uncle.' She had counted the wedding money; there was six pounds and a few shillings left. The sugar was finished, the flour was finished. Oldman Botha's tobacco too …

She was not Poor Relief!

'Oh, I almost forgot. Johannes sent you a message with the warden to say the man from parliament will be having dinner with him on Sunday and you are invited.'

Mister Werdt. But it was no longer necessary for her to see him. The Carnegie delegation had arrived.

'Who's that coming up the road?' the old man asked, narrowing his eyes as he looked in the direction of Deep Walls.

'It looks like Gieljam Botha and Daantjie Zeelie from Gouna.'

'Look again. They seldom come to this side of the forest.'

'It is them. Perhaps the chief warden has sent for them again to inspect the strange stinkwood.'

'What strange stinkwood?'

'Nothing. Just an old joke.'

'Make the fire and put the water on for coffee. The coffee's low, we must get some.'

'Yes, Uncle.'

The two old woodcutters sat outside with Oldman Botha. They sounded not in the least like the two anxious men she had accompanied to Mister Keet that day long ago. She had still been at school in Wittedrift then.

Wittedrift. Did life set the path you *had* to take? Or did you set the way yourself? Or turn your back on it? You'd never know. The only thing she knew was that there was about six pounds left before the road ended for her.

She broke the kindling and threw it into the fire contemptuously, saying to herself: When the money is finished, I'll walk into the forest and find a cave in the rocks along the Red Alder

River and stay there for the rest of my life.

When she went back outside, the three ragged old men were smiling like three mangy old cats that had just caught three mice. Blue pipe smoke curled in the air around them. 'And what, if I may ask, is the reason for this sudden joy?'

'Karoliena, the sun rises every day! One does not even have to believe it. It does! Gieljam and Daantjie have brought news.'

'What news?'

'A great festival is being planned, and they're looking for the best men to make wagons, and *we* are the best.'

'Are you hallucinating? What festival are you talking about?'

'A festival to celebrate the Great Trek,' Gieljam Botha said importantly. 'Next year,' he added.

Daantjie Zeelie was concerned that she did not quite understand. He explained to her: 'You see, Karoliena, just as Christmas is a festival to celebrate the birth of the Lord, this will be a festival to commemorate the Great Trek. The Voortrekkers. The farmers and their families who, years ago, fled with their wagons into the interior to try to find a better place to live.'

'I *have* been to school, Uncle. And they didn't flee, they moved away.'

'Same thing. Ox-wagons are going to trek from Cape Town up to Pretoria, following the same route as the Voortrekkers, and four of the wagons are going to be made specially with wood from this forest. The wagons will be donated by Knysna. Jaap Jonker came to see Gieljam and me the day before yesterday, he's looking for the best men to make the wagons. Stinkwood wagons. I told him: The best men are sitting right in front of you, Mister Jonker – and if we can get Oldman Botha at Jim Reid's Crossing to make the spokes, you will have the very best. But you will have to have the stinkwood cut immediately, it needs at least two years for the wood to dry.'

Old Gieljam took over. 'Then Mister Jonker said he already had the stinkwood. In his yard. Properly dried. He has taken responsibility for building two of the wagons. We can start growing our beards because everyone has to look like the Voortrekkers. Corduroy trousers and all. Johannes Stander says corduroy material is already on its way by ship. I said: Luckily Oldman Botha already has a beard. Women will wear long dresses …'

'Who's going to pay for the corduroy?' she asked.

'Jonker will pay half, Van Reenen in Sourflats Forest will pay the other half, because he is going to make two more wagons. He's a rich man.'

'When are you going to start making the wagons?'

'Monday, God willing,' Gieljam Botha said. 'Reverend Odendaal says the festival will not be the work of man but of the Almighty, helping the Afrikaners to stand together in these hard times.'

'Who's going to pay you for making the wagons?' What if she didn't succeed in getting a pension for the old man …

'Jonker and Van Reenen.'

'Who will pay Oldman Botha?'

'Jonker and Van Reenen. Fortunately I still have a good supply of ironwood; the spokes must be made of ironwood.'

At least it *was* a small encouragement.

And she would accept Johannes's invitation so she could ask Mister Werdt about the festival herself. Fortunately she had the borrowed dress and shoes; Johannes would not be ashamed of her.

But first she had to go to Veldmanspad on the Saturday morning to hear what the forest women were being told. And to find out who was talking to them.

It was the Rothman woman, who arrived at about ten o'clock. When Karoliena got to the school an hour earlier, only a handful of nervous women were assembled, her mother and Susanna among them. Uncle Salie's Martjie, Jan Koen's wife. Fransina, daughter-in-law of Anna van Rooyen – her hair fastened with a huge red bow.

'How is your mother-in-law, Fransina?'

'She can't get out of bed any more. Her legs are covered in sores now.'

Children were playing around the school ground, most of them with white or blue objects dangling from their mouths.

'What have the children got in their mouths?' she asked Aunt Martjie.

'Toothbrushes. They're not used to them. The government distributed free toothbrushes because the church nurse reported that the children's teeth were very bad. Now they run around with the brushes in their mouths. I want to know where the toothpaste is. Did you hear about the cheese?'

'What about the cheese?'

'The children are now going to be given cheese at school instead of milk. But dogs have eaten up all the cheese at Bracken Hill station that was supposed to have been brought here on the timber train. Why do you think we've all been called together here today?'

'I hope it might be to hear about some relief from our misery.'

'Your mother has become almost as high and mighty as when you married Johannes.'

'What do you mean?'

'She keeps a servant now, like the rich. The late Faan's Susanna. Apparently pays her a pound a month. I say: For a pound a month I'd also be a servant. You say you think we can expect to hear about some relief today?'

'Yes.'

The car came slowly up the road from the direction of the village. It was enveloped in a cloud of dust; the weather had been very dry. The Reverend Odendaal was behind the wheel, Maria Rothman next to him. She got out first. Black dress, flat black shoes. A finely whetted axe who greeted the group of apprehensive forest women with an unhurried bow of the head to the left and to the right – a gentle smile for each one of them so that for a moment dignity rose up within them like the heat from an old fire. The Reverend Odendaal followed her, lifting his hat with his left hand while shaking the rough forest hands with his right.

Hestertjie Vermaak's mother was there, wearing her black hat, and clutching a red book under her arm.

The Reverend came up to Karoliena on the veranda and shook her hand. 'I am particularly glad to see you here this morning, Karoliena. We – Mrs Rothman and I – have good news for you.'

Behind him, on the road from Deep Walls, she saw Elmina Vlok approaching, the 'baby' wrapped in a blanket in her arms. Samuel trotted behind her. 'I think we must ask the women to go inside,' she suggested quickly.

She waited for Elmina at the gate. Elmina with dull, frightened eyes … 'Whose funeral is it?' she asked.

'It's not a funeral, Elmina. An important woman from Poor Relief has come to speak to the forest women. Are you coming in?'

'I can't. I must take the baby to the church nurse. She does not want to suckle.'

How do you undo a deed you should never have committed? And where do you draw the line between right and wrong?

She entered the schoolroom through a side door. Maria Rothman had taken her place at the front of the room, and the Reverend was sitting in one of the front rows. Twenty or so forest women sat on the benches, a motley of crows dressed in the best clothes they owned. Head-cloths, ribbons, slides and bows in their hair …

Maria Rothman waited until Karoliena had taken her place on one of the benches at the back. It was strange to be sitting in the 'dead' classroom feeling the same anxiety that had always threatened to choke her when she was at school. She could not remember a single morning that she had not begged not to go to school …

'It has been found that the well-being of a family rests on the shoulders of the mother,' Maria Rothman took up her lecture. 'It is the *mother* who determines the place of the family in the community. The conduct of the children enables us to deduce the general conduct of the home – especially the conduct of the daughters. From the condition of the house, we can infer the condition of the mother – clean and neat, or dirty and disorderly.'

Maria Rothman's words fell between the forest women like drops of water on a dry and dusty place – drops which for the most part could not sink in because it had been dry for too long ...

'At the same time we dare not forget that poverty is the greatest demoraliser and enemy of our principles and self-respect. I have travelled throughout this country, and everywhere I have found the same pattern amongst the poor: ignorance and confusion because they did not have access to a decent education. If I refer to my notes, I find that two groups occur among the poor: those in deteriorating circumstances as a result of personal factors like disability, and those who are declining because of external influences.

'A home, a family, functions and is managed like any business undertaking. It operates well as long as there are firm rules and order amongst the members, and where responsibilities are laid down by the mother and the father – but especially by the mother. The father supplies the means, no matter how meagre, and the mother is the distributor thereof. If she does not do this skilfully, the whole family will suffer.'

Karoliena began to feel increasingly choked by the old anxiety. She had to get out. Go and play on the railway line, wave to the people in the coach ... Maria Rothman might have been saying the right things, but she did not know that some crows could only digest small pieces of food at a time ...

'The first task of the mother is to train the children in the art of running a home. The daughters to whom she gives this important training are the mothers of the future who will, in turn, train *their* children. The first task of the Carnegie Commission of Inquiry is to determine where training in poor communities is inadequate and to strive towards making this training available. For example, it should be noted that girls are getting excellent training at the housecraft school in Knysna, as are the boys in the industrial school outside the village. A community's wealth lies in its leaders, because without strong leadership any community will fall apart. The leaders within a community set the examples and give guidance, like seeing that children remain in school. It is the duty of the leaders ...'

She simply had to get out. She must wait for a chance to slip out the side door before the meeting ended.

'I had the privilege yesterday of visiting two of the progressive families here in Veldmanspad with the church nurse; in both homes the mothers were good, simple women; the houses were neat and tidy, some of the children are attending school in the village ...'

Only when she sat down under the Tree, did she allow herself to say the words out loud. 'Tree, it will be best for me if I can find a safe place somewhere in the forest to hide for ever. Become a tree. At least I will then live in peace until I die. These Carnegie people are good people, they know the right words – but they are completely unaware that they're cutting dead trees, and I don't want to be a dead tree!'

'Are you talking to yourself, Karoliena?'

Two woodcutters and a wood-dragger from Gouna took her by surprise.

'No, I'm talking to the tree.'

'And what are you saying to the tree?' They laughed and put down a bundle of sacks. One was carrying two long poles and a bucket.

'I'm telling the tree that you are poking pigeon nests for eggs.' The one with the bucket lifted the sack cover so that she could see the eggs. 'A good harvest,' she said.

'Good food,' he said proudly and with a touch of defiance –

as if daring her to challenge him.

She had seen forest men stealing pigeon eggs before: two held the stitched-together sacks under the tree or branch, the other prodded the rickety nest of sticks with a pole, the two holding the sacks deftly caught the falling eggs.

But she had nothing to say, a tree could not speak. Or didn't want to. She had to get home to make Oldman Botha something to eat and hang out the dress for lunch with Johannes tomorrow …

There was a strange kind of weariness in her. Maria Rothman spoke book-words, the forest used forest-words, but the forest women had only poor-words, and all the words were written with different kinds of pencils. The one did not understand the other and she doubted if they ever would.

She had just reached the hard road when a motor car caught up with her from behind. There was no time to jump into the undergrowth and hide; she could only stand at the side of the road and wait for them to stop and get out of the car. It was the Reverend Odendaal and Maria Rothman. They could not conceal their disappointment.

'Karoliena!' the Reverend called out, a note of relief in his voice. 'We looked for you, but you had gone.'

'So we decided to bring the good news to you at the house,' said Maria Rothman. 'But happily we have now found you on the road.' A finely whetted axe that knew how to strike the first blow …

'What good news?'

Something warned her that they would not be glad tidings.

'There is an opening for you for good work,' said the Reverend.

'Even lodgings with a good Afrikaner family,' Maria Rothman added.

Trees did not do human-work.

'I'm not looking for work.'

'Dear girl, you cannot survive in the forest with all its

uncertainties for the rest of your life.' The woman had a soft, gentle way of speaking. 'We realise that life cannot have been easy for you in the past, but the Church and Reverend Odendaal are going to do everything in their power to make the future better for you.'

'I'm not looking for work.'

'Come now, Karoliena!' The Reverend's patience was wearing thin. It was said that he once became so tired of struggling to understand the woodcutters that he went to spend a night with a team in their shelter in Gouna Forest in the hope of learning to know them better. At dawn, he ran into an elephant that was quietly stealing sweet potatoes from under the ash with its trunk. Some of the woodcutters said he screamed like a wild pig; others that they had to take him to the nearest water so that he could wash himself ... 'One easily forgets one's blessings and starts to take them for granted. One does not notice that one is actually going into a decline!'

'I'm not looking for work.'

'What are you looking for, Karoliena?' Soft, but sharp as an axe ...

'Peace of mind. The hope that something will be done for the woodcutters.'

'That is a priority at the moment, Karoliena. In the mean time it is of the utmost importance that you start considering your own future. What are the chances of reconciliation with your husband?'

'None. He does not want me back.'

'Where do *you* feel that you belong?' Maria Rothman asked patiently.

'In the forest.'

The Reverend was becoming restless. 'Do you remember how you resented going to Wittedrift, Karoliena? Do you remember how much trouble we went to for you? Because you were such a bright scholar.'

'But I did go.'

'Right. And now, once again, we have gone to a lot of

trouble to find you work in Port Elizabeth.'

'What kind of work?'

'It's a good job in a sweet factory.'

'I work in the forest. I'm the one who sees what you don't.' Angry words formed in her head all by themselves. 'I go where you can't go, and I do not want to go and wrap sweets.'

'That's enough!' The Reverend's temper got the better of him. 'You cannot go through life discarding every opportunity that comes your way, as you did with Johannes Stander! You *will* take this opportunity. You have no choice. A lift to Port Elizabeth has been organised for you on Wednesday and I will personally come to Jim Reid's Crossing to make sure that you take it. Be sure that you are ready and decently dressed.'

I'll hide somewhere, she said to herself as she walked away. I will not go and work in Port Elizabeth.

She would talk to Mister Werdt.

When she got home she found Hestertjie Vermaak's sister sitting outside the door. 'Uncle Wiljam won't give us milk; he says we must first bring the money.'

Another pound taken out of the drawer. She set out for Veldmanspad with the girl following.

'Ma says the important woman from Swellendam didn't take a penny out of her pocket; she just said we must see that the house is tidy. Our broom is broken. One can buy brooms from the shop at the station, Ma says we'll have to get a new broom ...'

'You can pick branches, tie them together and *make* a broom!'

'Don't be nasty, I'm only telling you what Ma said.'

'What else did your mother say about the meeting?'

'The woman said we have to cut up the meat better. Pa trapped a wild pig. Ma says we must all be educated. It's because we're not educated that we're so poor. Ma says, it's quite true, look how educated Karoliena is.'

When she got home again, Oldman Botha was carefully cutting

a wagon spoke with an adze. 'One must grab opportunities when they come your way, Karoliena.'

'As you say, Uncle.'

She was not going to work in a sweet factory.

'Are you going to Johannes tomorrow?'

'Yes, Uncle.'

She carried the dress and petticoat over her arm, the shoes in her hand. In Dam Forest she changed into the good clothes, combed her hair And hid her old clothes under a bush. She had walked only a short distance when she turned back and put the old shoes on again, carrying the new ones in her hand. They were more comfortable.

Johannes opened the door. He was pleased to see her, and pleased to see that she was properly dressed. But why did she have those terrible old shoes in her hand? Of course she could hide them. What about outside the back door?

Two servants were preparing food in the kitchen. Her mouth watered; it was *real* food …

She joined Johannes in the sitting room. A feeling of peace washed over her, as if she had unexpectedly stepped into an oasis of tranquillity.

Was Johannes the opportunity she had missed because of her own stupidity? Was he the way she had turned her back on?

Perhaps.

No. One did not cry over yesterday's bad weather …

He said he had a surprise for her.

What?

The Council had passed a resolution to remove all the old oak trees along the Main Street and replace them with others. The oaks were increasingly obstructing the new overhead wires. The Council had asked him to find out which forest tree, indigenous of course, would be the most suitable for beautifying the village. Not yellowwoods, because they would cause a bat plague when they started fruiting. The major problem facing the village was the refusal of landowners around the village to sell their land, or even part of it. It was utter stubbornness that was impeding crucial expansion! What tree would she recommend?

The forest chestnut, which some called the Cape chestnut.

Tell me about the tree.

It's a very beautiful tree. Large, providing lots of shade and flowers between October and December – wonderful pink flowers that attract the most beautiful butterflies.

'I spy on the butterflies along the streams in the afternoons when they gather to eat the mud.'

'Forest chestnut. I'll put it to the Council.'

'The village will love them.'

'Have you noticed that two more streets have been tarred?'

'Yes.'

A servant in a white uniform brought in the tea. There was a cake with yellow icing on a silver stand. Johannes cut the cake himself, setting the slices on small plates, with little silver forks.

'Are you still expecting Mister Werdt?' She had to know.

'Yes. And please don't bother him with unnecessary questions. I believe the delegates of the Carnegie Commission have been quite active in the area during the past few weeks.'

'Yes. They have even helped to find me work in a sweet factory in Port Elizabeth – transport, board, everything.'

'Are you considering taking the work?'

'No.' She got the feeling that his mind was elsewhere; he kept looking out the window into the street.

'I must say that you look very lovely, Karoliena – especially compared with how awful you looked the last time you were here.'

'I appreciate your lending me the dress.'

'You may keep it.'

'Thank you.'

Mister Werdt arrived. He had another surprise. Things were definitely looking up for the woodcutters. He was on his way to parliament with a brilliant proposal that the Knysna harbour be enlarged and deepened between the Heads so that the woodcutters and forest workers could become fishermen.

'They only know how to catch eels in the forest rivers. Perhaps they should rather be packed off to Port Elizabeth to work in the sweet factory.' She did it on purpose, pretending not to notice the shock and consternation on Johannes's face – the way he tried to stop her talking with his eyes. She continued to smile sweetly.

'I don't think forest people will take to life in the city, Mrs Stander.'

Johannes got up and poured rose-coloured wine into beautiful long-stemmed glasses. He did not offer her any. He was pleased, he said, that an Animal Welfare Organisation had recently been established in the village. Mister Werdt agreed. She asked if it included the welfare of the forest oxen? No one answered.

The ringing of a bell in the passage outside summoned them to the dining room. It was a superb meal. A stiffly starched white tablecloth covered the table; the white table napkins were also starched. Mister Werdt was clearly confused. He thought *she* was the housewife who had planned and organised the wonderful meal.

'I take it that you will have met the Carnegie delegation, Mister Werdt?' she asked while they waited for dessert.

'Unfortunately not, their time is very limited and mine is completely taken up with appointments of all kinds. But the information that has reached me is very positive. I agree with the Commission that merely handing out charity will not solve the poor white problem. It will only encourage dependency and kill the enterprising spirit of the Afrikaner. The government's schemes, its plans to give the poor whites work on the roads, to employ them to build dams and canals, to plant plantations, work on the railways – all of these clearly show sound decision making. We must not allow the unemployed to become too dependent on the state for job creation.'

'Do you know anything about a Voortrekker Festival that is being planned for next year?'

Johannes raised his eyebrows, apparently surprised that she should know about it. 'Oh yes!' the man from parliament answered, excitement in his voice. 'I serve on the Commemoration Committee. Commander Reverend Odendaal came up with a very good idea last week that young girls in traditional dress should collect money during the street parade for the Women's Missionary Society, and that the money be distributed among the poor women in the area.'

'Most importantly, to my mind, is that the Trek will unite the Afrikaner again,' Johannes added his opinion. 'Bring pride back into our hearts for being Afrikaners under one flag and with a beautiful new anthem which we hope everyone will accept. I believe an English translation will be published soon. Reverend Odendaal tells me that the Trek from Cape Town to Pretoria has been carefully planned – it will be a sort of pilgrimage, calling at all the places where the Afrikaners fought and died for their country.'

It sounded almost like a sermon.

After lunch, Johannes put on a strange kind of silk gown over his suit and he and Mister Werdt retired to the sitting room to smoke cigars. He asked her please to supervise the packing away of the silver.

She put her old shoes on at the back door and left without saying goodbye. Just walked away. Because that was how she felt. It had been a mistake to come. The abyss between her and Johannes – between village and forest, between poor white and rich white – was deeper than she had thought.

She put her old dress back on in Dam Forest and for a moment wished she could leave the smart one behind under the bush. The shoes as well. Then she realised that it would be childish.

Before she got as far as the Deep Walls station, four motor cars had stopped to offer her a lift. No, thank you. Smartly dressed women, hats tied on their heads with long, flimsy scarves and eyes that stared past her. The driver of the third car asked if she was one of the forest people. Yes. Was there any danger of elephants? Yes. Was is possible that an elephant might attack a car? Hard to say; some people reckoned elephants only hated cars that reversed. The woman sitting next to him nervously suggested that they turn back. But the man drove on.

At Deep Walls station she noticed someone sitting next to the railway line, head bowed so low it was almost touching his knees. Bare feet resting on the line. A picture of dejection. It was Ampie Stroebel. But it couldn't be – Ampie was supposed to be somewhere in the Magaliesberg planting ground nuts on a plot of government land.

She told herself: Pretend you have not seen him and keep walking. She couldn't pick up everyone who fell along the way!

'Ampie?' He looked up, his eyes bloodshot. The stripes of mucus on his jacket sleeves said he had stopped crying. 'Ampie, why are you sitting here?'

'I couldn't bear it any more, I ran away.' An honest confession and at the same time a call for help. 'I tried, but it didn't work out. It's not our place, Karoliena.'

'Where's Jakobus who went with you?'

'He's still there, begging every day to be sent back. I could no longer beg. The man from Welfare writes all the pleas in a book and says we must be brave. But my courage ran out and I ran away. I got a lift with a lorry as far as Oudtshoorn – from there I could at least walk back to the forest across the mountain.'

'And now?'

'I've been to Reverend Odendaal and he says I'm in big trouble; I have to go back to the Magaliesberg because I was there under government orders.'

'Where are your shoes?'

'Walked them to pieces crossing the mountain.'

'So now you're sitting on the railway line?'

'Perhaps the train will run me over.'

'Don't be silly, Mister Kennet will brake before the train hits you.'

'The driver of the lorry said I could go back with him. But there is nothing up there in the Magaliesberg, Karoliena – just bare red earth and no forest. No air to breathe. Jakobus is still planting ground nuts. They didn't want me to plant; they taught me how to repair zinc baths and fix gramophones. Then I ran away.'

'And now?'

'When life spits you out, you fall where you fall. Reverend says I must get back to the lorry driver. I'll start walking tomorrow.'

'How are you going to get over the mountain with bare feet?'

'Maybe someone will give me a lift.'

When the words formed in her head, she knew she would not be able to stop her mouth from uttering them. 'I'll meet you here at the shop tomorrow morning and buy you a pair of shoes.'

'Really? Where will you get the money?'

'I'll make a plan.'

When the wedding money was finished, *she* would be barefoot …

Oldman Botha looked at her closely when she got home. He asked if she had been to Johannes. Yes. Had he asked her to come back to him? No. Why did she look so troubled?

'Just because.'

'Seems as though you don't want to talk.'

'No.'

'Did you hope he would ask you to come back to him?'

'Perhaps.'

No. Johannes had become a silk-gown man. He was climbing higher and higher up his own tree. And she did not want to climb with him, for it was too painful when one fell.

Beyond Johannes was the sweet factory, and beyond the sweet factory were the cliffs of the Red Alder River ...

But first Ampie had to have shoes. It could not be helped.

16

SHE PUT TWO POUNDS in her pocket for the shoes. There were three pounds and six shillings left of the wedding money.

On her way to Deep Walls she had a strange fancy to step only on the dappled patches of sunlight on the road. She had to take big steps, sometimes jumping from one patch to the next because the sun was still struggling to climb over the forest. She turned it into a game, imagining that a snare-pit awaited her in the shadowed parts of the road.

She heard the motor car coming but didn't pay any attention; all her concentration was focused on staying in the sunny patches. She was afraid; the sweet factory was a snare-pit.

It was only when the car stopped alongside her that she looked up and saw that it was Johannes. There was surliness about him that surprised her, but didn't scare her.

'Good morning, Karoliena.' Stiff lipped.

'Good morning, Johannes.'

'I note that you have now lost even your manners in the forest. You did not have the decency to say thank you or goodbye before you disappeared yesterday!'

'I know. Ampie Stroebel is waiting for me at the station shop. He ran away from the place where the government sent him to plant ground nuts. He has to get back to Oudtshoorn and he needs shoes. Please go pick him up and take him to your shop …'

'Have you lost your mind as well?'

'Probably.' He had stopped his car in one of her sun patches; she had to move. He got out of the car and walked around it to stand right in front of her.

'Karoliena,' he said, 'I want you to listen very carefully. I'm not the sort of person who changes his mind easily. I couldn't sleep last night, because I had a lot of serious thinking to do. I'm here because I can no longer watch you going backwards and do nothing about it! My principles, and my Christian duty, will not allow it. I'm here to give you another chance. To ask you to change your mind and come back to me. After all, I am still your legal husband. It is clear that you are not looking after yourself in the forest, that you cannot take care of yourself and that I should once more take on my duty as your husband. Everything about you suggests that you are declining into the ways of a poor white, while in reality you are a very bright and attractive young woman who deserves better. Why are you doing this to yourself? Is it because you're too proud to turn back and are now just struggling on from day to day like all the others?'

'No, Johannes.'

'What then?'

'In the forest I'm real. With you, I'm a lie.'

'You're muddling your words, Karoliena. With me you had a chance to live a *really* dignified life.'

'There is an old stinkwood that is about a thousand years old in Stripe Bush. *That* is dignified.'

'I beg your pardon?'

'Most of the forest people – the poor whites – have given up, Johannes. I'm one of them, except for the fact that I have not yet given up, because I still have three pounds left. One only gives up when one has nothing left.'

'I don't know what you're talking about.'

'If I go back with you, I'll have nothing left.'

'You are talking in riddles, Karoliena!'

'You won't understand. I don't understand all the riddles myself. The Carnegie woman says the backward forest women were not properly trained when they were children.'

She had taken the wrong footpath and didn't know where she was. She would just have to carry on until she found her way.

'Oldman Botha says good does not become bad and bad does not turn into good. I'm not bad, I'm just having trouble finding the right footpath through the forest – so that I don't get lost.'

'Where are you going, Karoliena?'

'To the station, Ampie is waiting for me.'

'That's not what I meant and you know it!'

She did. 'In any event, Ampie is waiting for me.'

'Get into the car and come home with me.'

'Ampie is waiting for his shoes.'

That really made him angry. He threw his arms in the air. 'What the hell is wrong with you, Karoliena? Nothing one tries to do for you has any effect!'

'I suppose so.'

'You are going to get yourself so entangled with the poor whites that you'll never escape!'

'How are *they* going to escape?'

'That is no concern of yours!'

'Whose concern is it then?'

'Neither yours nor mine! Leave Ampie Stroebel – he's a pauper, a loser and a burden on the state! Come home with me and regain your dignity before it is too late for you as well!'

'I can't.'

'*Why not?*' It seemed as if he wanted to break her with his hands, but he couldn't reach her . . .

*

One day, many years ago, she came upon a little blue buck that had just been caught in a trap. It was the first time she had seen a blue buck trap. A young elder tree had been bent down and loosely fastened to the forest floor, a noose of string fastened among the leaves of the tree touching the ground. The little buck grazed, unaware of the noose waiting for its head. His head got caught in the noose, the elder tree shot up, and the buck was jerked up as well, strangled to death as it hung in the tree. That day, however, the little buck was not yet dead. She knew only that the noose was pulling tighter and tighter round his neck because it kept kicking. It bleated pathetically. She shouted to it: Keep still! She would fetch a ladder from the house and release him.

There was no one to help her. Her father was cutting wood, her mother was visiting one of the other forest women. She dragged the ladder, shouting: Keep still, I'm coming!

When she got back to the buck it was dead.

⁂

'Why not, Karoliena?' Johannes asked again. 'Don't you have *any* feeling for me in your heart?'

'I would be wrong if I said no. But I'd be right to say I fear being strangled in a trap.'

Ampie's shoes cost nine shillings. The pair of socks was one and sixpence.

She bought flour and sugar and tobacco as well. Then she started walking home. She took the footpath to visit the Tree in the hope it would make her feel better. She let the stonechat sit on her shoulder, fly around her head …

Johannes had asked her to come back to him. Half of her shouted: Hurry back to him, become Karoliena Stander and save yourself! The other half of her said: No. Rather hide in the forest where you belong and remain Karoliena Kapp.

Nothing made her feel better until she rested her head against the Tree's old body of coarse bark and whispered her fears to him: I'm scared and confused. Please help me. I don't know which way to turn. Please, stretch up and see if you can see Ampie. He's on his way to Oudtshoorn. Make sure that the shoes don't hurt him, that the socks help a little.

Afterwards, she could not remember how long she sat there before the miracle happened. It *was* a miracle. If the tree-spirit had emerged from the tree at that moment it could not have been a greater miracle! The sun suddenly fell from the sky and struck the forest with a blinding brilliance. From the side of the hard road a motor car turned slowly on to the sledpath …

CCO 10.

Mister Fourcade.

It was a miracle.

She was dumbstruck. She could not shout with joy. She could only get up on her feet and stand quietly, numb with happiness when he stopped and got out of the car.

'Mister Fourcade!'

'Karoliena, dear child.'

Don't cry, don't cry, she told herself. But joy as great as hers at that moment heeded nothing. When the old bushbuck with the human head put his arms around her shoulders, she began to cry, tears that just streamed from her eyes while she could have sworn she heard the tree-spirit laughing high up in the tree. Somewhere a wood-hoopoe joined in the laughter, and a distant lourie. The whole forest! The whole world!

At first she wiped her face with her skirt, then took the clean white handkerchief that Mister Fourcade held out to her.

He sat down on one of the Tree's huge buttress roots that bulged out above the ground and listened patiently to the endless stream of words that rolled from her mouth. Now and again he clicked his tongue – like when she told him how her mother had carried on when she heard that she had left Johannes. Sometimes he patted her hand. Shooed away the stonechat.

He laughed when she told him about the wedding money she had stolen. He said it had been a very clever move.

He smiled even when she reproached him for not having come sooner to see if she was all right.

He just let her talk. About Elmina's doll, the little stinkwoods, Faan Mankvoet, Hestertjie's child, Abel Slinger, the orchids, the day she had been a stinkwood tree, the Carnegie people . . .

He let her talk until she was drained.

Then she had no more tears. Only anxieties.

'There is still no solution offered to the woodcutters. Mister Werdt reckons they must go and catch fish.'

Then he told her a story, as if she was a child.

Long ago, when God had finished creating the world, he appointed his three best sons to take charge of it. The eldest son was named Love. The second one was Diligence. Together these two sons inhabited the earth and made it good and happy. Then, one day, the third son appeared from far across the mountains: he was a big strong man with a face like a god and his name was Smart. It did not take long for Smart to see how prosperous and contented his two brothers were. He said: This is not fair. They said: Come and work for us and together we will be even more prosperous. I'm too smart, said Smart, you must work for me because I can give you treasures you've never dreamed of. What treasures? Money, equipment, weapons of a kind that will make you even richer. They believed him and began to work for him. They worked harder and harder, until one day they realised that they had become Smart's slaves and that Smart was getting richer and richer. But the gardens and fields were yielding fewer crops and everywhere people were complaining of hunger. Smart became angry and scolded them; he even beat them to force them to work harder. The eldest son, Love, could no longer endure it and he fled into the mountains where he sits to this day, waiting for the bad times to pass. He is the only one of the three brothers who can remember what it was like when life was good. What he does today is send out his messengers all over the earth to whisper in the ears of man that he should not give up.

'Why does he rather not leave the mountain?' she wanted to know.

'His messengers are still working on the road off the mountain.'

'It's a pretty story, but it's stupid because it doesn't offer a solution to the woodcutters.'

'But at least there are helpers like you who can see what others can't.'

'I'm no one's helper. I can hardly see where I'm going myself!'

'You'll survive.'

'How? Go and wrap sweets?'

'No. I'll show you a way.'

'What?'

'You'll see. I'll be back in about a week's time. I'll come and pick you up at the house.'

'Don't go! You'll forget about me.'

'I won't.'

It was a long week.

The days were like fangs that snapped at her from all sides as if trying to devour her.

First there was the big reddish-brown motor car that stopped in the road below the house. A well-dressed man got out. He looked at the house, peered into the forest, looked back towards the house; walked around the car, bending down at each wheel as if inspecting it.

She was standing in front of the house with a mug of coffee for Oldman Botha who was working behind the house. The man walked towards the house. He was wearing a dust-coat and a hat. A stern face.

'Is your father home?' he asked abruptly.

'My father's dead.' She was deliberately terse because of the way the man was staring at her. 'Who are you looking for?'

'Oldman Botha. I believe he lives somewhere around here.'

'He's working behind the house.'

He turned and ducked under the branches of the wild olive to go to the back of the house. She followed him. Oldman Botha was cutting a spoke with the adze, ironwood shavings strewn all around him. He had been working since dawn.

'Mister Botha?' the stranger asked. She was sure she had seen his face before. In the village, perhaps in church . . .

'Good day.' Oldman Botha took off his hat and brushed the wood-shavings from his trousers. 'Can I help you, Mister?'

'I am the manager of Jonker's wood factory in the village – we are responsible for two of the wagons for the festival. I believe that you have been approached to make the spokes.'

'Yes.'

The manager stepped closer to the pile of spokes that lay neatly stacked to one side and kicked at them as if he was kicking a dog. 'The instructions for making the wagons have been laid down by senior management and must be properly carried out from the start. Our reputation is at stake.'

'I can make you a spoke in my sleep, Mister.'

'I'm visiting all the men in the district who are making our wagon-parts to ensure that the work is being done to specification. The route the wagons will take to Pretoria has been carefully planned; the wagons will leave Cape Town in August. It will be a long and arduous trek . . .'

'Where are they going to get the oxen?'

'Experts are organising everything.'

'You can't yoke tame and wild oxen together,' the old man warned.

'Just concern yourself with making the spokes.' He was putting the old man in his place. 'The wagons have to be finished at least a month before the departure date; there will be festivities in the village and the wagons will be part of the parade. Jonker Brothers wants to be proud of its wagons. I trust you know how many spokes are expected of you, old man?'

Oldman Botha responded with a jerk of his shoulders and an iciness in his voice. 'One wagon has four wheels, two wagons have eight wheels – every front wheel has ten spokes, every back wheel has fourteen …'

'Don't get agitated. I was just testing you … I've clearly overlooked the fact that an old man who lives with a pretty young woman must have something more than brains!' He laughed at his own joke. 'There's a woodcutter at Old Place who cuts his spokes with a right-axe, not with an adze like you.' He obviously wanted to appear knowledgeable.

She stood behind the old man feeling uneasy. The coffee in the mug was getting cold. The manager from the wood factory couldn't keep still, he fidgeted as if he had fleas in his pants.

'Only a stupid man cuts spokes with an axe. And if I wanted Mister's opinion, I would have rung a bell.'

'Careful, you might be ringing your own death knell.' He smiled, but it sounded like a threat.

She stepped forward. 'The old man's price is at least half a crown a spoke.' She had to *say* it. He had to know it.

'Just a minute, young lady!' he tried to check her. 'Price fixing is not woman's work.'

'It is today.' She threw the challenge into his pale blue eyes without blinking. He looked away, looked back, looked away. At that moment he represented to her every wood-buyer who had ever entered the forest, every harsh warden that had ever prowled through the forest, pricking his ears for the sound of axes so that he could go and check on the licences; check, too, whether it was a marked tree being cut, or if perhaps a trap had been set for some meat …

'Surely you have chores to do?' He was trying to put *her* in her place as well. 'The old man and I want to discuss business without your interference.'

'I'm staying. I want to hear what you have to say. The forest people have been cheated far too often by Smart and his conspirators.'

'I don't know what you're talking about.'

He was guilty, no doubt about that.

Afterwards Oldman Botha told her she had been too tough with the man, but that he was grateful they were going to pay him a decent price. Very grateful. The pension wouldn't be necessary.

And then the second fang arrived at the door the next afternoon. Faan's son Willempie stood there, fidgeting with his shirt buttons. When she asked what he had come for he said he was having trouble with his sums again. Something told her he was not telling the truth. But she offered to help him with the sums. No, he said, he'd manage. She said: Willempie, say what you have to say. He stared at the ground, continued to fidget with his buttons. He said she must please not tell her mother that he had been there; he had come the day before as well, but she was not home. Willempie, *speak*! she demanded.

'It's pay-day tomorrow, Karoliena. Aunt Meliena says the flour is finished and the sugar is finished – and if you don't bring the money you must take us back to Kom's Bush. My ma is scared, she says we can't go back there.'

'I'll bring the money tomorrow.'

'Don't say I've been here.'

'I won't.'

The worst thing was the anxiety in the child's eyes. The next worst was the worry in her heart because the money was running out, and the fear that Mister Fourcade would not come back, the possibility that she wouldn't succeed in getting Oldman Botha a pension – the money for the spokes would not last for ever.

It was as if a rock had come loose from the mountain and had started rolling down the slope, rolling and rolling …

But at least the rock seemed to have missed Meliena Kapp's house in Long Marsh Forest because everything was neat and tidy when she got there. Washing hanging over the wire fence round the garden, the garden had been dug, rows of cabbages planted, sweet potato runners set …

'Morning, Karoliena.'

'Morning, Ma. Where is Susanna?'

'She's gone to do the washing at one of the wardens' houses up at the forest station; the wife has had twins. Pays her four shillings a month.'

'That's too little.'

'Says who?'

'I say.'

'Then I say that a pound a month for boarding the three of them is a disgrace.'

'I don't know how long I'll be able to keep it up.'

'What? Do you think I can carry them for nothing?'

'Things look better around the house, even the garden is coming along nicely …'

'I'm telling you, Karoliena, I will not keep them for nothing!'

'No need to shout, Ma, I heard you.'

After a long wait at the magistrate's office, a clerk told her she would have to bring the old man himself to the office so that they could try to determine his age.

He's too old to walk here.

That is not our problem.

Bloody fool, she muttered to herself. 'I'll see if I can get him here,' she said out loud.

When she left the magistrate's office, she realised that it was too late to walk home before dark. In any case she was too tired to walk. She would have to find somewhere to sleep in the village – with the church nurse, or with Johannes.

No, not with Johannes.

An astonished Amelia Claassens opened the door. 'Karoliena, what a pleasant surprise!'

'Would you be able to let me stay over for the night? Please?'

'Of course. Come in – where is your stuff?'

'I have nothing with me.'

'Don't worry, I'll lend you a nightie.'

An hour later she felt as if she had walked out of the forest and entered another world. No, she'd crossed from the forest world to the outside world and she was getting lost because, she suddenly realised, one needed two heads for the two different worlds. A gentle one, and a tough one.

'Is it my imagination, or has the village been decorated for some reason – all the flags and palm leaves.'

'We are being honoured by a visit from very distinguished couple; a banquet is being held for them in the town hall this evening. They are family of the King of England – the Earl and Countess of Clarendon. The Council invited the Earl to go and shoot an elephant in the forest, but their time is limited. Mayor Wilson told me, though, that the Earl did express a wish to experience the *magic* of the forest they have heard so much about. The Mayor told him it could unfortunately not be arranged.'

'Perhaps Mister Wilson is afraid they may come across some of the forest people.'

'Can one blame him?'

'Not really, I suppose.'

'By the way, I went to visit Susanna at your mother's last week. It's going well with her and the children, your mother is taking good care of them. She's strict with the children, but she says you are becoming estranged from her. From everything and everyone else as well. She reckons old Abel Slinger and his wife have bewitched you. You and I know it's not true, but can we blame others if they start thinking like that? I mean, where are you getting the money to pay your mother to keep Susanna and the children?'

'Will Poor Relief do so in future?'

'Poor Relief struggles to keep going on a day to day basis. Your mother says Johannes is not paying you any maintenance; others say Oldman Botha has found gold – there used to be gold in the forest many years ago – and that he is supporting you.'

'That's not true.' She was starting to regret that she had asked for a place to sleep with Amelia Claassens.

'I believe you, Karoliena. Maria Rothman, one of the Carnegie delegation, says she suspects there is an interesting dark side to you that we don't understand. She really would like to talk to you.'

'She does not speak my language.'

'How can you say that? She is a very clever woman, she writes books.'

'She does not speak my language. Did Elmina come to see you with the baby that does not want to suckle?'

'How do *you* know about it?' she asked, surprised. 'Where on earth did she get the doll from?'

'Well, she could not lie in bed for the rest of her life waiting for a baby, could she?'

'Did you … don't tell me *you* …'

'Yes, I bought the doll.'

'How could you have done such an idiotic thing? Do you realise that stupid woman really thinks it's a baby?'

'Yes.'

'How are you going to undo this?'

'Why should I want to undo it? Let her play with the doll.'

'The Reverend is looking for a suitable institution to send Elmina to.'

'Tell the Reverend rather to club her to death – it would be more merciful.'

'Karoliena! The Reverend urgently needs to take *you* in hand!'

'It's time that something was announced by this so-called Carnegie investigation. They've snooped through the forest, but we do not hear a word about what they have found.'

'Reports of all the interviews have been sent to a central office where they are being processed. The poor white issue is an enormous one, Karoliena. And it's countywide. Measured against the problems in the cities, the forest's poor are but a drop in the ocean.'

'Really?' She felt as though she had been hit by the rock rolling down the mountain.

The next fang that snapped at her at Jim Reid's Crossing belonged to an elephant.

Oldman Botha was working on the spokes behind the house; she was cleaning the house. She was outside shaking out the old man's buckskin mat when the most incredibly beautiful motor car drove past on the hard road below the house; it moved silently and slowly as if to ensure that not a speck of dust would fly up and dirty it. The car did not turn off into Kom's Bush; it kept going in the direction of the mountain and the pass to the Long Kloof.

She went back inside and bent down to sweep under the beds. Her thoughts were preoccupied with Amelia Claassens's open warning to her that she might lose Johannes if she did not take care. 'He's an attractive man, Karoliena.'

'Do *you* fancy him?' She could not stop herself from asking the question, but Amelia did not answer. She looked away as though she was hiding something. Karoliena knew deep down that the day would come when Johannes would ask her for a divorce …

The next moment a man spoke from the door behind her: 'Excuse me …'

She was halfway under Oldman Botha's bed and had to get up in a hurry.

A tall dark man in a uniform with silver buttons stood in the doorway. He was wearing a cap like those usually worn by captains of ships.

'Can I help you?' she asked him in English. He *looked* English, and he also looked scared half to death. She quickly wiped the dirt from her knees with the floor-cloth and asked him again: 'Can I help you?'

It was the old story.

The beautiful car was parked in the road below the house, facing towards the Long Kloof. There was a beautiful silver badge on the bonnet and two people sitting in the back. The man in the uniform was the driver; his passengers were the Earl and Countess of Clarendon. Could she perhaps make a glass of sugar water for the Countess? As they had rounded a bend, a little way to the north, they had come across an enormous elephant lying in the road. Totally blocking the way. He was not dead, because he had waved his trunk in the air.

An ordinary day turned into the strangest of days. She made some sugar water and walked down to the road with it. The two most distinguished-looking people she had ever seen in her life were sitting in the back of the car. The woman was beautiful, with a complexion like the porcelain doll in Miss Ann's cabinet. She did not have a glass for the sugar water, only the tin mug. The woman did not want to touch the mug. It's a clean mug, she told her. Just open the window a little wider. The woman took the mug with both hands – slender, white fingers, beautiful rings, shining nails. She closed her eyes and sipped the sugar water.

The man sitting next to her had a more ruddy complexion, with freckles. His hands were freckled too. He asked if there was anyone who could go and shoot the elephant. No. He asked the driver to help him get out of the car, but the woman put her hand on his arm to stop him. The driver gulped down the rest of the sugar water behind the car. Were there lions in the forest as well? he asked her. No. What were they to do if the elephant charged? He won't, he's lying in the sun – you'll just have to wait until he decides to leave. The driver said they could not wait indefinitely, the Countess had a very delicate constitution. All their luggage had been put on the train at Knysna and they were to meet the train on the other side of the mountain. No other arrangements had been made. The trip through the forest was a private excursion because the Earl wanted to see the forest; they had not realised how dangerous it was.

She stood next to the car, not quite knowing what to do next. After a while she asked the driver if they would like some coffee. No, thank you. She got tired of standing around, so she suggested the driver should move forward a little way so that he could turn the car around at the turn-off to Kom's Bush and then go back to the village. No, he couldn't do that; the car was too big. What was more, no further arrangements had been made in the village for the Earl and Countess. Would she please go and see whether the elephant might have moved? Yes, but she couldn't spend the rest of the day walking up and down.

The elephant was still lying in the road.

She suggested to the driver that his passengers get out of the car for a while. No, the Countess was too scared. Was there *nothing* anyone could do? No. The driver had apparently not noticed that she was getting irritated at standing around for no good reason. She tried to think of something, but nothing came to mind. She walked round the car again ... thinking. She stopped at the door on the Countess's side, put out her hand and carefully opened the door while looking into the Countess's eyes. They were like a doll's eyes and they were terrified. There was an unfamiliar smell in the car. The smell of the King's people – like the tops of the stinkwoods must smell when they flower. Then she carefully reached out a hand and gently put it on the woman's lap; felt the slight shiver through the beautiful cloth of her dress. The woman was like a book that she could read through the palm of her hand; the words were like the delicate little flowers in the forest underbrush. She stood there, holding the woman's eyes with her own, telling them not to be afraid. The woman was like the genet's kitten; the cat with a long slender body and short legs that hunted in the trees – the cat that had once hidden her kitten in a hole in a tree and she tried for days to lure it out with pieces of meat she stole when her mother's back was turned. It took a lot of patience to coax the kitten out of the hole in the tree. When she arrived home with the kitten in her hands her father's mouth fell open. It's a wild creature! he cried. Take it back to where you found it before it infects you with all sorts of diseases! So she took it back to the hole in the tree. The next day it was gone.

The woman was not wild. Only scared. She just had to be patient …

Come, put your feet out … slowly … turn sideways … the other foot too … beautiful pointed shoes covered in the same cloth as her dress, lovely silk-stockinged legs … move forward a little … slowly. Stand up now.

She did not look at the Earl or at the driver, but she knew they were keeping their eyes on *her*.

She took the woman by the hand. Gently. Come with me, slowly now – the elephant is asleep, he will not come down the road. I want to show you something – it's not far. It's a little flower that looks just like you. The woman spoke for the first time: Are you an angel? Yes. Then why are you so dirty? I'm a dirty angel. The woman seemed about to smile. The Earl and the driver had got out of the car and were standing in the road.

She led the Countess by the hand. Carefully. She had held the kitten carefully too …

The length of the car. A second length. The heels of the woman's shoes sank into the earth, but she continued walking bravely.

She had seen a wild alecost flower on the edge of the forest the day before and had got down on her haunches to have a closer look at the little pink flowers. To really *see* them. To enjoy their dancing in the breeze. So dainty and pretty – and so carefree. She wondered why they were flowering there, and not deeper in the forest along the streams where they were usually found. She did not know then that they had flowered there because they had seen their human coming …

When they reached the little flowers, a sudden strange quietness surrounded them. The Countess let go of her hand and silently bent down over the flowers. Karoliena knew that if the Countess had been a flower, she would have looked like them. The woman cupped her hands around the flowers and the astonishment that spread over her face said that she knew it too.

She looked up and saw the Earl and the driver, still standing in the middle of the road, suddenly stiffen with alarm. Oldman Botha was walking down towards them from the house. The Earl said: There's a wild man coming towards us, making it sound like an urgent warning, but with the dignity of an old yellowwood preparing to defend itself against the wind.

She told him it was only an old forest man. Does he live in the trees? No, he lives in that little house up there. He's Mister Botha.

And that was the day of the king's people.

When Oldman Botha went to have a look, the elephant had gone and the road was clear again.

On the Saturday morning the Reverend arrived. Oldman Botha was working on the spokes. No, the Reverend did not want any coffee. Would she mind if they sat outside? It felt as if there was a bergwind in the air …

'The church nurse says you slept at her home during the week.'

'Yes.'

'She says you gave Elmina the doll.'

'Yes.'

'That was a very foolish thing to do. You don't have the training to appoint yourself welfare worker in this part of the forest. When you had the chance to study further, you turned your back on it. Have you any idea how much trouble the Church has gone to for you?'

'Yes.'

'Why did you leave Johannes?'

'You've asked me that before, Reverend.'

'I'm asking you again.'

'As I told you then, I tell you now: I just did.'

'That is no answer, Karoliena!'

'It is the only one I have.'

His face turned red with anger. 'You're going in the wrong direction, Karoliena! A dangerous one. Alone in the forest with an old man – it's affecting your mind! We found work for you in Port Elizabeth, but you turned your back on that! As you turned your back on a good man. I understand you no longer attend church at Veldmanspad on Sundays. What's to become of you?'

'What's to become of the woodcutters?'

'That is no concern of yours!'

'Whose concern is it then?'

'Everything possible is being done for them. At the highest level. But you keep on meddling in matters that have nothing to do with you. Apart from that, you're fast becoming a heathen, wandering through the forest like a lost soul and rejecting every hand that reaches out to you. You can't go on like this!'

'You're stupid, Reverend.'

'How dare you speak to me like that? Dr Murray of the Carnegie delegation says they found you covered in leaves and twigs in the forest one day, you didn't know where you were – you were probably engaged in some sort of evil ritual.'

'Dr Murray is also stupid.'

'How dare you make statements like that! You're talking about an important and learned man who is playing a vital role in the search for solutions for the woodcutters.'

'You're searching in the wrong places, because you're afraid of the right place.' She chose her words deliberately. To get back at them. 'The wood-buyers who are making the profits are not bothered about cheating the woodcutters. The solution would be to pay more money for the woodcutter's wood – money that he has earned honestly. But it's a bit late now. The forest is giving up, most of the woodcutters too. In the mean time the wood-buyers are too smart to give up a single slice of their enormous loaf.'

'You're talking utter nonsense! Since the wood auctions were instituted, the woodcutters are paid a fair price for their wood because they no longer have to depend only on the wood-buyers to sell their wood to. The question you should rather ask is, what are they doing with the money?'

'Paying their debts at the wood-buyers' shops. And you, Reverend, should take the trouble to attend one of these newly instituted wood auctions.'

'I've heard that you've already been banned from attending them.' Haughtily, with a touch of scorn that indicated he knew about everything she did.

'That's right. One of the wardens came to tell me that I must stay away in future.'

'Because you keep meddling in things that are no concern of yours!'

'The wood auction happens like this.' She would have her say. 'The woodcutters drag out their stumps and blocks to the depot where the wood is numbered. The wood-buyers come and take a good look at everything before the auction, talk to one another, tell one another on which of the wood they want to bid, agree not to bid on one another's wood. The woodcutters sit on one side, too weary to do anything; an ox that works too hard can hardly breathe. The wood, Reverend, is divided among the wood-buyers days before the auction. They pay what they want to, the woodcutters often don't even get back the price they paid for their licences. Wood-buyers are smart, and nothing stops Smart.'

'No wonder they banned you ...'

But he could not hide the look in his eyes, a look almost of enlightenment, and she knew she had told him something he had not been aware of.

The bergwind was picking up, the air was growing heavy. An uneasiness began to creep over her. Suppose it was a day on which the tree-spirit decided to emerge?

'I am sure you are anxious to get away?'

'I am.'

After he left, she made the old man something to eat.

'What did the anointed one want?' he asked when she took him his food.

'Nothing. I'm going for a walk.'

'Turn back before dark, there's a storm brewing.'

'I will.'

Above the forest, where one could catch a glimpse of the sky, thunderclouds were massing white against the blue. And the spirits of the forest were hiding deep inside the trees where no one would see them.

Stop thinking negative thoughts! she said to herself.

Reverend Odendaal's words had cast doubt in her mind, and it just kept on growing. Was there something wrong with her? How did one become a heathen? She didn't think she was a heathen, just as she didn't think she was playing the welfare worker. But sometimes one could not just walk past without stopping. She could not have left Ampie on the railway; or left Hestertjie's baby to die; left Susanna and the children in Kom's Bush . . .

Why did Maria Rothman think there was a dark side to her? There wasn't at all; she only wanted to know what it was like to be a tree! She did not understand why her hand had been able to read the Countess's mind so clearly the day before. It had been intuitive, perhaps, like when you're about to put your hand into a bird's nest and know suddenly you shouldn't because there is a snake in the nest. You take a stick and poke the nest, and out slithers a snake! There was no snake in the Countess; only fear that she could feel through the palm of her hand.

'Good afternoon, Tree.' She spread her hand on its trunk and waited. He was silent. 'Mister Fourcade has not come back yet. I think the Reverend is angry with me. I seem to be getting deeper and deeper into trouble, and I don't know what kind of trouble it is. I'm scared. Scared that I'll find out I'm bad and I don't want to be bad. It's like being hungry but you can't find any food to eat because you don't know what you are hungry for.' She hadn't meant to tell the Tree about the hunger thing . . .

*

Long ago, when she was still at school in Wittedrift, she went home for the holidays. Her mother was irritated with her because she didn't want to eat. She said she was hungry but didn't know what for. Her mother tried this, her mother tried that. Nothing took the hunger away. So she went into the forest. The first wild olive tree was full of ripe olives. She picked a handful and ate them. A little further on she found a tree-fuchsia alive with birds eating its sweet tasty berries; she shooed the birds away and harvested a handful for herself. They were so acrid that she had to lie down on her belly at the nearest stream to drink. Then she was frightened out of her wits by old Abel Slinger's Bella who had quietly been watching her from the underbrush. Bella cackled like a wood-hoopoe, told her she was thirsty because she had stolen the birds' food from their beaks. She told Bella not to be silly, she had done it because she was hungry. Don't they feed you at Wittedrift? They do, but it's not nice food. Bella cackled again and said that bad food made one unhappy. Only nice food made one happy. If Karoliena would carry the firewood home, Bella would make her some nice food. Good food. What food? Forest food. What? You'll see. Come, pick up the wood, my arms are tired, my legs too, one has to walk far to find dry wood in the forest. I notice you are becoming a proper white human now, you're wearing pretty shop-shoes. Your ma says you're getting educated. What for, I ask? The forest educates you. Come, don't fall behind.

She carried the heavy bundle of wood to Bella and Abel's little clay house. Half a wild pig was hanging in a sack from the roof. Bella said Abel had gone to the sea-caves to look for beads. The doctor in the village bought them from him. Bella made a fire outside on a large flat stone next to the house. They waited for the stone to heat. Bella asked how long she would still be at school at Wittedrift, if she had a boyfriend, if she had lots of clothes, whether her mother still getting on with old Cornelius Kapp ...

Questions, questions, questions. The fire burned while Bella lay comfortably on her side in the shade. Bella sent her to pick some grass and tied it into a bundle. When the stone had reached the right heat, Bella scraped away the coals and swept off the ash with the grass. She cut off a piece of meat and put it on the stone where it crackled and spattered. Then she dragged another flat stone over the meat on the first stone and made a new fire on the second stone. Then she went back to lie on her side and wait.

When the top stone had reached the right heat, she scraped away the fire, separated the two stones and cut off a piece of the meat for Karoliena to eat. The only thing missing was a bit of salt. But Bella didn't care about salt, she just ate until the fat dribbled down both sides of her chin.

When Karoliena got home she was no longer hungry. She told her mother that stone-food was nicer than stove-food. Her mother told her they were not Hottentots.

*

'Tree, I don't know what kind of person I am. I feel as if I am being rejected everywhere. I walk through the village, people stare at me and then look knowingly at one another; I keep on walking, telling myself: they don't know about tree-spirits! I get on the train, strangers stare at me. I come to you, but your spirit does not appear, and the wedding money is almost finished. I don't know what I'm going to do! And you just stand here without a care in the world!'

On the Monday, she and Oldman Botha were sitting in front of the house as dusk was falling. They heard a car approaching from the village. It seemed to have two large round eyes. It slowed down – it was CCO 10! Mister Fourcade! Sheer joy mixed with disappointment; why had he come so late in the day?

She ran down to the road and asked him why he had come so late. He just smiled as he greeted her, and began taking things out of the car: a lantern, two blankets, a picnic basket, a net-bag on a long stick – the kind strangers brought with them when they came to catch butterflies. And seldom did. The butterflies flew too high, and they didn't know where the butterflies went to eat mud in the afternoons. She asked Mister Fourcade where he thought he was going find a butterfly at that time of the day? He said he hadn't come to catch butterflies.

Mister Fourcade and Oldman Botha greeted each other like old friends. They sat talking in front of the door, ignoring her as if she was a nuisance. He told her to go and put on something warm, it was cold in the forest at night. Why would they want to go into the forest at night? To look for something. He was treating her as if she was a child! She went inside and put on a jersey and combed her hair, and heard Oldman Botha explaining to Mister Fourcade where he should stop the car in Kom's Bush and which footpath he should take …

She went back outside. It was almost dark. Mister Fourcade had opened the picnic basket. He handed them each a plate, and passed around thin slices of bread and pieces of cheese and tomato and little meatballs; he gave them each a starched table napkin. Then he looked at his watch and said they should leave in half an hour.

Oldman Botha went inside and fetched a lantern. He said he wanted to see what he was about to eat. She saw that he did not know what to do with the table napkin and told him it was to wipe his mouth. He said his mouth wasn't dirty. He sat down, shook his head slowly and said: 'Mister Fourcade, I was under the impression that I knew everything about the forest and now you come and tell me about something I've never heard of.'

'The forest hides many secrets.'

'You say they exist *inside* the bark?' with the disbelief of a child in his voice.

'Yes.'

'I wonder how many other things there are in the forest that we don't know about.'

'We actually know nothing about the forest, Mister Botha.'

'It's so strange – and to think I'm almost dead!'

'Don't pretend I'm not here!' she called out indignantly. 'What are you talking about?'

'Don't worry,' Oldman Botha consoled her. 'You'll find out soon enough and then you'll show me too. Luckily there is a good moon, you just have to find the right footpath and stay on it till you get to the first stream. Then you ought to start smelling it. It should be in full bloom.'

'Smell what?'

'Patience, Karoliena, patience,' Mister Fourcade patted her on the arm. 'I hope to show you something tonight, something so special that it might even keep you on your feet until you're ready to go back to Johannes.'

It was an unexpected slap in the face. 'I never said I wanted to go back to Johannes!' she shouted. If she had been a tiger she would lashed out at him with her claws because she could not believe he would betray her in this way. 'I am staying in the forest!'

'What will happen to you if anything happens to me?' Oldman Botha asked, wiping his face with the table napkin. Then he turned to Mister Fourcade and said: 'I don't think I've ever had such wonderful food in my life. Karoliena, don't drop your plate, it's proper crockery, not tin.'

'You can have my food as well. I don't want any more to eat.' She was too upset to eat.

'Yes, let me have it. I don't understand why you're so upset.'

Mister Fourcade looked at his watch. 'It's time we left.'

'For where?' She was deliberately obtuse.

'The forest.'

'I'm not going.' She was angry. Angry because others were making decisions for her! Angry because Mister Fourcade was suddenly so superior. 'I don't go into the forest at night.'

'That, Karoliena, would be very unwise tonight. Come.' When he got up, she knew she had to go with him.

They drove without talking.

When they turned off into Kom's Bush, she had trouble staying angry, because the beautiful moonlit forest was all around them.

'Make peace in your heart, Karoliena,' Mister Fourcade said.

No, she said to herself.

They had not gone far into the forest when he stopped the car and switched off the engine. He got out and lit the lantern, took the butterfly net and a small box. He gave her the two blankets to carry and started looking for the footpath. If he had asked her, she would have found it for him.

Then they started to walk through the forest – the forest that was in turn frog-forest, owl-forest, cricket-forest …

Until she could sulk no longer. 'Don't send me back to Johannes, I don't love him. I no longer love anyone, not even Mister Fourcade.' She wanted him to *know* it.

'Love has many faces, Karoliena.'

She ignored him.

They walked deeper and deeper into the forest. The sweet smell of the keurboom's flowers began to fill the air. They came to a stream, where the scent of the keurboom was even heavier.

'Do you smell it, Karoliena?'

'Yes, it's a keurboom in flower.'

'It's the tree we're looking for.'

'Why didn't you say so? It's a stupid tree with limp branches. I could have found it for you with my eyes closed!' There used to be three keurboom trees on the other side of the stream, but poor Faan Mankvoet had one year cut down the largest one and sawed it into a mountain of fencing poles. A man from Oudtshoorn came and hauled it out to his wagon to fence ostrich camps. Susanna got a pair of shoes from the money, the children some clothes. Faan made most of their shoes himself. Her mother's second husband, Freek van Rooyen, always believed that one had to use a young keurboom for a blue buck trap. Not an elder. He was the best blue buck trapper in the forest; the wardens tried for years to catch him, said he was the biggest killer of blue bucks in the forest, but they never caught him.

Then an elephant killed him.

Mister Fourcade began to walk around the remaining two keurboom trees with the lantern. It was difficult, because the undergrowth was very dense. 'What are you looking for?' she asked.

'Quiet! The forest has ears.'

She stood to one side and waited. The peace of the forest enveloped her with every breath she took, washing away her worries about the woodcutters and Oldman Botha's pension and Susanna and the children and whether Ampie had got a lift back to Magaliesberg …

She wished she could fall asleep right there under the tree and just let the stillness of the forest sink into her body.

Mister Fourcade took the blankets from her and spread them over the underbush beneath the larger of the two keurboom trees. He put the butterfly net and the box under the tree and called her to come and sit close to the tree.

'First, we shall work,' he said.

'Work?'

'Yes. I want you to pay careful attention.'

When she sat down on the blanket, all the pleasure of working in the forest with him suddenly returned. The sheer joy of it. As if brother Love had come down from the mountain to keep her company for a while. 'I'm sorry I said I didn't love you any more. It's not true.'

'I know.'

You're my father, she said to herself.

'But I still don't love Johannes the way I'm supposed to.'

'Love, Karoliena, is ladder with many steps. It's difficult to climb, because we often lose our footing and fall back. And sometimes we are too lazy to climb and we remain on the step where we find ourselves and become dull and sluggish.'

'I thought you said we were going to work, but now you're giving me a sermon.'

'Sermons are sometimes necessary, Karoliena.'

'Now you sound like the Reverend.'

In the light of the lantern she saw that he had once more become the old bushbuck with the human head. He took out his watch to check the time.

'They will start to come out any minute now.'

'Who?'

'The moths.'

She would always remember it as the night of the moths.

At about waist height around the tree's rough trunk there were white specks, the size of a fingernail. There were some a little higher up the trunk, some a little lower.

Mister Fourcade told her to watch the specks closely, they were little lids of silk woven over the tunnels of the moth pupae.

'The *what*?'

'The little containers in which the moths have been developing for months.' He looked at his watch again. She wondered out loud whether the occupants of the little containers also had watches. He said: Yes, and a calendar too.

She didn't believe him. She thought it was a game.

How would the moths know that it was February or March or April and time for them to emerge?

And the watches?

So that they know what time it is. They don't come out before half past seven, nor later than half past ten in the evening.

She did not argue, she still thought it was a game.

Keep watching, Karoliena; you'll see.

I can't see anything.

He lifted the lantern a little higher and closer to the tree. There seemed to be some movement under one of the lids, and the next moment it broke open and a horrible, thick, brownish worm-like creature started to wriggle out of the bark. When it was free of the tunnel, it did not fall to the ground, but clung to the tree. Then it slowly started to break open and turned into the most incredible thing with wings – not a butterfly, and surely not a moth, because no moth could be *that* big! It was bigger, she would have sworn, than the doublecollared sunbird, the smallest bird of the forest. It was the strangest, most beautiful creation.

'What on earth is *that*?' She could hardly speak.

'*Leto venus*. The ghost moth.'

'A *moth*?'

'Yes.'

'It can't be.'

'It is. Look, the next one is about to come out.'

Another lid started to open … and another a little way down the trunk. The first moth crawled up the tree and clung to the bark while its wings unfolded. It was lovelier than even the loveliest butterfly in the forest – the butter-yellow swallowtail.

Another lid started to tear open – her eyes could hardly take it in.

Moths, as beautiful as that?

'Are you sure they are moths?' she asked Mister Fourcade. 'Aren't they perhaps night butterflies?'

Four wings on a bright orange body – the two bottom wings a light orange; the top wings, huge and light orange, with silver squares painted all over them.

'This, Karoliena, is one of the forest's many secrets. One you must never reveal to anyone.'

'I won't.'

'You must give me your word for it.'

'I give you my word.'

Then Mister Fourcade took the butterfly net and caught the first moth on the tree and carefully put it in the box.

She was horrified. 'It'll die! Let it fly away.'

'It can't fly away, it lives on the tree. How much money do you need?'

'Put it back on the tree!'

'This is your salvation, Karoliena. Mister Ferndale at the chemist in the village is desperately trying to get hold of these moths. But he doesn't know where to find them. He will pay a pound a moth and I will go with you tomorrow to introduce you.'

'It's dreadful. It's murder.'

'It's survival. How many pounds do you need?'

She had no choice, she had to lift the axe and cut her first tree. 'Four pounds,' she said.

And cried all the way home.

17

THE SECOND TIME she went alone. And later she stopped feeling bad about it. She picked a handful of wild grapes to lay at the keurboom's feet as a gesture of gratitude. And so that it didn't feel so much like stealing.

Before long she could catch the moths even more deftly than Mister Fourcade. She learned that the male moths had small orange feathers all along the edges of their bottom wings. Then she always made sure that she caught two males and two females. She soon found a way to evade Mister Ferndale's questions, giving him stupid answers when he pestered her to take him with her when she went to catch the moths.

The money she received for the moths became her means of survival. And for others too: Anna van Rooyen's blanket; wool and knitting needles for Fransina, who was overjoyed with the shillings she earned by knitting jerseys.

One day when Karoliena took a collection of new jerseys to Mrs Stopforth at the Sourflats school, she walked into pandemonium. Children, chickens, pigs, all three teachers in a state of shock, everyone shouting and waving arms, sticks, hats, brooms, spades and hoes – anything they could lay their hands on!

Three enormous bull elephants were at work plundering the vegetable garden and the flower gardens – fearless miscreants that had come out of the lower part of Gouna Forest above Sourflats.

'It's years since they last did this! Bastards! They have no respect!'

'The children are hiding in the school!'

'They're going to trample down the school!'

'Where's the warden?' old Jan Plan called out hoarsely. 'Call Mister Monk, tell him to come and shoot them!' The rags that hung from the old man's sinewy body could no longer be called *clothes*. It was said that he was one of the best woodcutters in Gouna Forest in the old days, until he became too old and weak to lift an axe and moved out to Sourflats where there was more sun. He lived in a corrugated iron shack behind someone's clay house. It was believed *he* had been given the old-age pension …

She had not given up hope of securing a pension for Oldman Botha. She asked Wiljam Stander to drive them to the village. Waited at the magistrate's court for half a day for a clerk to estimate the old man's age and fill in the forms. He promised to write to Deep Walls if the pension was granted.

That had been almost a year ago.

In the mean time the pile of spokes was growing behind the house – and the old man was becoming restless and anxious that they might forget to fetch them. And pay for them.

'Then *I'll* carry the spokes to the village myself, Uncle, and strangle the money out of them!'

'Don't get so excited, Karoliena. A hard-pressed man must be a careful man. They promised they would come and fetch them.'

Then she had an unexpected stroke of luck. One day she called at the post office in the shop at Deep Walls to ask if there was post for Oldman Botha.

'No,' said old Mrs Perkes, 'but there's an enormous parcel for you that came almost two weeks ago.'

For *her*? How could that be? She knew no one who would send her a parcel.

It wasn't exactly a parcel. It was a wooden box so heavy she had to get two men to carry it to Jim Reid's Crossing for her. The box had come from far away. It had travelled on a ship and then on the timber train from the village to Deep Walls. It was bound with wire and string. The address painted on it read: *Carolina, protégée of Mr Boutha at Deep Walls, Knysna Forest, South Africa.*

She asked Mrs Perkes what *protégée* meant. The old woman said it was the same as foundling.

Inside the box were the most beautiful clothes and shoes – a present from the Countess. Six engraved glasses too, not one of them broken. The shoes were too small and the clothes were too smart, but Susanna unpicked them and turned them into dresses for herself and the children, for Hestertjie Vermaak and for one of the sisters.

And Oldman Botha rejoiced for days over the wire and the box.

The three elephants grazed leisurely.

'Pray that they don't find the bag of corn lying at the front door!' one of the forest women shouted. 'There was no time to drag it inside, I paid a whole pound for it – it's six weeks' supply!'

Mrs Stopforth came around the corner looking determined. 'Karoliena!' she called out in surprise, trying to shake off the frightened forest children clinging to her skirts. 'As if we don't have enough problems, *this* had to happen to us this morning as well!'

'So I see.' How had Mister Fourcade put it? Luckily there are helpers throughout the forest who can see what others can't. Mrs Stopforth had been Sourflats' eyes for more than twenty years. Its helping hands, too. If she had had a gun that day, she would have shot those elephants without a moment's hesitation. 'I've brought you a few more jerseys; give these to the coldest ones. The woman at Veldmanspad will knit more.'

'Thank you. You have no idea how much they are needed.'

Sourflats was about a two-hour walk to the west of the village. It was state land that had been sectioned into plots years before and allotted to woodcutters – small plots, bigger plots, allotted to white and brown and half-caste, all together.

She wondered if Mister Werdt had been to Sourflats yet. Especially after the conversation they had had at Johannes's table that Sunday long ago. She remembered his air of importance; the way he talked over her head as if she wasn't there – and getting his facts wrong all the time. Johannes had hung on to his every word. He said he was on his way to parliament with yet another proposal: that an urgent law be promulgated to forbid mixed marriages because it was a threat to the Afrikaner's tradition and status as a nation. She said there were two girls at Sourflats who had married brown men. Mister Werdt said that fortunately mixed marriages only happened in the lower classes. She pointed out that the half-caste children were among the brightest in the school at Sourflats and that one of the brown men – his name was Prinsloo – had built the best house at Sourflats. Then Johannes had kicked her under the table.

Soutflats – a collection of poor little houses for poor folk on the edge of dense forest where the men went out in the mornings to cut or plant; poverty as far as the eye could see, misery hanging like a mist over it all …

The school stood like a beacon in the centre of the sorry little community: straight shoulders, courageous heart; it was neatly fenced and flowers grew on either side of the flagged path. There was a large vegetable garden at the back. About seventy forest children attended, some came from as far as Millwood – which was a two-hour walk, twice a day – through dense, beautiful forest.

'What's going to become of us all, Karoliena?' Mrs Stopforth asked her. She sounded deeply troubled.

'I don't know.'

'Maria Rothman of the Carnegie delegation came here for a day. She visited the people, spoke to the women. Her main purpose was to write a report afterwards about what she had observed. She promised me she would recommend that the school should have a place where the children could wash, and books for them to read. I showed her the children's little cloth bags with their food for the day; they usually hang outside on nails. The good woman inspected the contents of the bags with real concern; asked why the bread was so badly baked, the griddle bread so heavy, why only two bags had bottles of milk in them. The rest had bottles filled with cold black coffee. I told her the mothers were ignorant when it came to the preparation of food and she said training would have to be provided. I agreed with her and now I wait every day for the miracle to happen. But to this day the only miracle that has turned up are the jerseys you bring. I do not know how you do it. The wool, the needles.'

'That's another miracle.'

'Those Carnegie people – if only they were better coordinated. Not that I want to find fault with them. First, one came to inspect the children's health. Three weeks later another came to examine the finances. Then the Rothman woman came. They were like oxen pulling in different directions.'

'The church nurse tells me you feed the children who have nothing to eat.'

'I can't always do it. A hungry child is a brave child, Karoliena. You hurt a little more for them.'

She took the pound from her pocket. She'd planned to buy more wool for Fransina, some groceries. Fortunately there was still a little money left at home, because it would be a year before the moths would emerge from the bark again.

The elephants had finished their meal and were on their way back into the forest.

And she left too. She didn't go via the village as she had planned, but decided to take a short cut through Millwood forest – *if* she could still find the path.

Her father always said the world could take the whole forest, just as long as it left Millwood to him.

But her mother said: No thank you, there are too many ghosts of the old gold diggers buried there.

Her father thought it must be terrible to die so far from your homeland and your people. Some even came from overseas to dig for gold.

They should have searched more towards the mountains, her mother replied. The only man who walked out of the forest with gold nuggets in his pocket was Saul Barnard. And see where he is today.

Her father said: The difference is, Saul knew the forest and every stream in it; the strangers left only damage behind them. Now Forestry has to cover the damage with plantations.

She entered the forest shortly after the elephants, walking as fast as she could, ever alert to the hissing lourie telling the elephants that she was there. Now and then there was an ordinary kok-kok-kok, but for the rest the forest was silent. Sometimes she heard the scrabbling of a mouse; the whirring of a chorister robin's wings, the soundless flashing of a sparrow-hawk. And the frogs …

She found the path easily. The first elephant dung she came across was in the old sledpath at Krisjan's Road. It was day-old dung. Definitely not the three that had been at Sourflats earlier that day.

She noticed that there were more and more butterflies and she knew why: the wild chestnuts were in bloom, decked out in their frilly pink dresses to lure the butterflies from their hiding places …

She would have loved to send the Countess a branch of wild chestnut with a butterfly on it. And a letter to say that Mister Fourcade had told her that butterflies did not eat sand-mud along the streams in the afternoon, they pushed their tongues into the mud to drink water. Emperor swallowtails, they were called, because they were the king butterflies of the forest, the largest in the whole country; and thank you very much for the box of clothes.

*

Idiotic Johannes. And idiotic Village Council that made the laws! She had recommended to Johannes that the Council plant wild chestnuts along the Main Street. Oldman Botha sent her into the forest to collect some of the large scabby chestnut fruits. He shook out the seeds, soaked them overnight in lukewarm water and planted them in boxes behind the house. They grew. She took a box of young chestnuts to the village to give to Johannes. He said he did not think the Council had time for trifling issues at that moment, the oak trees would have to remain for the time being. There were too many other problems in the village. They had gone to endless trouble to close the bars on Saturday afternoons so that the sawmill workers and others did not go straight there when they got their weekly wages. Their efforts had been rendered useless by the so-called *agents* who suddenly sprang up everywhere. They bought liquor before the bars closed and resold it to the poor fools on Saturday afternoons. Police would have to be appointed to put a stop to this evil, the agents were making exorbitant profits!

She carried the seedlings back to Deep Walls. Shuffling along slowly beside her, Oldman Botha showed her where to plant them.

After they had planted the trees she said: Perhaps one day they will flower. And people will say: Do you see those chestnuts? They're Karoliena's chestnuts.

*

Suddenly she heard the crying of a child and followed the path towards the sound. She found a little shack of plank and corrugated iron in a clearing. A dirty, half-naked little girl was standing outside. A little boy, looking just as wretched, was feeding her pieces of dry bread.

'Where is your mother?' she asked. They would be pretty children, if they were washed and dressed properly.

'Gone to the village.' The village was at least a four-hour walk away, surely she would not have left the children on their own …

'Who's looking after you?'

'We look after ourselves.'

The children had been left *alone*? They could not have been older than three or four. There was a little vegetable garden beside the house; rows of cabbage, carrots and mealies. Someone was making an effort …

'When did she leave?'

'This morning.'

Perhaps the little boy was closer to five, he spoke quite well.

'Why did she go to the village?' Perhaps the grandmother lived there.

'To sell peaches.'

Then she saw the three peach trees beside the house.

'Where's your father?' It was a neat little shack.

'Planting plantations.'

'What's his name?'

'Willem.'

'And yours?'

'Willem.'

'And you sister's?'

'Sissy.'

It was almost dark when she got home and Oldman Botha was waiting anxiously for her. 'I was getting worried about you, Karoliena. There were people here, strangers, asking for the young girl who used to take people into the forest.' There was something wrong with the old man, he couldn't look her in the eye.

She didn't tell him about the two children she had found in

the forest. Instead she made a fire to make him coffee, boiled sweet potatoes, broke open the last of the bread. But her thoughts kept returning to Millwood Forest ...

She had met the woman on one of the sledpaths, had seen her approaching in the distance. A thin woman, shoes in her hand; a dress that must once have been pretty and which had probably come to her in a church-parcel.

A good face, bright eyes. She was startled when she looked up and saw Karoliena waiting for her. 'Are you the mother of Willem and Sissy?' The woman's eyes turned wild with panic. 'There's nothing wrong,' she added hurriedly. 'I accidentally walked past your house.'

Fatigue and relief seemed to overcome the woman as she sank down on a windfall-tree next to the path. She said not a word, but her big blue eyes reflected years of suffering.

She had been to the village with one hundred and fifty peaches to sell. She had managed to get a little sugar and flour and coffee for them. The shop at Deep Walls didn't take peaches, nor did Mister Stander's shop in the village, only Mister Smit's shop. Did she meet any elephants on the way? No. The nearest was in Gouna Forest.

She felt bad because she had nothing to give the woman.

When Oldman Botha came to the table to eat, he said the strangers who had called while she was away told him that a car had driven off the bridge across the Knysna River. The driver couldn't free himself and had drowned. Apparently someone called Van Huysteen. 'It's a terrible thing, Karoliena. And we thought the bridge was a miracle after the drift where everyone had to wait for low tide before they could get through. Now it seems that motor cars are dangerous things. One of the wardens said a special law is going to be made for them, because they are so dangerous.'

He ate, he talked, he ate. He tugged at his beard ...

'Is something bothering you, Uncle?'

'There comes a day, Karoliena, there comes a day for all of us when the bridge under us gives way.'

'What bridge are you talking about?'

'One day, years ago, a car stopped in the road below the house. A strange-looking man with a beard got out and came up to the house. I said to him, you're almost as ugly as I am. He asked me something, I didn't understand him; he spoke English. Then he started to take off his clothes, rubbed his naked backside on the branches, laughing like child enjoying himself. I said: You don't seem right in the head, what's the matter with you? He just laughed. Later he went back to his car, stark naked, fetched a book and wrote something in it, tore out the page and gave it to me. I said, it's no use, I can't read. He walked through the underbrush again, scratched his back against a yellowwood behind the house – just like an elephant. Then he put his clothes back on, got into his car and drove away. He did not even ask if I would like a ride.

'The next day Mister-doctor came. I told him about the strange behaviour of the naked man. I showed him the page the man had written on and he said I must keep it; the man is a book writer from over the sea. He had an accident in the district with his car, broke his leg and had to lie in bed for six weeks while it mended. He probably wanted to run around naked because he was so glad to be back on his feet again. The letter is still in my drawer. One never knows when he might come back.'

He got up and went to look for the letter, came back to the table with a tightly folded piece of yellow-brown paper. 'Mister-doctor said I must not ask him what the words meant, they were rather difficult to understand.'

She unfolded the paper: *To the wild old man of the forest – from another wild old man. Bernard Shaw.*

'I'm afraid Mister-doctor lied to Uncle, it says here you're the wild old man of the forest.'

'Oh.' After another mouthful of food he told her what had probably been on his mind from the start. 'Now don't get alarmed, Karoliena. The new man who has taken over from Mister-doctor sent the warden to tell me that I must get out.

He will be taking over the replanting of the forest now. I said the forest does not want itself replanted. The warden said the message was that I must get my stuff out of the house; Forestry will have it demolished themselves.'

When the shock really started to hit her she got up from the table and went outside to be alone. It seemed to her that the world had slowly started to topple sideways and was about to fall over and she stood there helpless, gagged and without hands. Without hands one could do nothing. Without a mouth one could not scream. The only thing one could do was start running while one still had feet!

Brother Love on the mountain, where are your eyes?

The day she had run away from Johannes it had been her plan to hide somewhere and let the world forget about her. Then Oldman Botha became her shelter against the storm that raged inside her, a refuge where her hands could grow strong again. Deep inside she had nurtured a secret hope that one day, when Oldman Botha died, she would stay behind in the little house; care for the vegetables in the camp, keep an eye on his little Cape beeches, red alders and ironwoods. She would pose for cameras at the edge of the forest for strangers who wanted proof that they had seen the wild woman of the forest ...

Now, the rock that had come loose from the mountain was rolling towards her and Oldman Botha. There was no other place in the forest where they could go and hide from the world. Especially not for her.

The only thing she could do was use her feet, while she still had them, and run to the village to find out about the old man's pension.

The first difference she noticed at the magistrate's office was that she hardly had to wait at all before they called the right clerk to come and talk to her. How long would it take, she asked, before the old-age pension might be granted to Oldman Botha? Lady, she was told, a letter was sent to him more than a week ago to tell him that his application had been successful.

I beg your pardon?

Yes, he has been granted an old-age pension.

How much?

A pension of twenty-five pounds a year.

From when?

The end of the month – two pounds and five shillings a month.

Are you sure?

She had trouble standing still, she wanted to run to the forest to tell the old man! And to laugh at the rock rolling towards them! She would offer her mother a pound a month to take the old man in. Uncle Cornelius could build him a shack behind the house …

She would worry about herself later.

She'd worry later, too, about the water in the tank behind the house getting low. Every night when the old man blew out the candle, he said it had to rain soon, it was too dry. She tried to reassure him; said the rain would surely come.

The drought entered the forest slowly – by the time one realised it was there, it had been there longer than one remembered. One's eyes began to notice the signs – the streams in the ravines ran slowly; rocks in rivers that had not been visible before.

Clouds appeared, the west wind blew, but it didn't bring rain. You listened in the forest for the marsh lourie who always called when rain was on the way. But he was silent; you saw him only by chance in the early morning, sitting on a branch warming himself in a patch of sunlight. You asked him: Where's the rain? He said nothing. You pricked your ears in the night listening for the rain-frog's chir-chir among the calls of the other frogs.

Oldman Botha tapped on the water tank each day to find out how much further the level had dropped. It's a drought, Karoliena, he said shaking his head. The elephants came past more often. Oldman Botha told her: You must be careful, the drought is chasing them to the edges of the forest. At

Veldmanspad one night elephants destroyed every vegetable garden and kept an old woman trapped in a lavatory until morning.

At Deep Walls old Mrs Perkes handed her the brown envelope and said: Looks like a letter from the government, is Oldman Botha in trouble?

No.

It was the news of the pension.

She took the news home. The old man was sitting outside. 'They fetched the spokes,' he told her.

'Did they pay you?'

'Yes. I've put the money on the table for you to count and see if it's right. The manager wanted to know where you were, asked me if you were always so difficult.'

It was as if rain had suddenly started to fall from a clear sky: the money for the spokes, the news of the pension.

'You will be getting a pension from the end of the month – two pounds and five shillings every month.' She had to repeat it a few times before he believed it.

'The government has given me a *pension*?'

'Yes, Uncle.'

'And my house?'

'It says nothing about the house in the letter.'

'What's to become of us?'

'I'll make a plan.'

That was before she knew that Smart made his plans in the dark, and by the time he knocked at your door, it was too late to kick it shut.

The water in the tank ran out one Friday morning. That afternoon she took the two buckets and walked to a stream about half a mile into the forest – a side-stream of the Gouna River.

'Turn right when you get to the bottom of the sledpath, you'll see an elder tree and a quar standing together; you take the footpath from there and you will find a good place for filling the buckets,' Oldman Botha instructed her. 'Carrying water is a heavy task, Karoliena. I know; in the old days I did it myself when the drought came.'

'Now it's my turn, Uncle. Go inside and rest for a while.'

The forest in the drought was a different kind of forest. It seemed to have a long-suffering air about it. You remembered that it was a forest growing in shallow soil; all those roots that could not reach water when the drought came remained thirsty.

The worst affected were the seven-week ferns along the sledpath; no longer the tall, proud ferns the strangers always gaped at. The drought had shrivelled their leaves and bleached the green from them.

Mister Ferndale, who bought the moths from her, often begged her to bring him one of the dwarf chameleons that lived in the forest. He would buy as many as she could find and pay her really well for them. She asked Mister Fourcade about the little animals, he said he had only once had the privilege of seeing one. On a wild pomegranate. She asked Oldman Botha; he said they made themselves a bed in the tops of the tree ferns. She took the lantern one night and went to look in the tree fern growing close to the house. She pushed away the fronds and searched, went back to the house to fetch a box to stand on and searched again. Eventually, she found the clever little thing neatly rolled up in a small, ghost-white bundle tucked in under the uppermost fronds. She wondered what it had done with all its beautiful colours. She put out her hand to take it, but found she didn't have the heart to wake it up.

When Mister Ferndale asked her again to find him a chameleon, she told him she couldn't bring him one because it looked so pretty when it was asleep. He shook his head and said it was no wonder the forest people said she was not right in the head.

The dry forest was an unhappy forest that coped as best it could.

Shortly before she reached the stream, the footpath again took her through a patch of seven-week ferns that were so dry that they rustled round her legs like paper. The strongest, prettiest ferns in the forest had been given the wrong name. Because the huge green leaves did not live only for seven weeks, they usually lived for two years. They should have been called two-year ferns. Or thieves' ferns, because they were the ferns that were most often stolen by visitors to the forest who dug them out to take home. When she tried to stop them, telling them that the ferns would not be happy anywhere but in the forest, they became angry with her.

The stream, mercifully, still had enough water for the buckets. But halfway home she had to leave one bucket behind on the footpath because it was too heavy and the wire handle was hurting her hand.

She had hardly reached the sledpath when she was startled to see a man standing at the edge of the forest. It was Johannes. It could not possibly be him, but it was. He was standing with his hands in his pockets staring at the forest floor.

'Johannes?'

'Good afternoon, Karoliena. I took the sledpath, Oldman Botha said I might find you here.'

There was a strange expression on his face, and his hair seemed greyer. 'Is something wrong?'

'No.'

'Then why are you here?'

'Because I must talk to you.' He seemed anxious.

'About what, Johannes?' She had an urge to put out her hand and touch him reassuringly. But she didn't.

'There are things, Karoliena, that I feel you ought to know, although you are not supposed to know about them yet.'

'What things?'

'There is going to be a war.'

He could just as well have said that the sun was going to fall from the sky. 'What war?'

'A world war. Here, let me carry the bucket for you.'

'I left another one on the path. Two were too heavy to carry at the same time. What is the war about?'

'Apart from the war there are other, more important things you should know.'

It was an unfamiliar Johannes. Smart, important Johannes had dropped from the sky into the forest where he did not belong. Just as an elephant would never belong in the village.

She had to say something. 'Is it dry in the village too?'

'Very. Some of the old people say it's drier than they can ever remember. If it does not rain soon, water restrictions will have to be implemented.'

'If it does not rain soon, I will have to walk much further to fetch water.'

Suddenly he stepped right in front of her. 'Karoliena,' he said, urgently, 'your time in the forest is over!' It sounded like a warning and it frightened her because they were almost the same words she had been trying to stifle since Oldman Botha had been told that he must get out of the house.

'Is *that* what you've come to tell me, Johannes?'

'You're far from stupid, Karoliena, but there are things you know nothing about. National affairs, world affairs. Things don't happen by accident, they are carefully planned and most of us are in the dark.'

'Who planned the drought?'

'Don't be flippant! We are on the brink of a catastophe that might change our lives for ever. What I am about to tell you is confidential and must not be discussed with any of the forest people. Do you hear me, Karoliena?'

'Yes, Johannes.'

'Things are going to change and I don't want you to be unprepared for them.'

'Why not?' Why did he look so worried? 'Why are you telling me this?'

'Out of compassion. Everyone is going to be removed from the forest. You as well. The government has decided that all the remaining woodcutters will be given a state pension.'

The rock would miss the woodcutters, but it was still rolling towards her!

It was unbelievable news, not something to be frightened of, but she couldn't help feeling suspicious. 'When will they get the pension?'

'That will be announced in due course.'

'Oldman Botha has also been granted an old-age pension. When will the woodcutters be told?'

'As soon as the necessary structures are in place.'

'What structures?'

'Mister Werdt and Paul Sauer, the member of parliament for Humansdorp, have succeeded finally in getting a state Welfare Department established. They both had dinner at my house last night and told me about it. One of its first tasks will be the construction of a village for old and disabled woodcutters. They will build them houses. In fact, construction of the village has already begun. The reason I felt it my duty to come and tell you this, is because Oldman Botha will most probably be one of the first to be moved. You will therefore no longer have a home with him.'

The rock rolled ever closer …

Did Johannes think that *this* would make her go back to him? Was this one of those carefully planned things that happened while one was in the dark?

'Fortunately, I still have feet to run away.' He had to know.

'You don't realise how serious this is, Karoliena!'

'A village, you said? Where?' She hoped he would say at Deep Walls or Veldmanspad …

'At Elandskraal …'

'I've never heard of it. Is it in the forest?'

'It's about a day's walk to the west of Knysna and it will be known as Karatara.'

Karatara was the river where the first gold nugget had been found all those years ago. A nugget that set the world alight with a cold fire. A day's walk from Knysna for the old and disabled did not make sense. It sounded as if it was a dumping place that was being prepared for them. It made her angry. Because she could not utter a word, because her mouth had been shut, because her eyes had been closed while the plans were being made …

'Welfare will build about fifty houses as a government experiment and supervise the whole project,' Johannes continued. 'All those woodcutters and forest workers who are still able to work will be given employment in the state plantations. Some will continue to work for the Forestry Department in the indigenous forest for a few months of the year, because their knowledge and experience are still much needed. Some of those employed will be allowed to occupy the houses at a nominal rent. According to Mister Werdt the whole area around Elandskraal is very fertile and most suitable for gardening. They will also start building a church as soon as possible …'

She didn't want to hear any more. 'I must fetch the other bucket.'

'I'll come with you and carry the bucket.'

'You do not need to.'

'I want to, Karoliena. Don't push me away every time I reach out my hand to you.'

'I'm sorry. But I'm getting angry because a day's walk is too far.'

'I know, but things are seldom as bad as they seem.'

'No. And fortunately woodcutters are used to hardship.'

'Forget about the woodcutters, Karoliena! It's time you started thinking about yourself.'

'Yes, Johannes.' But I doubt if you're really concerned about me, you have never forgiven me. 'Tell me more about the war?' They had almost reached the bucket. She wanted to get home to think, to rejoice about the pensions, and be glad for the forest which would now be left in peace.

'The war will be fought in other countries. Mister Sauer says the government will do everything in its power to stay out of the war, and that we must trust that no one will be called up to go and fight.'

'As long as the war stays out of the forest.'

'It will.'

He picked up the bucket and carried it home for her.

But before everything – before the pensions, before Elandskraal – it first had to rain. She had to go and ask Abel Slinger when he was expecting the rain.

That evening she asked Oldman Botha if he had heard of a place called Elandskraal. Yes, he said, it's below Kleinhans Neck, not far from Barrington's place where he once had to help put out a forest fire.

'One of the world's fools tried to smoke a bee's nest out of a yellowwood during a northwest wind and started the fire. Seventy of us struggled through eight days of hell to put it out and stop it spreading this way. Why do you ask about Elandskraal?'

'I just wanted to know.'

'Years ago an educated woman stopped her motor car here one day. It was the first time in my life that I had seen a woman driving a car. She asked if I knew of a road that would take her to the upper waters of the Karatara River. Not quite to the top, I told her, but there is a kind of a road although it is quite a long way there. She asked if I would drive with her. She wanted find an October lily and she had been assured that she would definitely find them there. I said: Let's go. When we got to the other side of Elandskraal we found the veld on both sides of the road covered in lilies.'

'What does an October lily look like?'

'It's not much of a flower. A rather flabby green-and-white plant with strings of green-and-white flowers on the stem. A type of orchid. The woman was overjoyed. On our way back, we passed Elandskraal and I had to warn her about the mud: Elandskraal's mud is not for motor cars. We skidded this way and that, but she kept it on its wheels and dropped me off at the house without a scratch.'

'Would you say Elandskraal is a place for people, Uncle?'

'No. It's more of a cattle place.'

'I want to get up early and go to Abel Slinger to ask when he's expecting the rain.'

'He'll know.'

But she could not sleep because Johannes's words were going round and round in her head. *Your time in the forest is over, Karoliena*. Somehow she knew it was true. Without really being aware of it, her heart was starting to leave the forest with no idea of where it would come to rest. Like the fruit of a chestnut that burst open and shed its seeds, not knowing where they would fall. Mister Fourcade had once said that there was a right time to arrive and a right time to leave – the secret was not to do either too quickly.

Had Johannes told her *only* about the pensions and Elandskraal, her mind would not have been so muddled. What worried her most was that she didn't know what Welfare's plans were. And who was making the plans for the war?

Perhaps the woodcutters' pensions were the first outcome of the Carnegie Commission's investigation. Perhaps Elandskraal would not be too bad after all. Perhaps it was *her* eyes that were not seeing clearly. Surely somebody would open a shop at Elandskraal. She could not allow Oldman Botha to be discarded ...

She had to see Abel. She also had to see the church nurse in the village, perhaps she knew more about Elandskraal and the pensions.

'I've decided to take the train to the village, Uncle,' she announced when they got up the next morning. 'I may sleep at Amelia Claassens's place tonight and I also want to go to Long Marsh Forest and Dirk's Clearing.'

'What's bothering you, Karoliena?'

'It feels as if the world is falling over and we're all going to be thrown off.'

'It's not the world that's throwing me off, it's Forestry that's throwing me out of my house! But I'm more worried about where *you* are going to fall.'

'I'll take care of myself, Uncle.'

'That's my only consolation. You're not the kind to lie down where you fall.'

She said to herself: Old man, I hope you're right.

When she got to Deep Walls station, she had the feeling that the forest was actually in pain because of the drought. It was Wednesday, but there was no passenger coach, it was only a timber train. Old Mrs Perkes said the coach had not been hooked on for the past two weeks. The tourists wanted to see the forest at its best, when it was damp and green, not dry and lifeless as it was now.

Mister Kennet saw her and came to say good-day, but he was not his usual cheerful self. He said that, for the first time in almost thirty years, on the way up from the village he had almost hit an elephant which was standing half across the line. The drought was driving the beasts from the forest, and they were causing problems everywhere they went. It was time the government had them shot. He didn't know how he was going to get the train back to the village in any case; there were problems with water all along the way because the fountains were drying up.

The timber train usually had to take in water three or four times between Knysna and Deep Walls; the tanks at each of the water-points were fed by fountains. According to Mister Kennet the tank on the other side of Veldmanspad had not been filled that morning. If not enough water had collected by the time they got there, they would be in trouble. Fortunately, they didn't use as much water going down as coming up, but they'd come with Number 4 and that engine drank water like an elephant!

She got on to one of the open trucks and sat down on top of the wood. The wooden sides of the trucks were old and worn, it was a miracle that they could still carry the massive loads of tree trunks.

If the woodcutters could no longer cut, there would be no wood for the train to fetch. If the train no longer ran …

The guard, Mister Botha, also came to greet her. 'I can't remember it ever being this dry in the forest, Karoliena. The Reverend is considering holding a day of prayer for rain. The whole village has become a dust bowl. Mister Wilson says many overseas visitors are cancelling their holiday plans for December and January. Not just because of the drought, mind you, but because of the rumours that war might break out.'

'What war?' Johannes had said the same …

'There are dark clouds gathering over our heads and our future, Karoliena. Mister Wilson says they will stop road building completely, if war breaks out. It will be bad for the village, because more and more tourists are coming by road to see our beautiful district. Your mother took the train to the village last week. She's getting old – Cornelius too.'

'Yes, Mister Botha.'

The world shook a little more …

When the Number 4 engine started to pull the heavily loaded trucks out of Deep Walls station, she wanted to close her eyes and apologise for the holes that had been left. All the ghosts.

If only it would rain.

Abel would know when.

On the other side of Veldmanspad the train slowed down to stop at the water tank. The sander jumped down to get the canvas hose out of the tank and throw it into the engine's tank. She saw Mister Kennet get off to talk to the sander. Mister Botha came from behind to find out what was happening. When he came back, he said: We're running short of water and there's nothing in the tank.

'What will you do?' she asked.

'Buckets, what else?' he said. 'The drought is even attacking the train now.'

When the train started to move she knew they were going to Earth Dam a little way further on. She had been forbidden to play there when she was a child, but she had none the less gone there in the hope of seeing one of the rubbery-looking turtles that lived in the dam. Sometimes, if she walked very softly and slowly, she surprised a turtle on the dam wall. But it always took off in fright, so that all you saw was a splash before it disappeared under the water.

One day she asked Mister Heunis if he thought there were turtles in the forest. He said no, he could assure her there weren't any. Then she knew she was brighter than Mister Heunis.

There were four men who could fetch water for the train: Mister Kennet, Mister Botha, the fireman and the sander. Fortunately, the dam was not far from the line. The sander climbed on to the engine's tank. Mister Botha took the two iron buckets to the water, filled them and passed them to Mister Kennet. He then passed them to the fireman, who passed them to the sander, who poured the water into the tank. It was a tedious and exhausting business.

She got down and went to sit on the railway line a little way off and let her thoughts wander … Forestry would allow Oldman Botha to stay in his house until the houses at Elandskraal were finished … so she would be able to stay with Oldman Botha until it was time for him to move to Elandskraal … the Church would have to buy the church nurse a motor car if Elandskraal had to be visited as well. Or a horse …

Certainly not an ox. Old Abel's wife Bella boasted that her people's people had been wealthy in years gone by. They rode through the forest on oxen. Important forest Hottentots always had an extra Hottentot with them who followed on foot in case the important one wanted to get off the ox. Then the follower bent over so that the important one could step on his back and dismount comfortably.

If one thought about it, the pattern of life had always been the same. Some rode on oxen, others bent over to be trodden on.

The men muttered loudly with every bucket. The sander struggled to lift the heavy buckets and empty them into the engine's tank. The earth around Mister Botha's feet got muddier and muddier. The shirts on their backs were wet with perspiration.

They must have filled about thirty buckets before they had taken on enough water. She and Mister Botha got back on to the same truck and the train started to move again.

'We didn't fill her up properly, but we'll make it to Bracken Hill and get more water there. In any case the water was getting too muddy. By the time we get to the village it will be almost dark. Then all that muddy water will have to be drained and the pipes washed out with clean water, otherwise there'll be dirt in the injectors and we will be in trouble with Mister Wilson.'

18

IT WAS DUSK by the time she turned into the street where Amelia Claassens lived – and saw Johannes's car parked in front of her door …

Her heart began to pound with shock and she turned around and walked away as fast as she could. She didn't want to find Johannes with another woman – even though he and she meant nothing to each other any more.

They were man and wife only on paper.

She could not walk back to the forest because the elephants were too dangerous. Where did you go if you had nowhere to sleep because your husband had arrived at your accommodation before you?

But no. She did not have a husband.

Nor did Amelia Claassens …

No!

She could not go back to the forest at night.

She walked down the Main Street. All around her the village was getting ready for sleep. In the knapsack over her shoulder was a night-dress, a wash-cloth, a comb and clean bloomers. There was only one other place she could think of and that was the small station where at least there was a bench to sit on.

Johannes and Amelia Claassens?

No.

They were still washing the muddy water from the engine tank when she got to the station. They were like phantoms with lanterns – the nearest street lamp was too far away to give them the benefit of its light. She hid in the bushes on the other side of the line until the lanterns had moved off in the direction of the village.

A terrible loneliness descended on her. Why? Surely she was not jealous!

One of the wardens at Deep Walls had started to visit her at Oldman Botha's house in the evenings. Jan Gerts, a decent sort of man. On his third visit he asked if she would like to go for a walk, it was such a lovely moonlit night. Oldman Botha snorted and told him to go home. Karoliena was a married woman.

She never thought of herself as a married woman. She was just a woman who had once stood next to a man at the altar – accidentally.

The next morning Oldman Botha told her he wanted no nonsense under his roof.

She left the bushes on the other side of the railway line and went to sit on the bench on the veranda in front of the little station building. The loneliness followed her. She could hear the noise of the sea crashing through the Heads behind the station. One day, a long time ago, she and her mother had visited a cousin of her mother's at Old Place just outside the village. It was private land where plots for poor people cost five shillings a month and you had to put up your own house. She pestered her mother to walk with her to the lagoon, she wanted to see a ship. In the end her mother gave in. There was a beautiful wooden ship with tall masts lying at the quay. Her mother said: We must get away from here, I don't like the way those sailor-men are looking at you. The next moment a loud shot went off, dogs barked, birds flew up into the air, and her mother grabbed her by the hand and started running towards the village. Another shot went off behind them, and another, and yet another ... He mother shouted to an approaching man to turn back, war had broken out at the waterside! The man laughed. He said: Don't be silly, they are firing the cannon in honour of Queen Victoria's birthday. The ship at the quay is an English ship. She shouted back at him: Don't be stupid, the Queen's been dead for years!

Her mother was sometimes quite knowledgeable. If she had been educated she might have had a different life. She asked her mother how she knew the Queen was dead. Her mother told her she had read it in the newspaper. At the shop they wrapped forest people's and brown people's purchases in newspaper.

Some of the night sounds in the village were the same as those of the forest – frogs and crickets – but they sounded different. Flatter. If she had had a lantern, she would have walked home.

There was no place for her in the village. There was no place for her in the forest. Not any more. Perhaps there was no place for her on earth ...

Would Johannes spend the night with Amelia Claassens?

Don't think about it!

She rested her head on her arm and fell asleep some time during the night. When she woke up, the birds were singing and day had broken.

'Karoliena?' A surpised Mister Kennet touched her foot lightly. 'Did you sleep here the whole night?'

'Yes. I must go home now.'

'Go and get in the coach, we're taking five foreigners to the forest. Three of them are photographers and they want to photograph an elephant.'

She crossed the railway line to the toilet, washed her face under the tap, combed her hair, put on her shoes. Then she got on to one of the open trucks because she did not feel like joining the strangers in the passenger coach.

She got off the train at Deep Walls and from there took a short cut through the top of Long Marsh Forest to Dirk's Clearing. She was in a hurry to see Abel Slinger. When the foreigners got out of the coach at Deep Walls, Salman Fransen came up to her to ask if she would please help the photographers find elephant tracks. Two cows had gone into the forest close to the station earlier that morning – could she just help the men find the tracks? No, it was dangerous to follow a thirsty elephant; if it found you in its path, it would kill you just to get you out of its way. Fransen was really desperate. He walked faster and faster to keep up with her. Please, Karoliena, they're professional photographers and they want to take the first proper photograph of a Knysna elephant in the world.

'Mister Fourcade says they're the most dangerous elephants in the world as well!'

He turned back after that.

Abel's door was standing open. He was sitting cross-legged in the dark little house when she knocked softly on the door. Bella wasn't home, she had gone to fetch water.

'Why is it so dry, Uncle Abel?'

'Drought and rain, each one has its turn.'

'When will it be rain's turn again?'

'Not yet.'

It was stuffy in the house. 'What are those black things hanging from the roof?'

She had noticed them there before.

'Elephant shoes.'

'What are they for?'

'What are shoes for? You wear them. One of my old grandfathers wore them when he had to walk over a stony path.'

'Let me borrow them. Please.'

'You've got shoes.'

'Just for a while, please.' The thought had suddenly occurred to her: Perhaps one could know what it was like to be an elephant if one had elephant feet ...

When she had made herself the body of a stinkwood tree, she knew what it was like to be a tree. 'I'll bring them back, I promise.'

The old man seemed not to hear her, just lifted his head and stared at the roof. 'How is Oldman Botha? One never sees him any more.'

'He is too old to walk very far.'

'That's how it is. There's a time for being young, a time for being old. Young does not care for old, old does not care for young.'

'How do elephants live?'

'Like elephants. I can see that you're muddled in your mind again.'

'I think Johannes has taken another woman.'

'Man wants a woman, woman wants a man. That's how it is. Take the elephant shoes and look after them. Soak them in water overnight to make them soft.'

She had nothing to wrap the shoes in and she did not want to put them in the knapsack with her clothes. So before she reached her mother's house she hid them under a wild pomegranate.

Her mother was leaning over the garden fence while Susanna planted cabbages in the dusty earth.

'Good morning, Ma.'

'Karoliena? I'm sure I don't know why, but every time you appear at my door, I expect bad news. What's in the knapsack?'

'I slept in the village.'

'With Johannes?' Hopefully.

'No. I just came by to see how you are. Why are you planting when it's so dry?'

'We carry water from the stream down in the gorge. Fortunately, the children are home in the afternoons to help. Lord knows what's to happen to us, the plantation work is killing Cornelius. Old Jan Zeelie just fell over up there on the mountain where they're planting. They carried him down, but he was dead. I hear Oldman Botha's getting a pension now. I just wish Cornelius knew how old he was.'

'Everything will come right, Ma.'

'How the hell do you imagine *that* will happen?' She threw the words at her.

'I don't know, I only know that it will happen. Somehow.'

'No, Karoliena. All I can see is darkness. The world has forgotten about the forest like you have forgotten about yourself! You look as if you slept in your clothes! And to think that you could have been a rich woman today!'

'No, Ma, I would have been a poor woman. But you won't understand.'

'You're right, I won't. The Reverend came to visit, says the Church wants Willempie to go to Wittedrift next year. Susanna says she does not mind, but I said, leave the child. The church nurse says the government is pushing hundreds of the poor to work on the railways; I say, let Willempie go to the railways and start earning something. It's the end of the month next week, don't forget to come and pay me.'

'I won't.' There was still money left in the drawer for two months, but at least the money from the spokes and Oldman Botha's pension would help until it was time for the moths to come out again.

'The Reverend says Cornelius must start growing his beard for the Festival and Susanna must get a Voortrekker dress for the parade through the streets. I asked: And what about me? He told me I was too old. I said: Reverend, you're not so young yourself, are you? He didn't like that. He says this Festival will make people take each other's hands again. The church nurse said she might be able to lend Susanna a dress, everyone must take part. They'll be collecting money for the poor women of the district. I said, in that case, I'll march right at the front, even if I am on crutches!'

'Yes, Ma.'

'The church nurse wanted to know if you and Johannes were going to get a divorce.'

'I must go now.'

She fetched the elephant shoes from under the bush and stood there, holding them in her hands. They felt strange. They weren't actually shoes, just two flat pieces of hard elephant hide turned up at the sides with thin, dry thongs threaded through eyelets. There was thick, coarse elephant hair on the outsides. Why did they feel so strange? Why did they revive her yearning to go and hide deep in the forest and never come out again?

She had to go to the Tree. She had to get Johannes and Amelia out of her mind!

'Please,' she said when sat down next to the Tree, 'you must listen to everything I say today. I'm scared. I'm scared of the drought. And scared about Elandskraal. I got elephant shoes from Abel, but I'm afraid to put them on and walk into the forest, because I might never turn back again. Everybody is going to be removed from the forest. Me too. I feel as if I'm going to topple over like a tree and just lie and rot like a windfall. How would *you* feel if you suddenly fell over? Mister Fourcade reckons you are hundreds of years old, but at least no one will come and cut you down after the woodcutters have left the forest. And then there is something that I really don't understand: I'm scared that Johannes will take Amelia Claassens. Why?'

The Tree did not answer. The stonechat was gone. She was surrounded by the terrible drought. And the terrible loneliness.

When she got home, she found the Reverend sitting with Oldman Botha outside the door. A friendly, smiling Reverend.

'Karoliena, I had almost given up on you! How are you?'

'I'm well. And you, Reverend?' I'm not going to work in a factory.

'I couldn't be better. We decided at one of our meetings that you will be one of the collectors on the main day of the Festival. The Council has given the Women's Missionary Society permission to collect money for the poor women in the area. We reckon that you, with your pretty face, will easily get people to put their hands in their pockets. You will be given a Voortrekker dress to wear. Don't look at me like that, there's nothing to be afraid of. And what are those black things you have in your hand?'

'Elephant shoes.'

'What on earth for?'

'To make an elephant.' She could not help herself. He stared at her, shock in his eyes.

'Karoliena,' he said gravely, 'you desperately need to get out of the forest, we are really very worried about you!'

'Is it true that the woodcutters are going to get a pension and then be moved to Elandskraal?'

He leapt to his feet. 'Who told you such lies?' But his eyes said *he* was lying. 'I just came to tell you that the Church will see to it that you get proper clothes to wear for the Festival, once again reaching out a hand to you, although it is obvious that you don't want to be helped!'

'Reverend …' Oldman Botha was trying to say something. He was shaking with anxiety. 'Reverend, Karoliena is a good girl, I'll see to it that she does as you want her to.'

'I'd appreciate it, Uncle Botha. I've run out of patience with her.'

She put the elephant shoes under her bed and did not go back outside to say goodbye to the Reverend. She made the fire to boil sweet potatoes and pretended that she did not notice Oldman Botha come back into the house.

'You can't speak to the Reverend like that, Karoliena! I'm ashamed of you. Reverend says they will be yoking the first two wagons next Saturday, your clothes for the parade will be left with the church nurse. Please, Karoliena, I beg you to comply. The warden was here, he says this drought is the worst he has ever seen, and that two elephant cows almost killed a man at Deep Walls. The man was trying to photograph an elephant when three of them chased him. Fortunately, he dropped his camera and while they trampled it to pieces, he managed to get away. I told the warden it's the drought that's making the elephants so irritable. And then you arrive and announce that you intend to *make* an elephant! What must Reverend think? Not to mention all those lies about Elandskraal.'

'Forget about it, Uncle. They are stories I've heard.'

'Did you go to Abel Slinger?'

'Yes. The elephant shoes belong to him.'

'Throw them away!'

'No.'

'Karoliena!'

'Leave me alone, Uncle. I'm thinking.'

'What are you thinking?'

'How far one has to fall before one reaches the bottom.'

'Jesus!'

She soaked the elephant shoes right through the Tuesday night. On Wednesday morning they were soft. She tidied up the house and waited for a chance to get away.

'Why are you so restless, Karoliena?'

'If anything should happen to me, give the money in the drawer to my mother.'

'What nonsense are you talking? Nothing's going to happen to you, you are going to take part in the parade as the Reverend has instructed you. And you will fetch the dress from the church nurse.'

'Yes, Uncle.'

'If I was strong enough, I would have gone to the village myself on Saturday to have a look at my spokes. Gieljam says Jonker's two wagons are the most handsome he has ever seen. Gieljam himself now has a beard. I almost didn't recognise him yesterday when he came here with the Reverend, just before you got back. He says Freek Stander has been appointed to take charge of the oxen. Why are you so restless, Karoliena?'

'The water in the buckets will last until tomorrow.'

'That's not what I asked you.'

'I want to go to the forest.' She had to get the elephant shoes past him …

'I can see that your mind is somewhere else.'

'I want to go to the forest.'

'Why?'

'I don't know.'

'Karoliena!'

'Don't try to stop me, Uncle.'

She put the shoes in the knapsack and took the footpath that went north out of Kom's Bush to Velbroek's Road, because she felt it would take her deepest into the forest. And because the louries called from that side. And the elephants sometimes liked to go out to the hard road on the other side of Velbroek's Road. And the old people said the thick-legs had cleverly made a path through Pear Bush above Velbroek's Road, and because one of the tributaries of the Gouna River ran through Pear Bush there should still be some water there.

Then she remembered: you're not here to *look* for an elephant, but to *become* an elephant! Why? To feel how an elephant feels. Why? So I can take it with me if I have to leave the forest …

She knew deep down that she had already started to leave the forest, one step at a time. She knew this, although she did not know where she was going.

It was time to put the shoes on, but she was suddenly afraid. It was not the sort of fear you could run away from; it was more like the fear you experienced when you had climbed too high up a tree, and didn't know how to get down again.

Almost the first thing you were taught if you grew up in the forest was that you never – *never* – mocked an elephant.

She didn't want to mock an elephant. She would swear to that. She only wanted to feel what it was like to *be* an elephant. She was even prepared to exchange her greatest wish for it: to see the tree-spirit once more.

Mister Fourcade always said one should wish out loud: 'Please, Forest, take me and make me an elephant in exchange for the tree-spirit.'

The forest was dense and beautiful. No lourie gurgled or hissed to betray her to an elephant. She sat down in a place which had not yet been taken over by the drought, where the ferns were still brave and a wild chestnut stood decked in flowers; a glittering blue dragon-fly hovered at her feet; the Emperor butterflies played around the chestnut ...

She put on the shoes. Twisted the thongs once round her feet and fastened them with a knot. She felt strange when she stood up, and it frightened her. Don't imagine things, she told herself. She took a step forward, and it felt as if the earth rose through the shoes and into her body. Every stone, every twig, every dry leaf, every seed, every root. It was as if the earth had started to breathe with her. As if she had begun to follow a path through the forest that her eyes could not see, but that she felt with her entire being.

Slowly, the strangest things started to happen to her. All the fears she had ever known in her life rose up and out of her head. The fear, when she was small, that the night-adder would come into the house; the genet would come looking for its kitten; that her father and mother would find out she had done something wrong; fear that the lightning would fall from the sky and kill someone, fear of going to school, fear for the poor whites, of Wittedrift, of Miss Ann; the screeching of the sawmills when they ate up the trees; fear of Johannes and the Carnegie people, the wardens, the Reverend, the plantation ...

One by one her fears left her. She felt as if she had been cleansed and set free. She was good. She was a human being. As she walked through the forest in elephant feet happiness spread through her. She walked through the trees, up a hill, every step bringing a different fragrance: a gardenia was blooming somewhere; white elder-honey dripping from a bee's nest. Somewhere a genet slept. A wild pig, a bushbuck. A mouse was giving birth in a nest of leaves. A cross-berry was in flower. Toadstools that smelled like bread. Another chestnut. Butterflies that smelled of the earth. A wild honeysuckle was in blossom and the small blue butterflies that played around it smelled like milk.

There was a spirit in every tree, the human-elephant knew it even if she could not see them.

It was a magic forest, a dreamforest where life was a dream, even if you were awake.

A lourie in a quar tree started to hiss and gurgle angrily, jerking her back to earth and she almost stepped in the enormous footprint of an elephant in a patch of sand. A fresh print. A little way further on was a smaller footprint. A cow with a calf? She lifted her foot and put it down in the centre of the smaller print – then realised that she had stepped into the footprint of a cow. It had been a bull and a cow that had gone past.

The lourie gurgled and hissed, angrily.

She reached a stream and saw that the elephant footprints went through the water. She stopped, knowing that she must not follow them, but step into the footprint of the cow again and keep for ever the wonderful sense of fearlessness inside her – knowing what it was like to live in safety when the bull went out ahead of you pushing open the path and letting the forest close around you . . .

The utter peace.

A brown canary called loudly: Who are you – who are you?

I am Karoliena Kapp, an elephant cow who will never again be afraid of anything.

She sat down on the trunk of a windfall-tree and took off the shoes.

19

THE OLD MAN looked at her closely when she put the shoes outside the house to dry.

'Karoliena?'

'Don't talk to me, I'm still in the forest.' I'm still an elephant.

'Then I'll talk to myself. The church nurse was here, she brought the dress you must wear for the parade on Saturday when you are collecting money. It's on your bed. She's gone to Barnard's Island to see Elmina. The Reverend has found a place for Elmina in an institution; she must be given notice. The church nurse was in a hurry. She says the parade will start at ten o'clock sharp and the collectors must meet at nine – they will not wait for you if you are late.'

'I'm going to make the fire.'

'Karoliena, did you hear what I said?'

'Yes. I heard very well.'

'I promised the nurse I'd see that you got to the village, even if I have to drag you there with my poor old body!'

'That won't be necessary, Uncle.'

'Good. The nurse says the name of the institution where

they're taking Elmina is Karatara. I think it must be somewhere upcountry.'

'What about Samuel?'

'I was afraid to ask. Poor man.'

'Yes.'

A long pink dress with puffed sleeves and a white neckerchief with lace round the edges lay on the bed. A white poke-bonnet, white stockings, black lace-up shoes. At least the Voortrekkers had better clothes than the woodcutters.

She wouldn't be obstinate. She'd put on the clothes and do what they wanted her to. Later, when they came to take Oldman Botha away to Karatara, she'd quietly find herself a place to stay. Somewhere.

A timid little knock on the door, late that afternoon. It was Willempie, book and pencil in hand.

'Karoliena, your mother and my mother say you'll know because you're clever. I must hand in a composition at school tomorrow, but I can't find the right words. Will you please help me?'

'Come inside and sit at the table. What is the composition about?'

'We must write about why a Voortrekker festival is being held, but not one of us actually knows why. The teacher says it's to commemorate the Voortrekkers.'

'Sit down. How is your mother?'

'She cries in the night, I think it's because my father cut his throat.'

'Start writing: "A great festival is being held in our country in commemoration of the brave Voortrekkers. They began moving away in 1838 because they did not like the government . . ." '

'Don't go so fast!'

' "They moved away to look for a place where they could be free and happy, but all along the way they were killed by the people who were already living there. Consequently, they never reached the promised land." '

'Aren't you mixing this up with a Bible story?'

'Stories have a way of repeating themselves. Write: "Four stinkwood wagons have been made in Knysna to form part of a procession of wagons from Cape Town to Pretoria . . ." '

'My mother's going to take part in the festival. She is going to wear a long dress.'

'Write: "All the stinkwood for the wagons comes from the Knysna forest. The Voortrekkers are long dead. The trees as well, but they might still be living if the woodcutters had not cut them down, because trees live longer than humans." '

'I can't write that!'

'Then I don't know what you should write.'

'You're not helping.'

She got up early so that she would be in the village on time. Oldman Botha said the collectors had to meet at the church first, they would be given tins in which to collect the money.

She would not be wilful.

When she arrived at the church Amelia Claassens looked at her in astonishment. 'The Reverend was doubtful whether you'd turn up, Karoliena.'

She didn't say a word, just took the tin with the paper wrapped round it which said in big black letters: POOR RELIEF.

Many people had gathered along the street at the centre of the village, many of the women wearing long dresses, poke-bonnets and virtuous faces, pretending to be Voortrekkers. Men pretending to be Voortrekkers too, their faces behind bushy beards – it was difficult to recognise anyone. Here and there were a few ordinary forest people in ordinary forest clothes: shy, aloof and curious.

Ordinary village people mixed with them. Eyes stared at her in disbelief. 'Good heavens, aren't you Karoliena?'

Pennies, tickeys, sixpences fell into the hollow tin. Sometimes a shilling. Susanna, her cheeks painted red, wore a yellow dress that dragged through the dust; she kept rattling the tin in her hand.

Suddenly a cheer went up and everyone looked around to watch the horses and their riders coming down the street. On the first horse was the Reverend Odendaal, looking proud; beard, feather in his hat, corduroy trousers, blue neckerchief.

She wanted to go home …

Shortly after the horses had gone past, there was another cheer. She heard the lash of the whip and turned to watch. From Jonker's yard the first ox-wagon slithered into the street like a giant snake. Slow and stately. Pulled by a most beautiful span of raven-black oxen with huge white horns. The brand new wagon with Oldman Botha's spokes in the wheels going round and round. A proud Freek Stander was the driver; flicking the whip to this side and that. The son of a woodcutter from Gouna was leading the oxen in front, his head down. Four men sat on the back of the wagon, swinging their legs over the sides: Willem and Koos van Huysteen, each with a concertina; Martiens van Rooyen, son of Anna van Rooyen, and old Salie van Huysteen, each with a guitar. Beards, corduroy trousers, Martiens's dirty toes poking through his shoes. Right opposite the Standard Bank they began to play and a sudden, unexpected joyfulness changed the whole atmosphere of the festival.

People clapped their hands, money-tins clattered, people began spontaneously to dance, dust flying everywhere.

It became a real celebration.

Then the second wagon appeared from the yard. Old Daantjie Zeelie, bearded and wearing corduroy trousers, was driving fourteen red-speckled oxen. The leader was a boy from Veldmanspad. Women in Voortrekker dresses and poke-bonnets were sitting on the wagon, joyfully waving their arms in the air.

Karoliena stood beneath one of the oak trees in the Main Street and tried to find someone to give her tin to. She wanted to go home. Susanna came past, so she gave her the tin and started walking down the street with her.

'Isn't this wonderful?' Susanna was filled with excitement. 'I didn't know there would be so many people.'

They reached Miss Ann's boarding house and saw the old lady sitting on the veranda.

'You go on, Susanna. I want to have a word with this woman.'

'I think she's English,' Susanna warned her nervously.

'I know her.'

'Really?'

She climbed the steps to the veranda. 'Miss Ann?'

Recognition, surprise, even delight, shone in the woman's eyes. 'Karoliena – is it you?'

'Yes.' Miss Ann had grown old. Smaller. 'How are you, Miss Ann?'

'I'm well. And it's good to see you again, you look pretty in that costume. Come and sit with me for a moment.'

'Thank you.' Still the same dignified Miss Ann, only a little short of breath now. 'I'm also glad to see you again. I came to take part in the parade.'

'It is truly an important event for you Afrikaners,' Miss Ann said. Still the same slightly superior Miss Ann. 'And it's good for you to get out of the forest for a while. Don't you think the oxen were exceptionally fine looking? One can hardly imagine that animals so well looked after could come from the forest. They must surely have been borrowed from elsewhere.'

'The forest people usually look after their oxen.'

'A pity they don't look after themselves as well.' Still the air of haughtiness. 'A few are reasonably dressed, but most of them look like scarecrows. How are *you* doing in the forest?'

'Well.'

'I heard that you'd moved in with an old man. Is that true?'

'Yes.'

'How appalling. You were actually quite a sweet girl, but we simply could not get that wild streak out of you. I think there are days when Johannes still pines for you.'

Miss Ann was mistaken. 'Do you still take in boarders, Miss Ann?'

'No. One does not get any younger.'

'Can I make you some tea, Miss Ann?' The same shoes, the same dress.

'A pot of tea would be nice, we can have it here on the veranda. Use the cups with the gold rims.' The same old habit of talking down to you.

Nothing in the house had changed. It was like walking back into an old dream. But then she noticed that things had deteriorated. The dust. The tea cloths that had not been washed, the dirty kitchen floor. The musty smell.

Other pieces of the dream she could find only in her head: the bubble-cloth mat in front of the bed in the stoep-room. The framed mirror which had once held the reflection of a bride. She had known then that she would climb out of the mirror and run away.

But she would not one day sit on a veranda like Miss Ann, not knowing what it was like to be a tree. Or an elephant.

'Miss Ann,' she asked while they were having their tea, 'do you have someone to give you a hand in the house?'

'Old Maria comes on Fridays. But she is getting old and sickly now. Johannes seldom calls any more. After you left, he used to visit regularly. Do you ever see him?'

'Not often. He does not come to the forest very often and I am not often in the outside world.'

'What are you talking about, child?'

'Nothing. What else can I do for you, Miss Ann? Apart from washing the cups.'

'Nothing, thank you. You know, Karoliena, you really had potential – such a pity we could not get the forest out of you. If we had tried harder, you could have been a really smart woman today. But then, unfortunately, one is what one is, not so?'

'That's true, Miss Ann.'

'Perhaps that is why I pity you Afrikaners today. You are

celebrating the past while you know you have no future.'

'Perhaps it's just that the future is hidden from us. At least the past is something we know about. I'll go and wash the cups.'

'Will you be going to see Johannes as well?'

'No.' She wanted to go home. Storm clouds were gathering, the first distant rumblings of thunder echoed in the distance. 'The weather's working up, perhaps we'll get some rain.'

'Yes. Then the dust will turn to mud. I don't know which is worse.'

She had reached the hard road on the other side of Veldmanspad when the first large drops started to fall, sending little clouds of dust flying into the air as if the earth was shuddering with the forgotten wonder of it. The rain fell more heavily – on her head, on the poke-bonnet that was hanging on its ribbons down her back. Lightning lashed the forest, the rumbling of thunder became louder.

The Voortrekker dress turned a darker shade of pink with every drop of rain that fell on it; the hem dragging through the dust slowly turning to mud, the lace-up shoes on her feet flopping with every step because they were too big for her.

Rain. Water from heaven washing the drought from every leaf. The wonderful sound of it as it thrummed through the trees. High at first, it filtered down through the branches turning the leaves into gutters that drained the water so that the branches did not become too heavy. No call of a bird, not a gurgle or a hiss, not even a frog. It was as if everything was stunned with joy.

On the other side of Deep Walls station she took a footpath that led west through the glittering, wet-leafed forest and she begged the rain with all her heart to keep falling until everything had had a good drink. The forest floor was not soaked yet. She walked and walked, the dead leaves on the forest floor clinging to her shoes like little pieces of brown paper.

The next moment she stopped dead in her tracks. Through the rain, through the water streaming down her face, she saw it: the bunch of stalks hanging from the bark of a yellowwood tree right in front of her, long, narrow, pointed leaves on the tips of the stalks. Tiny white flowers, each on its own little stalk among the leaves. They were like small white bonnets with thin white braids neatly curling away. Little orchids. Some were still folded up against the stalks, others wide open as if they were smiling.

At first she thought the raindrops had stirred the little flowers, or perhaps it was the rain in her eyes. She wiped her eyes with the back of her hand … and realised that she was hardly breathing. She blinked. And blinked again.

Tiny white flower-spirits, vibrant and dainty, were rising from the orchids into the air, hovering above the wax-like petals. Tiny feet clung to the flowers for a moment – slipped back into the flower – rose again – mischievous little white spirits that came out to play in the rain. She could not take her eyes off them. They slipped back into the orchid at one moment, reappeared the next. They allowed her to watch as long as she wanted to, but her instinct told her to keep still. They were made of the same wax-like substance as the flowers, only perhaps thinner, more transparent. They seemed to be full of fun, as if they *wanted* her to see them properly, so that she would know she had not imagined them.

Magical small miracles. Little mysteries of the forest …

Then an elephant trumpeted somewhere between her and the road. In a flash, the orchids gulped back the little spirits. Gone. As if the elephant had frightened them.

She waited, but they did not come out again.

A lourie started to hiss and gurgle somewhere. He was warning the elephant that she was there.

The little flower-spirits had been vivid and real. Not her imagination. Not a dream either.

Suddenly the whole forest world was a miracle! She knew

now that it was not only *her* Tree that had a spirit within him …

She could not move. Dripping and stunned, she stood still in front of the yellowwood.

Not her imagination.

Not a dream.

And Mister Fourcade wasn't there to see it, he had gone to Cape Town.

Oldman Botha was sitting at the table, waiting for her. The house was filled with happiness because of the rain.

'The tank's overflowing. Go and dry yourself, Karoliena, it's a borrowed dress you're wearing. Where did you find the rain?'

'Shortly after the station.'

'Why didn't you take shelter?'

'I wanted to get home.'

'How was the festival?'

'Lots of people. Beautiful wagons, beautiful oxen, your spokes neatly in place.'

'Did you collect any money?'

'I did. I gave my tin to Susanna.'

'Did you see the Reverend?'

'Yes. On a horse.'

She answered without thinking. Because her head was full of flower-spirits.

She was no longer afraid of anything.

Elephants were not afraid.

She knew that she had turned around without realising it. And without knowing where she would go.

20

ALMOST A YEAR later, the plantation lorry stopped on the road below the house to pick up Oldman Botha and his few possessions.

'Don't cry so, Karoliena.'

'I'm not crying, Uncle. It's just that the tears won't stop running from my eyes.'

There wasn't much space for Oldman Botha and his things on the back of the lorry. Her mother and Uncle Cornelius and their furniture had already been loaded. Most of the tears were for them – two frightened old people on the back of the lorry who had died without anyone noticing.

No, she did not regret having thrown the piece of ironwood at the Reverend when he came to tell her that her mother and Uncle Cornelius would also be moved to Karatara in accordance with the Welfare Act.

'Why?'

'In order to qualify for a pension, as you should know. The government is going to close the forest, Karoliena. The time of the woodcutter and the forest worker has come to an end.'

'You bastards!' She could not stop herself, she was too angry.

He had brought Oldman Botha back to the house after the communion service at Veldmanspad. He had come specially to tell her that her mother and Uncle Cornelius were also going to be moved. She picked up the piece of wood and flung it at him. It hit him on the side of the head. He cried out in horror: Are you mad? She saw the blood oozing through his thin grey hair, and she didn't say a word.

The week after that she went to Long Marsh Forest and said what had to be said. They had been told nothing yet.

Karatara? Where's that? The only Karatara in the forest is a bloody river. Are we supposed to go and drown ourselves now?

No, Ma.

Then the church nurse came and told Oldman Botha that he would be moved there as well. Unfortunately, he wouldn't be given one of the little welfare houses, there were too many other people needing houses. However, room would be made for him in the old people's home that Welfare was building at Karatara. He had to supply his own bed as well as a small cupboard for his clothes. No, no implements. No, not even his adze.

When Amelia Claassens left, she walked with her to the horse-cart.

'Don't fret so, Karoliena. Things have to change because they cannot continue as they are. The forest people have gone too far downhill.'

'I'm not fretting. I'm just angry with the planners. Long ago I told Oldman Botha that it felt as if the world was falling over. Now that it's *really* falling, you simply fall with it, while trying to keep your footing.'

'I find it strange that you are managing to survive in the forest after all this time.'

'I can quite believe you.' She looked the woman in the eye and said without speaking: In the mean time you're trying hard to get Johannes. The woman heard her.

'What are you going to do when Oldman Botha moves?'

'I haven't decided.' I think you're hoping I will disappear. You're getting grey – like Johannes.

'You realise, of course, that you will not be allowed to move to Karatara with him.'

'Amelia, I'm not as stupid as you think I am.'

Amelia's neck reddened with annoyance.

The next time she came to visit Oldman Botha, she had a motor car which she drove with bent elbows, clinging to the steering wheel for dear life. Welfare had provided the car.

'You know, Amelia, I've been wondering how much money was collected for the poor during the Voortrekker festival,' she said, deliberately trying to provoke her. Not a word had been heard about the money or what had happened to it.

'If you bothered to go to church sometimes, you would have known, because it was announced during one of the services. A total of forty-three pounds was collected.'

'Who got the money?'

'Ask the Reverend.'

'The Reverend does not speak to me any more.'

'Do you blame him?'

'No.'

'Then at least you're thinking straight now.'

The day after the festival Mister Fourcade arrived from Cape Town and the muddy day turned it into a truly happy day even though it was still raining.

It rained for four days.

Only when the rain had stopped, was she able to take him to see the little orchids, hoping in her heart that the flower-spirits would again appear. So he would believe her.

There were even more of the floppy stems covered in little orchids hanging from the yellowwood's bark, but there were no little spirits. Mister Fourcade was astonished and overjoyed. He lightly touched the little flowers with his fingers – tried to teach her the plant's proper name, and gave up.

'You did not really come to show me the orchids, Karoliena.'

'I did. And at the same time I wanted to get you out of the house because Oldman Botha would not stop talking.'

He looked at her closely. 'You're different, Karoliena.'

'Yes, I am.'

'Why?' His eyes were full of questions.

'I think I have grown up – even if that sounds a little silly.' She suddenly knew that there were things she could not tell even Mister Fourcade. Not about the day she was a stinkwood tree, not about the day she was an elephant, nor about the day she'd seen the orchid-spirits. It seemed that some mysteries lay too deep in one's heart, and they didn't want one to think about them too often. Only to *know* that they were there.

'What is going to happen to you when Oldman Botha has to get out of his house, Karoliena?'

'I don't want to think about it yet. But I do feel that the forest has started to push me out.'

'Then you *have* grown up.'

'Yes.'

'Will you go back to Johannes, if I may ask?'

'Johannes does not want me back.'

'Mister Ferndale says you brought him quite a few moths during the year, but he would very much like to get more.'

'That's right, but he doesn't want to pay more.' Not that it bothered her much. Oldman Botha's pension helped to keep the house running. Forestry had stopped paying him, although the wardens still came knocking at his door to ask his advice. The trees being replanted by the new research man, Mister Laughton, kept dying.

'Promise me one thing, Karoliena,' Mister Fourcade said. 'Promise me you'll always stay as you are, no matter where you go.'

'How am I?'

'I don't really know, Karoliena.'

That was the last time she saw Mister Fourcade.

To her immense shock, early in February that year when she went to catch the first moths she found that both the keurboom trees had been cut down. Wood splinters and trampled undergrowth and a new gap in the forest roof was all that was left.

When she got home Oldman Botha told her not to upset herself too much; there were many other keurboom trees in the forest. There was a huge one on the side of the road at Velbroek's Road, and she would not even have to go into the forest to reach it.

She went to look for the tree. Someone had cut it down as well.

The one in Fork Bush too.

She went to the forestry station at Deep Walls and asked one of the wardens why so many keurboom trees had suddenly been cut down. He said: Don't worry about it, there are plenty of young ones coming up. Farmers were looking for keurboom poles and the woodcutters were more than happy to supply them.

One Sunday she went to see how Hestertjie Vermaak's child was, she had heard that he had whooping cough. When she got there, the yard looked worse than ever. But the old woman was wearing a new hat, and old Anneries was lying on his back in the shade. There was food cooking under the shelter. Bundles of poles, tied with thongs, lay next to the house.

'And this?' she asked. They were keurboom poles.

The old woman answered. 'Luck sometimes falls upon the poor too – not only on people like you. A man from Oudtshoorn pays Anneries three shillings a wagonload.'

'How many in a load?'

'Two thousand,' the old man answered. 'But fortunately for us, Forestry looks the other way when we cut keurboom.'

It was the beginning of March before she found a decent moth-tree again; a full-grown one full of little moth-lids. It was growing a little way into the forest just before Barnard's Clearing.

She fetched Samuel, Elmina Vlok's husband, and said to him: Do you see this keurboom tree? Yes. Then listen to me carefully: This is my tree, anyone who touches it with an axe, is dead. He stood there, his eyes blank, and asked: Who are you? She said: Karoliena. Look after the tree for me and I promise to bring you sweets when next I go to the village. His eyes lit up. Sugar sticks, he said, those with the stripes around them.

She took Mister Ferndale the first four moths. He said he urgently needed more to send overseas to a man who wanted to prove that the nearest relative of the ghost moth of the Knysna forest was found in Australia. When would she bring him more?

She bought Samuel's sugar sticks and when she got to Barnard's Clearing in the late afternoon she found him sleeping under the tree. He jumped up, bewildered, shouted at her to go away because the tree had already been sold! She handed him the bag of sweets and calmed him down. At first he just stood there – then a glimmer of recollection broke through and he started stuffing the sweets into his mouth.

'Thank you for looking after the tree, Samuel. You may go home now.'

Because it was still a few hours before the moths would start to come out, she decided to walk home with him. It was more out of curiosity to see how Elmina and the 'baby' were doing. And to find out whether it was true what people were saying – that the doll had more clothes than many a forest child and that Elmina bathed and dressed it several times a day.

According to Amelia and the Reverend, Elmina and Samuel would be amongst the first to be moved to Karatara when the woodcutters' pensions took effect.

'And what about the doll?' she asked Amelia that day, intentionally provocative.

'That, Karoliena, was *your* foolishness with which we now

have to deal. At this stage, I suppose the thing will have to go with them.'

Samuel walked into the house first. It was dirty and unkempt, but not as bad as it used to be. Elmina was giving the 'baby' a bath on the bed in the second room – the doll from which the paint had long ago been washed, pale-faced and without eyebrows or lips. The care with which the simple-minded woman was washing the lifeless thing was more tragic than funny.

'How are you, Elmina?'

'Good. We are moving.'

'Where to, Elmina?'

'Don't know. They'll come and fetch us. Lots of space for the child to play, says the other nurse.'

It was dark by the time she lit the lantern and took the footpath to the keurboom to catch the moths. Two males and two females.

She took them to the village on foot the next day.

'Will you be sleeping in the village tonight?' Oldman Botha wanted to know when she left in the morning.

'No. On my way back I want to call on Abel Slinger to give back the elephant shoes.'

'I'll be glad to get those things out of my yard. One never knows when the elephants will smell them and come and trample my house.'

'I thought you said Forestry was going to come and break down the house.'

'Don't make fun of me, Karoliena. At least the thick-legs are back in the deep forest since the rain, they no longer come and lie in the road and stop the cars. Why don't you rather take the train from Deep Walls?'

'No.' Then she would get to the village too late and she didn't want to have to ask Amelia Claassens for a place to sleep. Never again. Because she never wanted to see Johannes's motor car in front of her house again. Another riddle she couldn't explain – suddenly Johannes was always on her mind ...

She delivered the moths. Mister Ferndale wanted to know whether there was a chance of a dwarf chameleon? No.

Old Bella was waiting for her outside the mole-house.

'Abel said he saw you coming. Yesterday already. He's lying down, says he has to take note of what he sees.

The old man was lying in a corner in a huge cloth-case filled with bedding-bush. He was nothing but skin and bones. And wrinkles.

'I believe the woodcutters are going to be given pensions.'

'Yes, Uncle.'

'White people have always been better than Hottentot people. Inside the forest, outside the forest.'

'Yes, Uncle.' What else could she say? Other than borrow some of his own words: *That is how it is, how it has always been*. Even if she did not understand what they meant. She asked if there was anything she could do for him.

'Not really. Susanna who lives with your mother has promised to look after Bella when the angels come to fetch me.'

'I'm glad of that.'

'The church nurse was here; she said the woodcutters were going to be taken to Elandskraal. Unfortunately there wasn't room for me and Bella. I asked her why she would think we wanted to go and stay *there*? We might be brown, but we're not brainless. Bella still catches a buck in a trap now and then, your mother sends cattle food with Susanna.'

'What cattle food?'

'Vegetables. Sometime a few sweet potatoes. I see you will be leaving the forest.'

'Oldman Botha has to leave his house. Can you perhaps see which way I'm going?'

'No. One goes where one has to go, no use trying to take some other way. You'll simply be driven back to where you should go.'

'I must leave now. I've brought back the elephant shoes.'

'Good.'

The week after that a warden came to say that old Abel had died in his sleep.

She went to see Bella. The old woman was sitting quietly outside the house. No outward sign of grief. She said the warden had brought two men to bury Abel. They started digging a grave, but she stopped them and said: Not there by the wild olive tree. Lay him down over there at the dogwood tree and lay him down deep, the Englishmen must not find the place and dig up his skeleton. Your mother came, she brought a few flowers. I told her: I don't eat flowers. What's in the bag you've got in your hand?

A piece of meat and some griddle breads.

That cheered her.

Buy me a tin of flour when you go to the shop again.

I'll do so, Bella.

You're rich. Some fat from the butcher's shop as well.

Yes, Bella.

A little sugar and coffee too …

When she left, Bella continued to shout after her, telling her what else she wanted.

Oldman Botha was sitting on the tree stump outside the door when she got home. He was looking very pleased with himself. The warden had been to tell him that news had come that the wagons from Knysna had reached Cape Town safely. Thousands of people came to bid them farewell and to offer their prayers, and now they were on their way north. I'm telling you, Karoliena, he said, it will be a long trek. But our wagons will not fall behind. Their wheels have *my* spokes in them.

Yes, Uncle.

The following month the plantation lorry fetched him and his meagre possessions.

The pensions were paid out to the woodcutters two days before.

The first night that she spent alone in the little plank house it felt as if someone had died there. It was an ending. Of something. Of everything. Of the part of her life that started the day she left Johannes. Before that day she had been a different Karoliena Kapp. After that day she became yet another Karoliena – and now she was going to look for a place where she could once more become a new Karoliena.

If she could be granted one wish, it would be that the Forestry Department would grant her a year's grace to stay on in the little house …

She was awoken by a knock on the door. When she opened her eyes, she saw that it was already light. It was Hestertjie's older sister at the door. No longer a child, but a rather lost young girl beset with adult anxiety.

'What's the matter?' At least she would not have come to ask for money, Hestertjie's child had long been off the bottle.

'Ma is having fainting fits.'

'When did this start?'

'Yesterday. The warden sent word that the lorry would fetch us and take us to Elandskraal today. Ma says she does not want to go and live there, but the church nurse went to great trouble to get permission for all of us to go. Now Ma's started fainting. Hestertjie says you must come and help us. Pa started walking to Elandskraal before dawn. He's on pension now.'

'Tell Hestertjie I can't come. I have to go to Veldmanspad.'

'You can't abandon us now, Karoliena. Ma keeps falling.'

'You said the church nurse was going to find you work in the village. Did she?'

'Yes. But Ma says it's not necessary that I go and work for the rich because we have the pension now.'

'Go and tell your ma she must stop falling. The lorry will not pick her up and nor will it wait for her.'

'You're rude.'

'No. I've just run out of pity.'

She had to leave the forest. She knew that.

She walked to Veldmanspad and asked Wiljam Stander how much he'd charge to take her to Elandskraal in his motor car.

'It's a long way, and petrol is expensive.'

'How much?'

'Why are they moving the people *that* far away? I believe they call the place Karatara now.'

'How much?'

'The road is bad.'

'How much?'

'I can't take you for less than ten shillings.'

She turned around. 'Then I'll walk.'

'Wait! Perhaps we can agree on five shillings. Times are bad.'

'Agreed.'

Whether it was called Elandskraal or Karatara, she knew she had to go there to see how Oldman Botha was getting on. Her mother and Uncle Cornelius too.

The last time she had spoken to the Reverend was after the last service he conducted at Veldmanspad, shortly before the lorry had fetched Oldman Botha and taken him to Karatara.

She told Oldman Botha early that morning that she was going to church. The old man stared at her in astonishment. Why? he asked. She said she wanted to talk to the Reverend about the pensions for the woodcutters. The old man was immediately alarmed. He warned: Karoliena, don't pick up a snake and then come crying that it bit you!'

'I simply want to ask him for the truth.'

'Karoliena, I know you're going to make trouble! Leave the Reverend alone, he's anointed.'

'One has to find out what one doesn't know, Uncle.'

'You must believe like a child, Karoliena!'

'I'm not a child.'

After the service, she waited for the Reverend at his motor car. He got into the car, clearly wanting to drive away and pretend that he had not seen her. She knocked on the door of the car. He got out; apparently she did not realise that he was angry.

'Yes, Karoliena? I'm glad to see that you've been in church for a change.'

'I'm here because you are the best one to ask for the truth about the woodcutters' pensions, Reverend.'

'Please, Karoliena, not today.'

There was still a mark on his hairline where the ironwood had struck him. 'I only want to know the truth, Reverend.'

'What truth?' He was annoyed, but had to pretend to be patient and agreeable because many of those who had attended the service were watching them with interest.

'The truth about the woodcutters' pensions. Oldman Botha was granted an *old-age* pension, what kind of pension are the woodcutters going to get?'

'The same value – twenty-five pounds a year. From the first of April. From that day there will be no more woodcutters in the forest, because they will all be deregistered on that day. Now listen carefully!'

As he grew angrier she became calmer. 'According to one of the wardens at Deep Walls there are two hundred and forty woodcutters. Only twenty-five have been put on pension. What about the others?'

'If you've been to ask the warden, why come and ask me? On a Sunday too?'

'That's why I came to church. I wanted to ask you.'

'I thought seeing you in church was too good to be true.'

'What about all the others?'

'Have you come to ask or to make trouble?'

'I have to know.'

'The first twenty-five are those who are feeble in body or mind; they will be given what one could call pension on compassionate grounds. Others over sixty-five will receive an old-age pension. But everyone who is still able to work will be employed by the Forestry Department as plantation workers, day labourers or ordinary labourers. They will become employees of the state and will – over and above their pensions – be compensated for their labour.'

'By whom?'

'By the state. From now on *all* wood belongs to the state.'

'How much will the compensation be?'

'A shilling a day – foremen up to one and sixpence a day. It is extra income for them.'

'So now they become slaves of the state instead of slaves of the wood-buyers.'

'Have you come to make trouble?'

'No, Reverend.' I should have thrown the ironwood harder.

'Good. Promise me then that you'll stay as far away from Karatara as possible.'

She should have listened.

If Wiljam Stander had not assured her every so often that they would get there, she would have sworn they never would. They first had to get to Gouna, then down White Place Rise to cross the Gouna River. Then up a shallow gorge till they reached the Knysna River at the point where it had already started to flow into the lagoon. Then through the long drift.

She asked Wiljam if he was sure he was on the right road. Yes. Sit tight, Phantom Pass is up ahead.

'Something does not make sense, Uncle. According to Johannes, it is a day's walk from Karatara to Knysna. The route you're taking would be *three* days' walk!'

'There is a short cut from Karatara, but it's only for feet, not for motor cars.'

Uphill. Downhill. Uphill, downhill. Zig-zagging down a forest slope. It was a dreadful journey. Then the iron bridge across the Homtini River …

Until, finally, they were there.

An enormous empty plain at the foot of a mountain where the little houses stood in a wide circle like lost children holding hands in desperation. The white-washed houses with red corrugated iron roofs looked like square toadstools which had sprung up from the black earth. There was a large, square grey building in the centre. A surly woman opened the door on to grey passages, grey people. It smelled of pee. Oldman Botha was in one of the grey rooms. He was like a living ghost lying on his wooden bed covered with a grey blanket. He gave a cry of anguish when he recognised her. Grabbed her arm with a dead man's hand.

'Karoliena! I knew you'd come to fetch me and take me home.' A skeleton who tried desperately to sit up. A tree that had been cut down. Even if one could get him up, he would never grow again.

She didn't want to see it, she wanted to turn away.

In the room next door Samuel was sitting on a chair with his hat on. Elmina was on the bed with the doll wrapped in a blanket.

It was too late to let the doll die.

She had to get away …

Two rooms further down the passage, Anna van Rooyen was lying on a narrow iron bed; a bubble-mat on the floor in front of the bed was like a silent testimony that the woman had once been alive.

At least the elephants had a secret place where they went to die. They were not tossed on a scrap heap by other elephants.

She *had* to get away.

Uncle Cornelius was standing in front of one of the little houses on the western side of the wide circle of houses. He tried to be brave. Said the soil looked good and he was trying to decide where he'd start digging and planting so that it would not look so bare. The man at the office said wire fences would be put up around the houses. Yes, her mother was inside.

Meliena Kapp was sitting on a bench in the small curtainless front room.

'Karoliena!' She sounded like one who has unexpectedly seen her chance of deliverance. 'Karoliena, my child, my only hope left on earth!'

'I paid Uncle Wiljam to bring me.'

'You've got to take us back with you. Plank houses breathe, brick houses don't, we're suffocating here. Just look where they've dumped us! God will punish them for it. A man with a horse has gone to look for Salie van Huysteen, he simply walked off, said he's not staying here. Martjie was here a while ago, she's out of her mind with worry. We'll go with you in Wiljam's motor car.'

She knew she must not look back; not with her eyes, not with her mind. Just get into the car and leave before the toppling world knocked *her* off her feet.

They had hardly left when Wiljam had to swerve to make way for the plantation lorry. Hestertjie Vermaak and her mother sat in front with the driver, bouncing up and down. The two sisters were on the back with the child. Old Anneries too. They must have picked him up along the way.

They were almost home when Wiljam remarked: 'Karoliena, you've hardly said a word. I don't blame you. There's really nothing there except the little houses on that empty plain. No wonder they've reserved a large piece of ground for a cemetery, they're sure to die fast there.'

'It felt like the place where the road ends.' She didn't want to talk, just wanted to get home and keep her footing.

She would take some of the moth-money to buy groceries for her mother, go back and help to make the house a little more cheerful . . .

21

ONE SURELY EXPERIENCES only once in one's life the shock of finding that one's house is gone – no longer standing where it had been when you left it that morning.

Wiljam Stander was equally shocked. 'And *this*, Karoliena?' he cried out when he stopped the car in the road at Jim Reid's Crossing. Where Oldman Botha's house had stood there was only a bare patch against the edge of the forest. Her bed, the table and chairs, the cupboard and the crockery, the small kitchen cupboard, the wash-basin, the water buckets – all were standing alongside the road. Her clothes, blankets and pillows were stacked in a bundle on top of the table.

You don't actually die of shock. Your mind and your body die for only a moment, then you start breathing again and absorbing whatever it is that has caused the shock. Mocking words echoed through her mind with every step she took towards her abandoned belongings: The forest is not *pushing* you out, Karoliena, it is *throwing* you out.

It was no dream. It was harsh reality.

It was a picture of desolation, the place where Oldman Botha had once had his home and had one day invited her in.

'Jesus, Karoliena, what's happened here?' Wiljam asked behind her.

'Forestry said they'd come and pull down the house.'

'Why today? What are you going to do? How are you going to move all this stuff?'

'Just leave it. Go home, I need to think.'

'I can't just leave you here; this is a terrible business – just look at it! I can offer you two shillings for the water buckets and wash-basin. And perhaps I can buy the bed and the table too.'

'Leave it. We can talk about it tomorrow.' His voice seemed far away, she didn't want to hear him.

'It's as though you've been stranded in the middle of the road. You must be strong, Karoliena. What are you going to do?'

'I don't know, I need to think.' She didn't want to look at his shocked face. She wanted to be alone.

When he drove away, she sat down on the bare mattress on the bed. She was thirsty, but the water tank was gone. She was grateful that Oldman Botha had not seen it. That only she could feel the unearthly stillness around her. Not a bird. Not a breeze. Not even a frog. Perhaps the forest did not hate everyone, perhaps it even felt sorry for some of them. Oldman Botha had never harmed anyone.

When the tears began to fall, she wiped her face with her dress and let the solitude envelop her and everything around her. She knew she had fallen hard, and she wanted to lie down and rest for a moment.

On the other side of the road a lourie landed silently to roost on the branch of a yellowwood.

It was too late in the day for her to start walking to the village.

Why to the village?

Where else?

To find a place to sleep and to stay.

Where? *Don't think about it …*

Her heart knew where, but her head was not ready to acknowledge it. She wondered how long it would be before the shock went away.

The bed was right in the middle of the elephants' path. She must drag the mattress into the undergrowth, take a blanket and a pillow …

Some time during the night she woke up, instantly alert, and knew there was only one place for her to go.

To Johannes.

Please, God – *if* there was a God somewhere – don't let him turn me away.

She did not hear them coming. It was only when she heard the loud rumbling of an elephant's stomach that she knew they were there. Between her and the place where the house had stood. Elephants walking on their own path to Kom's Bush. She knew they would not trample her.

22

ONE FEELS DIFFERENT when one puts on a new dress. So does a village.

Although she did not immediately understand why the village felt different. She wished she still had the church-suitcase so that she need not arrive at Johannes's door like a beggar with a bundle.

The village was still waking up.

And she was getting scared.

She had not stopped falling yet.

The fall into the outside world had only just begun. Years ago she had not adapted to life there. Then she ran away. It had not been *her* in the mirror in Miss Ann's stoep-room. She found herself again only when she moved into Oldman Botha's little house in the forest …

The first placard was nailed up on an oak tree along the street: *Don't miss the greatest adventure of all time!* said the big black letters. Apparently no one had noticed that the tree was in pain because of the nails. On the next tree another placard: *Your country needs volunteers!* The next one was attached to a lamp post: *World outraged – Germany on side of Soviet*.

Something strange was happening, and it made the whole village feel different.

Her feet began to drag. What would she do if Johannes turned her away?

She had almost reached Miss Ann's boarding house when she saw the old woman sweeping the stoep. If she turned quickly …

But Miss Ann had seen her.

'Good heavens, Karoliena, what are you doing in the village at this time of the morning?'

'Good morning, Miss Ann. I left the forest early.' Invite me in. Please.

'And that bundle you're carrying?'

'Just things.' Ask me to come inside so that I can postpone Johannes a little longer. 'How are you, Miss Ann?'

'I'm well, thank you.'

'Do you still have that nice mirror in the frame that used to stand in the stoep-room?'

'Yes. Why do you ask?'

'I just wondered.'

'Is there something wrong, Karoliena?'

'No.' Wiljam Stander had given her three pounds for her few possessions; he was probably already carting them home to Veldmanspad. And she had nowhere to stay. 'Would you mind if I had a look at the mirror again?'

'I was offered five pounds for it last month, the frame is made of yellowwood and stinkwood.'

Invite me in. 'Are you going to sell it?'

'No,' she said indignantly, 'but you're welcome to look at the mirror, I've just unlocked the room. I can't leave it open as I used to because people have begun to steal things.'

The moment she stood in front of the mirror, she felt as if she was standing on the edge of an old abyss which she knew was very deep. If she fell, she would die. Perhaps some nightmares never went away – because they had not been dreamed through to the end?

The next moment she saw that it was *she* who looked back at her from the mirror. Unmistakably. Her entire being, even if she was wearing her old clothes. She also realised that she was standing on the bridge between the forest and the outside world and that there were bridges that one should not cross too quickly.

And that she had nothing to hold on to.

'Karoliena, are you sure there is nothing wrong?' Miss Ann asked suspiciously from the doorway.

'It is strange for me to be standing in front of this mirror again.'

'I can believe that. You were such a beautiful bride ...'

Then she noticed the bubble-mat on the floor next to the bed. Don't cry, she told herself. But although she held back the tears, she could not stop the crying inside – for Anna van Rooyen, for her own sadness, for everyone in Elandskraal's little houses. But mostly for Oldman Botha.

'Why are you staring so in the mirror, Karoliena?'

'I just am.'

'You've always been a strange one. It was a pity you could not adapt to life in the village. You were a pretty girl, and you're even prettier now, despite being so neglected. We did what we could at the time, and so did Johannes. But he didn't realise that people are what they are.'

'That's true.' She would not blame him if he no longer wanted her.

'Times have changed, Karoliena. The world is facing dark times. I take it that even the forest people have heard that war has broken out?'

'What do all the placards along the street mean?'

'It's *war*, Karoliena!'

'War about what? One placard mentions a great adventure – since when was war adventure?'

'You wouldn't understand. I doubt if you even know what the word *adventure* means.'

'It's an interesting event.'

'I suppose one could put it that way, yes. Smuts is a brilliant man. And he says we have no choice, we will have to fight on England's side against the Germans and the Italians if we don't want them to invade us too. Hitler is dangerous man. Hertzog is a fool, he wants us to remain neutral, which means we will be leaving a door open for Hitler to get to us.'

'Doors are always left open, Miss Ann. The forest has been closed now, but for many years the government saw to it that a door remained open to the wood-buyers by doing nothing to stop the exploitation of the woodcutters. The door had to remain open so that money continued to roll into the state treasury!'

'I doubt whether you have your facts right, Karoliena. Come, let me pour you some coffee, you seem to need it.'

'Thank you.' Careful, I'm an elephant and elephants know their facts.

The fire was already burning in the stove and steam rose from the spout of the coffee-kettle.

'I believe they have at last made a plan to remove the remaining woodcutters from the forest, and that they will be given a state pension,' said Miss Ann.

'Yes.'

'I'm glad for their sake. Perhaps they'll have nothing to complain about now.'

'You do not know all the facts.'

'You can tell me nothing about them, Karoliena. Almost all my life I've watched them passing my house with their wagon-loads of wood from the forest. They look the same as they did sixty years ago. No sign of progress! As I said, you are what you are – no matter what mirror you look in.'

'You would not understand, Miss Ann.'

'Help yourself to coffee.'

'Thank you.'

'And tell me what you're really doing in the village.'

Would she tell her the truth? 'I've come to see if Johannes will take me back.'

Disbelief spread over the old woman's face. 'How can you expect him to do such a thing?' she cried. 'After all these years!'

'I have nowhere else to go.'

'If you're prepared to work for food and a bed …'

'No, I'm not.'

The first knock was too soft – no one answered the door. Her heart was pounding as she knocked again, harder this time.

Johannes himself came to the door – towel over his shoulder, shaving-soap on his face. The impatience in his eyes vanished the moment he saw it was her, to be replaced by startled disbelief. 'Karoliena?'

'Don't ask why I'm here, just invite me in. Miss Ann is standing in the middle of the street to see whether or not you're going to chase me away.'

'Karoliena?' The frown between his eyes deepened. He hurriedly wiped his face with the towel. 'Is something wrong?'

'Forestry has demolished Oldman Botha's house. I have nowhere to go.'

A look of surprise lit his face, turning into something more like joy. 'Come. Come inside.' The words took her by the hand and welcomed her into the house. He closed the door behind her.

'I'm sorry about the bundle. I could only take what I could carry. My blanket, some clothes.' His mouth distorted as if he was grinding his teeth. 'Please, don't send me away.'

'One does not send a miracle away.'

'If you are involved with another woman, I'll understand.'

'*You* are my woman.' Magical, merciful words. Salvation.

But something about him was different. He was distracted; she could see it by the way he hesitated about what to do next – called the servant to take her bundle and to tell the woman to lay an extra place at the breakfast table. Said he had to go and open the shop first – and had to finish shaving.

'Come, sit in the lounge in the mean time.' As if he was saying: Don't disappear, I need time to recover from the shock.

Relief flooded her, almost paralysed her.

The house was unchanged. The little stinkwood table in which she hid the wedding money was still standing in the passage. She walked into the lounge. A wireless had been installed in a corner. A one-eyed creature, staring blindly into the room. Johannes came back.

'I see you've acquired a wireless. They've got one at the forestry station now too.'

'In times like this, one has to know what's going on in the world. Why don't you sit down?'

'I'm afraid to.' Don't cry. 'I'm afraid I might have to get up again.'

'Not if you promise not to run away.' It was not a reproach, more like an urgent but cautious plea for reassurance.

'There is nowhere I can run to, other than to crawl in under the cliffs of the Red Alder River.'

'Don't say that. I've never stopped believing that you would one day come to your senses, Karoliena.'

'I don't know if I've come to my senses, I only know that you are the only chance I have in life.' Don't come closer, don't touch me, I don't want to fall in front of you.

'Karoliena, you have brought salvation to me where I thought there was none. You'll understand when I explain.'

'Don't explain now. Rather give me something to eat, please. I can't remember when last I ate.' There was the same restlessness in him that she had noticed the day he had carried the water bucket for her in the forest. Even more, perhaps. He was a completely different Johannes from the one who had dropped her off at Miss Ann's boarding house all those years ago.

She waited until they were sitting at the breakfast table before she asked: 'What is it that is causing you such concern, Johannes?'

He first tapped with a silver spoon on the shell of a boiled egg in a porcelain egg-cup. Picked up the starched white table napkin …

'The war, Karoliena, is going to shatter our lives!'

The anxiety in his voice made her think of the wall of a dam that was close to breaking. She did not know this Johannes. But she had not forgotten how handsome he was.

'Miss Ann mentioned something about the war.'

'I will have to enlist.'

'Enlist?'

'Yes. And I can no longer give my support to Werdt – do you remember him?'

'Very well.'

'I cannot support him in his demand that a referendum be held to decide whether or not we join the war, that we should support Hertzog's policy of neutrality for the country. Werdt is a fool. I support Smuts.'

I have no idea what you're talking about.

'Your food is getting cold.' Sausage, bacon, fried tomatoes. Real bread. Real food.

'If we don't fight for our freedom, we will succumb to the level of slaves of Russia and to the malevolence of Hitler! A recruiting office will most probably be opened in the village next week. All over the country volunteers are queuing up to enlist; if we don't join the war, we will never be free again.'

Don't get so agitated. He did not hear her.

'My mother and Uncle Cornelius have also been moved to Karatara.'

'We hope that some of the younger forest people will join; ordinary soldiers are paid five shillings a day and will be sent to Oudtshoorn for training. Do you understand why I have no choice but to enlist?'

'I'm trying to understand.' The forest brought me up, and the forest is a place of peace, not war …

'If we do not put a halt to the evil, it will not go well for the country, for the whole world!'

'Fortunately, the forest has been closed and is safe.'

'The forest has an important part to play. Knysna depends on its wood, on the sawmills and furniture factories.'

'Where are the wood-buyers going to find wood? There are no longer any woodcutters.'

'Fortunately, the government has anticipated the demand. Forestry is in the process of reorganisation, they cut and sell themselves now and the industries are well supplied with wood. Alex Wilson says the timber train has never transported as much wood as it is doing at the moment.'

'I know a story about three brothers. One of them is named Smart and he is the one who makes plans in the darkness.'

'The time for stories is over, Karoliena. We have to look at reality!' As if he wanted to *ram* it into her head.

Don't try to scare me. I'm an elephant and elephants are not afraid.

After breakfast she went to the spare bedroom and untied her bundle on the bed. Put her things away in the wardrobe. Pretended she did not see him at the door every so often. Not speaking, just making sure she was really there.

One of the servants brought her a huge towel and said her bath was ready. Hot water. The greatest wonder of the outside world. He came to the door and said that her clothes were still in the main bedroom.

But she did not want to see those clothes again, much less wear them.

She wandered through the house, lingered in the yard, rested the whole day.

When they sat down for supper, she ignored his disappointment that she was wearing one of her old dresses.

It was a little bit of the old Johannes who sat opposite her at the table.

'How are the people adapting to Karatara? Your mother in particular.'

'Like discards.'

'Isn't that a bit harsh?'

'No.'

'When they had to cut wood, they complained. Now that the state has made provision for them, they still find fault.'

'We can't see into the hearts of others.'

'I wish I could see into *your* heart, Karoliena.'

'Why?'

'To understand how you really feel, what you really think. Whether you've really come back to me.'

'I have. But I'm not completely here yet, Johannes. I'm still somewhere on a bridge between the forest and the village.'

'The first time you did not want to adapt to the village.'

'I couldn't. I first had to finish living in the forest. Learn what it was to be a tree, an elephant. *See* some of the secrets the forest hides.'

'What makes you think that you'll adjust this time?'

'The forest has pushed me out. I now *have* to learn to live outside the forest.'

He was not reassured. 'You didn't succeed the last time.'

'That time I was *thrown* into the village. Don't do that to me again, because then I will have to leave, and there is no bath with lovely warm water under the Red Alder's cliffs.'

At least it brought a smile to his face.

The next moment he was preoccupied again. Serious. 'I cannot but believe that it was the hand of God that brought you back to me, Karoliena. Everything I've worked for, my shop, my house, all my interests in the village are in jeopardy because of the war. You are the one person I can trust with it all if you'll allow me to teach you to look after everything when I have to go to war …'

'I stole some of the wedding money.' He did not hear her.

'I will also teach you to drive my car so that you can sometimes go to Karatara on a Sunday.'

'That will be wonderful.' Like learning how to fly. 'And I'd be grateful if you would allow me to sleep in the spare room.'

'Why?' Direct, almost challenging.

'Because strangers don't sleep in the same bed.'

He heard her.

When she walked out on to the stoep the next morning, she

saw a wagon approaching down the street from the west. People from Sourflats. Nols Zeelie's wagon and oxen, his brother Koos at the back with the brake. It was the strange load of wood on the wagon that made her rush into the street. She didn't want to believe what she saw.

'What is the wood you have on the wagon, Uncle Koos?'

'We had a bit of luck, Karoliena. Wood factories want Cape chestnut to make rifle butts. Haven't you heard that there's war? My late father always said chestnut was the toughest wood in the forest and now suddenly the wood-buyers are waking up to it. Reverend Odendaal took old Jan Plan to the old-age home at Karatara; Jan died that same night. I believe your mother and Cornelius have also been moved there; are they still alive?'

'Yes, Uncle Koos.'

'I tell you, Karoliena, as long as one has something to eat, one has a lot to be thankful for.'

'Yes, Uncle Koos.'

When she turned back, Johannes was standing on the stoep in front of the shop, watching her with a strange softness in his eyes. She walked up to him.

'You look upset, Karoliena. You will have to learn to look past the wood-wagons.'

'I want to go and see Miss Ann.' Guns killed people. It must be terrible to be killed by a chestnut rifle.

'Ask her who you can get to make you some new clothes.'

'I'll ask Martjie van Huysteen at Karatara.'

'Will she be able to do it well enough?'

'Yes. And you can start teaching me about the shop tomorrow.'

So life started to pick her up – slowly and gently.

The bridge between the forest and the outside world began to feel stronger beneath her feet, although there were days when she wanted to flee back to the forest. But Johannes was there to stop her.

Like the day the first soldiers marched down the Main Street and the reality of war really struck her. It was not the first time she had seen Johannes in his uniform; she had grown used to his going to Oudtshoorn at weekends for training, grown used to supervising the brushing and pressing of his clothes. A strange pride welled up in her when he came into the room in his full military uniform.

She hadn't realised that love climbed into your heart through your eyes and hid there until you were ready for it. All she knew was that discontent was growing in her. Hatred, even. Because she was powerless against the war that had come flooding through the village.

The sea and the wind gave warning, but no one listened. They only gathered at the waterfront in amazement when the storm from the southwest began to blow huge masses of water from the sea through the Heads one afternoon. Roads round the lagoon were flooded and there was concern that even the railway bridge across the lagoon would be washed away. The old people were terrified; they said they'd never seen anything like it.

The next day the same crowd gathered open-mouthed along the Main Street to watch the two hundred or so young soldiers who marched down the street from the town hall. Among them were many that had once been forest children and whom she vaguely remembered. Rifles slung over their shoulders. Robust and brisk, smartly in step after months of training at the military camp in Oudtshoorn every weekend. Johannes was among them.

'The country can be proud of these young men,' he said at dinner that evening. 'I found it a moving experience.'

She did not say that she had run home to hide in her room. As she did in the evenings when the men from the village gathered round the wireless in the lounge, waiting for the ghostly glimmer through the mesh front so that it could start croaking the war news. How many ships had been sunk.

Russia's betrayal that had shocked the whole world. Germany that had joined forces with Russia.

'Things are looking bad, Karoliena,' Johannes said every morning at breakfast. And every evening too. She did not listen. Just put on her shoes and took another step across the bridge. Took Miss Ann some soup in the middle of the day.

'You are lucky that he took you back!' Seldom a day went by that Miss Ann did not reproach her.

'Yes, Miss Ann.'

'I did not ask you to feed me!'

'I know.' The old woman was fading fast.

'I did not ask you to clean my house!'

'It's dirty.'

'It's the motor cars speeding past, kicking up dust. I notice you are even driving Johannes's car now.'

'Yes. He taught me.'

'You'll have to find someone to make you better clothes. You still have a look of the forest about you.'

'Yes, Miss Ann.' She learned to step over some of the holes in the bridge, and sometimes to walk *around* them.

Like the way she walked around Johannes's vexation when she went with the new church nurse on Mondays to visit the people on the plots at Old Place – small pieces of land that they rented from the owner at five shillings per morgen per month. Good poor and bad poor lived side by side. Old woodcutters, old forest workers from the lower part of the forest. Plantation workers too.

'The church nurse is still very young, Johannes. She gets on better with them if I go with her.'

'You don't belong in that colony of poor whites!'

'Some make a reasonable living from their gardens and the children's wages at the sawmills and wood factories. Some of the women take in washing and some of the girls are employed as servants.'

'My wife does not belong there!'

She thought to herself: Your wife does not quite know

where she belongs. At night she longed for the forest. During the day Johannes taught her the skills of running a shop. How to work out prices, receive stock, check that every item had been delivered. Empty the cash-drawer, enter every penny in the book. Get the deposits ready and take them to the bank. Johannes was astonished because she was so clever and learned so fast … added up long rows of figures without making a mistake …

She had to tell Mister Ferndale for the umpteenth time that she no longer caught moths. No, she would not show him from which tree's bark they came. No, she did not want to be offered more money for them.

In the late afternoons Alex Wilson often came to discuss village matters with Johannes. He liked it when she asked him to stay for supper and told her frequently what an asset she was to the community, that it was so wonderful to see her back with Johannes – that his wife had told him to find out who made her such pretty clothes. Mrs van Huysteen at Karatara. Really? He didn't know that such talented people lived there. He had, however, heard that they woud soon start building a church at Karatara. It was only Knysna that was struggling to extend its boundaries because the landowners around the village did not want to sell and buyers were always being turned away.

It was an old story.

'I see the Royal Hotel is almost finished,' she said. 'If one looks at the number of cars that drive through the village, one would never believe there's a war on.'

'Yes. All those who got agitated too quickly and cancelled their holiday accommodation are suddenly trying to book any available place. The influx of people to our district is incredible. Trade in petrol and oil just keeps on growing. Our biggest problem is whether or not to let the main road run through the village.'

Another dusty story.

Karatara. Where she dared not stop the car in front of her mother and Uncle Cornelius's house because her mother simply got into the car and said she was going with her to the village.

The fenced-in camps round the little houses increased. Fruit trees, vegetable gardens, a sheep, a lamb, some chickens. Someone regularly had to go and look for Uncle Salie when he wandered off. Fortunately he always took the same road: the road back to Veldmanspad.

Oldman Botha was like a fallen tree. He had retreated into his own world where even she could not follow him. Elmina holding the dead 'child' in her arms; the child had died suddenly one night – wasn't she Meliena Kapp's daughter? How come she was so pretty? Do she also live there now?

She took flowers to put in the jam jar on Anna van Rooyen's grave.

Hestertjie Vermaak. Pregnant again. They said she had a coloured man now; it was no use her father Anneries trying to drive him away. Her mother had taken to making bubble cloths. Piles of them.

'Why are you always so downhearted when you come back from Karatara?' Johannes asked her.

'I'm trying to fight a war I can't win, even if I hang pretty curtains in my mother's windows, even if they've started building a shop just outside the village. Even if I pick up everyone along the way who wants to walk the twenty-four miles to Knysna.'

'Perhaps you should stay away for a while.'

'I can't turn my back on them.'

The only place she did not trust herself to go to was Deep Walls. Jim Reid's Crossing. To visit her Tree. Because she was scared that if she did so the bridge might give way under her. It was also the only place Johannes didn't want her to drive to. The road was too dangerous, he said, the possibility of meeting elephants too great.

It was the wireless that eventually made the bridge sway

underneath her.

She was serving tea and cake to the men gathered round the stupid thing when the news broke. War news, as usual, to which she had learned not to listen. But that night she heard it: one hundred thousand people had died in one afternoon in German bombing attacks on Rotterdam. *A hundred thousand people*. It stopped her in the doorway. It fell through the roof, it fell into her head, fell through her body. She walked outside the back door, told herself: No, don't do it again. She knew where the keys to the shop were, knew there was money in the cash-drawer. Told herself again: Don't do it, cling to the bridge!

She clung on until the next morning. Until Johannes had left to open the shop.

Then she got into the car and drove out to Deep Walls.

Slowly.

Until she reached the Tree.

How many trees were a hundred thousand trees?

How many people were a hundred thousand people?

She asked the tree-spirit, she knew it was there. How many years would it take the woodcutters to cut down a hundred thousand trees? It took one afternoon to cut down a hundred thousand people. She said it out loud. She asked the tree-spirit out loud. Until the storm raging within her had blown itself out. Until the war within her had ended. A lourie started to gurgle and hiss nearby. There was an elephant in the thicket.

She would have to step very carefully if she was to stay on the bridge.

23

WHEN THE SUN started to go down, she found peace in her heart and drove back to the village.

She pretended not to notice Johannes's relief when she got home. Pretended not to hear his reproaches. Just quietly began to prepare the supper.

'Karoliena, talk to me!'

'There is no talk left in me.'

'Where have you been the whole day? I was worried out of my mind!'

'In the forest.'

'You could have told me.'

'You would not have been able to stop me.'

'You know I don't want you to go to the forest!'

'It does not matter any more. I'm finished with the forest. And with the war.' I am almost across the bridge. All I'm looking for now is a piece of ironwood to kill the radio.

That was some time in early June.

Not long afterwards Johannes and the village men gathered solemnly around the wireless to listen to Smuts's speech. She heard the creaking voice, but did not really listen. Italy had been at war with France and England since midnight the previous night and South Africa would have to fight against Italy; calmly, but with determination.

She wasn't stupid, she knew the war would not go away if she killed the wireless.

Later, when she chopped it to pieces and threw it in the rubbish bin, it felt as if she had taken the last step across the bridge.

But this was only after the war came and took Johannes and the other young men away on the big train to travel north to fight. A crowd of weeping women at the station and quick emotional embraces. Johannes smelled of fear. Please, don't let him be killed by a chestnut rifle.

She didn't cry.

Only when she got home and started to smash the wireless into pieces with the hatchet from the back door, did the tears come. Every blow, every splinter that flew through the air, came from the anger inside her.

She cried for every hasty wedding of the last few months, performed in case the groom had to go to war. She had seen them clinging to each other in front of the altar. The fear, the *knowingness* of some of them.

How many thousands would still be killed?

The last blows were for Johannes. Her handsome, proud Johannes who had smelled of fear when the big train steamed into the station and he had held her tightly for a moment.

Some time in the small hours of the night she tidied up the lounge, swept up every fragment and threw it in the dustbin.

Then she went to sleep.

She got up the next morning, opened the shop and kept an eye on everything. She took care of Miss Ann.

'You're lucky that he took you back.'

'Yes, Miss Ann.'

'I did not ask you to wash me!'

'You say so every day.'

'You're different since Johannes has been gone. I hope it's your conscience.'

'Forest people don't have consciences.'

'I believe Smuts has gone to visit our troops in the North.'

'I took the timber train to Deep Walls on Sunday. They now hook on the passenger coach on Sundays as well to accommodate all the people who want to visit the forest. The village seems quite cheerful these days.'

'It's disgraceful! Don't they realise there is a war going on?'

Miss Ann lived until well into August. Then she just closed her eyes one Friday afternoon and died. Karoliena was alone with her. It was like reading the last page of a book, a strange book. Miss Ann with her kind heart for the poor, but who had never understood the forest people.

The night after Miss Ann's funeral she slept in Johannes's bed for the first time. And smelled him in the bedclothes. And missed him.

Please, God, not with a chestnut rifle ...

It was true. She didn't believe that Johannes would come back. Not after his first letter, nor after his second letter. Strange words written with strange ink. Obscure words.

The war had entered too deeply into him before he left. He had made her uneasy when he sometimes dreamed out loud. 'We're living in the most incredible country with the most incredible people, Karoliena! Every soldier that is willing to give his life for the country is a volunteer!'

He got angry when she said that Oldman Botha believed that if the angels wanted to take you, then they would. If they didn't want you, they'd walk past even if you were delirious with fever.

'That's forest-talk, Karoliena!'

No, she did not think he would come back. One after the other telegrams arrived in the village to announce that someone was missing in action. A few days later the news that he had been killed.

God, please, not with a chestnut rifle.

A second telegram came for her. And a third. The women in the shop watched her closely.

But the angels did not take him.

They just came and dropped him off at the door one morning. A broken Johannes.

One only once gets that kind of fright. The fright of seeing a man in front of you and seeing that one of the sleeves of his uniform is hanging limply at his side. With no arm in it.

The shop assistants said afterwards that she *had* fainted, that they had rushed to pick her up but she managed to pull herself up against the counter. White as a sheet.

No, the angels passed him by.

Johannes was empty without the war in him. A dead tree with no spirit. He didn't want to talk, did not ask about the wireless. Looked at the books in the shop, saw that the business had done well while he was away, but said nothing. Yes, he had received her letters. Yes, she had written about Miss Ann's death. No, he did not want to go for a walk. No, he did not want to go to church. No, she must not invite people for dinner. He wanted to be alone.

Then one morning he came into her room and said: 'Take me to the forest.'

He didn't say that he wanted to be *left* there.

She realised that only when they got to Deep Walls and he told her to go home. He got out of the car mumbling that he'd find his own way home.

Then he turned around and walked away.

She was alone in the empty house; there was no one she could tell that she suspected her husband had run away. No one she could send to go and look for him. When the forest took you, it saw to it that nobody found you.

She opened the shop in the mornings. Took care that the restlessness in her heart did not show on her face.

For four days.

Then she cracked.

She drove out to Deep Walls to the Tree to ask the tree-spirit please to look out over the forest and see if Johannes was safe. So that she would not die of worry. Johannes would not know how to survive in the forest, that forest grapes and cross-berries would see him through if he drank enough water …

He would not know how to evade an elephant.

When she stopped at the Tree, she saw a man coming up the sledpath from Gouna. He was still far away. She looked away, looked back, and saw that it was him.

'I knew you would come,' he said when he reached her. As if nothing had happened. The old Johannes in his new body. 'There was a little wild bird that kept flying around me.'

Only that night, after he had had a bath and had eaten, did he talk to her. 'I'm home, Karoliena. I first had to make peace with myself. I'll be able to learn to write with my left hand, I practised on the forest floor with a stick. If you don't feel that you are able to stay with me, I'll have to make peace with that as well. But it will be the hardest peace to make.'

Then she knew that it was a new Johannes.

She waited until he had gone to bed. Then she took off her night-dress, walked quietly through the dark house and got into bed with him. Warmed his cold body with her own and felt life beginning to surge through him.

'Karoliena …'

'Do not be afraid, Johannes. I am your missing arm.'

Acknowledgements

I would not have been able to write *Dreamforest* without the help of a few special people.

Adam Stander was the first to put the little forest train from Knysna to Deep Walls back on its tracks for me. Jan Westraadt, a fireman on the train at the time, 'drove' the train with a heavy load of logs from the forest to the village for me, again and again. Johan Baard, chief forestry official, showed me my first ghost moth – *Leto venus* – making me realise that it really existed. And I borrowed generously from the knowledge of Willie Cooper, a former ranger at Deep Walls.

I also received valuable information from former State President P W Botha, who has a deep understanding of the poor whites in the Knysna Forest.

I thank the J S Gericke Library at the University of Stellenbosch for giving me access to the reports of the Carnegie Investigation, especially those of M E R.

I am also indebted to John Ulyate, who was never afraid to drive the most difficult forest roads to take me many places.

Then, without *The Four Faces of Fourcade* by Clare Storrar, I would not have been able to use the character of Mr Fourcade with the necessary respect. And I am also most grateful to Trevor Ankiewicz.